THE CASE OF THE UNSUITABLE SUITOR

Recent Titles by Cathy Ace

The WISE Enquiries Agency Mysteries

THE CASE OF THE DOTTY DOWAGER *
THE CASE OF THE MISSING MORRIS DANCER *
THE CASE OF THE CURIOUS COOK *
THE CASE OF THE UNSUITABLE SUITOR *

The Cait Morgan Mysteries

THE CORPSE WITH THE SILVER TONGUE
THE CORPSE WITH THE GOLDEN NOSE
THE CORPSE WITH THE EMERALD THUMB
THE CORPSE WITH THE PLATINUM HAIR
THE CORPSE WITH THE SAPPHIRE EYES
THE CORPSE WITH THE DIAMOND HAND
THE CORPSE WITH THE GARNET FACE
THE CORPSE WITH THE RUBY LIPS

** available from Severn House*

THE CASE OF THE UNSUITABLE SUITOR

A WISE Enquiries Agency mystery

Cathy Ace

For Mum, with love

This first world edition published 2017
in Great Britain and the USA by
SEVERN HOUSE PUBLISHERS LTD of
19 Cedar Road, Sutton, Surrey, England, SM2 5DA.
Trade paperback edition first published
in Great Britain and the USA 2018 by
SEVERN HOUSE PUBLISHERS LTD

British Library Cataloguing in Publication Data
A CIP catalogue record for this title is available from the British Library.

ISBN-13: 978-0-7278-8744-3 (cased)
ISBN-13: 978-1-84751-854-5 (trade paper)
ISBN-13: 978-1-78010-918-3 (e-book)

Typeset by Palimpsest Book Production Ltd.,
Falkirk, Stirlingshire, Scotland.

ONE

Friday 19th August

Henry Devereaux Twyst, eighteenth duke of Chellingworth, was terribly worried about his croquet lawn. Oblivious to the beauty of the summer sky above, he stood on the terrace outside the morning room, hands on hips, scowling and tutting loudly. His head gardener, Ivor, matched his gestures but mouthed strong oaths in Welsh.

'It's a disgrace, Ivor, that's what it is. This act of destruction cannot go unpunished. I take it personally.'

Ivor cleared his throat. 'I don't really think Your Grace should do that.'

Henry glared at the man. 'How else should one take it? Now, of all times; we have the Anwen Allcomers arriving for their knock-around tomorrow morning, then it's the turn of the Chellingworth Champs on Sunday, with tea being served for both teams later that day. The croquet tournament is next weekend. This is the work of some sort of gang, you can be sure of that. We cannot let them defeat us. The tournament must go on!' Henry stuffed his thumbs into the pockets of his summer-weight waistcoat and struck the sort of pose he associated with Winston Churchill.

Ivor rolled his eyes toward the lawn. 'Might just have been one of them.'

'You think just one mole did all this? Preposterous. It must be a . . . what does one call a gang of moles?'

'It's a labor of moles, Your Grace. And they certainly live up to the name; hard working little so-and-sos they are.' The gardener sucked his tombstone teeth.

Henry leaned toward Ivor. 'I despise the idea of killing anything that's not for eating,' he said solemnly, 'but, under the circumstances . . . well, what *does* one do? I assume one doesn't shoot moles, does one?'

Henry noticed that Ivor hid the bottom half of his face with his large hand as he replied, 'No, Your Grace, you don't shoot moles. They're too wily to be shot. Live their secret lives underground, they do. Never know where you are with moles. It's not just the mounds that cause damage, it's their tunnels too. Their natural activities weaken the soil meaning it can collapse at any moment; so much of the damage they do is hidden from sight until everything just caves in.'

Henry nodded as sagely as possible. 'Rotters. So, what do you propose? Poison? Traps?'

Ivor sucked his teeth again. Henry thought that on this occasion he did so with a certain amount of relish. 'Well, the first thing you have to understand, Your Grace, is that nothing is fast, or guaranteed, with moles, especially since they banned the old mole poisons a few years back. Said they were bad not just for the moles but for other wildlife too, so they aren't an option any longer. If you're happy to have them killed another way, I could gas them, or trap them in plain old rat traps.'

'Moles are tempted by cheese?' interrupted Henry, surprised.

'No, Your Grace, that's mice. Earthworms. Moles like earthworms; I'd dig some up elsewhere and use *them* as bait.'

'Ah yes, worms, of course.' Henry rolled back and forth on the balls of his feet.

'So, traps can work, but they aren't fast, and they can maim or kill the animal. If you don't want them injured or dying there's an alternative, but it calls for a lot of patience. I'd say this was the work of one night only. I certainly haven't noticed any trails of yellowing grass – a dead giveaway with moles and their tunnels – and I've been tending the lawn closely, ready for the tournament. This is recent. He might still be close by. If I get Ian over from the Dower House right away, we could stalk the little devil, then plunge shovels into the ground capturing the creature in part of its own tunnel. The aim is to dig it up and cart it off in a box, but that all takes time.'

'Won't the croquet lawn be dreadfully lumpy after your shoveling?' Henry didn't like the sound of the process at all.

'Well, so long as the conditions are the same for both croquet teams, it might add a little spice to the competition, don't you think, Your Grace?'

'No, it won't do at all, Ivor. This is one of the best croquet lawns in Wales. It's certainly the oldest. It's a jewel.' He shook his head sadly. 'At least, it was until this morning. After everyone's had a chance to practice, I'm sure you'll be able to find some patches of grass to do a better job ready for next weekend, eh?'

Henry thought Ivor's voice sounded a bit flat when he replied, 'I'll certainly do my best, Your Grace.'

'Hello, my dear,' said the duchess Stephanie as she wandered out of the morning room. 'Ivor.' She nodded a greeting. Henry turned to beam at his wife and noticed her expression change when she spotted the damage to the lawn. 'Oh dear, what a shame. We seem to have had some mole activity. I'm sure you'll be able to flatten it all out, Ivor, with a bit of help. The teams won't mind a few "natural elements" to test their skills.'

Henry thought Ivor smiled rather too widely at his wife's words. He did his best to not sound snappy when he said, 'Not the point, dear. This lawn is a thing of beauty. It's famed across Wales. It won't do our reputation any good to have it seen in this state.'

Stephanie stroked her husband's arm. 'Oh Henry, the tournament is as much about sharing glasses of Robinson's lemon barley water, and a few sandwiches and cakes, as it is about playing and winning, don't you think?'

Henry gathered his thoughts. He was painfully aware that Stephanie hadn't been feeling too well during the first months of her pregnancy, and he certainly didn't want to upset her, but he felt compelled to try to make her understand the situation. He began by smiling brightly. 'I know this is your first tournament as duchess, but you've attended them before.'

Stephanie returned her husband's too-bright smile. 'Indeed I have, dear, and I recall with great clarity the amount of excitement and enjoyment the people who work at the hall have when they represent you, and how jolly it is for the villagers to come here to try and swipe the trophy away. I enjoyed three tournaments while I was public relations manager here.'

Stephanie turned from her husband to the gardener. 'I'm assuming you're going to try to track the mole and shovel it out, Ivor?' The gardener nodded. Henry was astonished that his wife appeared to know a great deal about moles. 'I see you haven't marked the boundaries yet for the playing area over the two practice days.'

'No, Your Grace. That would be one of my final tasks.'

Stephanie nodded. 'In that case I suggest that, for this weekend, you reduce the size of the field of play a little – see, over there on the right where most of the molehills are? You could mark that as out of bounds for the next couple of days. What do you think, Henry?'

'Excellent idea. Let's do that, Ivor. Who knows – if you and Ian are blessed with good fortune, you might have snapped up our hidden enemy before the Anwen Allcomers even arrive.'

'We'll certainly do our best, Your Grace,' replied Ivor, retiring to the far end of the terrace to make a call on his mobile phone.

Henry hugged his wife. 'How are you feeling this morning, my dear? I must say you're still looking a little peaky.'

Stephanie gave Henry what he judged to be an indulgent smile, 'I don't look peaky, I keep telling you this is my natural skin tone. I don't care to have the sun on my face, so of course I won't become tanned like you. But I'm extremely well. All my pre-natal examinations confirm both the baby and I are in fine form – everything is moving along just as it should. Now, come and share a pot of tea with me before the morning runs away from us. This week will be busy, and we need to have a plan of action.'

'Really?' said Henry, suddenly worried he might be called upon to do more than be a jovial host and wield a fiendishly accurate croquet mallet.

TWO

Saturday 20th August

Carol had just finished in the bathroom when her phone rang in her dressing-gown pocket. With her wriggling infant son Albert clamped to her side with one arm, she answered without checking the caller's number and was surprised to hear the voice of Tudor Evans, landlord of the Lamb and Flag pub, hissing at her.

'Is that you, Carol?'

'Yes, it is. Are you alright, Tudor?'

'No, I'm not. It's an emergency.' The man sounded rattled. 'Can you come over to see me? Right now?'

'It's before eight on a Saturday morning, Tudor. What's the matter?'

'Annie's involved. It's urgent.'

Carol's tummy flipped. 'Is she alright? Are you alright? Have you phoned – what, an ambulance?' As she spoke, Carol's mind raced through a list of potentially catastrophic events involving Annie; it seemed endless.

'It's not that sort of emergency. But I really need to talk to you. Now.'

Carol looked into Albert's cornflower eyes and replied, 'Just let me get dressed and make sure David's awake enough to cope with Albert, and I'll come over to the pub in fifteen minutes. Alright?'

Tudor sounded panicked as he responded, 'OK. But if you can get here faster, don't hang about, just come. The side door is open.' Then he was gone.

Carol woke her husband and placed Albert on the bed so he could be cuddled and protected. He immediately poked his tiny fingers up David's nose, which Carol noticed was helping her poor spouse come-to rather more quickly that he'd have liked. As she pulled on one of her trusty full-length, jersey-cotton dresses, she explained that she had to rush out unexpectedly. David was too befuddled to argue, or to even seek more detailed information.

The grassy heart of bucolic Anwen-by-Wye should have been green, but a fortnight of surprisingly dry and sunny weather had bleached it to the color of straw. As she rushed across the cement-like turf, Carol tried to stop herself imagining horrific scenarios involving her long-time friend and now colleague, Annie Parker, but couldn't.

When she walked into the deserted pub Tudor was hovering beside the bar. He beamed with relief as he welcomed her. 'Good of you to come, Carol. Will you take coffee here at the bar with me?'

Carol couldn't for the life of her work out what was going on, everything looked quite normal, except Tudor, who seemed to be vibrating. Annie was nowhere to be seen. 'Where is she? What's the matter?' she asked, almost afraid to hear the answer.

'She's not here, not right now. But like I said, it's *about* Annie.' Tudor handed her a coffee.

Carol wriggled onto a barstool and took the steaming mug. She allowed herself to relax just a little, but couldn't help feeling a bit cross with Tudor.

'You know she's been seeing this bloke, Huw Hughes?' the landlord began. Carol shook her head, shocked; she had no inkling of any such thing. 'Well she has been, for about a month, I reckon – all on the QT, because they don't want any gossip in the village, I expect. I wouldn't usually say anything – she's a grown up after all, and more than entitled to spend time with whomever she pleases. But I had a bit of a shock last night. I had a conversation with Huw here at the pub and . . . well, it's given me cause for concern. I think Huw is plotting to kill Annie.'

'You think *what*? Annie's *life* is in danger?'

'I do. I think it's just a matter of time. He's got it in for her, he has.' Tudor's expression was grim.

Carol slurped her coffee as though her life depended upon it; she certainly suspected her sanity might. She put down the mug before she replied, 'Let me get this straight – you're telling me that Annie Parker – *my* Annie Parker – is secretly carrying on with some bloke who I've never so much as heard of, and has been doing so for some time?' Tudor nodded. 'So – if she's seeing this chap, why do you think he wants to kill her? Sorry, Tudor, you've lost me. Can you explain more clearly?'

'Right, give me a minute, let me get it straight. I had it all worked out – what I'd say to you – and now it's gone.'

As Tudor finished his coffee, and poured himself another, Carol silently acknowledged to herself that she and Annie had spent hardly any time together since Albert's arrival more than four months earlier, so she had to contemplate the idea that the woman she had thought of as her best friend for more than a decade and a half was no longer an open book to her. Not so very long ago Carol would have been the first to know about a momentous development like a new man in the life of her ultra-single friend. But now? Maybe they'd drifted apart more than just a little. At that realization, Carol felt something akin to a tiny bereavement. It wasn't pleasant. When Tudor cleared his throat in a somewhat formal manner, she realized she had to maintain her focus.

'Huw Hughes has been coming into the pub, off and on, for a couple of months. He's originally from here – Anwen-by-Wye itself, not just the general area – and he went away to work and so forth. He's come back to "semi-retire." Bought himself one of those big houses out on the executive estate, he has.' Tudor rolled his eyes. 'Horrible place that – it's a blight on the landscape and the community; something should be done to prevent any more farmers from selling off land to allow for "much needed housing" in the area. "Much needed housing" my eye! Only millionaires can afford those brick-built monstrosities. Spoiling a perfectly lovely hillside, they are.'

Carol slurped patiently, hoping Tudor would get to the point soon. 'And?' she prompted.

'Right. Yes. Last night. He was in, as usual. I think he'd just dropped Annie off at her cottage with his car and he came in for a pint. Stood right where you are now and as good as told me he's about to ask her to marry him, then asked what did I think.'

Carol was amazed. 'You're kidding?'

'I am not. Serious as the plague, I am. So I say it all sounds a bit quick to me – which I think it is – and he says the best way to pluck 'em, is when they're in the first flush of love. "Pluck 'em!" Just like that he said it. Highly inappropriate I call that.'

Carol could guess Tudor's internally edited response to such a comment would have been much stronger; pretty much everyone in the village knew he'd been sweet on Annie since her arrival – everyone except Annie, of course

'Who exactly *is* this bloke?'

Tudor sagged. 'Huw? I thought he'd be an asset to the Anwen Allcomers croquet team, so I asked him to join. I didn't spot that he was so smarmy until we started our meetings. Never crossed my mind he'd end up pursuing Annie. And that's the other thing he told me last night that's got me really worried; three wives he's had. *Three.* And every one of them dead. I didn't like the way he said it.'

Carol restricted herself to a quiet, 'Uh-huh,' realizing Tudor hadn't finished.

'There's something "off" about him, Carol. I know he gets my goat with all his boasting about how he's done this and that, here, there and everywhere. Been all over the world he has, if you believe half of what he says. I'm trying to not let that color my opinion of him. But, I mean, *three* dead wives? There's got to be something wrong with that, hasn't there? And now he's got his sights set on Annie. She's in danger, I tell you.'

Carol shrugged as nonchalantly as she could.

Tudor pressed on. 'I think he's one of those blokes who goes around marrying women for their money, then bumping them off. And I don't want that happening to Annie. You've got to help.'

Carol decided it was time to try to rein-in Tudor. 'How, exactly?'

'See, what I was hoping was that you could find out a bit more about him. He's got a website for his business, that much I know, but nobody puts anything bad about themselves on their own website, do they? Can you help? Please? We've got to save Annie, from herself and from Huw Hughes.'

Carol could see Tudor was suffering and her heart went out to him. Why on earth hadn't Annie fallen for him? Tudor was exactly what Annie needed in her life; he doted on her. Carol felt guilty; she hadn't had the faintest idea that Annie was seeing someone. If she'd known, maybe she could have put in a good word for Tudor. There again, she had to admit to herself she knew nothing about this Huw chap, other than Tudor's somewhat biased rantings, and he might turn out to be even better suited to her friend.

Carol suspected Tudor had taken her silence to mean she was less than happy to carry out a background check on her best friend's boyfriend when he added, 'It should all be proper and aboveboard. I'd pay and everything. A pukka job. You could start off by meeting him, see them together. Everyone from the croquet team is coming here for a nine thirty meeting; you could join us.'

Carol looked at her watch. 'I'll have to pop home to see to Albert, then I'll come back later, alright? I'll give it some thought and maybe bring a contract with me, for you to look over. How about that?'

'Right you are. But let's keep this to ourselves? No letting Annie know.'

Carol left, shouting, 'See you in a bit.'

She dashed across the not-green green and ran into her house, toying with the idea that she'd like to talk about Tudor's request with Mavis, but it was still early, so she decided a chat could wait.

By the time Carol returned to the pub, the Anwen Allcomers' meeting had begun. She waved at Annie, and suspected the slim, tanned man sitting next to her must be Huw. Gertie, Annie's rambunctious black Labrador puppy, bounded to welcome Carol, and gave her a thoroughly good sniffing. Gertie's yellow-furred litter-mate Rosie, who lived at the pub with Tudor, joined in the fun of hunting out the parts of Carol where her calico cat had left most evidence of being petted. Eventually, both pups returned to their prized spots beneath the tables, upon which sat pots of coffee and platters of pastries – they both sat up, on full alert, keeping their eyes peeled for the tiniest morsel that might drop from above.

Carol sidled up beside her friend. 'Got room for me?' she asked. 'I'm just sitting in on the meeting to see how it's all going.'

Annie looked puzzled, but replied, ''Course there is, doll. Come on, let's all budge up a bit for Carol to fit in. There's even a muffin or two you can have.' She gave Carol a welcoming hug.

Moments later Carol was comfortably seated, an oversized cranberry muffin in front of her, happy she could indulge her sweet tooth without feeling too guilty. She surreptitiously scanned the group that formed the Anwen Allcomers croquet team, and quickly gathered that Annie was not to be one of the players, which calmed Carol; given her extensive knowledge of Annie's alarming ability to trip and fall when she was standing perfectly still, and to be impossibly clumsy when it came to pretty much any situation, she didn't much care for the idea of her friend wielding a large wooden mallet within ten yards of anyone.

'I'm in charge of refreshments,' whispered Annie with pride. 'I do the planning and ordering, then Shar gets all the goodies into her shop for me.' Carol nodded and smiled a greeting at Sharon Jones, the young but efficient local postmistress and shopkeeper, seated at the far end of the three tables that had been pulled together to accommodate the team. 'Tude done the coffee, of course,' Annie added.

Carol congratulated her friend on a superb muffin choice, tucked into it, and settled back to listen to the matters being discussed.

She recognized all but one of the people in the pub. Besides Annie, Tudor, and Sharon, there was Marjorie Pritchard, who sallied forth from her cottage overlooking the green each morning ready to share her opinion about absolutely everything that went on locally, whether it involved her or not. Carol was surprised to see the woman sitting quietly for once, though she suspected Marjorie was thinking about who she could victimize with her bossiness next.

Old Dr Priddle was there too, a retired GP who lived just outside Anwen; Carol had developed a nodding acquaintance with him when their paths crossed in the village, which they frequently did. She suspected the doctor would have once been blessed with an excellent bedside manner; she hardly knew him, yet felt warmly toward him. The thing about him that always made her chuckle was the way his belt and trousers were pulled up almost under his armpits, but, for all that, he was always well-turned out, even if his clothes had seen better days, and were utterly unfamiliar with an iron.

Aled Evans, Tudor's youthful helper at the bar during busy periods, was also in attendance – in body, at least; he was looking rather bored, and Carol wondered if he might be nursing a slight hangover. She was sure he shouldn't be quite that pallid beneath his summer tan, and he was pounding down coffee as though his life depended upon it, which she suspected it might.

Sitting next to Annie was the man Carol assumed was Huw Hughes – who'd recently returned to the village to blight Tudor's life, and, if Tudor were to be believed, wanted to marry then murder her friend. As she nibbled her muffin she took the chance to size him up. She recognized the man's wardrobe choices from her years of working in the world of high finance; the weekend-casual uniform of the wealthy, middle-aged man. He sported a crisp, brightly striped cotton shirt tucked into well-cut, belted indigo jeans, and was displaying bare ankles above loafers made of the sort of leather usually reserved for gloves. His cologne made her think of cedar and lemon warmed by the summer sun, and his expressive hands moved quickly as he spoke. She put him in his late fifties; he had a good head of still-dark hair, a deep tan and the bright blue eyes that were typical of the Welsh. As he spoke, Carol noticed that his accent was no longer what it once had been, if he'd been raised in Anwen; it had taken on more of an international twang, and reminded her a little of Richard Burton. *Dangerous*, she thought to herself.

'I think we're all on the same page, wouldn't you agree?' he said. Carol noted his tone was assertive, rather than enquiring. 'After all, we're a team, sharing a common goal. Victory.'

With enough muffin left to cover the entire bottom half of her face, Carol was grateful to be able to hide her astonishment at what happened next; Marjorie Pritchard giggled like a dizzy schoolgirl and tilted her head, touching the hair on her right temple with a playful finger.

When Marjorie spoke, it was in a tone so soft Carol couldn't believe it came out of the mouth of the woman known by all to have an affinity for barking instructions so loudly that anyone within a one-hundred-yard radius could hear her. 'But of course Huw,' purred the woman, gushing, 'you couldn't have put it any better. We're a team.' Carol almost choked on a cranberry as the divorcee managed to endow the word 'team' with a measure of sexual innuendo she found both alarming and grotesque.

'Exactly. A team. As I've always said.' Tudor sounded grumpy as he carried a couple of additional coffee pots from the bar and took his seat between Sharon and Aled. Carol could tell the man was struggling to retain control of the meeting, and his role as host.

Huw ignored Tudor, but acknowledged Marjorie with a broad grin which allowed Carol to spot his perfectly aligned, almost unnaturally white teeth. Having elicited another giggle from Marjorie he continued, 'Throughout my career I've worked on projects on an international and global scale, and some things can be distilled to essential truths, one of those being that every group – be it the entire population of a country, a multi-national organization, or even a little village-based gathering like this – has its dynamics. In order to gain, and retain, the respect of the group, its leader must lead by example.'

Dr Priddle took everyone by surprise when he smacked the palm of his hand on the table and shouted, 'Hear, hear! Done a good job over the years as our captain, has Tudor.' Carol noted that Tudor sat up a little straighter when he smiled at the doctor.

'But you haven't *won*, have you?' said Huw. Carol thought his facial expression portrayed a mixture of sympathy and triumph.

'The game's the thing,' said Aled rather half-heartedly with a sideways glance at his boss.

Sharon added, 'Yes, it's about the get-together as much as the croquet. Lovely time we've always had, haven't we? So long as the weather holds, of course. Remember that year – when was it? I know I was only little at the time – oh my word the heavens opened, didn't they? Complete washout that year was. When was that?'

'Not the point,' said Huw abruptly. 'A win would be good for morale in the village, don't you think.' Again, Carol noted he was asserting his opinion rather than asking a question. 'I have decades of experience in building winning teams for all sorts of organizations and institutions around the world. That international – no, that *global* experience – means I can bring my skills and talents to bear even here, in little Anwen-by-Wye. I know we're all looking forward to practicing on the real field of play later today, but I suggest we also take time for some trust-building exercises while we're out at the hall; the sort of thing those Chellingworth Champs won't have a clue about. We could gain an important edge if only we all put our trust in each other.'

'Whatever we do when we get there, we're going to have to think about making a move before too long,' said Tudor sharply, his nostrils flaring a little. 'If we're walking, we need to allow half an hour for that, and the croquet lawn is ours from eleven until three. We should make the most of our opportunity to practice on the lawn where the tournament will take place. I know we've all enjoyed our knock-abouts on the village green these past couple of weeks, but we need to familiarize ourselves with the actual conditions we'll be facing next weekend.' He glared at Huw as he added, 'Of course, that's particularly the case for those team members who haven't been able to make our practice sessions.'

Huw waved his hand in the air as though he were an Elizabethan courtier about to take a bow, which Carol thought terribly patronizing. 'Ah yes, my apologies, my fellow Anwen Allcomers. My so-called retired life is still rife with a myriad commitments and opportunities, and I continue to have interests around the world which call upon my time, so it's not always possible for me to be where I would *prefer* to be at any given moment. But, there, I've played croquet on several continents over many years, and I'm sure I'll still be able to handle a mallet more than effectively without too much effort.'

Tudor stood, red in the face, and began to tidy away crockery and pots. 'I still say we'd better make a move,' he muttered. Other members of the group also rose, Annie among them. Carol noticed that Huw grabbed her hand as she stood.

'Give me your phone,' he said quietly.

Annie looked down at him, puzzled.

'Go on, just for a moment,' urged Huw, standing so he looked directly into Annie's eyes. Carol reckoned he was about six feet to Annie's five-eleven, so they were, literally, face to face. He smiled, and Carol saw Annie's expression soften.

'What are you up to?' asked Annie sheepishly as she handed Huw her phone.

'Unlock it for me?' His voice was husky.

Annie did so, smiling uncertainly. Carol was surprised; Annie was many things, but 'uncertain' wasn't usually one of them.

Huw took the phone and pressed the screen a few times. 'There,' he said, taking Annie by both hands, the phone hidden between their palms, 'I've left you a little message. *Entre nous*.' He held onto Annie's hands for longer than Carol thought necessary.

Annie's reaction floored Carol; her friend stood silently, her eyes round, a broad smile on her face. 'Ta. Thanks. Ta,' said Annie. She tucked away her phone, picked up a couple of plates and scuttled off to the bar, grinning.

As people grouped together to walk to Chellingworth Hall, Carol got rather caught up with clearing away used crockery. The next thing she knew, Annie was at her side.

'Nice to see you this morning,' said her friend and colleague brightly. 'Are you getting involved with this team in some way then?'

'Not really,' answered Carol, honestly. 'Just thought I'd like to know what was happening, that's all. Tudor said I could join you all this morning.'

'So you're not coming to the hall with us?'

'No. But why are you going? Do you have to make arrangements for refreshments there too?'

Annie nodded. 'Yeah. Can't go longer than half an hour without something to shove into their mouths, this lot. Huw's going to run me over with the bags I've got, which is nice of him.'

'I thought I was doing that,' said Tudor, joining the pair.

'It's OK, I'll go with Huw,' replied Annie quickly. 'I know that with you and Aled both up at the hall today, you've got Rhian coming in to hold the fort. You can hang around until she gets here.

I'll head off, and see you there later. Can Gertie stay upstairs with Rosie for a bit? Huw said he'd rather not have her in his car.'

'Coming?' asked a suddenly present Huw.

'Right behind you,' replied Annie, waving cheerfully at Carol.

Once Carol and Tudor were alone in the pub he pounced. 'See?' he said.

'See what?' asked Carol warily.

'That man. He's all over her, he is. It's not decent. That's not the way a person who's serious about another person behaves.'

Carol felt inclined to agree with Tudor's assessment of Huw, though she told herself she was probably more familiar with his type than Tudor might be. The man didn't handle himself in the way anyone else in the village did – but she wondered if that might be more because he was a successful businessman, well-traveled and worldly wise, rather than because he was a serial wife-killer. She and Tudor chatted for about ten minutes, then she left the pub to return home with a commission for a day's-worth of background checking and a signed contract.

She felt she should let Mavis know what she'd agreed to do, and why. It wasn't as though Mavis was in charge of the WISE Enquiries Agency, but she was its sort of unofficial leader, and this was a matter concerning one of their own.

Half an hour later she'd brought her colleague up to speed on the phone.

'I see,' said Mavis. 'Ach, poor old Tudor's jealous enough to want us to do a bit of a background check on this man? Without letting on to Annie?'

'Precisely. Though, to be fair to Tudor, I'm not convinced he's merely jealous, I believe he's worried for Annie. So, how do you feel about us, or at least me, doing this?' asked Carol as she gazed down at her happily gurgling son. 'Can't do much harm, can it?'

'Unless Annie finds out,' said Mavis.

'Hmm, you're right about that. She might not think it's a very nice thing for friends to do.'

'Aye, or she might be flattered.'

'She'd never admit that though, would she?' Carol knew she wouldn't.

'Ach, I don't know. You're the one who's been her friend for the longest. Donkey's years, I believe. What's up with her and men anyway? Does she really have as little time for them as she'd have us all think?'

Carol weighed her response. 'You're right that I've known Annie for longer than you, Althea, or even Christine has, and I certainly have insights into her attitude toward relationships you don't. But – and I'm sorry to say this, Mavis – I don't think it's right for me to tell you things about her life she's not chosen to tell you herself. What I can say is this – Annie's got good reasons to tread carefully when it comes to trusting a man. Usually.' Carol sighed. 'She's learned a hard lesson in the past. But we've all done stupid things in our lives, haven't we?'

Carol noted that Mavis didn't admit she'd done anything of the sort herself. 'Tell me – do we even know if this Huw Hughes' three dead wives are real?'

'Tudor said the man told him himself. When I do a check, we'll know for sure.'

'And Tudor's going to pay for this? It's a real case?'

'Yes, and it is. He's already signed our standard contract. I thought a day might do it.'

'Right-o. I've no problem with it. This being August, and traditionally by far our quietest business month, I thought we'd not have anything to tackle while Christine's on holiday, so let's leave her out of this little job altogether. No need to interrupt her while she's . . . well, I've no clear idea what she and Alexander will be getting up to in the wilds of Ireland, but I'm sure they'll have enough energy to enjoy whatever it is. And she'll be glad of a complete break from work. So you're happy to take this on?'

'It's for Annie and Tudor, so yes,' said Carol. 'Tudor understands I can't start on it today; David and I have plans to run down to see Mam and Dad in Carmarthenshire later on, and I can't let them down. Not for this. It's not as though it's really urgent. I'll do my best to at least get things started tomorrow morning. What do you think Annie would call this case if she knew about it? The Case of the Unsuitable Suitor?'

'Aye, something silly like that, I dare say. Or mebbe it's more like The Case of the Lovelorn Landlord and there's nothing remotely "unsuitable" about this suitor at all. Best we know, I suppose. Email me when you have something.'

'Will do. And good luck with your meeting with Chief Inspector Carwen James. That's today, isn't it?'

'Aye, that it is. Saturday morning coffee here at the Dower House, no less. The man can hardly get on his high horse with Althea by my side. She has her uses, being a dowager duchess and what-not.'

Carol caught, 'I heard that,' in the background. She said, 'Give my best to Althea, and tell her I'll expect a full blow-by-blow account later on, in her own inimitable words.'

'Ach, don't encourage her, wee scamp that she is.'

Carol hung up, and began to pull together the staggering number of items she needed to pack to be able to take Albert away from home for a full day. As she pushed spare nappies, stuffed toys and feeding cloths into a giant bag, she told herself there was nothing to worry about, that Annie wasn't going to be murdered within the next forty-eight hours; even if Tudor was right, Huw would have to be married to her friend before he followed through with any deadly plans he might be hatching. Sadly for Carol, she didn't find that to be a comforting thought.

THREE

Christine Wilson-Smythe was in her element. She wondered if it was her soul that missed the smell of stables, or if she were merely experiencing a wave of nostalgia for her childhood. Either way, she felt grand. Free. Her heartbeat gradually slowed as she diligently brushed long strokes from Ciara's chestnut neck to her shoulder, recalling the hours she'd spent as a girl tending her horses, cleaning their tack and even the stables themselves. She was glad in her heart to be away from London. Even to be away from Wales, and work. She'd hated working in the City surrounded by braying men for years, but hadn't expected things to be quite so busy when she'd changed careers and thrown in her lot with three other women to form the WISE Enquiries Agency. She'd hardly had two days on the trot off work since they'd set up shop, and now an entire fortnight of relaxation stretched before her. Minus the few days she'd already had, of course.

She paused, and allowed herself to take in every sound and smell around her: hooves moving impatiently on the straw-covered cobbles; Ciara's wide nostrils breathing hard with joy and anticipation; the smell of fresh hay and leather. And behind and through it all the sweet, fresh air of an Irish countryside morning. When tearful recollections of the freedoms of her youth threatened to overcome her, Christine tossed her long chestnut hair and told herself to not be silly.

'How are you this foine mornin''?' called Alexander as he leaned on the half-open stable door.

Christine laughed. 'In foine fettle, so I am.' She mimicked Alexander's dreadful fake-Irish accent.

'You'd gone when I woke. Brid was in the kitchen and I could smell bread baking, which is the most amazing thing to look forward to. She'd made a pot of tea. I've brought you a mug. It's still good and hot.'

Christine rubbed Ciara's nose, got a nuzzle in return, and moved to the doorway. 'Lovely idea, Mr Bright.' Christine took the tea. 'Cheers.'

Alexander's eyes were shining; they looked especially light and alluring set against his skin, which had deepened from its usual latte hue to more of a pale walnut as he'd tanned through the summer. Christine hoped his eyes were gleaming because he was happy. She knew she was. Being back at her family's rambling, if rather run-down, Georgian manor house on the Irish border was exactly the tonic she needed. Just a few days in the old place and she was feeling utterly refreshed and ready to face whatever the world might throw her way.

'Want to come for a canter?' she asked brightly. Christine felt a little of the light go out of her life when she noticed the apprehension on the face of the man she loved. 'Ciara's my girl. I know how to handle her,' she said. 'You could take Paddy. He's older. A bit less headstrong.'

Alexander sipped his tea. 'You mean even *I'd* be able to cope with him?'

Christine 'Uh-hu'd' into her mug and hoped Alexander wouldn't notice she was trying to not smile.

'Is that the plan then? Going for a ride this morning? It looks like a lovely day for it, but Brid said it might rain later. She made it sound like a curse.'

Christine smiled. 'Oh Alexander, it's Ireland in August; of course it's going to rain later. But if we get going within the hour we'll be back before it hits us. It'll come in from Sligo, in the west; you'll see it coming across Upper Lough Macnean. Minutes after it hits us here on the banks of the lough it'll tap on windows in Holywell, then soak the shoppers in Belcoo.' She looked at her watch. 'Probably reach us here about one o'clock.'

Alexander laughed. 'That's pretty precise.'

'Ah well now, it's what Frank Mitchell promised us on UTV Live last night, so it must be true.'

'Good, is he?'

'Best graphics in the business. Come on, I'll get Paddy sorted for you. You should go and grab yourself some boots, so you should.'

'OK, but if you get any more "Orish" I might run away screaming.'

'It's being back in the house where I had so many happy times with Mammy and Daddy that's doin' it,' called Christine with a chuckle as Alexander headed off. 'And see if you can talk Brid into making some sandwiches for us. Let's not bother with breakfast, we can eat while we're out riding. I'll put saddlebags on Ciara. Get some water bottles, too?'

'What did your last servant die of?' called Alexander, his voice bouncing off the cobbles in the stable yard.

'I beat him to death while he lay his lazy bones a-bed in the morning.'

''Nuff said.'

Christine returned her attention to Ciara, teasing her mane with her fingers. 'Poor old Callum and Brid. They've been running around like headless chickens since we arrived. Maybe I should have given them more than half a day's warning that we were coming, but it is my home after all. And the place is clean and tidy enough, sure it is. Ah well now, my sweet girl, where shall we go today? Fancy some jumps, do you? You used to love to jump, but maybe you're too old now?' Ciara's stamping and nickering told Christine she was still young enough at heart to be excited by the idea of some walls to leap and fields to chase across.

'We'll do some gallops, sure, but we'll have to keep an eye on Alexander.' She leaned backward and called along the stable block, 'You keep him safe, mind you do, Paddy.' Paddy whinnied when he recognized his name. 'Hang on boy, I'm coming,' called Christine.

As she walked along the stables she congratulated herself on having managed to escape from her normal life for a fortnight, telling herself how lovely it would be to not have to investigate anything or anyone for quite a while.

FOUR

Just twenty minutes after her phone call with Carol, Mavis MacDonald glared at the man across the coffee table from her in the sitting room of the Dower House with a look that made Althea think she was willing his head to drop off. The man glared back at Mavis with equal venom.

The dowager duchess Althea Twyst hardly dared breathe; the tension in the room was palpable, and she was sitting between two people who might explode at any moment. She looked at one, then the other. Who would win this match of wills? She found the entire situation utterly exhilarating.

Althea couldn't help but cheer internally when Chief Inspector Carwen James forced his face into the shape of an insincere smile. She'd known Mavis wouldn't crack before he did.

The small, intense-looking man, who made the dowager think of a vole, pleaded, 'Please, Mrs MacDonald, you have to see it from our point of view. We police no longer represent a force, but a service. And, if we are to perform our service to the community, then all members of that community have to play their part in allowing us to do so. It's a partnership. The feeling at divisional headquarters in Brecon is that it is vital for us to develop an understanding between your private enquiries agency and those of us bound to uphold the law of the land. You have a duty to keep us informed of your actions and discoveries the very moment a criminal act is observed by you or one of your colleagues.'

Mavis nodded. 'Aye, that it is. And we have done exactly that on every occasion it has proved necessary since our arrival in the area.'

'Except this one,' added the policeman dryly.

'Including this one,' retorted Mavis.

'Oh, this is better than Wimbledon,' said Althea aloud, not meaning to.

Mavis flared her nostrils in Althea's direction and continued, 'As soon as we became aware that a theft was likely to take place, we telephoned the police station and alerted your "service members" to the situation. It wasn't our fault that no one was able to get to the scene of the crime until after said crime had taken place.'

As he straightened his back, the highly polished buttons on the man's uniform glinted in the sunlight that flooded the comfortable sitting room. Althea thought he looked more than a little out of place surrounded by cabbage-rose upholstery, and wasn't at all surprised that her beloved Jack Russell, McFli, was sitting at the man's feet with his ears pricked, his expression telling her he was at his most vigilant.

The policeman sounded painfully sincere as he said, 'You're keenly aware of the large geographic area covered by a dwindling number of officers here in Powys, Mrs MacDonald. I know you do because we discussed that very topic, at some length, I recall, at the community outreach meeting in Anwen-by-Wye where I spoke last month.'

'That I am. But I'm also aware that if I send photographic evidence of a trio of men with a transit van in the process of breaking into a disused pub, together with information that suggests they are specialists in denuding such premises of any and all fittings with a resale value, you'll excuse me for believing I have done my professional, and community, duty in alerting the proper authorities to a crime in progress. It was you yourself who made it crystal clear to me and my colleagues that we are not to go "banging about trying to arrest people." I believe those were your exact words.'

'Hoist by your own petard' flashed through Althea's mind. She bit into a ginger nut biscuit to stop herself saying anything.

The policeman bristled. 'I have every faith in Constable Trevelyan's abilities; she has an excellent reputation. I have her word that it would have been physically impossible for her, or any of her colleagues, to have made the journey to the scene in time to prevent the crime, or apprehend the culprits.'

Mavis's nostrils twitched the way Althea knew they did just before she was about to give someone a good tongue-lashing. 'The photographic evidence we gathered while observing the men in question, and their actions, has led to their subsequent apprehension and planned prosecution. I understand that not only have you retrieved the fixtures and fittings they removed from that pub, that day, but you have also found a storage facility where a good deal more contraband was being hidden. What else would you have had us do? Make ourselves known to them and try to take them by force?'

The man blustered, 'Absolutely not. That's exactly what I do *not* want you women doing—'

'Ah,' said Althea, nodding sagely, then crunching on her biscuit. She could feel her friend's hackles rising, and wondered how Mavis would proceed.

Mavis picked up her teacup, too calmly. '"*You women*", Chief Inspector?'

The man stood, retrieving his hat from the sofa. 'We are, of course, extremely grateful for the evidence you have provided us, Mrs MacDonald. However, I cannot help but believe that, had you alerted the local constabulary to your suspicions ahead of time, they might have been able to act in such a manner that members of our force could have been on the spot to prevent the damage which occurred that day.'

'You mean the members of your "service," I believe, Chief Inspector,' said Mavis quietly, also rising to her feet.

The chief inspector attended to his hat, in search of invisible dust. Eventually he looked up, a somewhat cowed expression on his face and spoke in a rather stilted manner, 'I understand the nature of your business. There are other firms of private investigators within our catchment area, of course, as there have been throughout my career. What I can say is that the WISE Enquiries Agency does, indeed, meet the standards of professionalism we would hope would be employed by all such businesses, and I thank you for that. I also understand your services might be retained by people who are facing situations with which my officers are not legally allowed to become involved, until a certain line is crossed. As you know, we pursue an active community-wide strategy of crime prevention, but not all crime can be prevented. We can only act when a crime has occurred or is imminent. There is, some might say, a time and a place for the services you offer; I would ask you to search your conscience about exactly when you call upon my officers.'

'Aye. Well then,' said Mavis noncommittally.

'Your Grace,' mumbled the policeman with a nod in Althea's direction.

Althea didn't stand, but waved the hand in which she was clenching the last quarter of a biscuit. 'Such a pleasure,' she said, smiling sweetly.

As the door closed behind the policeman, Althea looked at Mavis, her eyes twinkling. 'Good job,' she said, grinning.

'Aye, mebbe,' was all Mavis had to say for herself before she sat down and angrily dunked a ginger nut into her tea.

'Given what the chief inspector said, shouldn't you have mentioned the new case we're working on? You know, the case of the serial killer who might be targeting Annie.'

'Tudor made it quite clear to Carol that was to be a strictly confidential undertaking, Althea.'

Althea picked up her cup. 'But he *has* asked us to look into his concerns that a man might have murdered three women. That sounds like the sort of thing you should mention to the police.'

Mavis rose to her feet. 'Ach, Chief Inspector James might have had a point about us getting in touch with the station sooner than we did when we were tailing that van transporting those thieves—' Mavis paused and shrugged her small shoulders ever so slightly, which surprised Althea, who knew her friend rarely admitted she was wrong – 'but on this occasion? Tudor's troubles? It's no' the time to speak up.'

'Do you think Tudor is overreacting?' asked Althea. 'I believe the only person in Anwen-by-Wye who doesn't know he's sweet on Annie is Annie herself, and I further believe that's because she chooses to not see it. She's not a stupid person, so she must be purposely ignoring the signs we all see every time they are within five feet of each other. But, that aside, do you think Tudor has taken it into his head that this Huw Hughes chap is a bounder, a cad – and possibly a murderer – just because the man has set his cap at Annie? There again, what if he's right? What if this chap's *actually* a Black Widower?' Althea allowed her face to show her morbid glee at such a thought.

Mavis shook her head. 'My dear Althea, we're not living in some sort of flapper-age novelette. When did you start talking like someone from the roaring Twenties? A bounder? A cad? Setting his cap at

Annie? Good grief.' She picked up the last ginger nut on the plate – much to Althea's chagrin – and snapped off a corner with her teeth. Althea could tell her friend was ruminating as she munched noisily. 'If Tudor's suspicions hold water, it's hardly a joking matter. Such a person here? With Annie in his sights? That wouldnae be at all amusing.'

'When Carol gets going I expect she'll rather enjoy it; it's the sort of thing she's good at – hunting down records from the four corners of the earth,' said Althea as she regarded the empty plate beside the teapot with disappointment. She checked her wristwatch. 'Want to join me in the kitchen garden to potter for an hour?'

Mavis checked the watch pinned to her chest. 'Ach, look at the time. No, I'll take myself to the office and back for a good walk, and I might do a bit of paperwork while I'm there. Why that man insisted upon meeting me here I don't know. The office is the place for business.'

'He said that coming here on a Saturday morning was to show you he saw this as more of a polite call, rather than a professional one.'

'Aye, true enough.'

'Are you sure you won't come and potter with me? I'm planning on clearing a couple of spots for some beehives, you could help.'

'Can't you get Ian to do that?'

Althea shook her head. 'He's been seconded to the hall by Ivor for a couple of days. Come on, it's a lovely morning and it's not too hot yet. Just until lunchtime.'

'Go on then,' agreed Mavis.

FIVE

Sunday 21st August

Carol Hill sat on the closed toilet seat in her bathroom, and balanced Albert on her knee as she dragged a brush through her unruly blonde curls. 'That'll do for now,' she told her infant son as she relinquished the hairbrush and picked him up to carry him downstairs. 'Daddy'll be happy we gave him a lie-in this morning, won't he? Now we'll go and give Bunty some food, then Mam'll have her breakfast.' Albert gurgled his approval of his mother's plans, and Carol took comfort in the prospect of a quiet Sunday morning.

With her son, herself and her cat all fed, and the bells of St David's church summoning the faithful across the village green to sing Eucharist, Carol hoped Albert would settle. She plonked herself at the dining table cum home-office and opened her emails. Mavis had reminded her she wanted a telephone briefing on the background check into Huw Hughes as soon as Carol had anything concrete.

Carol looked down at Albert's wide blue eyes. 'Poor Mavis, she's as worried as I am. Let's get going.'

Between nine thirty and twelve, Carol Hill's fingers did what they – and she – most enjoyed; they fluttered across her keyboard allowing her access to websites and servers around the world, as she built a portrait of the life of Mr Huw Beynon Hughes, originally of Anwen-by-Wye. She tracked him as he moved from Wales to London, to Paris, then to Chicago and New York. She followed him to Amsterdam, London again and finally back to Anwen-by-Wye. His life, it seemed, had come full circle, even as his international profile – and presumably fees – had escalated. As she worked, Carol built a standard background file on the man, replete with digital clippings from corporate websites, publicly available business documents, magazine profiles, newspapers from around the globe and social media sites.

After a couple of hours she knew she'd done all she could in one sitting, besides, Albert was cooing happily with his father in the kitchen and she was missing her son and spouse. A luncheon sandwich was in order, she told herself.

'You were full-on when I took him,' said David Hill as his wife entered the jolly yellow kitchen. 'How's it going? Having fun?'

Kissing her husband and son on their respective heads Carol smiled as she replied. 'Oh, you know me, I'm never happier than when I'm here at home with you two while simultaneously roving the planet in search of background material. So, yes, I'm just lovely, thanks. You slept well.'

David stretched. 'I most certainly did. Needed it, too. I was as stiff as a board after all that driving yesterday. Let's think twice before we go promising to drive back and forth to your parents' farm again on a Saturday in August. That traffic was nuts; I didn't think so many caravans even existed, yet there they all were – in front of us all the way there, and back.'

Carol ran the water from the tap until it was cold, then made herself a glass of orange squash. 'I see you've got one of these already. Want more?'

David shook his head. 'So, tell me all about it. What are you up to? Something interesting? Must be to have you at it on a Sunday.'

Carol settled herself at the table, sipped her drink and weighed how much to tell her husband. 'As you know, many of our clients require us to retain their confidentiality, and this one does. But there's a personal angle, and I'd really welcome the chance to talk it through with you, though I can't tell you everything. Would you mind?'

'Would I mind? You mean once you've told me you'll have to kill me?'

Carol grinned, put down her glass and reached to take Albert from his father's arms. 'No, I won't tell you enough to have to do that, but you might get frustrated, and you have to promise you won't breathe a word. To anyone.'

'Go on then. Debrief me.' David winked.

'It's something Tudor has asked us to do.'

'Tudor Evans? At the Lamb and Flag?'

Carol nodded. 'It seems there's a bloke named Huw Hughes who used to live here, went away, became a Big Deal in management consulting and some particular brand of motivational clap-trap—'

'Don't hold back now, say what you really think.'

Carol rolled her eyes. 'I've read the stuff he says in interviews and it's all a load of codswallop. I can't believe people pay good money to be told things that are obviously common sense, or else so airy-fairy they don't really mean anything at all. In any case, it seems he's very good at selling his services, and he's now come back to Anwen-by-Wye to sort-of retire and enjoy the lifestyle of a country gent. Tudor's recruited him to the Anwen Allcomers croquet team, and it seems he's after Annie.'

David dragged the basket of clean laundry across the floor to his feet and began to fold. 'When you say "he's after Annie" you'll have to be more specific. Do you mean there are witnesses to this

Huw chasing her around the village green, or is it more subtle than that?'

'Now that's what I *can* tell you. You know I went out, twice, yesterday morning?' David nodded. 'Well, it was because Tudor wanted me to see this Hughes chap and Annie together. They were at a meeting at the pub.'

'And?'

Carol paused. 'In a nutshell, I have to admit I've taken an instant dislike to the bloke, and, yes, he and Annie were definitely flirting. Tudor says they've been seeing a lot of each other though Annie hasn't mentioned anything to me. Even so, what I witnessed made me think she is at least interested in him.'

'You mean it wasn't just him coming on to her? She was playing her part, too?'

'I'd say she seemed a bit taken. She was acting in a very un-Annie-like way.'

'*Veerry eenteresting*,' mugged David, stroking his chin and jiggling his eyebrows about.

'Ha, ha, not.' Carol poked out her tongue at her grinning husband. 'We all know how the situation must make Tudor feel, him being the world's most patient, and silent, suitor over the past six months or so. I suppose, therefore, it's natural that he wants to know more about Huw's background. He, um . . .' She hesitated before she dropped her bombshell. 'Huw Hughes has been widowed three times, you see.'

David looked up with his hands full of tiny cotton socks. 'He's had three wives die on him?'

'Well, no, not *on* him—' the couple shared a giggle – 'but he's definitely had three wives, and they have all died.' Carol could tell David was intrigued because he'd just paired a yellow-striped sock with a blue dotted one, and he hadn't even noticed Bunty curl herself into a ball on top of the clean laundry.

David sat back in his chair, paying attention. 'Have you found out how they all died?'

Carol nodded. 'Only in general terms. I haven't found out every detail yet, but, because of what I've learned so far, let's just say I'm a good deal more worried now than when I started.'

'How d'you mean?'

'Well, that's where it gets tricky, see? All I can really say is that none of them popped off with a previously undiagnosed heart condition.'

David's eyes widened. 'You mean you think this Huw might have helped them on their way? Hey, if he's topped three wives, he's officially a serial killer, you know?' Despite the fact she was holding Albert, Carol managed to swing at her chuckling husband.

'David, stop it. I don't want us talking about such things in front of Albert.'

'He's not six months old yet, get a grip. But come on, I can tell there's more.'

She nodded. 'You're not wrong. Without being specific, let's just say that each one of his late wives left him a tidy sum. So far I've found out most about his third wife; she left him, quite literally, pots of money. She was a jam heiress.'

'A what?'

'Jam. Preserves. Marmalades. Her father built a big company in the States making them. In jars. Pots. She was worth a bundle. I haven't found out exactly how much yet, but I'm betting it was a pretty penny.'

'Jammy old Mr Hughes,' said David with a wicked grin.

Carol finally reached his arm with a playful thump. 'Don't, David. This bloke's dating Annie.'

'She'll be fine. She's hardly an heiress, is she?'

'She's got the money from her flat in Wandsworth. That's a fair bit.' Carol nibbled her lip.

'Not exactly worth marrying and killing her for though, is it? Not unless she got a lot more for it than I would imagine. Besides, if this bloke's only been here two minutes, what imminent chance does he stand of getting Annie up the aisle? Zilch. Not ever, probably. You know what she's been like since John died. She's shut down completely as far as men are concerned.' Carol opened her mouth to speak but David continued, 'I know, I know, she had good reason – finding out after two years of being with John that he wasn't truly separated from his wife, and only discovering that painful truth after his death. Horrible for her. But Annie? Really? This Hughes chap couldn't have picked a tougher nut to crack.'

'He couldn't have picked a woman more desperate to love and be loved is what you mean,' replied Carol. 'Don't forget, David, I've known her longer than I've known you. She rarely shows her true self. But I know what she's like under that shell she's built to protect herself.'

'An eternal kid, that's what she is. Her parents are her enablers. You lot too.'

Carol reached out and touched her husband's hand. 'She's a woman who was utterly and totally undermined by the only man with whom she ever had a serious relationship. Until she saw them at his funeral, she didn't even know he had children. Is it any surprise she acts like a kid? She wants to *be* a kid. She doesn't want to be a grown up. Being a grown up didn't work out so well for her, did it?'

David shook his head and shrugged. 'Well, if this Huw is talking marriage, it just goes to show he doesn't know Annie at all well.'

'He might know her better than we think. John's been dead nine years now. She might be ready.' Carol felt worried as she said the words. 'And if she falls, the chances are she'll fall hard.'

'So, what's next? There's bound to be a "next,"' said David. 'Got your tentacles out around the world trying to get information about the deaths of these women?'

Carol nodded. 'I have. My question to you is – even though I can't tell you all the details – do you think I'm overreacting? See, I'm beginning to feel maybe Tudor has something, after all. Annie might be in danger.'

David returned to pairing socks. When he finally looked into his wife's eyes, she could tell he was taking her question seriously. 'You don't overreact, my love. It's not in your nature. You're really worried; I can tell that just by the way your shoulders are hunched and your brow is furrowed with that funny little line down its middle. Annie's been a close friend of yours for a long time, and if this Huw person has a possible track record of marrying, then disposing of women, you should not only dig into his background, but you should probably bring that to the attention of the police, and have a word with her about it. There are some terrible people out there, Carol, and most of them don't go around wearing badges that tell the world what they're really like. This bloke could, truly, be a serial killer. Where better to come and hide away than a backwater like Anwen-by-Wye? Nothing ever happens here, and the local law enforcement lot only show up if there's a fete or a knees-up at the pub. Go for it, Carol, do what you can for Annie.

You never know – you might end up saving her life. And let me know if I can help.'

Carol was relieved her husband wasn't making fun of her concerns. He never did, which was one of the reasons she loved him. 'Well . . . I was wondering if you were still in touch with Hans, in Amsterdam.'

'Hans van Groening, the systems manager in the police data center?'

'Yes.'

'Sort of.'

'The "sort of" that means you could ask him a favor?'

'Of course I can, if it's for you, and to protect Annie. I'm not saying he'll be able to give you what you want, of course. Want to write him an email, and I'll send it?'

Carol handed her wriggling son back to his father, rose and made herself another glass of orange squash. 'Thanks, love. I will. Even if he isn't able to get me the information I would like, it's worth asking.'

'As you say, oh dear, professionally-enquiring wife,' responded David, swaying Albert in the air in homage.

SIX

Annie Parker's Sunday didn't start well: she swore at the showerhead when it didn't deliver an instantly boiling, instantly powerful jet; she swore again when her toaster produced something that looked more like charcoal than anything edible; she felt completely exasperated when Gertie tripped her up as she squirmed into her shoes at the front door.

'Gert, girl, give us a break, doll. I'm tryin' me best to get you out for a walk and there's you tryin' to break me neck.' Gertie licked Annie's outstretched hand by way of an apology, and, as usual, Annie's heart melted at the sight of sad amber eyes seeking forgiveness. 'Come on, let's go and collect Rosie at Tudor's.' The puppy's licking grew more frantic, as did her leaping, at the sound of her littermate's name.

When the landlord pulled open the side door to the pub, Rosie was already sporting her lead and raring to go. Annie was surprised to discover both Rosie and Tudor would be coming for a walk that morning.

It was still early, so the pair agreed they had time to round the green and head off to the duck pond and back before Tudor needed to get to church.

'So, how are things going, you know, in general?' asked Tudor nonchalantly as the pups gamboled.

Annie enjoyed the sight of two mallards squabbling in the reeds at the edge of the pond as she replied, 'Tickety boo, ta. We had a good day, yesterday, didn't we? It was lovely to be on the proper croquet lawn out at the hall. Good idea the way Huw made everybody do that teambuilding stuff. Mind you, I can't see how falling back into someone's arms makes you a better croquet player.'

She noticed Tudor stood a little more upright as he replied, 'Yes, exactly.'

'Nice of him to include me in the whole thing,' added Annie, 'even if I was only the "demonstration model" as he put it.'

'He didn't hurt you when he caught you, did he?' asked Tudor, not looking at Annie. 'It seemed to me he grabbed you a bit roughly.'

Annie laughed. 'Nah, made of tough stuff, me. I was fine.'

'Even when the two of you showed the rest of us how to pull against each other when you were sitting on the floor?'

'What, that sort of pull and push thing?' Tudor nodded. 'I'm quite strong,' said Annie, 'I won't break, you know.' Annie wondered why Tudor was showing so much interest in the way his toes wiggled in his sandals. 'He was telling me how capable he thought I was, in fact,' she added.

Tudor finally looked up to face her. 'That's all you two were talking about, for all that time?'

'Well that and about the time he lived in France. Had a place right in the middle of Paris. That must be like heaven.'

Tudor's brow furrowed. 'I didn't know Paris held such an attraction for you.'

'Aw, it's just a dream, you know. Going there sounds like a good idea. Some lovely interiors they've got there. Seen them on the telly. And I bet it's fun doing all the art galleries. I dunno, it all just seemed to bubble up out of me when I was talking to Huw.'

Tudor pulled at Rosie's lead as she strained to get closer to a couple of ducks that were daring to swim nearby. 'I know you like antiques and so forth,' he said once the danger had passed, 'but I'd never pegged you as someone who'd like to go to art galleries. I like doing that too. You've never mentioned it to me.'

'Well, you've never mentioned it to me neither.'

Tudor puffed out his cheeks. 'The Glynn Vivian in Swansea will open again later this year. Spent millions on it, they have. That would be a great place to visit. Not too far.'

'Glynn Vivian?'

As they walked back to the pub, Tudor explained that the gallery had first opened in 1911 in his native Swansea as the result of a bequest by the son of a wealthy copper-works owner in the area, who'd sadly died a year earlier. He reminisced enthusiastically about how he'd had his eyes opened to the beauty of ceramics as a result of frequent visits there as a young man. Annie was surprised at the level of passion Tudor seemed to have for the topic. 'Fabulous lot of Swansea china they've got there. Blue and white, some of it. You like blue and white, I know,' he concluded.

The couple paused outside Annie's small, thatched cottage. She wondered how Tudor happened to know she liked blue and white china, decided it was best to not ask and settled upon saying, 'That's all well and good, Tude, but we'd have to get someone to look after the pups.' She smiled indulgently at Gertie who was already excited at the prospect of her post-walk treats. 'We couldn't take them, could we? I mean, it would be dangerous enough having me near valuable breakables, let alone them. Besides, they wouldn't allow dogs, I'm sure.'

Tudor reached down and ruffled Rosie's head as she scrambled against his leg. 'These two? We could sort something. We could make a plan and set a date. It's opening in October.'

Annie felt her tummy clench. She froze. 'Yeah, let's talk about it again, eh? Gotta go now. See you later, at the tea for the croquet teams up at the hall. Four thirty, right? Tarra.' She dragged Gertie into the cottage, making sure she didn't bang her head as she entered the tiny front door. Leaning against the wall in the hall she looked down at the puzzled pup. 'Oh Gawd, Gertie, a date? Did he mean a *date* date, or just a date for a trip?' Gertie yapped her reply. 'Yeah, I dunno either. Do you think Tudor really likes me? He never says nothing. Why did I even mention I'd dreamed of going to Paris?' Gertie seemed to agree and shook herself in her harness. 'Come on then, treats,' said Annie. Gertie licked her lips.

Outside, Tudor Evans turned on his heel and stomped off toward his pub. Anyone close enough might have heard him muttering '. . . she'd go to Paris with that rich idiot Hughes in an instant, I bet, but won't even come to Swansea for the day with me.' Rosie's ears flopped, and she trailed behind her master studying his heels.

SEVEN

'This is going to be quite the get-together,' observed Annie, as she and Althea stood in the croquet pavilion. She watched tables being erected and covered with white linen cloths on the adjacent terrace and was taken aback at the number of silver serving platters laden with sandwiches and pastries being transported across the croquet lawn by a stream of servers. She felt a growing sense of gloom that, after this spread, her attempt at catering for the Anwen Allcomers might be seen in quite a different light.

Althea patted her arm. 'We have the resources, dear. And Henry does so like to show off. I wonder where he is. I expect he'll be along by the appointed time. Would you care for a walk while all this is going on? I think McFli and Gertie might behave a little better if we take them away from all these tempting treats.'

'Yeah, me too – I'm starving,' said Annie with a chuckle. 'If you don't want any of them plates to have my fingerprints all over them, best we go somewhere until it's time for us all to dive in.'

'It's a shame Mavis decided to not come,' said Althea as the women trailed along a pathway that ran down a slope leading away from the croquet lawn.

'Well, I don't get the impression croquet's her thing,' replied Annie. 'It's not mine either, truth be told. I'm here for a nice tea.'

'When should we expect your Tudor to join us?' asked Althea.

'I keep telling everyone he's not *my* Tudor,' said Annie. Gertie barked and pulled anxiously at her lead. 'Oi! Gert, what's up?'

'I'm glad to hear he's not *your* Tudor,' said a voice from behind a grouping of several large rhododendrons. 'Music to my ears.'

Huw Hughes extricated himself from the shrubbery.

'I'd rather you didn't walk *through* the plants,' said Althea, horrified that anyone would do such a thing.

Huw brushed himself down. 'No damage done, I'm just fine, and I don't think this lot would notice the odd broken branch or two. Good day to you, I'm Huw Hughes.' He threw a sparkling smile at Althea and added, 'Yes, *that* Huw Hughes. Maybe you've heard of me?' He held out his hand, 'And you are?'

Annie was puzzled when Althea drew herself up to her full less-than-five-feet and put on what Annie always thought of as her hoity-toity voice. 'I am the dowager duchess Althea Twyst, Lady Chellingworth, wife of the late seventeenth duke. And I've never heard of you.'

Annie felt embarrassed for Huw when she noticed him blush a little beneath his tan. 'I'm sorry, your ladyship,' he said, looking uncharacteristically sheepish. 'I'm sure I didn't harm any of your plants.'

Annie was even more perplexed when Althea replied airily, 'It's "Your Grace," thank you very much, and I certainly *hope* no damage has been done. Those particular plants were put there at the express wish of my dear, departed husband thirty years ago and have given many people a great deal of pleasure. One would hate to see their beauty diminished by a bungling oaf.'

Anxious to defuse the situation, Annie said, 'Huw's one of the members of the Anwen Allcomers, Althea. He's just returned to the area after a career traveling the world, telling people how to build better teams and run more successful businesses.'

Annie didn't care for the way Althea looked Huw up and down; she did it too slowly for it to mean she was thinking anything good. She'd never seen the dowager like this before; Althea had no side to her and was never the slightest bit snobby, considering who she was. Annie wondered what had got into her.

'That's as may be,' said Althea haughtily, 'but he's certainly no sympathy for nature, it seems. Come along, Annie, these dogs need the walk we've promised them. I'm sure we'll see Mr Hughes at the tea being hosted by my son, the duke, later on.'

Annie threw an apologetic smile at Huw as she, Althea, McFli and Gertie continued down the path. The next half an hour or so didn't pass as happily as she'd originally hoped.

Returning to the pavilion, Annie could see that almost every member of both croquet teams had arrived, and was delighted to see Huw crossing the grass toward her. Althea left with McFli to hunt for her still-absent son, and Annie found herself apologizing to Huw for the dowager's behavior. 'I've never seen her like that before, really I haven't. Possibly she's ticked off that Henry's not here overseeing all this lot. It's his responsibility really.'

'Isn't it marvelous, the way you're able to speak about a duke that way,' said Huw, twirling a straw in a tumbler of lemon barley water, a glint in his eye.

Annie let out a belly laugh. 'You're not kidding. Me from the East End of London hob-nobbing it here with this lot? I'd never have thought it.'

'Tell me about your childhood, it must have been fascinating,' said Huw leaning in to Annie. She liked the way he smelled.

'Nothing special, just ordinary. Like me,' she replied. 'Could I have a glass of that? Where'd you get it?'

'Have mine,' said Huw, handing her his lemonade. 'I just poured it.'

She accepted, then sucked hard on the straw, needing the cool drink to stop her flushing.

'Don't ever sell yourself short, Annie. You *are* special,' purred the man whose watch Annie reckoned had probably cost him much the same as Mavis had spent when she'd bought her Mini. 'Never let anyone make you think you aren't. Those eyes of yours are enough to make you special, even without the rest of you.'

'Ha! You mean me plates like flippers and me big bum?'

Annie felt her tummy flip when Huw touched her bare arm and said, 'Please, don't put yourself down like that. Your feet aren't overly large and, as for your delightful rear end? Well, some of we men prefer a lady to have a substantial posterior. You're a shapely woman, Miss Parker. And that skin of yours? Like liquid chocolate, it is.'

Annie didn't know quite what to do, or say; she'd never had anyone refer to her skin that way before, and the idea made her feel a little queasy. Almost immediately, her self-defenses kicked in and she blurted out, 'Well, I'm no Milky Bar Kid, am I? So – Galaxy or Cadbury's Dairy Milk?'

She swallowed hard, and really didn't know how she felt when Huw came close and said huskily, 'Bournville, of course.'

As if from nowhere, Tudor was beside the pair. 'You two talking about Bournville? My, my – I haven't had a bar of that in years. You've whetted my appetite for a nibble of it now. I'll have to ask Sharon if she's got any at the shop. Sandwich, anyone?'

Annie took the platter Tudor had stuck under her nose and spun around seeking an escape, anxious to compose herself. She almost fell over Dr Priddle, who was sitting in a canvas-backed collapsible chair nearby. He patted the arm of the empty chair beside him, 'Come and have a sit with me, dear, and tell me how wonderful you think I am at roqueting – I had a few at practice yesterday, didn't I?'

Annie didn't have the faintest idea what the man was talking about, but was glad to sit down in the shade for a while. She exercised her patience as he chattered about his glory days playing on various croquet lawns around the United Kingdom. She didn't really listen, though her ears pricked up when he mentioned Huw.

'Did you know him when he was growing up here?' she asked, glad to finally have something to talk about.

'He was one of the older teens by the time I arrived in Anwen. He and my dear departed wife did seem to hit it off rather well. Came over for tea, supper, that sort of thing. They played chess together. Rather a boring game, if you ask me. Are you a chess player?'

Annie shook her head rather than shouting at the man; he didn't seem to acknowledge the fact he was hard of hearing, though everyone knew he was, and made allowances.

He continued, 'Mad about it they were, and I was delighted she had someone to play with, of course. Not a lot of chess players in the area back then, there weren't. Not the sort of thing a lot of sheep farmers do, is it?'

'I don't see why not,' replied Annie. 'It's a game for clever people and all the farmers I've met around here seem pretty sharp.'

'There's an enormous difference between being clever and merely sharp, my dear,' said Dr Priddle as he patted Annie's hand. He paused, then added, 'Huw was always clever. Oh yes, up there with the best of them when it came to that, he always was. Good with the ladies, too. Always had a string of the local girls running after him.'

Annie tried to not seem too interested. 'Really?'

'Oh yes. Some terrible scrapes he got into I can tell you. Though they were different times, weren't they?'

Annie wondered how long ago the doctor meant, and tried to work out when Huw might have left the village. 'What, the Eighties? Not so different. I remember them well.' A kaleidoscope of memories featuring giant shoulder pads, massive mobile phones and drinking champagne in wine bars across the City of London twisted itself in Annie's mind's eye, making her shudder a little in the warmth of the summer sun. *Was I ever really that young, that stupid?* she thought.

'Earlier than that, the Seventies,' replied the doctor, dragging her back to reality. 'Huw didn't hang about; he left school and went straight off to beat the world at its own game, he did.'

'And now he's back,' said Annie, looking across the lawn, through gaggles of people in croquet whites and pastel linens, to where she could see Huw deep in conversation with one of the Chellingworth Champs players. She wondered what he and the woman she believed was some sort of cook at the hall were talking about, then saw Huw gesturing toward a platter of the pastries. They both smiled.

'Nice bloke, Huw, isn't he?' she said to the doctor. 'Look over there, do you think he's telling her what lovely treats she's made for us today?'

The elderly man replied, 'Oh, yes, Bronwen Price. Nice girl. Very sad.'

'How so?'

The doctor looked away. 'Oh, nothing. She's done well for herself, there's no denying that, but is she really happy?' He paused, bit into a sandwich, chewed for a moment or two then added, 'But, there, are any of us ever really happy? Maybe that's just too much to expect. It's only in the life hereafter that we can hope for true happiness.'

Annie had become accustomed to the fact that many Welsh people seemed to believe that heaven was the only place they'd know a life that wasn't harsh and filled with duties. She tried to think of a reason to leave the seat she'd taken, and realized how very hot and thirsty she was, so suggested bringing something cool to drink; Dr Priddle had drained the two glasses beside him.

At Annie's offer the man's rheumy eyes twinkled. 'I'd love a glass of barley water, no ice mind you, but a few bits of lemon would be a treat. Segments, not slices, if you don't mind. Thank you.'

Returning from the drinks table with two glasses clutched in her hands, Annie passed one to Dr Priddle and set a second on the wide, flat surface of the arm of his chair. 'Is that alright?' She'd stuck a couple of wedges of lemon onto the rim of each glass.

'Lovely, thank you,' replied the doctor. Annie watched, horrified, as he took a piece of lemon and bit into it, chewing the whole thing as though it were a segment of an orange, or apple. Her mouth, and then her entire face, puckered.

'Annie?'

She recognized Huw's voice. Standing upright she could see his head above the crowd, and waved.

She half-bent to say, 'Cheerio,' to the doctor and caught him nattering on about something she'd missed.

'. . . she could have had it. I told her so at the time. No need for her to do that, there wasn't.'

'No need for who to do what?' she asked.

The doctor looked embarrassed and waved his hand as though swatting away his words, 'Oh nothing, nothing at all. I shouldn't have said anything.' He touched the side of his rather bulbous nose with a crooked forefinger. 'Mum's the word. Forget I mentioned it.'

'Okey dokey, see you later,' said Annie, unconcerned that she should try to forget something she hadn't heard anyway.

She began to weave her way toward Huw. As she did, she passed the woman Huw'd been deep in conversation with; Bronwen was carrying a plate of pastries in her hand and Annie was pleased to see her fill the seat she'd left, feeling less guilty that she'd abandoned the doctor.

Before she could reach Huw, Annie was grabbed by Sharon, who whispered in her ear, 'This lot makes our pasties and muffins look a bit sparse, doesn't it? We'll have to try harder for the meeting on Friday. Want to pop by the shop and we'll hatch a plan?'

'Right-o,' replied Annie moving away, only to be accosted by Marjorie Pritchard before she'd taken three more steps. Huw intersected with them both.

'Ah, my two favorite ladies,' he said, beaming.

Annie smiled politely at Marjorie, who giggled and blushed. 'You're just saying that, Huw,' said Marjorie girlishly. 'Did you know that Huw and I go all the way back to school days?' asked the woman who usually terrified Annie. Annie shook her head. 'Oh yes, we grew up together, didn't we Huw?' Annie had never noticed before that Marjorie Pritchard had small teeth, almost like those of a child. When she smiled you saw an awful lot of her gums.

Huw put his arm around Marjorie's shoulders and said, 'Indeed we did. Though of course you were Marjorie Lloyd, back then, weren't you? Married a good man, did Marjorie. I knew him a little, too. Owain Pritchard. Sorry that didn't work out in the long run,' he said quietly.

Marjorie looked up at him and replied coquettishly, 'Ah well, it was all for the best, I dare say. I'm happy enough without him. Though, of course, being alone isn't a state of affairs a woman has to be totally happy about. Being single for so many years has made me value the company of a good man, and it's marvelous that you, such a *good* old friend, have come back to the village.'

Annie thought she might be sick.

'I understand Annie's waiting for Mister Right,' said Huw with a wide smile.

'Really? You think one might exist for you, Annie? Good heavens!' said Marjorie.

'Did I hear my name being taken in vain?' asked Tudor, approaching rapidly with a glass of foaming ale in one hand and a plate of sandwiches in the other.

'No Tudor, I said "heavens" not "Evans,"' replied Marjorie, using the snarky tone with which all of Anwen-by-Wye was familiar.

'Oh, sorry,' replied the florid publican. He laughed more loudly than Annie thought he needed to. 'My mistake. Anyway – anybody for a ham sandwich? Or a tomato one? I've brought a selection.'

Annie took a tomato one. Tudor gave her a conspiratorial wink as he said, 'Sorry, Annie, there's no hot sauce here. I know you'd probably love a drop on that, wouldn't you?' Turning to Huw, Tudor added, 'Annie's mother introduced me to putting hot sauce into a Bloody Mary instead of Worcestershire sauce. Deeply satisfying.' He grinned manically at Annie.

Huw took a ham sandwich with the tips of his fingers. 'Ah yes, hot sauce. I realize the Caribbean has a host of distinctive flavors, and I have tasted many of them in my travels, but I feel it would be remiss of me to not speak up on behalf of the sauces made in Louisiana. Some are so delicate, yet fiery. Quite amazing. Who knows, Annie, maybe one day you'll be able to stroll the streets of New Orleans and pick up some sauces that even your experienced palate would find tantalizing. Has "Nola" ever called your name?'

Annie was a bit nonplussed. 'Not so much. That would be more up Tude's street – loves his jazz does Tude, don't you?'

She noticed Tudor swell. 'Indeed I do. Traditional jazz on Bourbon Street itself – that's something I'd love to experience.'

Huw replied airily, 'I'm sorry to say Bourbon Street isn't what it once was, Tudor. It might be the stuff of legend and dreams, but these days it's a collection of bars that has replaced real musicianship with a culture of drink-until-you-vomit cheap alcohol packages. All the people worth hearing have moved to Frenchmen Street. I was there just a year ago and saw the most wonderful trombone player—'

'Excuse me,' interrupted Tudor, 'Annie, come and have a quick word with me and Sharon about the food for our next meeting, would you?'

Annie tried to tell Tudor that she and Sharon already had a meeting planned, but Tudor pushed the plate of sandwiches into Marjorie's hand, grabbed Annie by the arm and all but dragged her away.

'Oi, hang on a mo,' said Annie eventually, as she and her 'escort' nodded and fake-smiled at people chatting in small groups on the lawn. 'I'm going to sort the food with Shar in me own time. What's up with you?'

She noticed Tudor looking crestfallen. 'Nothing,' he said lamely. 'Sorry.'

'Well knock it off then.' Looking about, Annie saw that people were beginning to wander toward the pathways that led from the hall toward the village. 'Althea first, and now you too? What's got into everybody today? I'm off, I've had enough of this. It's not worth it for a few free sandwiches. Come on Gertie, let's go home,' she glared at Tudor, 'on our own, and the long way round, so I can walk off some of this steam. Tarra, Tude. See ya.'

EIGHT

Monday 22nd August

When she answered the phone and heard Tudor's voice, Carol thought he sounded tired.

'Any news?' he asked huskily.

'Not a great deal, yet, to be honest, Tudor,' she replied quietly, creeping away from her sleeping son. 'Hang on a mo, I've just got Albert down. Let me get back to my desk.' She did so, and opened up her laptop. 'I haven't sent you the file I'm preparing yet, because it's not complete, but I have established that Huw Hughes is who he says he is, does have a storied background in management consulting and motivational speaking, and has, sadly, been widowed three times.'

'Anything else?'

Carol hesitated. She didn't like giving clients information about which she was uncertain herself. 'Not at the moment. I know you've retained our services for a day, but the hours within that day might be used up across several days of the week. I'm waiting for some further sources to get back to me. Time differences and enquiries around the world can take a little longer. I should have something more concrete by tomorrow.'

Tudor remained quiet. Carol pictured him behind his bar, comfortable in his own surroundings, but worried about the woman everyone suspected he'd fallen for in a pretty serious way.

Eventually he said, 'If an old friend of hers were to mention something – you know, about him having had all those wives, she might listen.'

Carol could tell Albert wasn't asleep after all, and that he'd need her attention very soon. 'I'm not aware Huw's made a secret of having been widowed three times, Tudor, so I'm not sure how much good my mentioning that fact to Annie would do. Look, let's not panic about this, right? Give me the time I need to do what I do, and I hope I'll be able to give you some detailed insights soon.'

'I need ammunition, not insights.'

'Got it.' Carol hung up. *So, it's war then*, she mused as she made her way upstairs to her son's room to lullaby him back to sleep with a few choruses of 'Myfanwy'.

By eleven o'clock Carol Hill was happily chatting with an old contact in New York. Carol had left her high-powered past behind her, but Jenny had moved up in the world, quite literally; she'd been appointed to oversee an entire group of multi-national companies, and was now ensconced in a thirty-seventh-floor office of a gleaming HQ building in mid-Manhattan. She was showing Carol the expansive views she enjoyed every day via Skype.

'Do you miss the world of finance?' Jenny asked.

'Not at all,' replied Carol happily, 'especially the part where you have to be at your desk at all hours. Mind you, I'm glad you're there so early this morning.' She spun the camera around her living room. 'This is the world I want, and this is where I am happiest,' Albert gurgled as she pointed the camera toward her son, and his chubby fingers reached out to grab Jenny, far away.

'You know how I am when it comes to kids, but I guess he's kinda cute,' said Jenny, returning to her desk and pulling on her spectacles. 'So, what was it you wanted? This isn't just a social call, is it?'

Carol admitted as much and gave Jenny as little of the background to her enquiries as possible. 'One of your companies was a client, listed on his website. What can you tell me about him, if anything?'

Jenny tapped at her keyboard. 'We hired him to give an after-dinner talk at a group management retreat in the Hamptons. Nice gig. Got a cool $10,000 for that one. "How leadership comes from within" was the title of the talk. I could email you a transcript of that, if you like. Nothing here about it being confidential.'

'Thanks. Please do. When was that? The after-dinner thing.'

'Two years ago. The date's on the transcript. Got it?'

'Yes, it's here, thanks. That's it? He didn't do anything else for you? None of your other companies?'

'Nope, or, as I recall you always like to say, "Not a sausage."'

'Do I say that?' Carol laughed. She knew it was something her mother said a great deal.

'You used to. Often and with feeling.'

The women shared a chuckle. 'Thanks, I appreciate the info, Jenny.'

'No probs. Hug that baby, and enjoy him, sweet girl. Miss ya. Gotta go. Meeting at six thirty.'

'I understand. Thanks Jenny.'

As the face of her old friend disappeared, Carol sat back in her comfy chair and grinned at Albert. 'Your mam's so happy to be here, with you, not stuck in some office somewhere having to go to meetings any more. So let's get on with this. What's this bloke Hughes got to say about leadership?'

Half an hour later Carol had added a synopsis of Huw Hughes's speech on leadership to her digital bundle of notes. He'd managed to talk for an hour to – as far as Carol could see – tell a group of multi-millionaires something she thought was both wrong and, frankly, unethical; that the best leaders always have to keep their true agenda hidden from those they manage in order to be able to achieve their desired ends.

She added a note at the end of her synopsis: 'Dangerous claptrap', then thought better of it and deleted it. Her reports were supposed to be professional and unbiased.

She sent a few more emails trying to prise information out of old contacts who might be able to unearth information about the death of Huw's second wife while on safari in Kenya, then returned to digging into the circumstances surrounding the death of his third wife, in Amsterdam, and his first in the south of France.

An hour later she was able to write a note for the file which read:

> On 19th October last year the authorities were called to the home of Huw and Darlene Hughes in central Amsterdam. Huw had found his wife on the ground in a courtyard at their home. He had returned from a business trip the day before, and the Hugheses had given the maid a couple of days off. He got up in the morning, his wife wasn't in bed, and he found her in her nightgown, her head cracked open. The findings – reported in a newspaper, so they are public – were that she had fallen from a Juliet balcony that led off the couple's bedroom and had sustained massive head injuries, leading to her death. Darlene Hughes, née van Haak, was the Jam-Jam heiress. The family had sold out to a multi-national company back in

> the early 2000s, so she didn't have the business to run, but she had the cash. Millions. Seems she and Huw lived the high life. There are lots of photos of them (see attached) in various society pages. Yachts, exotic holidays, exclusive parties, charity stuff. Real jet-setters. When she died, her net worth was rumored to be around 20 million US dollars, which is a lot less than she'd inherited. Huw didn't get all that, though; she left a 'large amount' to the convent in southern California where she received her education. No idea how much Hughes got. (NOTE: the house he just bought at the gated estate off the Brecon road was listed for sale at one and a half million pounds. I don't know if that's what he paid for it, but it was the asking price.)

She sat back, satisfied with her results, but not liking them. She ploughed on, and was delighted when her search turned up more information about Huw's first wife.

'You look happy,' said David as he strolled into the sitting room and bent to peer at Albert who was examining his toes.

'I am. I just found out what I needed to know about the circumstances surrounding the death of Huw Hughes's third wife, and now I've got the inside info about his first wife, too.'

'And?'

Carol sighed. 'Not a word, right?' David nodded, so she told him all about Huw's third wife, the jam heiress. 'And when it comes to wife number one, well, I think it's tragic that a woman who has proudly given interviews about her successful use of Alcoholics Anonymous then dies while driving drunk on holiday in Europe.'

'I thought the "anonymous" thing was supposed to be just that. Why talk about it in public?'

'She mentioned it in an interview she gave to a society reporter. They even had a photo of her showing off the thingy they give you when you've been sober for a year, next to a glass of orange juice.'

'Society reporter? So the first wife was rich too? As well as the third one?' David sounded intrigued.

'Yes, posh *and* rich. I suppose number one – Vivian – must have lapsed while they were on holiday in Monte Carlo. Such a shame. She died on the same road where Princess Grace had her fatal accident. It sounds as though it's claimed a lot of lives over the years.'

'So he wasn't with her at the time?' David picked up Albert and squished his face into his son's tummy. Albert giggled and squirmed.

'No. She'd gone off for a run about in the rental car on her own, it seems.'

'So wife number one gets killed in a car crash, and wife number three takes a header off a balcony. They're both pretty violent ends. The more I hear the more I think this bloke might, in fact, be bumping them off. What about wife number two? How'd she go?' asked David, holding his son above his head.

'I don't know yet. Stop trying to get information out of me. You'll be pointing shiny lights at me next, and threatening me with a hypodermic full of truth serum.'

'Aw, come on, this stuff you do is much more interesting than creating a patch for an insurance company's system in Toronto that's taken a hit. And you know I'll only talk to Albert about it. And he's not saying anything to anyone, is he?' He bounced the baby in the air until he giggled.

'Well you get on with that patch, and I'll get on with this, and we'll update each other over a sandwich later. Alright?'

'Hmm,' mumbled David as he placed Albert back in his cot. 'Such a good boy,' he cooed.

Carol looked down at her son. 'Yes, he is.' Then she thought, *Not so sure about this Huw Hughes, though. I'm starting to get really worried now.*

NINE

When Annie and Gertie burst into the office at five past nine on Monday morning, Mavis was at her desk with an hour or so of filing and accounting work behind her, feeling good, and wearing the contented smile of a woman who knows she's ahead of the game.

'Don't say it, Mave,' began Annie, 'I know I'm late. Blame this one. I swear she's started hiding her lead from me.' Annie caught

Mavis's eye just as the Scot opened her mouth to respond, and held up her hand, looking exasperated. 'And don't say that neither – yes, I've bought a spare one, and yes, I put it somewhere she couldn't get it. At least, I thought I had. But I found both leads tangled up in a big ball under me bed. *Me bed.* That's got to be her doin'. They can't have got there on their own, can they?'

Mavis felt her mouth shrink to a thin line. 'Aye, well, mebbe a third lead, tucked away in a drawer somewhere, wouldna' go amiss,' she observed dryly, then decided she should try to begin the week on a more positive note so added, 'You enjoy your early-morning walks between your cottage and the office, don't you?'

Annie looked surprised. 'Yeah, I do. I never imagined I'd ever stop missing London, but I have to admit, I love it here.'

'So you've settled in, then?'

'As settled as I ever feel anywhere. Thanks for asking. What's up with you? Everyone's a bit off this week.'

'Ach, I don't see how that can be the case. The week's barely begun. How's that wee pup of yours? Thriving by the looks of it.'

Gertie yapped her agreement, and she ran to Mavis as Annie scuttled off, first to the loo, then to boil a kettle to freshen the pot.

Mavis noticed that Annie took her seat at her desk with great care. 'You feeling well?'

'Not too bright, Mave. I think I got a bit overheated yesterday at the tea thing. Cor, it was hot. Humid too. I don't like humidity. I thought at one point we might get some rain last night, but no luck.' Mavis noticed her colleague's expression change to one she judged to be nostalgic. 'Maybe it's for the best that me mum and dad left St Lucia before they had me, 'cause I don't think I could have coped with the heat there.'

'Ach, had you been born there you'd have acclimatized, I dare say,' replied Mavis.

Just as Annie was wriggling her bare toes beneath her desk and taking the first sip of her tea, the office phone rang. 'I'll get it,' she said. 'Hello, WISE Enquiries Agency, how may I help you?' Mavis liked the way Annie answered the phone, and knew her technique had been honed over decades as the receptionist of a large firm of Lloyds insurers.

Mavis set about preparing her own cuppa as she attempted to

keep Gertie's excitement at the prospect of biscuit crumbs to a bit of quiet yapping.

'And what sort of—' said Annie, followed by 'Well, yes, of course we—' and 'No, I agree maybe—' She rolled her eyes at Mavis as she continued, 'It wouldn't take—' then an exasperated, 'Oh come on—'

Mavis was horrified and mouthed 'What?' at her colleague.

Annie spun her seat so her back was facing Mavis and carried on, 'Now hang on a—' She finished with a, 'Right-o,' and slammed down the phone.

'Tell me that was no' a client,' said Mavis abruptly. 'In any case, why would you need to speak to anyone like that on the phone?'

Annie called Gertie to her and rubbed the pup behind the ears; Mavis wondered if she was trying to calm the dog, or herself.

'First off, it was Stephanie, then Althea, then both of them at once. And are either of them a client? Don't ask me, but they are saying we have to trot up to the hall. "Quick as you please" were Althea's exact words. Normally I'd say "Who does she think she is?" but she knows very well who she is, and who we are, so there's no point. But she was in full bossy-mode, I can tell you that much. Right off with me and Huw she was yesterday too. What's got up her nose?'

'I've no idea what you mean. Althea's not usually a demanding woman,' said Mavis in her calming voice, knowing how deeply Althea was worried about Huw's pursuit of Annie.

'Well, she's in a right strop, I can tell you that.'

'So why have we been summoned? What's afoot?'

'Stephanie was the only one with any real information; she said something about balls and paint and I didn't get much more than that.'

'Balls and paint?' repeated Mavis with a smirk she couldn't quite catch back.

Annie grinned. 'Yeah,' then let out a belly laugh. 'Oh come on, Mave, we've got to go to see what she's on about. I've got all sorts of ideas running around in my imagination now.'

Mavis agreed they should make haste, and they did, taking Gertie with them as they strode out across the sun-drenched, mounded landscaping of the Chellingworth Estate, past the lake and the ha ha to the estate office at the rear of the hall.

Neither the duchess nor the dowager were where they'd said they would be, however, so Mavis and Annie were forced to hang about for a good ten minutes. By the time Stephanie and Althea arrived, Mavis could tell Annie was fit to pop, so she decided it was her professional responsibility to try to defuse the situation. Fortunately, Gertie's enthusiastic greeting of McFli allowed everyone to turn their attention to the playful dogs, and take a deep breath.

'Well here we all are then,' began Annie, 'and you've given Mavis and me some fun trying to work out how paint and balls are connected, so come on then, spill the beans. What's up?'

Althea looked at Stephanie somewhat sheepishly. 'It was my idea to phone you,' she began, 'but now I'm not so sure we've done the right thing. I think maybe we should have talked Henry into phoning the police after all.'

Mavis felt the expression on her face shift from pleasant anticipation to slight concern. 'Come on, out with it. What's happened?' she snapped. She glared at both Althea and her daughter-in-law.

Stephanie said, 'Last evening, when everyone had left after the tea and before we had a light supper, Henry and I had a bit of a knock around on the croquet lawn. We tidied away the mallets and balls, and shut up the pavilion ourselves. I saw you there yesterday, Annie, but do you know the place, Mavis?'

'That's the green-and-white painted wooden building down below the croquet lawn, under the evergreens, right?' checked Mavis.

Stephanie nodded. 'At some point between about seven last evening and eight this morning – when the place was first seen by anyone – someone has gone in there and destroyed all the windows, smashing them to smithereens. They've also splashed the inside of the building with paint. It's the most dreadful mess. We've just come from there now.'

'Anything missing?' asked Mavis.

Stephanie shook her head. 'There's nothing worth stealing at all. We phoned you as soon as we saw it for ourselves.'

'What about inside? You said there was paint,' said Annie.

'I took photos,' she added, handing her phone to Mavis who scrolled through several photographs, then gave Annie the phone.

Mavis said, 'Aye, one for the coppers, I'd say. That's nasty.'

'Definitely not a gang tag,' said Annie. 'It's a bit . . . biblical, innit?' said Annie. 'Slapping "VENGEANCE IS MINE" on walls in red paint seems a bit – well, over the top, wouldn't you say?'

'Depends on a person's state of mind,' said Stephanie.

'Depends on what it means exactly,' said Mavis.

'Romans 12:19 – "Vengeance is mine; I will repay, saith the Lord." That's the King James version, of course,' said Althea.

'I agree with Mave,' said Annie. 'This is one for the local bobbies. Did you only see this after you phoned us, and now you've phoned them?'

Mavis expected Stephanie to agree this was what had happened, but the duchess shook her head. 'Henry's seen the damage too, and we've talked about it, the three of us.' She looked across at Althea. 'We've all agreed this is something that must have been done by someone who works here, at the estate. Henry's rather keen to treat this as an "internal matter."'

'Why do you all think it's someone from the estate itself?' asked Mavis, directly.

'No one from outside could have gained access to the pavilion between the hours during which the damage occurred,' replied Althea.

'Can you really be sure of that?' Mavis's eyes narrowed.

Mavis thought Althea looked a bit scared. The dowager glanced at Stephanie, who replied on her behalf, 'You know very well how things work here; when the time comes for the hall and grounds to be closed to the public, several members of the security staff drive the perimeter of the estate making sure all vehicles have been taken away and that there's no one obviously dallying or lurking about the place. They certainly made their rounds after the public hours yesterday and then again after the tea party for the croquet teams.'

'But it's impossible to be one hundred percent certain that everyone has left the estate, correct?' checked Mavis.

'Especially if a person, or persons, unknown has made a concerted effort to find somewhere to hide out and are determined to do so,' said Annie.

Stephanie sighed. 'If you have to put it that way, then, yes, if someone were intent upon secreting themselves I'm sure there are any number of places they could do so, though now that you've forced me to admit as much, I have to say I might sleep less soundly in my bed tonight.'

'Sorry,' muttered Annie.

The duchess rallied, 'All of that being said, Henry feels – and I have to say I agree with him on this matter – that this sort of vandalism, and especially the words that have been painted on the wall, smacks of something highly personal rather than something done by a "stranger." He is quite certain he wants you to investigate rather than reporting it to the police.'

'I don't like it,' said Mavis, standing and beginning to pace – as far as the small office allowed for it. 'The police have the ability to check for fingerprints, to test paint types and sources, things beyond our abilities. They might be able to establish where the paint was purchased, and by whom. Or they might find a set of prints they already have on record.'

'It could be some trouble makers, bored and looking for a bit of fun, and prepared to see scaling the wall that surrounds most of the estate – or the hike from those parts which are not walled – as an exciting challenge,' suggested Annie. 'Is it the sort of place where people come after dark to drink, do drugs, have it away in the corner – that sort of thing?'

Mavis noted Stephanie's surprise as Althea said in a matter-of-fact tone, 'Too far from the village for underage drinkers – they'd be out in the fields beyond the village; druggies wouldn't bother bringing their stash all this way, they'd just stay closer to wherever they'd met their dealer. And as for having a bit of the other? There aren't any soft furnishings or even a good view from the pavilion to appeal to those looking for a private bit of rumpy pumpy.'

Annie almost giggled, drawing a warning glance from Mavis.

'Know what I mean? Know what I mean?' added Althea nudging Mavis with a snigger.

Mavis herself struggled to suppress a smile as she enjoyed the expression on Stephanie's face. 'That's as mebbe,' she said as soberly as she could manage, 'but I don't see how we can be sure if it was an insider or an outsider. And what chance do *we* have of finding the culprit if it were someone from outside the estate? None. Of course, we could take a look at the pavilion ourselves, to see if there's anything you missed, or that isn't in the photos, but we will not handle the case. Criminal damage has been done. It's clearly a matter for the police. You recall my conversation with Chief Inspector James, Althea?' The dowager nodded meekly. 'Surely you cannot have forgotten how forcibly he impressed upon us the necessity of reporting criminal doings, rather than us handling them as a private matter.'

'I told Henry how insistent the chief inspector was, honestly I did. But he won't budge. He's been like that since he was a child. Once he digs his heels in there's no shifting him. I—'

'—blame the nanny, I know . . . we all know,' interrupted Mavis, 'but this isn't about blame, or even your son's hubris, this is about the law. As I said, mebbe we could take a look, in case there's anything we can spot, but I'm no' going to allow the agency to take this on, and that's that. It's the police, or nothing.'

'Well, in that case, maybe we should all go there now, because Henry wants the place cleaned up as soon as possible,' said Stephanie. 'If we get there quickly maybe nothing will have been disturbed and we can still talk him into phoning the police. He wants everything to be shipshape for the tournament. First it was the moles, now this dreadful vandalism. Who knows what'll be next. They say bad things come in threes don't they?'

Althea rose and spoke to Mavis and Annie. 'I don't think we need to get Carol involved in this, do we ladies? Good things also come in threes, like us, Stephanie. Annie, let's leave Gertie and McFli here – I don't want their paws anywhere near that broken glass. We'll find someone to keep an eye on them and we can collect them later. Come along, let's get enquiring.'

'We're no' enquiring, Althea,' said Mavis as firmly as she could.

'No, of course we're not dear,' was Althea's reply.

TEN

Christine's cheeks glowed pink, her nose was smudged and her hair a tangled mess. Alexander kissed her. 'I seemed to have a little more control over Paddy this morning,' he said.

Christine noticed how proud, if sweaty, Alexander looked as the couple led their horses back to the stables. 'By the end of this holiday you'll be riding like you were raised in the saddle,' she replied.

'It's sort of addictive, isn't it?'

Christine began to remove the horses' tack. 'It is that. And it sure does give a girl an appetite. I hope Brid has a lot of bacon to go with our eggs this morning.'

'Bread and butter, too,' replied Alexander with a grin. 'That woman makes bread the whole world should taste. It's quite incredible.'

'And she knows it,' laughed Christine. 'Tell you what, why don't you go and get cleaned up while I do this? I'll come over as soon as I can. If you see Brid, tell her we'll be ready to eat in about forty-five minutes, OK?'

'Will do. I'll be glad to get out of these clothes. Join me?'

Smacking him away, Christine giggled. 'Go away with you now. And leave that bathroom in the sort of state I'd like to find it.'

Christine focused on wiping down Ciara and Paddy; she knew the horses found the process soothing, and a delight; their eyes and nickering told her that. When she'd finished, she made her way across the courtyard to the manor, where she was greeted by Alexander who looked crisp and clean, and smelled heavenly.

Christine touched his cheek. 'You shaved. Grand.' She kissed him. 'I'm so pleased you're enjoying our holiday. I know you're indulging me by being in Ireland at all, let alone riding all over the county. Is it too horrible for you, being away from your beloved London?'

Alexander returned her kiss, gently caressing her hips. 'Not too horrible, no. I'm sure I'm happier here, with you, than in London without you.'

Christine pulled away, playfully. 'I'm getting out of these stinky riding clothes.'

'I'll help,' offered Alexander.

Laughing as she ran up the wide staircase, Christine turned and called, 'I can manage quite well all alone, thank you. Are we on for a big, late breakfast?'

'I couldn't find Brid, so I got cleaned up first.'

Reaching the landing Christine called, 'Check the scullery, that's where she usually is.'

'I did, but I'll check again.'

When Christine came downstairs, showered and changed, her still-damp hair hanging on her shoulders, she called out for Alexander.

'Out here,' he called from the rear of the manor. 'There's no sign of either Brid or Callum. No fresh bread, either. Not even a hint of it in the air.'

Christine admitted she was puzzled. 'I wonder where they've got to.'

'What do they do when you aren't here?' asked Alexander. 'I mean, they can't simply keep on dusting everything just in case someone in your family decides to turn up out of the blue. They must have lives, and duties, in the normal run of things?'

Christine judged Alexander was struggling to imagine what such duties might be, so helped him out. 'There's a lot of general upkeep for the manor; when a place is almost three hundred years old, you've no idea how often the plumbing or the roof decides, for no apparent reason, to stop performing the function for which it was designed. Ask Daddy, he's the one who pays the bills. And there's the land to tend, too.'

Alexander looked puzzled. 'They weren't over at the stable block, and we've just ridden across the majority of the estate where I didn't see hide nor hair of them. Besides, it's not as though this is a crop farm, with lots of machinery and so forth. There are just a few bits of it actually growing stuff, right? Otherwise it's grassland and woodland, and not much else.'

'The potatoes take a lot of work. Though I should imagine they're all up by now, wouldn't you?'

Alexander shrugged. 'Potatoes come from Waitrose. In little plastic bags. Rural isn't my thing.'

'Let's go and see if all the vehicles are here. Maybe they've gone into Holywell or Belcoo, or even further afield.'

Ten minutes later Christine was more deeply puzzled. 'Everything is where it should be. So, if they've left the place, how did they do that?'

'Is there somewhere local they might walk to?'

Christine laughed. 'You've seen Brid and Callum – does either of them strike you as the sort of person who'd walk anywhere?'

'No, neither of them looks like someone who'd go for a walk for fun, and it's a bit far for them to walk to even the nearest home. I reckon they'd take one of the Land Rovers, but they're all accounted for.'

Christine gave the matter some serious thought. 'Look, I don't think we should be worried about them, and I'm so hungry I could eat my shirt, so let's make ourselves some food, then we'll give this place a proper going over. How's about that?'

'Agreed.'

As she led the way to the kitchen Christine called over her shoulder, 'I suppose I've got Annie to thank for the fact that The Case of the Disappearing Domestics just popped into my head.'

ELEVEN

Feeling her phone vibrate in her pocket as she walked toward the croquet pavilion with her colleagues, Mavis pulled it out and was surprised to see Carol's number. 'Hello. Is everything alright?'

'I've just emailed you my completed file on Huw Hughes. Can you talk?'

'Ach, can you no' keep Gertie away from McFli?' called Mavis to Annie, hoping Carol would understand.

'Alright, I'll do me best,' replied Annie curtly.

'Got it, Annie's with you,' said Carol. 'Can you get away from her to talk?'

'Give me a moment,' replied Mavis. She explained to the other women that she needed some privacy, and allowed them to walk on ahead. 'She's gone away a bit, but I cannae read the whole file now, what do I need to know?'

'It's not looking good for our Mr Hughes. Or Annie.'

'What's your main concern?'

'The ways in which his wives died. Highly suspicious, I'd say. You can read my report later. Do you want an overview?'

'Aye, go on then, I'm listening.'

After Carol had brought her up to speed Mavis said, 'The south of France, Kenya, and Amsterdam. Quite a range of places in which to lose wives. And wives with money, too. Aye, I'm no' liking the sound of this. Can you give me any more highlights? Or maybe that's no' quite the correct term.'

Carol sighed. 'You're not wrong. The more I find out about this

Huw bloke, the less I like him. To be honest, I didn't begin with a very high opinion of him in the first place. And I'm worried, Mavis. Really worried.'

'So, start there,' said Mavis, keen to get personal input from her colleague. 'I can read the information you've gathered after we've spoken, tell me in your own words what you think.'

Another sigh from Carol preceded her next words, 'I honestly think Tudor's got something. Maybe he came to us as a knee-jerk reaction to seeing Huw with Annie, and after hearing Huw's lascivious remarks about her at the pub that night, but Tudor might well have uncovered an actual serial killer.'

'Good heavens, you're serious, aren't you?' Mavis sounded as shocked as she felt.

'I really am,' said Carol. 'You see, I'm not sure anyone else will have looked into the three deaths the way I have. I have to admit none of his three wives would have married him if they'd believed themselves to be in danger, and I think we have to assume he told numbers two and three about those who went before them. But obviously none of them have spotted the danger signs. I believe he's good at getting a woman to fall for him and marry him, and I have a horrible feeling he then kills them off when he's in a position to cash in.'

'I'm happy to play Devil's Advocate, as you know,' said Mavis, 'so here goes. Have you confirmed all the information you have gathered with more than one source?'

'Where possible, yes,' replied Carol 'In certain instances – like getting hold of the specifics of the causes of death of the women – I can only get that sourced unofficially, but that doesn't mean the details are inaccurate. For example, there was no way even a contact within the Amsterdam Police could get me a look at the actual post-mortem report on Darlene van Haak Hughes, but I did get an email response from them confirming that the newspaper report I was able to access was "not inaccurate." I take that to mean I have good, solid facts. I've pursued similar investigations into the causes of death of his first and second wives. The second proved the most challenging, because of where she died. Kenya.'

'You said the first died in a car crash, the second suffered some sort of food poisoning and the third died of head injuries due to a fall. That would be a highly inconsistent modus operandi for a serial killer,' noted Mavis gravely.

'True, but all are types of deaths that could be planned for ahead of time, then made to look like accidents,' retorted Carol. 'He'd have to do it that way, or he couldn't keep getting away with it all the time. And look at where all these deaths took place; no two of them in the same country – that's clever, because he could bet on police forces not communicating with each other.'

Mavis sat down on the bone-dry grass under the shade of a tree, and gave the matter some thought. 'Ach, you're right. This is serious. Tell me, did anyone raise questions about the deaths at the time they happened? The authorities? Family members?'

'That's another interesting thing that I don't like, and which presents a pattern, I believe,' said Carol. Mavis noted the gravity in her colleague's voice. 'Wife number one, Mitzy Hughes nee Redworth, the ex-alcoholic who suddenly returned to the bottle and drove herself off a cliff, drunk, she had a sister, Misty. Yes, I know – Mitzy and Misty. Anyway, Misty was convinced her sibling would not have done what she was assumed to have done, namely, drink a large amount of vodka then jump into a rented vehicle and drive at high speed along the Grand Corniche above Monaco. Misty was quoted as saying something I believe is quite telling in a newspaper interview – "Mitzy hated stick-shifts." The reporter noted that Hughes had been unable to rent an automatic vehicle when he and Mitzy had arrived at Nice airport, so he alone had driven the vehicle while they were in France and Monaco. The sister thought it unusual that Mitzy would have chosen to take off driving in the type of vehicle she did. Interestingly, I found another story in a newspaper local to where the surviving Misty lived, which carried a feature article about her new, large home – which she'd managed to renovate to an exceptionally high standard and fit out with the latest technology. The story ran about a year after Mitzy's death.'

'And?' Mavis wondered if Carol's thinking had shot in the same direction as her own.

'Could be a sign that Huw paid off Misty, to shut her up about her suspicions?'

'Hmm, could be,' was all Mavis was prepared to offer by way of an acknowledgement. 'What of the other two wives? Were any suspicions raised about their deaths, by anyone?'

'That's the problem, Mavis; neither his second nor third wife had any living relatives. Maybe that's just because they didn't – or maybe it's because he was more cautious in his selection of a potential wife.'

'What was it that poisoned the second wife exactly? Was anyone else affected?'

'The couple was on safari in Kenya; part of the time they were in a swish lodge where the giraffes come to feed at your bedroom window, but for a few nights they were glamping out in the bush.'

'Glamping?'

'Glamorous camping – you know, the sorts of tents you see in Hollywood films, with running water and all mod cons, but you're off somewhere in the middle of nowhere. Lots of staff, food prepared and served to them all. Huw told the authorities that Verena, his second wife, had managed to get herself involved with some sort of Kikuyu ceremony – that's the largest native ethnic group in Kenya, now all largely Christians, but, it seems, with some practitioners who cling to their old ways. He said she told him she'd willingly participated in a cleansing ritual called "vomiting of the sins" where her tongue had been wiped with a concoction made from local herbs, that had been mixed up with the intestines of a goat. I suppose you could say it's unsurprising she became ill. They stuck her on a jeep and headed for the nearest habitation, which was the lodge they'd been staying at previously. She died there. They didn't manage to get the body to a hospital until a few days after that, and her remains were cremated in Nairobi. Her ashes were returned to Delaware, where she was from. I followed up, tracing reports from Delaware area media; she was well-known in the area as a contributor to charities, so they carried a fair amount of news about her death there. A memorial was held for her in her home town of Newark. Her family had been in the paper mill business it seems; lots of money, pillar of the community, that sort of thing. However, Verena was the last of the family; no siblings. The newspapers and their websites carried lots of photos of Huw looking deeply tanned, and crying.'

'Aye, well that's to be expected if the man's been widowed for the second time in – what was it?'

'Four years between the deaths of Mitzy and Verena. But it seems he rallied; he married Darlene nine months later. The wedding photos are quite something; she was vivaciously attractive, wore clingy gold lamé for the ceremony, and they had a fancy suite at the Paris casino and hotel in Las Vegas for the shindig. It was rumored they enjoyed a private performance by a hypnotist named Anthony Cools, who's all the rage there, apparently. Must have cost a pretty penny, I expect. Funny thing to do, if you ask me, for a wedding reception. But there, what do I know? David and I had a small ceremony in church and a reception at the local pub.'

'Ach, you know a lot, Carol, and you certainly know the value of a pound, which is no' a bad thing. Now tell me, when they found this third wife dead in Amsterdam, was there no suspicion that he'd helped her off the balcony himself?' As she looked up through the branches of the leaf-laden tree above her and caught glimpses of white clouds in the blue sky of a perfect summer's afternoon, Mavis shivered.

'Not a sausage,' said Carol. 'I gather he was questioned, but no evidence was found of a struggle, or foul play. She hadn't left a note, so they couldn't conclude she'd intended suicide. It was ruled our equivalent of accidental death. The news of her passing got more play back in the USA than in Europe. That's another thing Mavis – three American wives, all well-connected back in the USA, all dying abroad. What do you think? I'm sorry to say – horrified to say – I think he really is a serial wife-killer. This file is something I think we should consider handing to the police, not Tudor.'

Mavis hooked her bobbed hair behind her ear and replied, 'What you've told me sounds damning, but I'd like to read the files before we decide our next move. However, what I've also heard you say is he's married women with substantial financial assets. So, even if he has somehow done away with his wives, I cannot see that Annie would be on his radar as his next target.'

'He might not need any more money, or he might think she's got more than she has. Do you think he could believe Annie's someone she's not?'

'Ach, no. Everyone knows who Annie is; there could be no thought that's she's someone else. He'd only have to ask about a bit; everyone met Eustelle and Rodney at Henry's wedding – there's no doubting Annie's her parents' daughter, and no one could imagine the Parkers have a hidden fortune.'

'Thanks, Mavis, I know you're right, but I can't help feeling worried for her; Annie's my mate. If he mentioned to Tudor that he was thinking of asking Annie to marry him, maybe Huw's already hatching a plan to do away with her. We should say something to the police. I should say something to her.'

'Now hold your horses,' said Mavis. 'Like I said, let me read what you've sent me before you go doing anything rash.'

Carol sounded subdued. 'Look, the thing is, Mavis, I don't really think there's much more I can find out about Huw at this stage, and I suppose – properly speaking – I should at least pass this file to Tudor. He's our client, and it's what he's paid me to do. Are you happy with me doing that, or do you think this is going to cause him unnecessary concern?'

Mavis sighed. 'When did you tell him you thought the information would be ready?'

'Tomorrow.'

'Very well then, I shall read everything by the morning, then we'll discuss how best to proceed. The man's paid us to do a job of information gathering, but there's nothing says we cannot edit what we pass to him. Let's speak first thing in the morning. Thank you, Carol – you've done the sort of job I'd have expected of you.'

'It's for Annie; I wanted to do my best.'

TWELVE

Finally joining the rest of the group, Mavis stood outside the croquet pavilion snapping photographs of the scene with her telephone's camera, trying to push away worries about a serial killer stalking her colleague.

'Get one of the painted words inside,' said Althea.

'Aye, I'll do that, but I need to be careful. As you should be. Don't go standing on that glass, Althea.'

Althea stepped back from a mass of shards littered across the grass as she replied, 'I'd say someone threw out all the balls and mallets from inside, otherwise there'd be more glass in there and less out here. This mess will be impossible to clear up safely. How sad. And awful.'

'I dare say the equipment can be saved,' observed Mavis as she poked a mallet with her toe. 'None of it appears to have sustained any damage. But you're right enough, it'll take some doing to gather up this glass. Stephanie, you'll be wise to keep the public away from this area altogether. Liability issues.'

'Do you think they could vacuum the grass?' asked Annie.

'There's no electricity connected to the pavilion, so they'd have a job,' replied Althea. 'Maybe a generator or two, and then they could bring over some of those giant, noisy big Hoover things they use up at the hall.'

'Ivor and your son are on their way to meet us here, Althea. We can discuss that option.' Mavis paused, then added, 'Good idea, Annie.'

'I do have them sometimes,' she said with a grin.

'Now step aside and let me get into the doorway,' instructed Mavis. She snapped a few shots of the interior of the wooden structure.

'Can you tell if it really is red paint?' asked Althea. 'It's what we suspected, but one can't be sure.'

Annie grinned. 'It's not blood, is it? Cor, that would be brilliant.'

Mavis gave Annie a stern look. 'Ach, it's clearly paint. Blood isn't that color, except on TV, and I can smell it, too. It must be oil based. Now tell me something useful, Althea, Stephanie – do you know if that shade of paint is in use anywhere on the estate?'

The duchess and the dowager gave the matter some thought as Mavis picked her way carefully through the glass and back to an area of grass it had failed to reach.

Althea shrugged. 'Possibly,' she mused. 'Behind the folly there's a copse with some small buildings. I think they were originally put there for . . . oh, I don't know. But they are rather ugly. I recall they have red doors. But, otherwise, most of the things that are painted on the estate are either black or green or brown – to blend in, not to stick out like that color would.'

'What about interior paints?' pressed Mavis.

Stephanie shook her head. 'I can't recall I've seen it in use anywhere in the hall. It's a hideous color. But Bob Fernley, our estates manager, would know if it's been used in the past. Is it important?'

Mavis said, 'I'm thinking that if it's in use on the estate, it might point to someone who works here being the perpetrator. If this was done by an outsider, they'd have had to bring it onto the estate with them.'

Annie added, 'Either way, having paint here, at the pavilion, would mean whoever did it had come here with the purpose of painting that message, not just vandalizing the place, wouldn't it?'

'Good thinking,' said Mavis. 'Whether they found it on the estate or not, they came to the pavilion armed with paint and a brush to do this specific job. The *message* mattered to them. "VENGEANCE IS MINE" was what they wanted to say – maybe the destruction was just a way to draw attention to the fact the message had been left here.'

'Why not just paint the message somewhere else more obvious like on one of the outbuildings in daily use, and let everyone see it more easily then?' asked Althea.

'The pavilion will be the center of attention this week and at the weekend. Anyone working on the estate would know that,' said Annie, thoughtfully.

Mavis smiled. 'You're firing on all cylinders today, aren't you?'

Althea tilted her head. 'She can do, you know. And thank you for it, Annie. This is something that's been done to my home; it doesn't feel nice. I'd like us to find out who's done it, and why. After all, the message is rather ominous, wouldn't you say?'

Mavis agreed. 'That it is. Though we don't know what's meant by it, it promises something to come. And not a pleasant something.'

The arrival of Henry and Ivor gave Mavis the chance to speak to the duke about what she believed was his wrong-headed decision to not call in the police. It took her about five minutes of a sustained assault, but Henry finally conceded it was the right thing to do, and Mavis offered to take the matter forward. She sent an email with some photographs attached directly to Chief Inspector Carwen James as proof of the destruction, and forewarned him of her intent to telephone him immediately so he could, personally, tell her exactly how he'd like her to proceed with the matter.

Following her phone call, Mavis announced, 'We're to touch nothing. An officer has been dispatched from the Builth Wells police station and will be here as soon as possible. I suggest someone goes up to the hall to show the officer the way to the pavilion.'

'I'll do that,' volunteered Henry rapidly. Mavis suspected the duke was taking any possible chance for escape from the largely female gathering. He'd seemed uncomfortable since his arrival and had been completely cowed by Mavis's arguments.

'No, you stay here, dear,' said Stephanie. 'With the air warming up, I can smell that paint and it's making me feel a bit queasy. I'll go back to the hall and bring the officer with me to meet you here.'

'It's not too far for you to walk, is it?' Mavis noted Henry's genuine concern for his pregnant wife.

'Good heavens no. It's just across the lawn and up the steps – I'll bring the officer back through the hall, and I'll also arrange for this general area to be roped off ahead of the gates opening to the public today. I'll be back as soon as I can.'

Mavis got her extra photos of the vandal's paint-job by tip-toeing to one of the smashed windows, then, as the group had little to do but await the arrival of the police, she asked, 'Who knows of the existence of the pavilion?'

Henry replied, 'Everyone who lives and works here, or ever has; members of the public who visit and choose to follow the paths which lead in the direction of the pavilion. It's not difficult to find; it has its own little signpost along with a plaque which details the history of both the croquet lawn and this building. The lawn was laid out in 1660, for the playing of "pall-mall" and, when croquet became all the rage in the 1800s, they used it for that. The pavilion was built ahead of a visit by Queen Victoria in 1859 to allow her a place to sit out of the sun and observe play on the lawn. We have all the implements used on that visit stored away safely up at the hall. Somewhere. It's just dreadful that a place with such a history now stands in ruins.'

Althea pointed out to her son that a few new pieces of glass and a bottle of turpentine would be all that were required to bring the pavilion back up to snuff, but Henry wasn't to be cheered so easily, Mavis could tell.

Half an hour later Stephanie arrived with Constable Trevelyan in tow.

'Good to see you again, Llinos,' said Mavis, managing to make the woman's name sound like *cleen-oss*. It was the best she could do. 'How've you been?' Mavis liked the compact woman who had joined the police after a previous career in the military; she enjoyed the no-nonsense approach the officer adopted, and positively glowed when she saw her working.

'Lovely, thank you, Mavis,' replied the officer. 'Now, what have we got here then? Oh, nasty bit of work. Someone with a bit of an anger issue I'd say. And what about that message painted in there? Mean anything to anyone? Anyone you can think of who has a bit of a beef with the family? The estate?'

Everyone shook their heads. Henry replied, 'We've been discussing the rather horrifying possibility that it might well have been someone who lives or works at the hall that's done it. But I have to admit I am loathe to accept such a suggestion.'

'Thank you, Your Grace,' replied Constable Trevelyan politely. 'I see we have two of the members of the WISE Enquiries Agency here, and their trusty helper,' she smiled at Althea with what Mavis judged to be real warmth, 'so maybe I should seek their input too. What do you think?'

Mavis noticed Henry's nostrils flare with annoyance as she stepped forward to lead the police officer, with whom she'd worked before, through the group's thinking, and details of the security measures enforced on the Chellingworth Estate.

Nodding curtly, Constable Llinos Trevelyan said, 'Of course there won't be an entire forensics team arriving in bunny suits and so forth to investigate the crime scene, but I shall certainly put in a request for one of our experts to come here, give the place a good going over, check for fingerprints and take paint samples. However, I'm afraid that, as you say, Your Grace,' she acknowledged Henry, 'given that this could be the work of someone from either inside or outside the estate, there's little chance we'll find them, unless fingerprints are discovered which are already on record.'

Mavis appreciated Henry's polite response, thanking the constable for her professional attention, then the entire group was asked to leave the pavilion area, which they did. Constable Trevelyan would await the arrival of her colleague, and secure the scene.

Finally back at the hall, Mavis, Annie, and Althea collected McFli and Gertie, then repaired to one of the small dining rooms on the first floor to which the public had no access. There they were served luncheon – with accompanying dog bowls. As they tucked into their substantial ham salads, the women continued their discussion about why on earth anyone determined to bring attention to a threatening message would choose to express themselves in a relatively out-of-the-way part of the Chellingworth Estate.

'I believe it's something that's somehow connected with the croquet tournament,' said Annie after a fair amount of mental deliberation.

'You don't think they chose the pavilion just because it will be the general center of attention over the next few days?' asked Mavis.

Althea nudged Mavis, 'See, I said we'd end up enquiring, didn't I?'

'Ach, away with you. We're no' enquiring, I just like to have my facts straight. Now, you've been involved with the Anwen Allcomers, Annie, and I dare say you know everyone on the Chellingworth Champs team, Althea. So let's share all that knowledge between us while we eat.'

Althea placed her knife and fork carefully on her already-empty plate. 'If you have a pen and paper I could write a list.'

Mavis allowed her mind to range through possible reasons for a person seeking 'vengeance', in capital letters, no less, as she watched the dowager suck the end of the biro she'd handed her. She couldn't resist observing, 'That's no' good for you, you know.'

Althea gave her a vinegar look and continued to write deliberately on Mavis' pad. 'There, that's the lot.' She handed the pad to her friend and colleague who had also finished her meal. Mavis took the pad, then cleared the plates to the far side of the table as Althea rang the bell for service.

Casting her eyes down the list of names Mavis said, 'I think we both know everyone but two people on the list of the Chellingworth Champs, Annie: there's the duke, of course, as captain of the team; Bob Fernley the estates manager; Edward the butler; Ian Cottesloe your factotum, Althea. Those we know, and I cannot imagine any of them as the culprit. Can you Annie? Althea?'

'Cor, wouldn't it be great if the butler done it?' said Annie with a wry grin.

'Not for us,' retorted Althea, 'Edward is an excellent butler and they are in desperately short supply these days. Besides, he's been here forever, as have Ian, Bob and – for heaven's sake, you cannot imagine my son did this, can you? It *can't* be any of them,' chided Althea.

'Moving on,' said Mavis, 'tell us about Bronwen Price, I don't think I know her, do you Annie?'

Annie shook her head. 'I know of her, that's all. Cook here, in't she?'

Althea leaned in. 'You probably wouldn't know her well, either of you, though she's been here forever too. Must be in her late fifties by now, I suppose. She's a Miss. Never married. I believe she came to work here back in . . . oh it must be thirty, or even forty, years ago. Started in the kitchen as a scullery maid; you know, a bit of a general dogsbody. Now she's Cook Davies's right hand. Excellent at pastries and cakes. She's the one we have to thank for that Victoria sponge over there on the sideboard. She's probably responsible for quite a few pounds around my hips. Who can resist a Victoria sponge for pudding? She knows I love them so.'

'Reliable? Likely to be given to this sort of damaging activity?' asked Mavis.

Althea turned her attention to the girl who cleared the plates, then sliced and served the sponge cake, only finally answering when the trio were finally alone again. 'I'd say yes, and probably not. She's always struck me as a reserved person. Good bakers usually have patience, I've found. They enjoy the precision of recipes and are prepared to follow them. Not one given to outbursts of any sort, I wouldn't have thought.'

'And what about Aelwyn Thomas? Is that a man or a woman, by the way?' asked Mavis.

'Neither. It's a girl, and a very sullen one at that,' replied Althea.

Mavis sat a little more upright. 'That sounds interesting. The sort of destruction we saw might indicate a sullen, spiteful person. Tell me more about her.'

'Honestly, I can't. Sorry, dear. You'll have to ask Mrs Davies-Café – the Mrs Davies who oversees the café staff, not Mrs Davies-Cleaning who oversees the cleaning staff at the hall. Aelwyn is a waitress at the café; as you might imagine, I don't go to the café on a regular basis, so I don't know the girl at all.'

'What makes you say she's sullen, then?' challenged Annie, gently.

'Just a mo,' said Althea, unable to resist the slice of moist sponge sitting in front of her for another second. She thrust her fork into it with glee, and winked as she stuffed a large piece into her mouth. Mavis watched as Althea's face lit up with enjoyment, and she and

Annie both happily tucked into their pieces too. The three women indulged in silence for a few moments, then Althea spoke.

'I've sat in the pavilion for a few hours over the past couple of days and have watched both teams enjoy their time on the lawn. It's a more jovial atmosphere than when the tournament begins and I do so prefer the fun of the game, rather than when it becomes overtly competitive.'

'Is that what happens at the tournament?' Mavis was surprised.

'Oh you've no idea,' replied Althea with a heavy sigh. 'All the fun goes out of it, and rampant competitiveness overwhelms even the most sensible of players. Henry's to blame, of course; he has to win. And Tudor Evans would dearly love to do so. They rile their players up to an alarming extent on occasion, and sometimes I fear they cross the line beyond true sportsmanship.'

'Yeah, Tude hates to lose as much as Henry does,' observed Annie. 'I can't imagine it's all fairy dust and unicorns when they face each other; I can picture them both now, red in the face and totally determined to triumph at all costs.'

Mavis tried to imagine how heated a game of croquet could possibly become, but, never having seen a proper game played, realized she was doomed to fail miserably. 'That aside, what allowed you to form an opinion of this girl as being sullen when you don't know her?' she pressed.

Althea gave her response some thought. 'At the Chellingworth Champs' practice session, she chewed gum constantly, twirled her hair every few minutes so it hung in rats'-tails, looked utterly bored and miserable, and was even using her mobile phone to send texts when the rest of the group was discussing tactics. Sullen, and rude, if you ask me.'

'Mebbe no different than many young persons these days,' observed Mavis. 'Age? Background?'

Althea puffed out her cheeks. 'About eighteen, and no idea. As I said, you'd really have to ask Mrs Davies-Café.'

'Will do. Now – let's consider their opponents, the Anwen Allcomers. You're involved with that team, Annie. Am I correct in believing they've never won the tournament?'

Annie grinned, and wiped a few crumbs of sponge from her chin. 'They did once, back in the Eighties, said Tude, but never since.'

'That's quite correct,' added Althea, 'it's become something of a bone of contention, as you can imagine. The accepted view in the village is that the home team – the one made up of people who work on the estate – has the advantage of being able to practice whenever they wish on the lawn that will be used for the tournament, whereas the village team has to play on the green in Anwen. I don't think that makes the slightest difference, myself, as one of the wonderful things about croquet is that each game differs from another in innumerable ways.'

'You seem to know a good deal about it,' noted Mavis. 'Are you a player yourself?' The only time she'd ever seen Althea anywhere near a croquet mallet was that very day, at the pavilion.

'I used to play when I was young. I wasn't bad. I didn't play much after the birth of Clementine, though I must admit I sometimes miss the old gang I used to play with in London, back in the Sixties.'

Mavis dragged the conversation back to the matter at hand. 'Annie, who else is on the team?'

'There's Tude, Marj, Shar, Aled, Priddle, and Huw.'

Althea giggled. 'Oh that almost sounds like that children's thing on the TV. You know, what's it called? Trumpton. With all the firemen. You know what I mean. What was it now? Pugh, Pugh, Barney McGrew, Cuthbert, Dibble, Grub. Isn't it funny the things one remembers?'

Mavis felt her entire brow rise. 'Indeed it is, dear.' She turned to Annie. 'Now, I know some of the people I *think* you mentioned, but not all: Tud*or* is the captain, of course; I'm not surprised to discover that Marj*orie* Pritchard is a team member, though I cannot imagine the dynamic between her and Tudor if he's supposed to be in charge—'

Althea butted in, 'She's surprisingly meek, for her, when she's doing something like this. To be fair, she's a woman who can be a good team player. Of course, she's not used to someone else being in charge, but she's aware Tudor runs this show, as he has for many years. She's played for about the last seven or eight tournaments.'

Mavis wondered if Althea was experiencing a sugar high, which wouldn't be a surprise given the dowager was halfway through a second slice of Victoria sponge. She decided she wanted to hear more from Annie. 'Would you agree with Althea?' she asked.

Annie nodded. 'Marj*orie's* acting really weird, if you ask me,' replied Annie, 'but I don't think she'd do something like that stuff at the pavilion. It's not her style. She'd just walk up to someone and threaten them face-to-face; she wouldn't skulk about painting things on out-of-the-way pavilions. Not nearly confrontational enough for her.'

'I also know "Shar",' said Mavis, 'if this is the Sharon Jones who runs the post office and general shop in the village.'

'It is,' replied Althea. 'Nice girl. Very much like her mother. I'm so glad she managed to get the shop back from those horrible people who ran it for a short while. Her shop's the heart of the village, bless her.'

'Annie?' said Mavis as pointedly as she could.

'Yeah, Shar*on*. It couldn't be her. Wouldn't even say hello to a goose, let alone boo. Then there's Aled Evans, who helps Tudor at the pub.'

'Hmm,' said Mavis calling up the young man's face in her mind's eye. 'I recollect him being a fairly even-tempered type. Not overly ambitious and neither sharp nor stupid. I cannot imagine why he'd want to do this sort of thing. Would you agree, Annie?'

'Aw, yes, he's a love is Aled. I suspect he's got a bit of a wild side to him, but he's reliable. Tude says he's there for all his shifts, bang on time, and doesn't swing the lead, neither. Hard worker, is Aled.'

'Who's "Priddle"?' asked Mavis.

Once again Althea answered, her eyes closed as she licked her lips, hunting out the merest morsel of sponge. 'Used to be the doctor in Anwen. Must be about a hundred by now. Older than me in any case. Lives in a stone cottage outside the village. Nice man, though a bit of an odd duck some might say. Not a very strong player, but sharp as mustard when it comes to the trick shots. I wouldn't be surprised to discover he practices a lot in his own garden. Tudor always refers to him as his "secret weapon."'

Annie shrugged as Mavis looked her way. 'That's him. Nice old bloke. Sort of saggy. There you go – with Althea talking about Trumpton, she's got me thinking of kids' telly now. Bagpuss. That's what Dr Priddle reminds me of, Bagpuss. "A saggy, old cloth cat, baggy, and a bit loose at the seams." Anyway, he's nice, in an old man sort of way. I sat with him for a bit yesterday and we had a little chat. I don't think he talks to people often; he was rattling on like a good 'un. Drank half his own body weight in lemon barley water too, and couldn't stop sweating, bless him. Mind you, it was very hot at the tea.'

'And did any of your topics of conversation suggest he might have felt it necessary to return to the pavilion overnight and smash it about?' asked Mavis.

'Nah, he wouldn't have had the strength to lug a tin of paint to the place, let alone make all that mess.'

'He wields a mallet with significant force,' noted Althea, 'but I agree with Annie, I cannot imagine the man doing it, or wanting to.'

'So tell me about Huw,' said Mavis gently. Given what Carol had told her, she was interested to get Annie's opinion of the man, and was delighted that, for once, Althea held her peace.

Annie helped herself to another piece of sponge. Stabbing at the innocent dessert with her fork Annie said, 'He's from here originally. Come back to retire. Well, not really retire but sort of half-retire. It seems him and Marjorie went to school together, so I expect quite a lot of people hereabouts know him from back then. Dr Priddle did. Apparently him and his missus were big buddies with Huw. He used to go over to theirs all the time. Chess player, it seems. And while he was still in school too. He's been all over the world. He's lived such a big life.'

Annie's voice trailed off, and Mavis judged she was gathering her thoughts. 'What type of person is he?' she prompted.

Annie wiped the corner of her mouth with the edge of a lace napkin. 'Good at what he does. Clear about what he wants. Sure of himself. Fun too.'

Mavis noticed that Annie was twirling her dessert fork on her empty plate. 'So,' she said sharply, 'a candidate for this sort of thing, or no?'

Annie twirled some more. 'Nah, not Huw.'

Mavis sighed. 'So you two are quite certain that not one person connected with either croquet team could have done it, with the possible exception of a sullen teen about whom we know nothing.'

'It could be someone connected with the teams in another way,' offered Althea.

'You mean like me, doing the refreshments?' said Annie, relinquishing her fork.

'I mean someone who wants to get a message *to* someone on

one of the teams,' said Althea with determination. 'By the way, shall I ring for tea?'

'We could pop over to the café and have a pot there,' suggested Mavis.

As the three women agreed and rose, Annie said quietly, 'The Case of the Vengeful Vandal.'

Mavis tutted.

Annie poked out her tongue by way of a reply.

THIRTEEN

Christine's heart was pounding; Ballinclare Manor wasn't built on the same scale as Chellingworth Hall's 268 rooms, but it did have about forty different spaces ranged over four, beautifully proportioned Georgian floors, and she and Alexander had spent the last hour making a concerted effort to enter each one to establish if Brid and Callum Ahearn were anywhere to be found. They weren't.

'Basement and outbuildings next,' said Christine descending from the dusty, near-derelict topmost floor where the tiny servants' quarters had now become storage rooms for the sort of detritus the landed gentry can accumulate over almost three hundred years.

Alexander sneezed as he followed her. 'I just need to wash up a bit after that last room. I'm beginning to think you come from a long line of hoarders, and that's why your flat in Battersea is so overrun with all sorts of decorative bits and pieces.'

'So says the man who bought an entire antiques business just because he likes old, beautiful things.'

'I like young, beautiful things too,' said Alexander, snatching Christine's waist as the couple rounded the final landing before the last sweep of the staircase to the ground floor.

Playfully pushing him away, Christine stopped abruptly and shushed him. 'Listen. I think I heard something.'

The couple strained their ears.

'Yes, I heard that too,' said Alexander, his eyes alight. 'I think it came from one of the rooms back here.'

The couple re-entered rooms they'd been in about twenty minutes earlier and opened every door and even every drawer in each chamber. Nothing.

'Hang on a minute,' said Christine, dashing out of a rear bedroom. 'I've got an idea. I think there was a servants' staircase at one time. I wonder if . . .' She broke off and headed toward a dusty corner, where she began to knock the paneled walls. 'This sounds hollow. Alexander, could you break through this wall, do you think?'

Alexander knocked on the wood. A muffled thump came in response. 'I think there's someone back there – but isn't there any other way to get there? From the top floor down, or from the bottom floor up? Breaking down a wall seems a bit extreme.'

Christine sucked her bottom lip. 'Maybe we could break into the servants' stairwell from the top floor. If we have to demolish a wall there, no one would ever see it.'

'OK, let's have a look. After all, if there's someone, somehow, languishing in a disused stairwell, they must have got in there without this paneling being shattered.'

'Good thinking, Batman,' replied Christine, 'though, on that basis, I didn't notice that any of the walls upstairs had been damaged. I wonder if there might be an access point in the basement.'

'Yep, I agree. Let's head down there. It was our next port of call in any case.'

Alexander led the way down ancient, rickety wooden steps to the cavernous space beneath the rear of the manor house. Christine followed along, having taken a few minutes to dig out some torches from a drawer in the scullery. Passing through chamber after chamber, Christine was surprised at how good the basement was looking; she certainly didn't need the torches, because each room was hung with several working light bulbs. Although the floors were rough and uneven they were well swept, and there was no evidence of the giant cobwebs and general dustiness she'd expected.

'What can I smell?' asked Alexander pausing. 'Did this used to be a wine cellar?'

'Not for a long time. Up until Grandfather's time it would probably have been used as such, but he'd have drunk his way through it all, and there'd not have been the funds to re-stock it since then. Why do you ask?'

'Can't you smell it? Is that wine?'

Christine sniffed the air. 'No, it's not wine, but I think I know what it is. Come on, let's keep going.'

As Christine attempted to follow Alexander into a particularly spacious room – brick-faced and whitewashed – he held out his arm to prevent her moving further. Peering inside, Christine could see pieces of wood strewn across the floor, and a great deal of broken glass. She pushed past Alexander's arm and bent to examine the glass on the floor. Some was clear and thin, some green and a good deal thicker. She poked a couple of pieces of broken wood with her toe, pushing them toward each other.

'The smell is stronger in here,' she noted, now sure of her assumption.

Alexander sniffed the air. 'You're right, it's not wine. It's some sort of chemical. Or fruit. A fruity chemical?'

'It's potcheen. At least, it was. Look – there are different types of glass here. I bet it's from the bottles.'

'You mean Callum and Brid have been making illegal moonshine down here?'

Christine shrugged. 'They could. There's plenty of ventilation in the rooms near the stairs we just came down, and I happen to know there's a platform that comes down to the basement for loading purposes. Looks like there was a struggle. Certainly bottles were smashed. Then the stock was cleared out and all the equipment with it.'

'Who on earth would do that?' Alexander looked nonplussed. 'I thought it was alright to make it now. You know, legally. They sell it at that pub we've been to a few times in Kilburn.'

Christine's jaw firmed. 'You're right, the government has granted a few licences of late. People outside Ireland think making potcheen is all about us loving a drink and enjoying the craic. But it's about more than that – it's about making a political statement too. I could regale you with tales about how the locals hid their spirits from the tax collectors sent out by Charles II in 1662 after he applied a tax on all production of alcohol a year earlier, and I could tell you how much they enjoyed making and drinking their own booze in the face of The Pot Still Act of 1779. It's classic, really – it's a bit of a standing joke that the English-backed owners of the land, who were all largely absent from their Irish estates, owned the land and produce from which most of the illegal alcohol in Britain was made.

And isn't that just exactly what Daddy is – absent, and making his living in London.'

'Do you think he knows about this? If it's true?'

Christine managed a smile. 'Ah now, Daddy's been known to imbibe the odd drop or two himself, but I have no idea if he knew Brid and Callum had set up shop here. What I do know is that, when it comes to making and selling more of the stuff than for what one might call "personal consumption," then it can become about the money. And it can attract some unsavory types. We're almost on top of the border here – the manor overlooks the lough through which it runs. Even before they signed The Peace it was pretty porous when it came to potcheen; there was talk of some of the nastier elements using the stuff to raise much needed funds for guns and bombs. Nowadays, with Eire being part of Europe and us being in the UK here, who knows what sorts of people have a vested interest in a large stock of an illegal spirit that can be made cheaply then sold on for a fair profit.'

Christine noticed Alexander's expression shift as he said, 'You seem to know an awful lot about potcheen. How come?'

She couldn't resist a smile. 'When I was a young girl it was the sort of thing I'd overhear people talking about in the villages, or out on the roads. Used all sorts of code words, they did, to be sure the wrong person didn't know what was going on. But I worked it all out. I liked codes. Nancy Drew's fault, I suppose, and *The Secret Seven*. I loved those books. What have Brid and Callum gone and got themselves muddled up in?'

'I hate to say it, but I think we should phone the police,' said Alexander.

'We can't,' snapped Christine, her mind awhirl. 'Not until we know what we're dealing with.'

Alexander moved to hold Christine in his arms. She wriggled away. 'Come on, I don't know what's gone on here, but we have to try to find out.'

A couple of rooms away from the place where they'd found the evidence of smashed potcheen bottles, Christine and Alexander finally discovered what they'd originally been hunting for – a narrow door set into a wall tucked around a corner, out of sight. It was locked and barred with what appeared to be a recently, and hurriedly, installed metal rod shoved into the cracks in the brick surround.

Kicking, pulling, and some more kicking, released the bar; Alexander wrenched open the door to reveal a dark, steep set of steps.

'Here,' said Christine, handing him a torch.

He led the way, treading carefully on aged wood, with Christine close behind.

'I think this is a window, boarded over,' said Alexander. 'Could you shine your light here for a minute?' He shoved his own torch into his pocket and, by the light from Christine's, pried a couple of nails from the window surround allowing the hardboard sheet to pop off, which created a cloud of dust. A small sash-window, its glass heavily stained and marked, allowed some light into the stairwell.

'You'd think I'd have noticed windows in one of the walls of my own home that I'd never seen from the inside, wouldn't you? But I don't recall anything like this tiny one at all. We'll have to take a look from the outside.' She peered through the glass, wiping at it with the bottom of her blouse. 'Look, there's the stable roof just below us. I think I know where we are. How odd to think I'm in a part of my home I've never entered before.'

Alexander had re-lit his torch and turned a corner ahead of Christine. 'Take a look at this,' he called.

Following him, Christine was surprised to see a doorway on the small landing where the stairs changed direction. It led into a tiny, square, windowless room where one wall was covered in shelves. A thump came from above the pair. 'Go on, get going. Maybe someone's in another one of these on a different landing,' she urged.

A flight up, Alexander used the large iron key he found hanging beside a locked door to open it. Inside, Brid Ahearn was sitting on the floor crying. Tear tracks cut through the dirt caked on her face.

'Ah, God love you,' she cried as she flung her arms around Christine.

Christine and Alexander led the sobbing woman down to the basement, then up to the kitchen. They all took their time.

'Don't stop me, I have to go,' was Brid's first properly comprehensible statement as she ran to the nearest loo.

Christine made a pot of tea and hurled four sugars into a mug while it brewed.

'What's going on? And where's Callum?' asked Christine of Brid as she sipped her tea, trying to not let the panic she felt creep into her voice.

'Oh Jaysis, Mary and Joseph, I'm so happy you found me, so I am,' said Brid, crossing herself as she spoke. 'Thought I'd die in there I did, sure enough. Thank yous. Thank yous both. Oh dear, sweet Jaysis. My poor Callum. Took him off, they have. What'll we do?'

Christine allowed herself to look at Alexander; his wide-eyed shrug told her he thought it best she continued to try to get information out of the shaken woman. 'Brid, calm yourself, and tell us what happened. Please,' she pleaded.

Brid set down her mug and leaned toward Christine, 'All kicked off about nine this morning. Put the heart in me crossways they did showing up in their vans. Callum was out with the chickens . . .' She paused and shook her head. 'Wrecked with the fear he was this morning – ossified last night, so he was – and I was doing the washing; wanted to get it on the line before the weather got fierce. Six big numpties comes in the back door here and starts talking rubbish about Callum owing them money and them being ready to knock lumps out of him.'

Brid slurped tea and Christine noticed Alexander was agape. 'Translation for the Englishman,' said Christine with a slight smile, 'Callum was nursing a hangover, having been drunk last night, and was out feeding the chickens. Brid was doing the laundry when six large men, who didn't look very bright, arrived demanding money with menaces.'

'Thanks,' said Alexander. 'I never knew I'd need English translated into English.'

Christine kicked him gently beneath the table. 'I've heard the way you talk to your mates in south London; less about the Irish using words no one else understands, thank you very much.'

'Fair enough,' said Alexander.

'What then?' asked Christine. 'Don't worry about him, Brid, he'll get used to how we talk in these parts. Eventually.'

'Yous had gone off already, so I took them to where Callum was. All went at it there they did, chickens flapping all over the place with the racket they was making. Eggs broken. Feathers a-flyin'. My poor Callum, I couldn't help at all. One of them held me arms so I couldn't have a go at them meself. And it all came out.' More tea slurping.

'What came out?' asked Christine as gently as she could.

'Callum's only gone and borrowed money from someone and not paid it back, hasn't he. I could have knocked him over the head for that meself. Dope. Told me why he did it. He's still a dope. Shouldn't have done it. Or should have paid it back. But he said he would when he could, which was when he . . .' Brid paused and looked from Christine to Alexander and back to Christine.

'We know about the potcheen,' said Christine.

Brid relaxed a little. 'Ah. Well. There you are then.'

Christine waited while the woman poured more tea from the pot, then felt herself losing all patience. 'Come on, Brid. Talk. Is Callum in danger? Have they taken him and the potcheen to pay off a debt? Why did they lock you up? And how on earth did they know they could lock you up where they did? Even I didn't know that place existed, and I grew up here. Get it all out. Now.'

Brid rearranged her shoulders and looked sulky. 'Borrowed money for new stills and all the gubbins he did. Eejit. Said the potatoes would all go to waste otherwise. Made the stuff. Got it all crated up and stored. Was due to sell it off as a bulk load two weeks ago, but that didn't work out, then he got it all sorted again for this weekend, but you two turned up, so he called off the deal. Didn't want you knowing about it. Didn't sell it. Didn't have the money to pay off the loan. They come today and took the lot of it, and him with it.'

'So it's *our* fault he's in trouble?' said Alexander warily.

Brid didn't look at him as she replied, 'Callum reckons so. It's what he told them this morning. Stuffed him in the back of one of them there vans they did, then filled up with the potcheen and locked me up. I've no inkling how they knew about them stairs; I thought it was only myself and Callum knew of them. Maybe he let something slip.'

'I'm sorry our arrival has messed up your plans for selling the illegal potcheen you made from crops you've grown on our land,' said Christine, allowing there to be a slight edge to her tone, 'but maybe Callum shouldn't have borrowed money from a man who sounds rather dangerous.' Brid shrugged. 'Did they say they'd be bringing him back?'

Brid looked all of her sixty years as she replied, 'They'll be back tomorrow morning. Not to bring him back, at least, they didn't say that. To have a look about and see if there's anything worth taking from this place, they said.' She blushed. 'We didn't tell them you was here, you see. So they thought they'd have the run of the place. Said they'd need a lorry for the job.'

Alexander leaned in. 'So you're telling us that tomorrow morning there'll be a band of men coming here to, basically, strip the place of anything of value? How much money did Callum borrow?'

'He said it wasn't that much to start, but he couldn't sell the stuff when he'd thought he would so the interest, it kept on building up. That's a lot, they said.' Brid was close to tears again.

'But they've got the potcheen, they can sell that. Won't that pay off Callum's debts?' Alexander scraped his chair backwards and stood, pacing the flagstones.

Brid began to cry. 'I don't know, so I don't. Too scared to hear proper, I was. Sure they all looked two shillings short of a pound, but evil with it. That's the worst type. But they won't have taken the drink over the border in the middle of the day, surely to God. Must have a plan to keep it this side, somewhere. Maybe even sell it over here.'

'Any idea where that might be, Brid? And what can you tell us about this man who loaned Callum the money?' pressed Christine.

'Nothin'. "The Boss" was all they said. He's got to be a bad lot, hasn't he?'

'And his men will be back here in the morning,' mused Alexander. 'Right then, we'd better be ready for them.'

FOURTEEN

Tuesday 23rd August

The little bell above the door of the general shop and post office that overlooked the green tinkled as it opened. 'Hiya Shar, it's only Annie.' There was no one in sight.

The multi-colored plastic flaps of a privacy curtain fluttered as Sharon walked into the shop from the rooms behind. She was holding her mobile phone against her ear and made gestures at

Annie which anyone would be able to interpret to mean 'hang on a minute.'

Annie browsed the fresh breads and sliced meats, wondering if she fancied a ham bap for lunch. She found it difficult to make up her mind because the dinner she and Huw had shared at a swank restaurant in Gower the previous evening had been rich and filling, and she'd known at the time she shouldn't have eaten it. However, Annie had set aside her concerns about her rumbling innards and had tasted everything Huw had ordered for them. By the time she'd looked at her toast that morning, she was beginning to wonder if starting two consecutive days feeling less than one hundred percent meant she shouldn't dare to eat anything other than the most bland of lunches.

As she considered her choices, and recollected the drive to and from Gower with Huw, and his delightful attentiveness the entire time they were together, she couldn't help but overhear Sharon's conversation.

'Oh it's awful,' said Sharon. 'He looked so well when I saw him. And there's no one, is there? Of course, his poor wife did, didn't she? Aw, poor dab. Well, you never know when it's your turn, do you? Alright, yes, when I hear something. Thanks for letting me know. Bye now.' She hung up.

Annie gave her attention to the young woman tucking her phone into her pocket. 'What's up?' asked Annie.

'You'll never guess – poor old Dr Priddle's dead,' said Sharon sounding shocked. 'Just like that. His cleaner, Mrs Davies-Duster, found him dead on the floor beside his chair, in front of the TV with it still on, not half an hour ago. Terrible he looked, she said. No idea how long he's been there like that. She only cleans his place on Tuesdays and Thursdays. He could have been there days. She's had quite a turn. Having a cup of tea now, she is, which I think's a very good idea. Said the police and what-not are on their way.'

'Is this Mrs Davies-Duster the same one what oversees all the cleaning at Chellingworth Hall?' asked Annie, unsure how someone who had such a responsibility could possibly find the time to clean other people's homes.

'No, that's Mrs Davies-Cleaning. Mrs Davies-Duster just does houses,' replied Sharon. She leaned in. 'Word is she's called

Mrs Davies-Duster because all she does is flick a duster around the parts people can see. And manages to drink gallons of tea while she's at it.'

'Gordon Bennett, sometimes I think everyone around here's called Davies. Breed like rabbits, do they? Davieses, I mean?'

Sharon looked puzzled. 'Not that I'm aware, but, you're right, we have our fair share of them, and more. Same as all over Wales, I dare say.'

'So, was that Mrs Davies-Duster on the phone to you just then?' Annie had often wondered how Sharon seemed to know about everything going on in the area almost as it happened, and realized this might be why – the people involved rang her with the news themselves.

Sharon nodded. 'She got there at seven thirty, and there he was. She's phoned the police, of course, and now she's stuck there waiting for them. Talked to me from his kitchen. Not going to stay in the sitting room with a dead body, is she?'

Annie could tell Sharon was itching to get the word out. 'I wonder what he died of,' she said.

'Probably his heart, I'd have thought,' said Sharon, 'if he went like that. Usually is, isn't it? And he was very old, after all.'

'I'd better tell Tudor,' said Annie, thinking about the gap in the Anwen Allcomers' croquet team. 'He'll be sorry to hear he's gone. Me too. I didn't know the man well; I'd met him when you lot were all practicing for the tournament, obviously, and we had a bit of a chat at tea on Sunday. He seemed like a nice bloke.'

'He was my mam's doctor when I was born, and mine when I was a kid, until he retired. Had lovely lollies for us little ones when we'd been good in his surgery. Mam'll be sorry to hear he's dead. Always said the new doctor wasn't half as good as him. I'd better ring her first.' Sharon pulled out her mobile, then looked at Annie with sharp eyes. 'Sorry, Annie – did you want to buy something before I start doing my duty getting the news out?'

Annie got herself a tomato, some ham and a couple of doughy, flour-dusted baps, agreed with Sharon that they'd catch up later to discuss future plans for refreshments for the croquet team, then headed across the green with the intention of delivering the news about Dr Priddle to Tudor.

Ten minutes later she and Tudor were sitting on stools drinking coffee at the bar, while Gertie and Rosie played with a stuffed toy – taking it in turns to try to kill it.

'I can't get over it,' said Tudor grim-faced. 'I had no idea he had a heart condition.'

'We can't be sure that's what it was,' said Annie quickly. 'It could be any number of things. Sharon's source just guessed, that's all. I expect they'll find out more at the post-mortem, if they have one.'

'A sad day,' said Tudor, his shoulders sagging. 'He was a character, you know,' he added a little more brightly, 'always a smile and a "How do you do?" when he came through the village. For everyone. Half of dark he drank. Never a full pint. Half of dark, and sometimes a packet of bacon crisps. Said that was because he didn't eat bacon any more – which might mean he knew he had a problem with cholesterol, I suppose.'

'I'd have thought, at his age, he'd have had a good few problems. It's the sort of time when a person's body starts to wear out, isn't it?' observed Annie.

Tudor sighed. 'Comes to us all, in the end. He walked a lot, always looked hale and hearty, even if he wasn't too quick on his pins. Managed very well throughout our team's practice sessions this year, and at our day up at the hall. No signs of anything wrong then.'

'I was chatting to him on Sunday,' said Annie thoughtfully. 'Or he was chatting more to me, I suppose.'

'What about?'

'Oh, just this and that. He was saying that Huw used to spend a lot of time at his house playing chess with his wife when Huw was still at school here.'

Tudor stood up and marched to a spot behind the bar, where he picked up a glass and began to polish it with a tea towel. 'I see,' he said.

Annie wondered why he sounded so strange. 'He seemed to enjoy chatting about the old days,' continued Annie. She couldn't fathom why so many glasses needed Tudor's immediate attention.

'Before my time,' he said. Rather curtly, Annie thought. 'Hadn't retired when I got here, but he'd certainly gone by the time I first needed to see a doctor. He was never mine. But I've come to know him and like him over the years. Can't not get to know a person in a place like this.'

'Do you think there'll be a service?' asked Annie.

Tudor put down the glass he was holding. 'At church at least twice a month, he was; of course there'll be a service. St David's was his church. There'll be a big turnout too. I'd better phone Reverend Roberts soon. He'll be the one to make plans.'

'They might not be able to have a service for a while; there might need to be a post-mortem. Dr Priddle died alone, at home. I happen to know that if a dead person's GP thinks the death is unexpected, they won't sign a death certificate, and they'll arrange for the coroner to order a post-mortem. That could take a while. Do you know who his doctor was?'

'No idea,' replied Tudor, who'd returned to his glass-polishing. 'Since he moved out of the village, and especially since the doctor's surgery closed down here, he might have had a doctor out in Builth Wells, or maybe even Brecon. I dare say the police will sort it out. Got to be used to dealing with this sort of thing, haven't they?'

'I suppose you're right,' replied Annie, already thinking about the fact she should let Mavis know what was going on and that she might be late arriving at the office.

'Nice to know,' replied Tudor.

'Sorry, what's that? Nice to know what?'

'That you still think I'm able to be right about something.'

Annie was puzzled. Tudor was behaving weirdly. In fact, quite a few people had been acting strangely of late. 'There you are then,' was all she could summon by way of a reply. 'Who will you get to replace him? On the croquet team, I mean,' she added.

Tudor paused again. He dumped the tea towel on the bar. 'I don't know, but you're right, I'd better give that some thought.' He looked over at Annie as she played with the pups. 'I don't suppose you . . .?' He paused.

'Me? Play croquet? Oh come on, Tude, you know I like to help out, but croquet? Really? You need someone posh to do that. It's a shame Chrissie's on holiday, she'd probably have been able to step in.'

'You don't have to be posh to play croquet. I'm certainly not posh, and I've played for donkey's years. It's not an expensive game to play, and you don't need loads of equipment or space to play it like some games. Tennis, now that's something you have to have loads of space to play, and a special surface, and posts and a net;

those rackets alone can cost a packet.' He paused and allowed himself a little grin. 'Croquet just needs a bit of grass, a few hoops, balls and mallets – which all last forever, by the way – and you're off. You can play it on your own, or with two or any number of people. Good game is croquet. Cheap as chips to play. You don't have to be posh at all.'

Annie shrugged; she'd always thought of croquet as something that people with titles played, and the tournament – and especially the lavish spread she'd seen on Sunday – had merely supported her original thinking. 'When you put it that way, you've got a point,' she conceded. 'But I always thought it was a very English game. How come there's a tournament here, in the middle of Wales, then?'

'It's just a game. It doesn't have a nationality. Some people reckon it started in Ireland, some in France. Either way the Welsh have as much right to enjoy it as the English.'

Annie sensed a bit of anti-English sentiment in Tudor's tone, which wasn't so unusual; having watched him follow the Six Nations rugby championship earlier in the year she'd got used to him – and pretty much everyone else in the village – being rabidly, and vocally, anti-English when it came to sports. She'd decided months earlier it was best to let it pass, and not comment at all.

She stood, trying to pull Gertie away from Rosie. 'I'd better get going or Mavis will have me guts for garters. I'll be late.' She looked at her watch. 'Nope, I'm late already. I'll phone her while we walk.'

'I could give you a lift to the office if you'd like,' offered Tudor.

Annie gave his suggestion some thought. 'That would be great, ta. But I wouldn't mind using the facilities before we go. My innards aren't all they could be. Weren't yesterday, neither. Alright with you?'

'Go ahead. There must be something going around. I wasn't all that good yesterday morning, and Aled couldn't even make it in for his shift last night he was so bad. I heard Marjorie Pritchard had to run off and leave the church cleaning crew yesterday with a bit of a problem. It's probably this heat. Not used to all this hot sunshine around here.'

Annie almost missed Tudor's final point, and certainly didn't have time to agree with him, as she felt her tummy gurgle, thrust Gertie's lead into his hand and rushed across the pub, promising herself plain food for a couple of days.

FIFTEEN

Alexander Bright woke early, leaving fitful dreams behind him. He rolled out of bed as silently as possible; he didn't want to wake Christine now she was sleeping soundly. Hoping for a sunny morning he was disappointed to see banks of dark clouds hanging over the lough. He pulled on some clothes and padded out of the bedroom as quietly as the ancient floorboards would allow.

Once downstairs, he went outside and stood beneath the portico at the front of the house making phone call after phone call. He hadn't been able to do it the previous night because he didn't want Christine to know what he was up to, and she'd needed him by her side the whole time. The discovery of the inconsolable Brid, finding out about the potcheen and knowing the manor was under threat of a return visit by a group of thugs had, understandably, put Christine on edge.

Even as he dialed yet another number in London he recalled, with pride, how quick Christine had been to take positive action to offset the imminent threat to her family home. He'd been amazed by how easily she'd charmed and lied her way to organize a meeting, at Ballinclare Manor itself, with members of the local police.

Alexander checked his watch; there was more than an hour before their expected arrival. Christine had gleefully announced that a couple of officers were coming, believing they were to discuss two key topics – the planning of security protocols for the manor, and her setting up a branch of the WISE Enquiries Agency in the area. She hadn't minded using her father's title to ensure she was taken as seriously as needed, and had been promised a visit at the critical time.

His fourth call didn't allow him to do more than leave a message, so he tried a fifth number.

'Hello Dave. Alex here. I need some help. I'm in Ireland, not far from your old stomping grounds. Up for it?'

Dave was most accommodating, as Alexander had known he would be; he'd used Dave and his plumbing firm on dozens of his construction and refurbishment projects over the years. Many of the plumbers who worked for Dave were Irish, some from the north, some from the south. Alexander reckoned Dave and his boys would be able to give him insights and information about potcheen and its darker business-side, fast. Hanging up, he knew Dave would come through for him; Dave understood urgency, and Alexander had left him in no doubt about how grateful he'd be in terms of his efforts. He walked back into the manor with more of a spring in his step than when he'd left.

Christine was running down the wide staircase as he entered, her hair still damp from the shower, her feet bare. 'Just going to grab some toast and coffee, then I'll spruce myself up for the coppers,' she said, planting a kiss on Alexander's cheek. 'I hope Brid's managed to have a bit of a lie in like I told her to. See you in the kitchen.'

'Right behind you – we can talk about The Case of the Purloined Potcheen.'

'The what?' Christine sounded horrified.

'Hey, I've been working on that for ages. Hang on, let me take this call. Two shakes and I'll be with you,' replied Alexander. His phone was vibrating and he recognized the name of the caller – Kevin – a builders' merchant located in Norwood, south London, who owed him more than a few favors. He answered and listened silently, astonished at what he heard.

Eventually walking into the kitchen he asked, 'Did you know that Enniskillen, the main town of this fair county Fermanagh of yours, is inundated with people who apparently earn almost nothing, yet live the high life?'

Christine looked up from her tea. 'Swaps,' she said.

Alexander deflated a little. 'Oh, so you do then. Has it always been like this?'

Christine smiled as she poured a cup from the pot. 'You mean have we Irish always preferred to swap what we have for something we want, rather than spend real money – and pay taxes into the bargain? Yes. We have chickens here, so we have eggs; Brid swaps eggs with people who keep pigs in exchange for bacon; she swaps some of that bacon for cheese the dairy farmers make. No money changes hands. No taxes are paid. It works.'

'Is that maybe why Callum didn't have the cash he needed when he wanted to buy everything he needed for more stills, and cash was what he needed to get the equipment?'

Christine gave the matter some thought. 'It could be, though, honestly, what Brid said doesn't make much sense. The equipment isn't expensive in itself, it's just large storage containers, piping, the copper "worms" for the distillation, then all the bottles and crates. I mean, when all's said and done, the costs and the value can mount up, but if he'd bought it a bit at a time he could have managed, I'm sure.'

'Look,' said Alexander, taking his tea, 'I don't mean to alarm you, but I've made a few calls, and I've got some information coming in from Irish contacts in London who know about the potcheen stuff. Not in the way you do, but on the shadier side of things.'

'You shouldn't have,' said Christine. Alexander thought she sounded as though she meant it literally, not in a grateful way.

'Well I did. And the news isn't good. I just got word from someone who knows someone who says that if Callum has borrowed from the wrong people, he could be in a great deal of very real trouble. Especially if he's become in anyway involved with some bloke known only as The Gadfly. After she calmed down a bit, did Brid give you any idea what sort of money we're talking about? Or what sort of timescale it was that he was overdue with his payment?'

'I honestly don't think she has any notion. But I tell you what, I don't like the alias being used by that chap you mentioned.'

'What? The Gadfly? Doesn't that just mean someone who's annoying – like a fly, biting away at you all the time.'

Christine nodded slowly. 'It does that. But in these parts it has another meaning.'

'How d'you mean?'

'It's the title of a book by an Irish writer. It became really famous in Russia. About revolution. Took hold hereabouts with those fighting their own revolution. If this bloke's using that as an alias, it might say something about his political leanings. Could be dangerous. He might— shush, here comes Brid.' Christine stood. 'Good morning to you, Brid. I've made a pot of tea. How are you?'

Brid burst into tears, and Alexander thought better of staying for toast. 'I'll just make a few more phone calls, and don't forget the police are due here soon. I'll stay out of the way, upstairs, for now – you alright with that, Christine?' She nodded.

Alexander made his escape, mug in one hand, phone in the other; he had no desire to meet with the local police largely because he never thought it a good idea to allow himself to appear on the radar of any organization that wore uniforms. In his world, as in the local environs, keeping yourself to yourself, and the government in its many guises out of as much of your business as possible, was a useful rule of thumb – until it became unavoidable, and you needed their help. He didn't think this was that day.

SIXTEEN

Henry was at his wits' end. 'Blessed creature!' He stomped from the breakfast table to the sideboard to select the perfect eggs and the correct number of pieces of bacon to start the day.

'What is it, dear?' asked Stephanie, pouring tea to accompany her toast.

'That blessed mole, that's what. It looks like the little blighter Ivor caught and transported to one of the upper fields wasn't working alone after all. Either that, or it's set an underground-speed record burrowing its way back to my croquet lawn. Have you seen the mess out there this morning? Mounds all over the place. It's awful. As bad as the vandalism at the pavilion.'

'I'm sure Ivor's doing his best, Henry,' said Stephanie gently as she passed the pepper to her now-seated husband. 'He'll sort it out, never fear.'

Henry didn't think his bacon tasted as good as it usually did, but applied himself to it nonetheless. He was surprised when his mother entered the morning room.

'Good morning, dear,' she said. 'No, don't get up. I'd hate to drag you away from your healthy meal.' Henry thought he noted a bit of an eye-roll being exchanged between his mother and wife, but chose to ignore it.

'Will you take breakfast with us, Mother?' He looked down at McFli who had rushed toward the sideboard, and was wagging his tiny tail at a good rate of knots. 'No bacon for you, McFli,' he said firmly, thinking he might manage another couple of slices himself.

'I'll take tea, that's all. Thank you, Stephanie, I'll pour for myself.'

'To what do we owe the honor of this unexpected visit?' asked the duchess of the dowager.

'Mavis was scurrying about the Dower House first thing and I didn't have a very good night, so I thought I'd take a walk, and ended up here. I see the mole is back – or you have more than one. Will Ivor need young Ian to help him all week, do you think, Henry?'

Henry nodded as he continued to grapple with indecision about making another trip to the sideboard.

'And is there any more news from the police about the vandalism?' asked Althea. Henry recognized his mother's 'unconcerned' tone, which he knew meant that was exactly why she'd come.

'Since Mavis insisted I put the matter in the hands of the police, I should have thought the whole thing is now, clearly, nothing to do with the WISE women,' he said with as much finality as he could muster. He rose from his seat and returned to the sideboard with his plate.

He couldn't see the expression on his mother's face, but suspected it would be the epitome of innocence as she said, 'I'm not here as a helper at the agency, I'm here as the dowager of Chellingworth. It was against us that the vandal acted, and I am, therefore, fully entitled to be concerned.'

As Henry returned to the table, with a few more slices of bacon than he'd originally intended taking, he witnessed his wife holding his mother's hand. 'Of course you're entitled to be concerned, and kept informed, Althea,' Stephanie was cooing, 'but we haven't heard anything at all from the police.'

'Not likely to, either,' added Henry. 'As I told you yesterday, they aren't going to throw the might of their force into a paltry little investigation like this. They have bigger fish to fry. I'll put money on them paying us lip service and nothing more. You WISE women should have taken it on. Mavis should have allowed my opinion to prevail.'

Henry didn't like it when his mother sighed; it usually meant she was about to give him what for. He steeled himself, but no broadside was forthcoming.

Althea simply said, 'Excuse me, I'm vibrating.'

Henry realized his mother meant her mobile phone needed to be answered. He munched his bacon as she took her call.

Returning the phone to her pocket, Althea apologized for having remained at the table while she spoke. Before Henry could tell her he thought it a terrible thing to do, she held up her small hand demanding his silence as she answered yet another call.

Irritated, Henry glared at his bacon. He wasn't at all sure he wanted it anymore. He sneaked a piece off his plate and waggled it at McFli head height. The dog wasted no time in darting to Henry's side and snatching the bacon from the duke's fingers.

Putting away her phone for a second time, Althea sniped, 'Please don't do that, Henry. McFli should not be allowed bacon. It's bad for him. Not that such large quantities are good for you, dear, but that's your decision. Unlike a human, McFli isn't aware of things like cholesterol and heart attacks.'

Henry tried hard to come up with a biting retort, but failed. 'You're in demand this morning,' was all he could muster. 'Do you usually take so many calls on that thing?'

Althea beamed. 'Since I've had a mobile phone my life has changed so much. You've no idea how easy it is to keep in touch with people when you have one of these things. It's like a little miracle. One never feels alone when one has a mobile phone.'

As Althea laughed at her quip, Stephanie joined in, 'You'd have been a natural in public relations, Althea. That's the sort of thing we'd have come up with after a meeting between ten people for ten hours. And the best thing about it? It's true.'

'It certainly is. And look at what I've learned already that I'd otherwise not know about.'

'What's that, Mother?' asked Henry.

'The first call was Sharon Jones. It seems Marjorie Pritchard was rushed into hospital yesterday afternoon with terrible . . .' Henry noticed his mother stare at his bacon before she concluded, '. . . gastric problems. Totally dehydrated she is, poor thing. They hope she can come home later today, but they kept her in overnight for observation and so they could put her on an intravenous drip.'

Stephanie answered, 'I'm sorry to hear that. Do they know what the problem was? Something she ate?'

Althea leaned toward her daughter-in-law. 'No one's saying, but I suspect it must be. Then there's poor Dr Priddle, that was the second call.'

'Oh, I say,' said Henry beaming, 'two of them down with a tummy bug? Sounds like the Anwen Allcomers will have to rely upon back-up players this weekend. I scent another win for the Chellingworth Champs.' He pushed his emptied plate away, feeling satisfied at last.

'Henry, watch your words,' snapped Althea. Henry was surprised at his mother's tone.

'Come along, Mother, you know I don't mean I'm *glad* that the Pritchard woman and Dr Priddle are both poorly, but—'

'Dr Priddle isn't poorly, he's dead, Henry,' said Althea tartly. 'As I said, watch your words until you are fully informed.'

Henry felt dreadful. 'I'm sorry, Mother. You're quite correct. That's terrible news about Dr Priddle, though he was getting on a bit, wasn't he?' Before his mother had time to reply he noticed Stephanie pulling a face at him. The penny dropped. He tried to rectify his mistake by adding, 'A good deal older than you, Mother, I'm sure.'

Henry noticed the dowager didn't make eye contact with him when she replied, 'Somewhat.'

Shifting uncomfortably in his seat, Henry indicated to his wife he'd like some more tea, which she prepared for him with an expression on her face that could have curdled the milk in the jug. As she handed him his cup and saucer she whispered, 'Would you care for a slice of humble pie with that, dear?' Henry felt his cheeks flush.

He was delighted when Stephanie asked his mother, 'Did you know the doctor well, Althea? I'm sure he'll be missed. Did the caller inform you what happened?'

Althea seemed to be rallying. 'Thank you for asking, dear. I can't say I knew the man well, though, of course, as the doctor in the local village he was often the first to attend when one of the children was taken ill. Henry's father's insistence that we had Mr Wellington in Harley Street as our doctor of record was all well and good, but when one has urgent need of a physician one isn't able to wait for a doctor – albeit one who's risen above the need to use such a title

– to drive from London. Dr Priddle was most generous and made prompt home visits.' Althea put down her cup. 'Indeed, Henry, it was Dr Priddle who put forward the idea that your brother had contracted measles, despite the fact he was in his forties.'

Henry felt a heaviness in his tummy he was quite certain wasn't the bacon. 'I didn't realize that,' he said quietly. Looking across the table at his wife he added, 'As I've told you, I was out of the country when Devereaux was taken ill, and died. It's one of the great sorrows of my life that I wasn't able to say goodbye to my brother.'

Henry saw true tenderness in his mother's eyes. 'You said your farewells when he went off on his trip to America, and you went off to France. It was a good leave-taking, Henry; you were both wishing each other well for the adventures you were about to undertake. It was tragic that Dev's visit to Indiana coincided with an outbreak of measles, and that his contraction of the disease led to pneumonia and his untimely death. We had no idea he would fail so rapidly. Dr Priddle was with him at the hospital when he unexpectedly died. For that, at least, we can be grateful.'

Henry felt the silence that followed closing in about him. 'I miss Dev,' he said simply.

'I understand why you would,' replied Althea. She turned to Stephanie. 'Although they were only half-brothers, Dev and Henry were true best friends. Maybe the fact they had different mothers allowed them to cement that relationship. Dev was a wonderful boy, and man; full of vigor, though somewhat foolhardy, it must be said. He'd have made quite a good duke, Henry – but I think you have done, and are doing, a splendid job. You are the sort of duke he'd never have been; you're here, present. The hall and the village mean something to you. Dev would always have been a rover. I, for one, believe the seat's relationship with the community is stronger because the title came to you.'

'Hear, hear,' said Stephanie, smiling at her husband and raising her teacup in a toast.

'Thank you,' said Henry, feeling truly grateful that his mother and wife recognized how difficult it was for him to try to be the man he'd never imagined he'd have to become.

He was glad when Stephanie asked, 'And do they know what happened to Dr Priddle?'

Althea shook her head. 'The news is he died alone, at home.

Which I do think is a terrible pity. I hope it was quick. If one goes alone, it should be quick.'

'Amen to that,' said Henry.

SEVENTEEN

Christine had steeled herself for the role she knew she had to perform that morning, and hoped she would do a good job. When the bell in the front porch jangled, she shooed Alexander to sit on the landing, hidden by banisters, so he could overhear the conversation she was about to have. Just before pulling open the front door she gave herself a final talking-to, and willed her mind-set to shift into the gear she needed.

She fussed and gushed as she invited the police officers into her home, her plan being to overwhelm them sufficiently with her charm that they'd remain at the manor long enough for their liveried vehicle to be seen by the men planning to raid the place. Brid had been dispatched to the topmost floor with a pair of ancient binoculars so she could be lookout and report developments to Alexander, who would relay vital information to Christine by text.

The inspector who'd been selected to meet the viscount's daughter at Ballinclare Manor initially struck Christine as possessing the personality of a dead trout, yet even he seemed to become enlivened by Christine's instantly fabricated plans for establishing a branch of the WISE Enquiries Agency on the estate.

Only the senior officer spoke; the junior one remained as dumb as the antimacassars on the worn sofas. Christine spoke generally about the agency, then opened her laptop and showed the officer details of cases they had concluded successfully. She emphasized the rigorous ways in which the WISE women observed the niceties of the finely-balanced relationship between themselves and local law enforcement in Wales; she noted the inspector seemed calmed by that idea. Then she tried to draw out the man on the nature of possible cases for a firm of private enquiry agents in the surrounding area.

'Are there many firms like this already doing business about these parts?' she asked.

The inspector's accent made it plain to Christine that he hailed from Belfast, or close by; his harsh, flat tones seemed to mangle the words he spoke.

'To be honest wid ya, not so's you'd notice,' was his initial reply.

Christine pressed, 'So, Inspector Beattie, does your professional opinion suggest to you that's because there isn't enough work for such an undertaking in these parts, or just that people aren't sharp enough to spot the opportunity? Is there a lot of work for a company that would undertake to investigate that which the police cannot?'

The policeman threw a sideways glance at his underling. 'Any chance you could rustle us up a cuppa?' he said sharply.

Christine stood. 'My apologies, inspector, my helper around the place has some duties to perform elsewhere on the estate this morning, but I did prepare a tea tray. Would you let me put the water in the pot and bring it through?'

'Could this one manage it?' He stuck his thumb toward the junior officer, who leaped to his feet.

Christine sensed the inspector wanted to speak more freely than he could with his subordinate in the room. 'Certainly – how about I show your constable where everything is, then maybe he could wait for the kettle to boil and bring it in for us?' She did as she'd said, then returned to the sitting room, leaving the junior officer – who even to her eyes looked to be about twelve years old – to tea-making duties.

'So,' she opened, 'do you think there's work for us here?'

Inspector Beattie rubbed his chin. 'There might be, but you'd have to have the right sort of people working for you. I know those Welsh are pretty stubborn when it comes to telling all to outsiders, but they're nothing like people around these parts. Not sure how much your colleagues would get out of the locals here. You'd need Irish talking to Irish. Might need to recruit locals for the jobs. And make sure you knew their backgrounds, too.'

Christine decided to take a leap of faith. 'Between you and me, I had wondered about that. The old wounds haven't gone away, have they? Maybe only the Irish would really understand that. Do you have much to deal with in this area of a political nature?'

'Difficult to say,' said the man.

Christine judged he was trying to work out how much he could reveal to the daughter of a viscount whose land had been given to him by the English, and who mainly resided in London, far away from his estate. She decided to help him out. 'I know times have been difficult here; despite the fact I spend a great deal of time not here, this still *is* my home – it's in my heart and in my blood. The terrible hurt of the past will never completely disappear, and I dare say there are still whispers about who did, or believed, what, when believing was all you had to do to become a target. It's been said by those a great deal more clever than me that Ireland's past has the potential to poison its future, but I know that so many individuals are working hard to not allow that to be the case. We can all try to be part of the solution by our own actions. I know my father felt that when he hired Brid and Callum Ahearn to live and work here; two faiths under one roof allows for understanding to develop. I had also hoped that helping people with little problems – not crime, not violence in their lives, but the small things that worry them – might be a way to help. To show them their problems matter, whatever their background. That's why I thought maybe our agency might have a useful role to play.'

Inspector Beattie's response was more encouraging. 'You might have something at that. So many people won't ever come to the police with their problems, you see? Either they don't trust us because we're us, or – even if they do trust us – they don't want us poking about in their business.'

'Ah, thank you constable, you can put it there,' said Christine when the tea tray was presented. She served, and allowed the conversation to revert to more general topics.

'As you know, I spend a good deal of time in Wales these days, and I have to say I've grown to like their ways there. In many respects it reminds me of life here; Chellingworth Hall is in Powys, the largest county in Wales and rural for the most part. The people there, like here, work hard to make the best life they can for themselves and their families, from the land in many cases, but that's never been easy. Of course, there are always those only too willing to take advantage of any situation, and questionable "opportunities." Just a few weeks ago we unearthed a network of thieves whose specialty was to plunder the pubs that are, sadly, closing down. Their preferred method was to get into the abandoned buildings under cover of darkness and strip out the metal, the wiring, fireplaces – anything they could sell on. Dreadful. Pubs are such an important part of our heritage, don't you think?'

Christine beamed at the juvenile officer. As she handed him his tea he dared to say, 'Some pubs are even closing down around here, which I'd never have thought possible. People stay home to drink more these days.' A glance at his superior shut him up.

'But that's the sort of thing we could do, you see, inspector – be your eyes and ears; we were able to gather information that allowed local law enforcement to catch that gang, and their prosecution will be easier because of our surveillance evidence. I've heard there are informal networks in these parts too. I was having a coffee in Enniskillen just the other day when I heard some woman talking about a chap her husband had borrowed money from, and how grateful they were for it – I think his name was Gadabout. See, there's an example of someone else in the community trying to give help to ordinary people who need it.'

The young officer almost choked. 'Do you mean Gadfly? God help them then—' he spluttered as another sharp look from the inspector shut him up.

Christine knew she'd hit a nerve. 'Yes, that was it. Gadfly, not Gadabout. It sounded as though he was quite popular. The women she was talking to all seemed to know him. It must be difficult for people to get what they need from banks, like it's difficult for them to get what they need from the police. We could do what he seems to be doing – offer a service to the community from within the community itself.' She realized she was skating on thin ice because the expression on the inspector's face suggested he was about to have a heart attack.

'I wouldn't go around saying things like that about that character,' he snapped, placing his cup back in its saucer. 'I'm sorry to say there's a lot you don't know about the specifics of this area. You've been away more than you've been here for a good many years. Things, people, change. If you were to set up a private investigations company here you'd do well to do a great deal of research before you took any cases. You wouldn't want to come up against any outfits that meant you'd be biting off more than you could chew.'

Christine forced herself to look innocently surprised. 'You mean this Gadfly's a real crook? Not a pillar of the community at all?'

'Likes to paint himself as something he's not – not that we actually know who he is. But I can tell you this – wherever we hear his name it's accompanied by a trail of misery and heartbreak – and sometimes, yes, real criminal activity. And that's what I mean . . .' He looked as though he was going to pick up his cup again, but Christine could tell he was deep in thought. He looked directly into her eyes. 'You're young, and you have all this. Why would you want to go prying into people's dirty laundry at all? Isn't it all divorce and sleaziness for people like you?'

Christine was taken aback; the man seemed to have suddenly changed his opinion of her. 'I believe we help those who cannot help themselves by using our skills, talents, and training,' she replied.

'Sometimes, that's not enough,' he said darkly. 'Sometimes you need a large force of highly trained individuals working with you to help you see the full picture. I would suggest you consider that if you decide to go ahead with your plans. This isn't the sort of thing you could go into with your eyes closed. There are some nasty types about.'

'But that's not something that's only true here – it's true everywhere,' said Christine, disliking the way this man was describing her homeland. 'We see it in Wales, and in England where we've also worked on cases. I dare say the same could be said for Scotland too. Every part of the world, in fact. There are good people and bad, of all religions, colors, creeds, and sexual orientation. Being rotten to the core, and acting upon it, isn't something that's reserved for one group or type.'

'That's as maybe, but there are certain environments where the wickedness men choose to do can flourish more easily, if only because of the number of damaged people who are available either to be taken advantage of, or exploited in other ways. This is a recently war-torn land, few of those who don't live here understand that. You should.'

Christine tried to take in what he'd said as she glanced at a text on her phone. It read, 'No sign of them. Can you keep it going?' Realizing she somehow had to keep the officers there for as long as she could, she went through the process of a detailed walk-through of the entire manor, with the junior officer pointing out all the lax security issues he observed, and noting them on a sheet.

An hour later she'd completely run out of reasons for them to stay, and they left. Christine had a workable plan for a security system in her hand, and a heavy heart when she thought about Callum and the clearly dangerous Gadfly. She wondered how much to tell Brid.

EIGHTEEN

Annie tucked into her ham and tomato bap with relish. She was hungry, and knew she should have eaten half an hour earlier, but she'd missed her chance; Huw had phoned so she'd wandered outside the office for a chat, and hadn't wanted to be eating when she talked to him. Now she knew she had to stuff her face, quick, or Mavis would be back from lunch at the Dower House and shout at her for getting crumbs everywhere – she needed at least five minutes to clean up herself and her desk after she'd so much as nibbled a biscuit. Gertie did her bit to help.

Annie was thankful that she had to answer the phone just as Mavis, Althea, and McFli arrived and the dogs greeted each other.

'Hello, Annie?'

'Yes.'

'It's Sharon.'

'Hiya, Shar. Alright?'

'Ta, yes. Have you heard?'

'What?'

'About Marjorie.'

'In hospital, you mean?'

'She's out now.'

'Good.'

'And about Dr Priddle?'

'Have you forgotten I was there when his cleaner phoned you this morning?'

'No. I mean the poison.'

'What poison?'

'As soon as his doctor got to his house this morning they rushed his body off for an urgent post-mortem. Mrs Davies-Duster said the doctor actually used the word "strychnine"; made her tell him everything she'd touched, eaten, or drunk since she'd been in Dr Priddle's house. She's only just been able to phone me now because when she told him she'd had a cup of tea – and there was a mug and a glass on the floor beside the dead body, see – they rushed her off to hospital too. In her own ambulance. Poor thing's been poked and prodded all morning. Only just let her out.'

Annie waggled her arm at Mavis and Althea to try to get their attention. She said loudly, 'So Dr Priddle was poisoned? What made the doctor suspect that? And why did he think strychnine?'

Annie could tell Sharon was enjoying herself when she replied, 'Mrs Davies-Duster said he had a horrible face on him. But she's never seen a dead body before – well, only her uncle, and he got mashed in a combine, so that doesn't count. She thought all dead bodies had a look on them like Dr Priddle did. Apparently not; the doctor who came to see the body said that's how they go with strychnine. Something about his back being arched. It's terrible, isn't it? Poisoned. Here. In Anwen-by-Wye. Who'd have thought? Anyway, now I've told you I've got some more calls to make. I'll keep you up to date with any more news, tarra.'

Annie hung up and passed the information to her colleagues.

Mavis began to pace. 'If it really is a case of strychnine poisoning, that's bad. Strychnine's not easy to get hold of; it means someone went to a great deal of effort to get the poison, then to get it into him, somehow. But why? Why would anyone want Dr Priddle dead? Althea?' Annie and Mavis looked over at the dowager who was fumbling around in her pocket, her face pale. 'What is it dear?' asked Mavis.

Annie could tell Althea was upset when she replied, 'Annie, Mavis tells me you weren't very well yesterday morning, is that right?'

Annie nodded. 'Sorry, Mave. I tried to hide it from you, but, no, I wasn't well.'

'Nor was I,' admitted Althea. 'I was all twitchy, and feeling like I needed to be near *facilities*. Remember, young Aelwyn at the café was late to work because she wasn't a hundred percent? Frankly, if she had wrong with her what I had wrong with me, she shouldn't have been working in a place where they serve food at all, but, maybe they didn't know what "having a bad tummy" meant. I know what it meant for me. You told me Tudor wasn't very well Annie, and Aled missed a shift. And then there's Marjorie Pritchard too. I have to make a phone call. Oh where *is* the blessed thing? I can't find it.'

Annie handed Althea her mobile. 'There you go.' She'd never seen Althea look so worried before.

A moment later Mavis and Annie were aghast when they heard Althea shout into the phone, 'Stephanie, Stephanie – you oversaw the preparation of the food on Sunday for the croquet teams' tea, where was it all prepared? You're sure it was at the hall and not at the café? Good. Nothing was handled at the café at all? Excellent, so we won't have to close it down on one of our busiest weeks of the year. Go to the kitchens right now and find out what happened to all the food left over from the tea. I don't know, just find it. But don't let anyone touch it, or do anything to it. Also ask everyone if anyone ate any leftovers, what was done with the leftovers when they came back to the hall and so forth. Yes. Yes, I want to know everywhere that food has been, and where it is now. I'm on my way. Just be ready for the police to come to inspect it all and collect it at some point. Yes, the police. Why? Because I shall be telephoning them presently and telling them I think we've poisoned everyone. And I think we've killed poor Dr Priddle, that's why. Now go on – go!'

Althea handed the phone back to Annie. 'Come along, there's no time to waste. We'll have to fight our way through all the visitors to get to the hall, quick as we can.'

Annie felt she had to do something to reel in Althea's panic. 'You mean we'll have to force our way through the herds of wildebeest sweeping majestically across the plain?'

Althea's face softened. 'Thank you, dear. You're a good girl for trying to calm me down, but that's Basil Fawlty, not Monty Python.' Annie liked the feeling of Althea's small hand on her face as it gently cupped her cheek. 'Come along now. I know I'm in a bit of a panic, but I do think that poisoning dozens of people is something one should feel panicked about. Don't you see? Everyone who was taken ill was at the tea. We prepared the food at the hall. We served the food at the hall. We've killed a man.'

'Wait!' called Mavis. 'While I'll agree there's been an amount of people who've no' been well, it's highly unlikely you'll have poisoned them with strychnine, Althea. Annie – explain your symptoms, in detail.'

Annie didn't like the idea at all. 'Really?' Mavis nodded. 'Hot and cold, dizzy, very shaky and all sort of nervous, I suppose you could say. I was all on edge – and I was sick a few times. Had the trots too. Horrible it was.'

Mavis looked grim. 'Sorry to hear it. And you Althea?'

Althea looked at the floor as she replied, 'The same. The worst part was feeling all unsettled, as though I was vibrating all the time.'

Mavis tutted. 'You should have told me, dear. And do you know what Marjorie Pritchard's symptoms were, Annie – exactly?'

Annie admitted all she knew was that the woman had needed to make a rapid exit from her church-cleaning duties and could only guess why she'd ended up sufficiently dehydrated to require hospitalization.

Althea looked at Mavis with a glimmer of hope. 'Is that different to strychnine poisoning? Might it just be some sort of nasty food thing we couldn't have known about, and Dr Priddle's death is nothing to do with Chellingworth after all?'

Annie felt her tummy clench when Mavis said, 'I'm sorry to say your symptoms sound not unlike those which might be associated with a mild case of strychnine poisoning – though, let's be clear about this, we do not yet know for certain if that's what killed the doctor. How are you feeling now, by the way?'

Even though she didn't really feel it at that moment Annie said, 'Fine, thanks. But why did only Dr Priddle die?'

'I've no idea, there could be many reasons, but Althea's right, let's get to the hall and start asking questions.' Mavis headed for the door.

'Shouldn't I phone the police before we leave?' squeaked Althea.

'Do it as we walk to the hall, come along,' pressed Mavis.

'Come on, Gert,' said Annie, following along, 'thank heavens I didn't feed you any treats from that tea on Sunday. Let's hurry up, we're off to look into The Case of the Dead Doctor . . . though, now I've said it out loud, it don't sound right. Too serious for a funny name is this one.'

NINETEEN

Henry wondered if everyone had gone mad; Stephanie was barking orders into her mobile phone, Cook Davies was in tears and Elizabeth Fernley – his estate manager's wife, who oversaw the household alongside the duchess – was running about as though her hair was on fire.

Henry felt utterly helpless. 'What can I do?' he kept asking. All anyone would say was, 'There's nothing you can do, thank you, Your Grace.' It made him feel a bit sick to think no one believed he could contribute to helping sort out a real crisis at his home. He decided it was best for him to sit in a corner of the kitchen and wait until someone noticed him. He'd done much the same thing when, as a boy, he'd listened to his big brother laughing and joking with the staff. Indeed, the chair upon which he'd sat all those years ago was still there, in the same spot under the window beside the massive inglenook fireplace which – back in the sixteenth century – had accommodated entire pigs on a spit. As Henry plopped himself down he realized he wasn't even as useful as one of those ancient pigs; at least they'd fed people.

He sighed as he watched it all happen. Stephanie first ensured that additional security personnel were sent to the working areas of the hall to keep away any members of the public who might have wandered into the maelstrom of activity by mistake. Henry had to admit, his wife was in her element. He'd been aware how good she'd been at building the popularity of Chellingworth Hall during her years as its public relations manager, but in a sort of general way. Acknowledging to himself he'd been rather taken by Stephanie almost upon her arrival, he also had to admit he'd been in awe of her business acumen rather than ever really understanding it.

Now he saw her almost as though she were Britannia herself, riding into battle. She kept mentioning something called 'crisis management guidelines' she'd apparently put in place when she was in office, and he was amazed to realize everyone knew what she was talking about. As such, most people involved with running the hall began to drop into place like cogs in a giant machine, all taking on a specific set of responsibilities.

Stephanie stood in the middle of the vast kitchen and spoke with authority; Henry's heart swelled with pride as he looked on. 'Elizabeth, you oversee the household with me, so you'll gather contact details for all staff members – our staff and casuals – who had any possibility of coming into contact with the food and beverage supplies before, during and after Sunday's event. They'll need to be interviewed by the police, and we should be in a position to give them full details when they arrive. Cook Davies, you and Bronwen can draw up a detailed supplier list for everything we served, and we'll also need a timeline for all prep and serving, as well as details of every location where food was stored, prepped and served, then what happened to the leftovers. Please detail your clean-up procedures and append information about sanitation protocols you used. Make sure you then retrieve all the platters, serving jugs etcetera that were used, and bring them to one place for them to be inspected and, if necessary, tested for residue.'

'There'll be no residues to be found,' said Cook Davies, sounding a little hurt.

'I'm sure you're correct, Cook, but we must show the authorities we're taking this seriously. If any sort of contamination took place here it is our duty to ensure that does not lead to cross-contamination. If any serving ware has been stored where it can come into contact with other items not used on Sunday, those additional items must also be pulled from storage for checking and re-sanitizing.'

Henry thought Cook's ears looked rather red. 'That could run to half of what we've got, which is a great deal,' she said huffily.

'Then so be it,' replied the duchess. 'We'll cover the table in the servants' kitchen with some sort of protective sheeting and place everything there. Thank you.'

Henry could tell Bronwen was trying to calm Cook Davies, but it didn't seem to be working.

Stephanie continued, 'Roger, as estates manager, you can provide a full list of all attendees at Sunday's croquet team event. Thank you all.'

Henry watched as people scurried off to fulfill their appointed duties, and felt even more useless.

He perked up when his wife said, 'Henry dear, I wonder if you could help, please?' He shot to his feet, a little too fast if the slight dizziness he felt was anything to go by, and saluted her. He didn't know why, it just felt like the right thing to do.

'Thank you dear, no need to salute,' said his wife, smiling. 'Could you pop up to our rooms and get me a thin cardigan, please? For some unknown reason I'm feeling a little chilled. My yellow one, it's in the press. Thank you.'

'Are you sure this isn't too much for you and the baby?' Henry was worried. Why would Stephanie feel cold? Did she have a temperature? 'If there's been some sort of poison floating about the place, should you and the baby be – well, checked in some way? I hate the thought that something might happen to either of you.'

Henry's heart lightened a little when his wife touched his arm, tenderly. 'Don't worry, dear. I haven't had any symptoms, and I didn't eat or drink a single thing at tea on Sunday; I'd enjoyed a good luncheon and I don't have room for as much food as I used to with this little one taking up space. Please, I just need a cardi. That's all. It's cool here in the kitchen, and this is where I need to be for now. Thank you, dear. It's the best way you can help at the moment.'

Henry left the bustle behind him with a specific function to perform, and felt good about it. He headed toward the servants' stairs, which he habitually used when the hall was open to the public.

Upon returning to the kitchen with Stephanie's cardigan, Henry realized his life wasn't about to return to normal at any foreseeable point; not only had his mother, Mavis and Annie arrived, but there seemed to be enough uniformed police officers dotted around the place to suggest a riot was about to erupt.

Henry managed to catch the eye of the most beribboned police officer, who instantly made a beeline for the duke. 'Your Grace,' he said, shocking Henry with the breadth of his smile, 'I'm so terribly sorry to meet you under such circumstances. Chief Inspector Carwen James, Dyfed-Powys Constabulary, at your service.'

'Chellingworth. At yours,' replied Henry extending his hand tentatively, not sure what to expect given his family was possibly on the hook for having poisoned a man. He felt relieved that the officer was clearly the sort of chap who expected to take charge, and did so.

'The duchess has been most helpful already,' said the man in a tone Henry interpreted as erring on the side of confidentiality. 'Of course, there's a great deal for my officers to do here, but yes, she's made a splendid start. We will, of course, be taking a good deal of foodstuffs and so forth away from here to our laboratories for testing, but we'll make sure you have an itemized list of all the returnables. Can't have any of the Chellingworth silverware going missing, can we?'

Henry forced a smile when he spotted the man affecting a comical wink, then became worried again when the policeman's face fell.

'Something has become obvious since my arrival, and I wondered if you might be of some aid, Your Grace.'

'But of course, what might one be able to do to help?'

The policeman stepped even closer to Henry – something for which the duke didn't greatly care. 'The list of those who came into contact with the foodstuffs served at Sunday's tea party runs to dozens, and I wondered if there might be somewhere here, at Chellingworth Hall itself, where we could hold interviews? As you may, or may not, know, our station in Builth Wells is not the most capacious of places, and it would mean a good deal of too-ing and fro-ing for everyone involved. Since the people we need to talk to are all either here already, or can get here easily because they are used to coming here to work, I wondered if . . .'

Henry felt relief, and offered as many rooms as might be required for the procedures to be carried out. With the help of Edward, who joined the pair at Henry's request, access to several rooms on the first floor was organized to allow for multiple interviews to be held simultaneously for the rest of the day, and all without any of the activities coming to the attention of the visiting public.

As the maelstrom passed, and the number of bodies buzzing about the kitchen dwindled, Henry could feel his shoulders lift a little. Finally, it was only a small group that remained; Henry sat with his mother, Mavis and Annie, and helped entertain the distracted dogs while the women talked.

'Can you think of anyone at all who might have it in for us, dear?' asked the dowager of her son. 'Mavis and I had a word with Inspector James and we all agreed there might be some connection between the poisoning of food, Dr Priddle's death and the vandalism at the pavilion.'

'Mother, no one has even proved our food *was* poisoned, nor that such a thing led to Dr Priddle's death,' snapped Henry, causing McFli to return to Althea's feet in a huff. 'And as for being connected with what happened at the pavilion, who knows?'

'I think it's a bit much to believe that the vandalizing of a building with the words "Vengeance is Mine," people falling ill after a tea hosted just outside that very building, and the death of one man present at the time, can all be coincidences, Henry,' chided Althea.

'Your mother has a point,' said Mavis, backing up the dowager.

Henry gave up trying to get Gertie to chase her tail and stood, pacing the considerable length of the kitchen. 'I suppose so. Is that what the police think? But why would anyone *want* Priddle dead?'

'See, I'm with Henry on that,' said Annie firmly. 'I got the impression Priddle was a nice old bloke – so let's start there; why would anyone want him dead? Anyone? Ideas?'

Mavis shook her head. 'I'm sorry to say I barely ever met the man, other than to nod to him when I saw him sometimes in the village, and therefore have no knowledge of him whatsoever. Althea, you're likely to know most about him. What can you tell us about him, other than that he attended you and your family here at various points in years gone by? What of his life? His family? Might he have held controversial opinions, or have done something that would have created enemies? Come along, talk.'

As everyone stared at her, Althea wriggled in her chair. 'Let me think,' she said aloud, chewing the corner of her lip – a telltale sign to her son she was doing just that. 'I cannot recall Dr Clive Priddle ever being spoken of by anyone in anything but the most pleasant terms. He had a good bedside manner, knew how to handle children and didn't put up with malingerers. Of course, he had the sympathy of the entire village when his wife died, but things were never quite the same for him after that, I don't think. I believe he was younger than retirement age when he left his practice. As far as I know he always lived a quiet life. A regular at church, though not devout, if you know what I mean. Got somewhat involved in village events, but not in a pushy way. Always there, but not oppressively so.'

Mavis gave Althea a sideways glance. 'How did his wife die?'

Althea brightened. 'Of course, you wouldn't know. She killed herself. Took a lot of tablets. He found her dead in bed next to him one morning. Hence the sympathy of the village.'

'I didn't know that,' said Henry. 'Why would you not have mentioned it, Mother?'

'Why on earth would I, dear? You were away for so long, and it's not really the sort of thing in which you'd be interested, is it? "Welcome back to the family seat from your travels, Henry . . . nice to see you, and, by the way, the wife of the doctor who treated you a few times as a child killed herself three years ago." Not really *us*, is it, dear?'

Henry had to agree it wasn't.

'Anyone know why his wife did it?' asked Annie 'Did she leave a note?'

Althea shrugged. 'It's a long time ago, and I have to admit I didn't hang on every word of gossip that was flying about the village at the time.'

'Was Sharon's mum running the shop in Anwen at the time?' asked Annie. Althea nodded. 'Why don't I ask Sharon if I can talk to her mum about it? If Sharon's anything to go by – and if she gets her news-gathering abilities from her mother, like everyone says – her mum might remember a good deal more about it than you do, Althea.'

'But why do you want to know about his wife dying?' asked Henry, puzzled.

'If that's all that makes him stand out from a crowd, mebbe her death has something to do with his own,' replied Mavis.

Henry didn't see it, but decided it was best to nod and look as sage as possible.

'We've already discussed the people who were involved with both croquet teams,' said Mavis, 'so I suppose the next question is – do we think Dr Priddle was the intended victim, or was someone else the target?'

Henry didn't like that idea. 'Why on earth would you ask that? Do you think someone's got it in for a person other than Priddle, and might do what they've done to him to someone else?' As he spoke the words, he felt horrified he'd been compelled to do so.

'Dr Priddle was old. He wasn't infirm, but possibly had a generally weak constitution,' replied Mavis. 'As a retired nurse, I know full well that poisons can attack individuals in different ways. Factors like body size, levels of hydration and so forth can play a part in how much or little effect they have upon a person. As I've said, I've only seen Dr Priddle from a distance, but I'd have said he was of medium build. Would you agree?'

'He was always a large man – not tall, but quite portly,' said Althea.

'He'd lost a fair bit of weight then,' added Annie. 'I noticed his trousers were always pulled up very high, almost to his armpits, and he wore them tightly belted, so I'd say he kept wearing his old clothes, even though he'd shrunk and lost weight. That might be why I always thought of him as saggy.'

'Keen observations, Annie,' praised Mavis, 'so maybe he had a smaller body mass than I'd have originally thought. I dare say no one here would have any idea about his general state of health, would they?' Three heads shook. 'Something the investigation will ascertain,' continued Mavis, 'but his diminishing weight, his age and maybe some general health issues might have meant the dose of poison he got was the same as that which others received, but it affected him to a deadly extent. Althea – I know you're some years younger than he was, and you're certainly a woman who's in excellent physical condition, allowing for that slight weakness in your left knee, but you're also a good deal smaller than him. One might have expected you to succumb too – so, what exactly did you consume at that tea?'

Henry watched as his mother closed her eyes and appeared to be counting her fingers. 'Three cucumber sandwiches, two Welsh cakes and a scone with jam and cream,' she said with certainty.

'Anyone know what Dr Priddle ate?' asked Mavis.

'I saw him eat three ham sandwiches, and a scone with butter,' said Annie. 'I wasn't with him all the time the food was doing the rounds, so he might have had a lot more, or nothing else.'

'And from where did he get the sandwiches he ate?' asked Henry, eager to contribute.

He noticed that Annie paused before she answered. 'Tudor gave me the plate, and I passed it to the doctor.'

'And Tudor got them from . . .?' Althea was agog.

'I didn't see. I assume one of the tables.' Henry thought Annie looked a little deflated as she spoke.

'So, the man ate sandwiches available to all, and a scone, also available to all,' said Mavis. 'In our discussions over luncheon yesterday, when we thought the vandalism might be connected with the croquet teams, I believe we established that Dr Priddle was an unlikely candidate for having done the damage. We also discounted several of the other players almost out of hand. Now I wonder if each player should be considered more closely. What do you think?'

'I can tell you I had nothing to do with any of these goings-on,' said Henry, sounding as offended as he felt. 'And I cannot believe for one minute you'd imagine the rest of my team as a possible vandal or murderer. Edward? Never. Bob Fernley? Why on earth would he want to kill Priddle? Then there's Bronwen Price, who's been here since the year dot, as has Ian Cottesloe. I'll grant you that young girl Aelwyn Thomas is a bit off, even though she's a wizard with a mallet, but she's just a girl. Again – why would she want to kill Priddle?'

'And why would she make herself ill too? Remember – when we went to the café yesterday we couldn't talk to her because she was still working; she'd come in late because she was sick,' said Mavis. 'Mind you,' she added quickly, 'that could be a device to cover up her guilt.'

'I went over and had a chat with her later in the day, after she'd finished her shift,' piped up Annie. 'I think I know why you thought she was so sullen when she was practicing on Sunday, Althea; she wasn't off sick with *that* sort of a bad tummy yesterday – it was the other sort.' Henry noticed Annie give him a strange look as she patted her lower abdomen and added, 'You know, girl's stuff.' She flashed him a smile, he put two and two together and did his best to not blush.

'Ah, I see,' said Mavis, then added, 'so she wasnae sick to her stomach at all? Interesting. Anyone else not taken ill that we know of?'

Henry noticed that Annie shifted in her seat as she said, 'I don't think Huw was, at least, he didn't mention it when we had dinner last night.' Henry wondered why Annie looked so timid when she spoke; she wasn't usually given to being backward when coming forward.

Althea sniffed. 'You had dinner with that Hughes chappie last night? Really? He struck me as rather an odious type. You do surprise me. Anyway, I expect it's something the police will ask everyone,' she said. 'And they'll be able to find out all the things we can't, like who could have got to the food, and when.'

'And with what,' added Mavis. 'Ach, I wish I could be a fly on the wall of the place where they'll be doing that post-mortem, and where they'll be testing the food. To know what killed him would be useful, and there might even be stomach contents they can test, too.'

Henry felt his own tummy flip at the thought.

'The police are ready for you all whenever you can come,' said Stephanie entering the kitchen.

'Then let's be going,' said Mavis.

TWENTY

Carol sat at the bar of Tudor's deserted pub and watched the man disintegrate a little more with the scanning of each page of the folder she'd handed him. She and Mavis had decided against editing her findings, and she'd guessed he wouldn't be happy to read what she'd discovered about Huw Hughes. However, she hadn't expected him to be so deflated; his usually robust frame seemed to shrink before her.

'The deaths of his wives are highly suspect,' said the landlord eventually. He sounded sad, and grim. He looked directly into Carol's eyes and added, 'How can we get her to see him for the man he really is?'

Carol thought she'd better clarify what Tudor meant. 'You mean, how can we get Annie to see that Huw has buried three wives who died under questionable circumstances?'

Tudor nodded, then sighed so deeply Carol thought he'd pass out for lack of oxygen. 'You're her friend, can't you show her this?' He waggled the folder under Carol's nose.

Carol pondered the ethics of what Tudor was asking. 'Do you think that's a good idea? Annie might not be too keen on the fact I've been poking about into the background of someone she knows, nor that you asked me to do it.'

'Counterproductive, then,' said Tudor unhappily.

'I reckon.'

'So how then? How can we get her to see sense? It looks as though this man really might be a killer after all. I'll admit that was my suspicion, but it looks like you have real evidence here.' His eyes pleaded with Carol.

'Not evidence, Tudor, but I do believe I've managed to join up quite a few circumstantial dots.' She was annoyed when her phone rang in her pocket. Reflexively pulling it out to check who was calling, Carol felt a ripple of annoyance when she saw a text from Mavis: Phone me. Now. URGENT!!!! 'You have a think about it, while I make an urgent call. Sorry, Tudor.'

She swung her legs down off the barstool and took a few steps toward the fireplace, which offered a little more privacy, and speed-dialed her colleague. 'Hi Mavis, I'm with Tudor, is this *really* urgent?'

'Aye, it is that,' replied Mavis tartly, 'but I'll be quick. I'm up at Chellingworth Hall where all hell has broken out; the police are here to gather evidence in a criminal case. It's believed Dr Clive Priddle might have died as a result of strychnine poisoning, and they're looking into the possibility the source was the tea served to the croquet teams here on Sunday afternoon, due to the fact many others who attended were taken ill. We're not involved, directly, because the police are quite properly in control, but Annie, Althea and I feel we'd like to gain our own insights. We'll need your help, please. Background checks. Fast. You'll be up for that, I assume. It sounds like you've finished the work . . . you were doing.'

Carol judged Annie might be able to overhear Mavis, and that explained her colleague's circumspection. 'I have. Tudor's got the file now.' Carol glanced over at the usually-ruddy landlord, who looked decidedly pallid at that moment, and wondered if he was getting himself worked up a bit too much. 'Mavis, I have a question,' said Carol, hoping she'd just had a bright idea. 'If we're going to need to do a background check on Huw as part of this Priddle thing, because he's a member of one of the croquet teams, could Annie work with me on that? You never know what "she" might find out, or how quickly I could "uncover" certain key facts. Know what I mean?' She hoped Mavis would cotton on to her train of thought.

'Aye, that's no' a bad idea. That way she'd . . . be helping you. You'd both be able to find out much more, and a good deal quicker. I'll speak to her about it. The key question is – I know we've agreed to you doing as much work as you can from your home while Albert's still needing you to feed him, but do you think you'd be able to come to the office for this? I think we'd all do a better job if we could coordinate face to face.'

Carol gave the matter some thought. 'Albert's with David at the moment; I didn't want to bring him with me to the pub. But I'd have to bring him with me if I came to the office later today. I could make plans with David for him to provide cover tomorrow, and I could set up some bottles in the fridge for Albert by then. How about that?'

'Aye. We'll see you in a wee while at the office then?'

'You're on.' The women disconnected from each other.

'You're off now?' asked Tudor, not even looking consoled by the passionate hand-licking he was being given by Rosie.

'I need to collect my son and get to the office. It seems there's an idea Dr Priddle was poisoned, and the police are involved. It also seems the WISE women might be helping out somehow.'

Tudor's expression changed from pure pain to half-shocked. 'Poisoned? Clive? Who says he was? Why would anyone want to do that to him?'

Carol shrugged. 'Sorry, I don't know all the ins and outs, that's what I'm off to investigate now. But I think I might have worked out a way for Annie to do some of her own digging into Huw's background. She might end up finding out what we'd like her to, without us having to let on what we've done.'

Carol was delighted when Tudor's face brightened a little. 'Really? Oh, that would be marvelous. Do you think you can steer her in the right direction so she'll get hold of this dirt on him? She needs to see he's dangerous, and it'll only mean something to her if she finds out for herself. You know what she's like.'

'Leave it with me; I'll do what I can.' Carol patted Tudor on the arm and Rosie on the head, then left the pair interacting more happily than they had since her arrival.

TWENTY-ONE

Christine sat at the kitchen table, and mentally prepared herself for the phone call she was about to make; she didn't really want to ask for help from her colleagues back in Wales, and still wasn't one hundred percent sure she would, but she'd reached about ninety-nine percent, so felt she had to do it. Aware that her quick thinking had forced the thugs planning to rob the manor to give the idea a second thought, she knew there might still be a threat.

Alexander was calling in information and possible on-the-spot help from his Irish contacts in London, which was helpful, but she felt keenly that *she* was the one who should protect her family home. She told herself it wasn't a weakness to ask for help when one needed it. The first priority was to safely retrieve Callum from the clutches of someone who might be truly dangerous, and her second and third priorities were running neck and neck; she had to make sure the police didn't need to become involved, and her parents had to be kept completely in the dark, too.

Finally ready, she speed-dialed Carol's number; Christine knew she'd be the one who'd be able to dig into this Gadfly character's background.

Carol answered almost immediately. 'Hello Christine, how are you? Having a lovely holiday?'

Christine affected the most jovial tone she could summon. 'Not a care in the world, thanks, and the weather's a treat.' She looked through the kitchen window at the pendulous, dark clouds hanging over the hills beyond the lough. 'Just a drop of soft rain now and then, but that's why it's so green and beautiful around here.'

'Right you are,' replied Carol. 'Send a bit over this way, will you? It's so hot you could fry eggs on the pavement here. Not that we should complain, I suppose.'

'But we all do,' said Christine, who actually managed to smile. 'So how's it going there without me?'

Christine noticed that Carol didn't answer immediately. It made her wonder what was going on back in Anwen-by-Wye, despite what she was facing in Ireland. 'There's a few bits and pieces we're looking into,' said Carol sounding vague.

Christine wasn't buying it. 'Out with it, Carol, What's up? Trouble?'

Another pause. 'Well, there's no harm telling you, I suppose.' Carol filled her in on everything that was going on at Chellingworth Hall and the surrounding environs.

When Carol had finished, Christine said, 'Good grief, I can't leave you lot alone for two minutes, can I?' The two women enjoyed a chuckle, then Christine told Carol what had been happening in Ireland.

'And we shouldn't let you out of our sight,' was Carol's response when Christine had finished. 'So, is there anything I can do to help you with what you're facing there?'

Christine had known Carol would be willing to step up, if she could, so she listed the ways she thought her colleague could come to her aid by using her research skills.

Carol replied, 'Right-o. When I get to the office of course I'm going to have to pitch in with what's going on here, but I'll do what I can as soon as possible for you, and I'll email you anything I get. Unless it's not emailable, then I'll phone. OK?'

Christine felt a wave of relief and gratitude wash over her. 'Thanks, Carol. You're brilliant at this sort of thing. Alexander is putting out feelers within the circle of people he knows – and the people they know, by the sounds of it. However, you'll be able to do something I, he nor they can; you'll be able to burrow down deeper than the surface stuff. And that's what I need; I need to understand this Gadfly's interests, involvements, and where he might be holding Callum. Think sideways – you know, think about how the name Gadfly might be attached to anything in the area.'

'Exactly what I have planned. I'd better go now, I'm nearly at the office. I promise I'll get back to you soon. Love to Alexander. Bye.'

'Bye,' replied Christine. Pushing her phone into her pocket, Christine got up from the table and walked to the window. The rain was getting closer. It looked as though it was going to pour.

TWENTY-TWO

As Carol entered the office, she was relieved to find Mavis had set up a couple of electric fans to provide a breeze in the place; the doors were all shut to prevent Gertie and McFli from making a break for freedom.

With Albert settled in his hastily-constructed pillow-filled cushion-pen on the floor, and the two dogs in no doubt at all about the fact Albert had to be inside the pen and they had to be outside it, Carol finally sat down in front of her computer screen.

Annie brought her a cup of tea. 'It's been a while since I've been able to look across the desk and see your face, doll. Nice to have you back for a bit.'

'Nice to be back,' replied Carol, 'though I have to admit it's lovely to be able to work from home. It's just easier for me and Albert when anything he might need is close-by.'

Annie looked around the infant-related detritus scattered about the office, and told Gertie to stop trying to clamber over the sofa cushions to reach the happily gurgling Albert. 'Yeah, you've got a point,' she conceded.

'Come along now,' said Mavis, 'we need progress. I propose Althea and I work on the people on both teams she feels she knows well, so she can guide me about where to begin to gather data on them, and I propose you two tackle those we know less well, so Huw Hughes and Aelwyn Thomas. When we've done that, all four of us should undertake the task of investigating Dr Priddle's life as a group, dividing responsibilities before we begin. Agreed?' Everyone nodded, and got going.

Carol had given a great deal of thought to her opening gambit, and quickly drew Annie into carrying out some background research into Huw Hughes. Carol was pleased, and a little worried, that Annie seemed to be quite keen on getting stuck into the job, so allowed half an hour to pass before she thought it would be a good time to offer to shoot some insights she'd 'just gathered' to her friend. Annie was suitably impressed.

'Cor, you're so good at his, Car. I'm pretty naff compared with you. Look what you've found; all I've done is read his website and get some ideas for where to look next.'

Carol grappled with her duplicitousness and told herself not to blush as she replied, 'It's what I do, and it's what I've done a lot of,' she explained. 'It's no surprise I'm quicker at it than you. Anyway, maybe what I've dug up will help you decide where to look next, and I'll get started on Aelwyn.' She'd carefully edited her original research to make it look incomplete, though she made sure Annie got all the key facts about Huw's dead wives. Then she thought it best to shut up again, and got on with burrowing into the life of Aelwyn Thomas, which she felt wouldn't take long at all; the girl was an avid user of all types of social media and clearly had no concept of what 'privacy settings' meant.

By the time Carol was convinced Aelwyn was harmless, if bordering on the narcissistic – given the number of selfies she posted on a daily basis, some of which were taken in the most inappropriate settings, she thought – she realized Annie was wriggling about in her seat and looking quite miserable.

'What's up?' she asked her friend as innocently as possible.

'Did you read all this stuff about Huw?' asked Annie.

'Sort of,' replied Carol guardedly. 'I usually spot main points, then download the materials. I haven't read all the details yet.'

'Well, what I want to know is how come he's never told me none of this stuff? I mean, we sat in a car and across a dinner table for hours just last night, and though he said he'd been married three times before, that was all he said. Never mentioned his wives were all rich, and posh. Nor how they died. In fact, I'm not even sure I knew they *were* all dead. I thought maybe *one* had popped her clogs – 'cos I knew he was a widower – but I suppose I assumed a couple must have been divorces.' Annie looked across at her friend. 'Sorry, Car, but the information you've given me has come as a bit of a shock.'

Carol forced herself to smile. 'Well, one dinner date doesn't mean you're serious about him, does it?' She wondered how Annie would react. Just what *did* Annie feel for this man? Carol felt cross with herself as she admitted she really had no idea, and tried to push aside her guilt by watching Annie's face; what might it tell her that her friend's words might not?

'Nah, not serious. Just a bit of fun, you know?' said Annie. Carol judged her tone to be forced.

'What, like that tall, dark and handsome police officer from Brixton nick you used to refer to as "sex on a stick"?' Carol picked a benchmark relationship she knew had meant little to Annie, except for providing a few evenings of fun and a slight frisson of heavy flirting.

Annie stared into the distance. 'Bill Edmunds? I wonder what he's up to now. Brixton seems like a long way away, don't you think?'

'As the crow flies it is, but you don't mean the place, do you? You mean "those days"?' Carol spoke to Annie as a friend in need, which she was; she didn't care that they were in the office with Mavis and Althea.

Annie's reply suggested to Carol that their lack of privacy mattered to her. 'Not the time or place, doll.'

Carol's heart fell as she saw sadness in Annie's eyes; the sort of expression she'd worn for years after John's death. 'Would you like to come for a little walk with me and Albert? He needs a breath of fresh air away from these fans, then maybe he'll nap.'

Annie agreed, and the two women – accompanied by Albert and Gertie – wandered out into the sunshine, seeking the shade of a copse not far from the barn. Finally able to stroll without baking, Carol opened with, 'When I passed what I had to you, I carried on digging into Huw's late wives,' she lied.

'And?' asked Annie, wide-eyed.

Carol took a deep breath and gave Annie the details of their deaths. The information spilled out of her quickly, and she noticed Annie didn't look at her as she spoke but gave her attention to Gertie's needs instead. Carol began to wonder if Annie was even listening; her friend's reaction when she'd finished left her in no doubt she had been.

'Done it again, in't I, doll?' said Annie, her voice heavy.

'What?'

'Picked a bad 'un. I'm useless, me. I can't stop myself falling for the charmers, can I? Remember John's flash car? The fancy dinners? Get me every time, they do.'

Carol's tummy didn't feel good. 'Do you mean you've really fallen for Huw?'

Annie's eyes were filling with tears. 'Oh, I don't know,' she said angrily. 'Not *fallen* fallen, like John; John was everything to me. You know that. Everything. Huw? Well, he's a bit flash, but he's been so nice to me, Car, and I'm not used to that. It's nice to be noticed. To be treated like a lady, even though I don't deserve it.'

Carol adjusted Albert's sunhat as she replied, 'Now don't go saying that. Come on, Annie – we both know each other well, and we know where we've come from. Look at us here; we're living a life neither of us could have imagined, and we're actually friends with people who have titles and tiaras. Neither of us was born to this sort of thing, but it's where we are now. And when it comes to being treated like a lady, well, a woman doesn't need a title to deserve that. Everyone should have the chance to feel special, man or woman. That's nothing to do with birthright or status. So come off it, Annie, don't pull that "poor little East End girl" rubbish with me. We're both as common as muck and come from working-class backgrounds. Try not to feel sorry for yourself; you've had a bit of a flirt and a nice dinner with a bloke who's got a dubious track record, but that's not the end of the world.'

Annie's tears flowed. 'Well, it might have been a bit more than flirting and dinner,' she smiled sheepishly, 'but that's not what I mean, Car. I'm not getting any younger, and I love Gertie and all, but I'm going to end up all on me own, in't I? Like that old girl who lives next door to me with all her birds in cages. It'll be just me and Gertie, and I'll end up with bats in me belfry and kids giggling about me when they wait for the bus.'

Carol tried hard to not lose her patience, but found she was struggling; she felt total responsibility for her son, but Annie? Just how much support did a longtime friend deserve? Carol toyed with the idea of 'tough love.'

'How about, instead of bleating about how bad you are at picking men, you take a look at the things you're good at? I understand that Huw's background has come as a bit of a shock to you, but, you know what, you're a big girl now, and I know you've got it in you to overcome this. Look at all you've achieved in your life. Sometimes it takes one friend to point things out to another, but I know how you've been through hell and come back from it. The trouble is you don't see what an achievement that is.'

'At this moment I don't feel like I'm any good at anything at all,' said Annie miserably.

Carol struggled to put her arm around Annie, but Albert was in the way, so she made do with squeezing her chum's hand. 'I know your mum and dad didn't have much when you were growing up; mine didn't either, in a different sort of way. You know – you were urban, I was rural, it's different. But we both found our way to careers in the City that gave us each a lifestyle we enjoyed. Let's be honest, Annie, back in those days – before David and John came along – you and I had a lot of fun times, didn't we?' Annie nodded, and brightened a little. 'I saw how what John did to you made you become . . . well, let's just say you come over as being angry with the world, at times. And I get it; he treated you badly, and neither you nor anyone else deserves that. Even when those horrible bosses at CFK made you redundant – in such a dreadful way – you bounced back, and your work with the rest of us at WISE since then has been incredible.'

'Ta,' said Annie quietly.

'You're not the defensive, stroppy person people think you are; you're great at undercover work, you enjoy doing research and are good at it – especially when you question people face to face. When you're working, people trust you, they let things slip to you. You're someone people feel they can chat with. *That's* the Annie I know; the woman people warm to. It seems to me the only ones seeing that person in the past little while have been the ones you're investigating, not your friends. Maybe you could let down the walls a bit, brush the chips off your shoulder and just be the old you a bit more often. You used to be playful; nowadays you come over as cross and hard done by all the time.'

Annie sighed. Tears flowed silently down her face. 'I know you're right, Car. I haven't been myself since – well, I'll be honest and admit that getting stabbed on the job, just before you announced you were pregnant, did for me more than I thought. I'd never felt physically vulnerable before that. Then being kidnapped when I first visited Anwen didn't help. And I do sometimes think the world is unfair. But you're right, sometimes it's good to me too. I like it here, Car. I miss my parents, but I don't miss London like I thought I would. See, I think my problem is I've always had to fight so hard for everything, and I got used to that. Now it seems I don't know how to stop fighting when I don't need to. Does that make sense? Like Don Quixote, tilting at windmills, I suppose.'

Carol nodded. 'See? You never seem to say things like that anymore. You've read a lot and you know a lot, but you're always going on about how you don't know anything at all. Why is that, Annie? I know what it feels like to have to be twice as good as a man at a job just to be able to get two-thirds of the pay, but I'll admit I have no idea what it's like to be raised in an environment like the East End of London, or to be black. I can't understand what those differences have made for you, but I know how I was treated by the Establishment – like a thicko from the back of Welsh beyond, with people laughing at my accent in London's better wine bars and telling sheep jokes behind my back all the time. Though why they do that about a Welsh woman, I have no idea. One thing I'm certain of is that it never helps if you put yourself down – especially when there are so many people ready to do it for you.'

Annie spoke quietly. 'It was hard for me in the white world of the City. I'm black, I'm a woman and I've got a Cockney accent. It really annoys me when one black person talks for us all, or even when a woman does for all women – everyone is an individual, everyone has a different specific experience. So all I can say is, for me it was like there was this whole secret world I couldn't get into. I saw white girls in the office get better shifts than me, get better treated than me, and I was the only one they made redundant. 'Course, all the men got treated better than any of the women. That apart, was I treated the way I was 'cos I'm black, or 'cos I refuse to try to talk posh like them, or 'cos my name's not something double-barreled? I dunno. But I do know the whole package of what I am and what I've lived through has made me believe the best thing to do is to be even *more* me, and shove it in the world's face before the world shoves me.'

Carol's heart went out to her friend. 'Even so, maybe you could give people a chance to see the *whole* you? The you I know and love. Dare to show them all of yourself, not just the angry, hurt part of you. *I* know it's your determination that sometimes looks like anger, but despite the fact you've been pretty prickly since you got here, people have warmed to you, you know. Take Tudor, for example; he's all over you like a rash. I know he's not the best-looking bloke in the world but he's steady, a hard worker, of good moral fiber and – let's be honest – he's potty about you.'

Carol was surprised by how shocked Annie looked. 'You think

Tude's really interested in me?' she asked. '*I* don't think he is. He's just a nice bloke, that's all. He's the same way with everyone.'

Albert started to struggle in his harness, and Carol suspected even the shade was getting too hot for him. Her concern for her son's wellbeing offset against her friend's seeming thick-headedness made her feel cross. 'You know what, Annie? I love you dearly, and I've always been there for you, and I *will* always be there when you need me in the future. But, sometimes, I think you need a good kick up the backside. You're not a kid anymore. Albert's a baby and needs me to do everything for him; you're supposedly a grown-up, and you need to start doing things for yourself. On the one hand there's Huw, who's at least got a more than questionable track record when it comes to women, and on the other there's Tudor who's . . . well, Tudor. You're a private enquiry agent – use your skills to research them both, equally. Dig beneath the surface. You're good at that, I know it; you're even allowed to admit that to yourself. I'm taking my son back to the office now, to get back to work. I suggest you do the same.'

As she stomped back to the relatively pleasant temperature of a fan-cooled office, Carol felt herself vibrate with anger – not at Annie alone, but also at herself, for having lost her temper. She loved Annie, but sometimes the woman drove her to distraction.

Carol told Althea and Mavis the basics of what had transpired outside, and had been back at her desk for twenty minutes before Annie reappeared. When she did, all three of the women's heads popped up, looks of apprehension on each face.

'I'm back,' Annie announced sheepishly as she took her seat and quietened Gertie. She cleared her throat loudly. 'Listen up.' They all did. 'Has Carol filled you in on the fact we just had a bit of a heart to heart?' Althea and Mavis nodded. 'Good. So I'm going to start by saying I'm sorry. Apparently I've been a right pain in the you-know-what for some time. Since that miserable slob back in London stabbed me, in fact. I'll try harder to not be like that from now on. So watch out, Mave – merry quips a-plenty are on the way, along with the odd double-entendre. You'll have to get used to it. Again.'

'It's true you've quite a comical turn about you, when you choose,' acknowledged Mavis.

Annie continued, 'I've also been a silly mare about a few other things, too, it seems. So let me tell you what's going to happen.

None of us will mention this again, and I will do my job to the best of my ability. I say we find out if Huw Hughes is truly mixed up in the deaths of his wives. I also say we look into his history with Dr Priddle, and work out if he might have wanted the man dead. Dr Priddle told me about Huw's friendship with his late wife, and we know she killed herself – maybe there's something there too, because that's yet another dead woman in Huw's past.'

'I never thought about it that way,' said Carol, kicking herself that she hadn't.

'Well, I did,' replied Annie, in a way that made Carol proud. 'Out there, surrounded by all this loveliness where I'm lucky enough to live now, and knowing I have good friends in you lot, I've given myself a good talking to, and – I admit it – I phoned my dad, who told me pretty much all the same things Carol just did, though he was a bit less polite. Thanks for being just the sort of chum a person needs when they're feeling pretty down, Car; Dad said it was about time someone told me to get a grip.'

'Rodney's a perceptive man, I've always said so,' said Mavis.

'True,' agreed Annie. 'Anyway, I've had what I think is a bright idea. What if Huw's the sort of bloke who picks up women who – yes, like me – have weaknesses when it comes to self-esteem? What if – despite the fact they all had pots of money – these women he married didn't feel appreciated? He knows what to say and do to make a woman feel special. Trust me, I know that from personal experience. I recently read an article about cult religions, and how they draw people to them who feel undervalued, unloved, and are looking for someone – anyone – to take an interest in them. Maybe that's what Huw's like.'

'I think that's an interesting idea, and an excellent line of enquiry, Annie,' said Mavis.

'Yes, I think so too,' agreed Annie, 'but we'll need Carol's skills to help us find out what sort of women he married, not just who they were and how they died. Teamwork.' Carol was delighted to see Annie beam a genuine smile for once.

'There are women all over the world being taken advantage of by online con artists who play on exactly that sort of weakness,' said Althea. 'It's especially hard when you're elderly and lonely; widows can become easy prey.' She glanced at Annie. 'I know you're not a widow dear, so you wouldn't understand what it's like to lose the only man you've ever loved—'

'Well, before we get started on our new line of enquiry, I'll tell you why that's not exactly the case,' said Annie. Carol felt her heart break all over again for her chum, as Annie explained how John had deceived her, and how the depression she'd suffered after the discoveries she made at his funeral had led her down some very dark paths indeed.

TWENTY-THREE

'I'll answer the bell, Brid, you finish that tea,' called Christine as she made her way across the hall toward the front door of the manor. Upon opening it, she was confronted by two men so large she was amazed they'd both managed to fit into the small, banged-up little VW Beetle parked just beyond the porch. Knowing that Brid had described the men who'd taken Callum away as being big, she was immediately on her guard – then she told herself thieves would hardly ring the door bell.

'Can I help?' she asked politely.

'We've come to see Mr Bright,' said the slightly narrower of the pair.

'Our boss Mr Flanagan told us to come,' said the taller one.

Christine nodded and opened the door wider. 'Do come in.' She turned and called, 'Alexander, it's for you.'

Both men laboriously wiped their feet, removed and shook the rain from their jackets, then hung them on the hooks in the porch before entering. 'Thanks,' said the taller man.

They followed Christine into the main sitting room, where they sat in chairs that seemed too small to hold them, awaiting Alexander's arrival. Christine was relieved when she heard him clattering down the staircase. She shot to her feet. 'Ah, here he is now. Alexander, you have visitors.'

As Alexander entered the room, the two men rose and the narrower one moved to greet him. 'Mr Flanagan told us you'd be expecting us. I'm Tom, and this is Barry. We're on loan to you for the duration.'

Christine looked across the room and Alexander's expression told her he was pleased with what he saw.

'Good to meet you Tom, Barry.' He nodded at the men. 'Francis Flanagan has been a friend and business associate of mine in London for some time. It's good of him to allow you both to be here when I find myself in need of some local support. Allow me to introduce you to Christine Wilson-Smythe. This is her father's estate, the Viscount Ballinclare, and we find ourselves under threat of a visit by some gentlemen who would like to relieve this house of some of its more lovely possessions. They've already taken Callum Ahearn away with them, as well as what appears to have been a considerable amount of potcheen. We believe he owes somebody known as Gadfly some money. So, first things first, is there anything you can tell us about who these men might be, or who this Gadfly character is? Is he dangerous? Are they?'

Barry and Tom exchanged what Christine judged to be a significant glance. Barry spoke gravely, his thick accent telling her he hailed from Belfast. 'In that case, Mr Flanagan picked the right men for the job.'

'He did,' agreed Tom. 'You talk, Barry.'

Barry did. 'Everyone hereabouts will have heard of him, but no one knows who Gadfly is. There's no question he's got a vicious streak through him. He's several men who work exclusively for him, and he pulls in others as and when he needs them. Lots of characters around here will do most things for a bit of extra cash, and many won't be too fussy about what it is they're asked to do. Not easy to find steady work, see?' Christine and Alexander both nodded. 'We know some of the locals he'd call on, but the ones who work for him full time?'

Tom took over. 'They're the type you move away from when they come into a pub, if you know what's good for you. You don't want to overhear anything they might be saying by mistake; don't take kindly to people knowing their business, so they don't.'

'You know they're coming here for sure, do you?' asked Barry.

Alexander looked across at Christine, and she took her cue to reply. 'To be honest, we hope we've made them change their mind. Callum's wife, Brid, told us they said they'd be back this morning with a lorry to strip the place. I managed to get a meeting arranged here with the local police. I believe the sight of the police car sent them packing. I have no doubt that, by now, they'll have managed to discover I'm here and that I have company. Brid swears she and Callum haven't told a soul anything about Alexander, and I believe her, largely because we didn't tell either of them anything they could pass along. However, Callum at least knows Alexander's name, so they might have some idea that a sometime-property developer from London is here, along with the daughter of the house. Possibly they'll forget the idea of robbing the place. Or maybe not.'

'Either way, we're glad you're here,' added Alexander. Turning his attention to Christine he added, 'We could make up a couple of rooms for the next couple of nights, couldn't we?' She nodded.

All four of them were standing awkwardly in the middle of the room and, now she knew the men were to become unexpected overnight guests, Christine suggested tea, which was accepted by all. 'I'll rustle up a tray, and I'll have a quick chat with Brid about dinner.'

As she left Tom called after her, 'I could go to the chip shop in Belcoo, if there isn't enough in.'

'I expect we'll mange,' she called back. She made tea, and discussed all the necessary arrangements with Brid, thinking all the time about Alexander's decision to call upon local muscle through a contact in London. She couldn't quite decide if it bothered her. Was she becoming so accustomed to Alexander's shadier side that she was now prepared to accept a situation which, just a year earlier, would have been extraordinary? Most odd was the fact she didn't mind putting up with a couple of thugs who looked imposing and were probably quite handy with their fists.

As she carried the tea tray back to the sitting room, Christine realized with a bit of a start that she had changed. She and Alexander had spent so much time over the months discussing how much she wanted him to change, she'd not so much as considered that maybe her own moral compass had shifted. Christine laid down the tray feeling as though she'd had a minor epiphany, and wondering whether it was a good thing or not.

What did become clear over tea was the fact that Tom and Barry were going to spend a lot of time on their phones. By the time their tea was drunk, they'd also managed to confer – in low voices and accents so thick even Christine had a problem understanding anything they said – and Tom delivered their joint report.

'Aye, well your Callum's gone and got himself in a real spot of bother it seems. Word out there? Whatever he's told his wife, he's into the Gadfly for a bundle.'

Christine looked at Alexander with worried eyes.

'I'll go and find Brid, and we'll sort out some sleeping arrangements,' she said, taking her leave. She took comfort in the knowledge that, across the Irish Sea, Carol would be helping her out with some useful research.

TWENTY-FOUR

Wednesday 24th August

Annie had been up until all hours working at her laptop, digging into the life of the man she'd recently come to know more than a little, and admire a surprising amount – Huw Hughes. Despite her lack of sleep, even when she'd finally gone to bed, she still arrived at Sharon Jones's shop at eight thirty sharp, where Sharon's mother, Mair, was due to share breakfast with Annie in the kitchen at the rear of the premises.

Mair was already bustling about the tiny space when Annie and Gertie presented themselves and, after cordial greetings, Annie settled to a pot of tea and plate mounded with thickly buttered toast. She picked up a squeezable container of Marmite and squirted it on so it mingled with the butter in rich, tempting swirls. She asked just one question before she tucked in; Mair Jones's reputation as a prodigious talker was legendary.

'Tell you all I know about poor Dr Clive Priddle and his late wife? Well, I'll do my best,' said Mair, her beady eyes alight with excitement beneath her tastefully colored blondish hair. Mair Jones picked up her teacup, held it with both hands, and peered across the narrow laminate-topped table at Annie. 'Hard to know where to start, really,' she began. 'Edna and Clive had been married a while when they got here and seemed happy enough. Can't be easy being a doctor's wife, but she did alright. In those days we had a married vicar – not like the one they've got at St David's now – and in the village pecking order, the doctor's wife came just below the vicar's.

Edna did well as the sort of second-in-command for committees and things. Quiet, but diligent. Kept themselves to themselves did the Priddles, which you'd expect.' She winked at Annie over her tea. 'Hard for a doctor to mix with people in the village when he's seen them in all states of undress, if you know what I mean; you can't enjoy a pint in the pub standing next to a man whose had his hands on your you-know-what, can you?'

Annie nodded her agreement, not wanting to staunch Mair's flow.

The woman continued gleefully, 'I always thought they were happy, but I suppose you never know what's going on in a marriage, under the surface, do you? Came as a shock to us all when she took her life, it did. One day she was there singing in church, the next she was as dead as a dodo. Tablets. Lots of them. Easy enough to get if you're married to a doctor, I suppose.'

Annie managed to squeeze in, 'Did she leave a note?'

Mair looked around the tiny, empty room then leaned in. 'You bet she did, and it said . . .' She paused, as if checking she wouldn't be overheard. 'Well, I didn't see it myself, of course, but I had it on good authority that she blamed the doctor for what she'd done. Said her heart was broken, and she couldn't stand to live with him any longer, if you please. And he's as lovely as they come is Dr Priddle. Well, he *was*, poor dab.'

Annie decided to dig deeper. 'What about Huw Hughes? Do you remember him being a friend of the Priddles?'

Mair nodded. 'Over there a lot he was. But you saying that now – calling him a "friend of the Priddles" – makes me think; it's a bit of an odd thing for a boy to do, isn't it? I mean he was still in school then, yet he was over there at all hours, day and night.'

'Dr Priddle told me Huw played chess with his wife,' said Annie.

'Chess?' Mair laughed, sipped her tea and gave Annie a look that spoke volumes. 'Well, I suppose it must have been that then.'

Annie pressed, 'Do you mean you think something . . . romantic . . . was going on between Huw and Edna?' Annie grappled with the idea. 'Wouldn't she have been much older than him? He'd have only been about seventeen or eighteen, I suppose. Clive Priddle told me Huw left the village straight after he left school.'

Mair picked up a second piece of toast. 'Now let me think about that, I'm not as good as I used to be with time. She died in the winter of 1978 to 1979. It was a bad one, I recall. Couldn't bury her for quite a while, because of the snow, and the ground being so hard. Almost forty years ago. The doctor himself would have been in his forties then, and she was a good bit younger than him. You can check on her headstone in the graveyard at St David's – that's where she is – but I'm going to say she was in her early thirties when she died, so maybe fifteen years older than Huw.'

Annie pressed, 'Do you think she'd have been the type to have a fling with a boy?'

Mair smiled broadly. 'Seen those Chippendale blokes, have you? They'd all be a lot more than fifteen years younger than me, and I don't know what I'd do if any of them threw themselves at me, but pushing them away wouldn't be top of my list. But her and him? Well, you never know, I suppose.'

'Did Huw have any girlfriends his own age?'

Mair leaned back in her creaky chair. 'Even though it's a long time ago, that's something I'm sure of; always popular with the girls. The girls at school with him, the girls in the village. There wasn't really anywhere for them to go but the youth club they held at the village hall back then, and they'd come in the shop here to get pop and crisps, and suchlike, for their evenings out. So I saw most of what went on.'

'And did a lot go on?' Annie was curious. She recalled her own life at much the same time; she'd left home and started work when she was sixteen, and had enjoyed living it up in London on her own. She'd seen all sorts. But she couldn't imagine what it would have been like to live in a village in the middle of Wales in the Seventies – she might as well have tried to imagine what it would have been like to be a teenager on Mars.

Mair waved her hand in the air. 'Compared with some of the things you hear about today, they were innocent times. A bit of smoking around the back of the hall, the odd flagon of cider drunk by those who weren't old enough to buy it legally, that sort of thing. Maybe there were youngsters at it like rabbits all over the place, but I never saw them. A bit of snogging in the graveyard, but that's to be expected. Huw? I saw him about a lot with Marjorie Pritchard – or Lloyd as she was then – and Bronwen Price; all over him like shirts on a clotheshorse they were. He didn't seem to mind, but I don't remember there being one special girl. Too special himself, he was. There was talk that he bought some of his clothes in Cardiff, which says a lot. Very dapper even back then. Sharon tells me he hasn't changed much in that respect at least. No idea how he afforded it; his parents had less than nothing, and he certainly didn't have a weekend job like some of them.'

Annie acknowledged that Huw certainly still took care of his appearance, but she wasn't sure that was a damning fact. Gertie began to bark aggressively toward the opening which led to the store room, and thence the shop.

Annie hung onto her lead tightly. 'What is it, Gert? Smell something interesting?' Annie caught a fragment of something being said in the shop, then she recognized Tudor's booming voice. She checked her watch. Time had flown by. She gathered her thoughts and asked, 'Is there anything else you can tell me, Mair? About Clive, Edna or Huw?'

Mair gave the question some thought. 'I'm sure there's loads, but I can't imagine it would be of any interest to you. Like I said, the Priddles were normal, till she killed herself. After that, the doctor went to pot. He was never the same. Moved out of Anwen a few years later, and then became the man you knew – sort of jovial, and still involved with village life, but just on the edges. By the sounds of it, you've been getting to know Huw quite well since he got back. It must be lovely to hear about all the things he's been up to all round the world. He's done very well for himself, I understand.'

Annie could tell Mair would like nothing more than for her to spill the beans about Huw, but she decided she needed to get to the office, so thanked Mair and headed off.

TWENTY-FIVE

Mavis listened carefully, and took notes, as Stephanie spoke to her rapidly on the telephone. Althea annoyed her by hovering too close, so Mavis swatted at her with her notebook until she retreated to the far end of the office sofa.

'Stop it,' hissed Mavis as Althea made wild 'wind it up' motions. 'Hold on a moment would you please, Stephanie?' She turned to

Althea. 'This will take longer if you keep distracting me. Just be patient, dear.' Althea sat on her hands and bit her lip.

Eventually Mavis ended her call and joined Althea on the couch. 'Well, that's a good deal of information to be going on with. You should be proud of your daughter-in-law, she's a good head on her shoulders.'

'I am, and she does,' said Althea brightly. 'Now come on, cough. What's up?'

'Ach, some of the things you say. You and Annie are as bad as each other, the pair of you,' chided Mavis. 'I'll tell you "what's up"; Dr Clive Priddle was most definitely poisoned with a lethal dose of strychnine, which he had somehow ingested at some point – there's no time of death as yet, at least, not one that they're sharing. That being said, I'm sure you'll be as delighted as Stephanie was to discover that none of the food served at the tea on Sunday at Chellingworth Hall has been found to contain any such substance.'

Mavis was touched to see the relief on the dowager's face. 'You mean we didn't kill the doctor?' Althea's voice cracked with emotion as she spoke.

'It appears that way. They've no idea how the strychnine got into the poor man's system, but they're giving your food – or what was left of it, in any case – a clean bill of health. Stephanie was told the laboratory staff had worked through the night to analyze the samples they took from the hall, and Chief Inspector Carwen James himself phoned her with the news. I think he was impressed by how she handled the entire matter yesterday, which is good for us too, because now we know more than we could have found out for ourselves.'

'And have they found out anything more about the paint and so forth at the croquet pavilion?' asked Althea, a note of wariness in her voice. 'I've been thinking hard about how there might be connections between the case of the vengeful vandal and the case of the dead doctor . . . or should it be the poisoned physician? No, that's not alliterative enough.'

Mavis tutted. 'No, they haven't, but they're no' cases at all, Althea. Well, they *are*,' she corrected herself as the dowager's eyebrows shot upwards, 'but they're no' *our* cases; they are both police matters, as is right and proper.'

Althea stood, brushed down her cerise skirt – which Mavis thought she'd rather cavalierly teamed with a chartreuse blouse – and began to pace. McFli trotted behind her, his little legs moving many times faster than Althea's, and Mavis had to admit they made a slightly comical pair; she told herself to think twice about pacing around as she herself had a good think, in future.

Althea turned and asked what Mavis realized was a highly pertinent question, 'If there wasn't strychnine in the food we served, then why were so many people taken ill after eating it?'

Mavis replied, 'I don't know, and Stephanie didn't offer any information on that point. Maybe just one ingredient was spoiled and that did it? It's been exceptionally warm, so maybe the ham? Or maybe someone didn't wash the tomatoes or the cucumber properly and they were tainted with something they didn't test for at the lab.'

'As far as I'm aware all the vegetable ingredients came from our own greenhouses and the garden. We're organic, as you know. However, could you phone Stephanie back and ask her to ask the policeman chappie if they're planning to do more tests, and, if not, whether they might? He seems to have taken a bit of a shine to her, and I suspect neither you nor I are in his good books these days. Well, you most certainly aren't, dear,' Mavis noted a twinkle in the dowager's eyes, 'so maybe she could do something about it for us?'

Mavis didn't care to admit it aloud, but acknowledged to herself that Althea had made a good point. She rang the duchess and made the appropriate requests. 'She said she'll get in touch with "Carwen,"' said Mavis as she hung up.

Althea tilted her head and gave Mavis a meaningful look as she replied, 'Nice to know they're on first name terms.'

'Aye,' said Mavis. 'You must be used to the fact that a title will get them hopping about for you every time. As for showing respect to a woman who's given decades of service to her country as a nurse in the armed forces? That wee man cannae see the good I can do for him.' She felt cross, and was pleased that Althea had turned her attention to McFli. She was even more relieved when Annie and Gertie arrived.

After the inevitable kerfuffle that accompanied the greetings between dogs, Mavis noticed Annie had a sort of glow about her that morning. She also spotted that Annie didn't – as was usually the case – fiddle about making tea before she took her place at her desk. 'How did the interview with Mair Jones go?' she asked, suspecting something juicy might have come of it.

'I'm writing it up now,' said Annie without taking her eyes off her screen. 'I know the best way to record everything is quickly, so just give me a bit of time to do that while it's fresh in my mind. Ta.'

Mavis was surprised; she could tell that something in Annie's demeanor had shifted since the previous day's chat between her and Carol, and was grateful for it. She liked Annie a great deal, but had been perturbed to see what she considered to be an increasing amount of chippiness in the woman since they'd decamped from London to Wales. Initially she'd put it down to a form of homesickness; Annie had rarely left her beloved London throughout her entire life, and now she was living totally beyond her comfort zone in a tiny Welsh village. But, as the months had passed, Mavis had suspected it was more than that. Mavis hoped she was now witnessing the return to Standard Operating Procedure for Annie, which she preferred.

'There you go,' announced Annie spinning away from her desk on her wheeled seat. 'Done and sent.'

'Do you want us to read it, or are you happy to tell us what you've discovered?' challenged Mavis.

Annie recounted her conversation with Mair Jones to the two women.

'A sad tale, but no specific reason emerging that would suggest Huw Hughes might wish Dr Priddle dead,' summed up Mavis when Annie had finished.

'I agree,' chorused Annie and Althea. They exchanged a smiling nod.

'So, what next?' asked Mavis. Just as she was about to get up to perform her usual exercise of pacing the office, she stopped herself; she didn't want to become too predictable.

'I've been doing a lot of digging into Huw's background,' announced Annie, 'and I have considered all the facts, but I can't believe he killed his wives. Any of them. And I cannot find anything in his past or present that would make him either want to vandalize the croquet pavilion or poison Priddle. I've read Carol's background notes on Aelwyn, the girl who works at the café, but I think there's a hole in them; we need to know more about her parents. Priddle was old; she's very young; she might have acted because of some connection with her family we don't know about yet. We need to do that research. Also, I know Althea's comfortable discounting the possibility that any of the long-term employees of the Chellingworth estate could be to blame, but I think we should carry out our own independent research to as thorough a level as we have done so for Huw and Aelwyn. That's next, I believe.'

Mavis took a moment to digest Annie's comments. 'You do know this isn't our case, right?' she said.

'I know the poisoning and the vandalism are both police matters,' replied Annie soberly, 'but we all believe we can do a different type of job than the police can, don't we? So we should do it. I'm not aware of any outstanding cases at the moment, so why twiddle our thumbs when we can be doing something useful. Someone killed the doctor, so why shouldn't we do what we can to find out who?'

'Despite the fact the police are looking into it?' said Mavis, by way of utter clarification.

'Despite that, yeah,' replied Annie, her chin jutting forward just a little.

'Maybe we should speak to Carol, who's likely to carry most of the weight of our information search,' suggested Mavis; she didn't want to dampen Annie's rediscovered enthusiasm, but was realistic enough to know that Carol's speed and efficacy would far outstrip the combined efforts of all three of the women in the office at that moment.

'I could help too,' offered Althea brightly. 'I'm not good with computers, but I could ask people questions, to their faces. They'd have to make themselves available and tell me the truth because I pay their wages: Ian I pay directly; Roger, Edward, Aelwyn, and Bronwen are paid by the estate; Tudor's pub is leased from the estate, and he pays Aled's wages; Marjorie Pritchard would tell me anything if only I'd invite her for tea. That's most of them covered right there.'

'So we're all convinced the vandalism and the murder are connected?' asked Annie. Two heads nodded as one. 'Yeah, me too.'

'We should all be there when you chat to them, Althea,' said Mavis. 'Well, maybe Carol doesnae need to be away from Albert for all that time; we can brief her when we've finished.'

'Very good,' said Althea standing. McFli sensed something exciting was about to happen, and readied himself to participate. 'Let's go to the hall; everyone will be there, even Ian, who's still working on this wretched mole problem with Ivor. We'll call them in for tea, one by one, and see what's what.'

Mavis thought Annie sounded disappointed when she said, 'No gumshoeing, just tea and talk? So more Christie than Chandler.' Mavis nodded. 'OK, I can do that too,' Annie added, grinning. 'So long as there's cake.'

Mavis wondered if she was going to be able to cope with the revised version of Annie, who seemed to be channeling positivity to an almost alarming extent.

TWENTY-SIX

Christine hadn't been to Enniskillen for many years, and she had to admit she hadn't missed it. As the windscreen wipers did their best to cope with the thundery rain, she and Alexander sat silently waiting for the traffic lights to change to green.

'You're sure you're going to be alright with me just dropping you at the door?' asked Alexander for what Christine reckoned was the fiftieth time.

'I'll be fine.' She tried to not sound testy. 'And there won't be a door; this isn't like any police station you'll have seen in London, it's the biggest PSNI station in the area. It'll be grim.'

'PSNI?'

'Police Service of Northern Ireland. It'll be like a mini fort. Be prepared. They built it on a little promontory so it's surrounded on three sides by the River Erne, which offers better protection. This won't be some bucolic, ivy-covered police house where the local bobby hands out sweets to the nippers and sound advice to teens foolish enough to consider even remotely wayward behavior. It'll make Brixton nick look like a bunch of amateurs built it.'

'Sounds delightful.' Alexander's tone suggested he was utterly miserable.

'Look, we discussed this till all hours; we've agreed I should play nice with the cops so's you and your mates will keep your squeaky-clean reputations intact if everything goes a bit wonky. I'm happy to do my bit, and I'll lay it on thick.' Christine was nervous, but didn't want Alexander to know that. She wanted him to be proud of her, and believe she was as good at what she was doing as she hoped she was. 'I admit I wish Carol's information about Gadfly had been a bit more illuminating, but she's so good that at least we now know we're dealing with someone who's not just your average thug; her description of the complex financial arrangements the man has made, through various companies and so forth, means he's determined to remain anonymous. I know she'll uncover more; she's only just started digging. He won't be able to hide everything from Carol.'

'I understand,' said Alexander. 'She's good.'

Christine watched as the sights she'd seen with her mother when they'd visited the Enniskillen museums years ago passed by; the place didn't just feel smaller now, it felt almost oppressive. Christine tried to push such thoughts from her mind and said, 'Not long now, especially if the lights are with us. I'll phone you when I've finished.'

'I don't know where I'll be parking, so allow a bit of time? I'll get back to you as soon as I can. Be careful. You're walking in there with only one thing to your advantage – you're the daughter of a viscount.'

'If you think that's always an advantage, you don't understand the folk around here at all,' replied Christine with a sigh. 'There it is, just pull over by that petrol station on the left.'

'Good grief, you weren't joking; it does look like a fort,' said Alexander.

As she walked toward the main entrance, Christine couldn't help but feel intimidated by the tall, gray-stone walls and the massive corrugated metal structures that rose behind them. She could see the security fence stretching along the road, surrounding the entire compound. It was the sort of place that, once you got inside, you'd probably wonder if you'd ever get out again – which she suspected was the desired effect.

Having an appointment with an inspector meant her acceptance into the compound went smoothly, but the security measures were stringent; she felt anything but comfortable as she was shown into a modern, impersonal meeting room, where she waited for Inspector Beattie.

She ran thorough the main points of her tale one more time as she listened to the serviceable clock on the wall tick the seconds away. 'I've spoken with my colleagues; we think the WISE Enquiries Agency could make a go of it here; I'm seeking information about working methods in the area and how we can set things up properly from the off; I'm interested in connecting with retired officers who might be interested in working for the agency; I'm seeking advice on promotional aspects.' All were points designed to build a smoke-screen of respectability and professional interest, just so she could ask one or two choice questions about the Gadfly's operations. She hoped the dour Belfast-man would be taken in.

When the inspector finally arrived, opening with apologies about a meeting that had run on, Christine responded graciously and took the first step in her plan – she set herself up to look like an upper-class fool, and threw herself headlong into the interview.

By the time she left the station, Christine felt as though she needed a cool shower. The thundery humidity, the oppressive nature of both the police station and her task had made her 'glow' – her mother's euphemism for a pouring sweat. She waited for Alexander in the rain, her umbrella almost useless.

Flopping into the car seat and buckling up, Christine said, 'Let's go home. Now.'

'Did it go OK?'

'Not exactly.'

'What did he say about the epicenter of Gadfly's operations? Here, in Enniskillen, or spread about as Carol's initial findings suggest?'

'He didn't answer me; he deflected.' Christine sounded as annoyed as she felt.

'And Gadfly's known associates?'

'Apparently he doesn't have any.'

Alexander sounded surprised. 'Really? That's not what Tom and Barry said.'

'I know.'

'I saw he kept you waiting.'

Christine turned and looked at the side of Alexander's head. 'How do you know he was late?'

'Ah ha, I know everything,' mugged Alexander. 'In fact, I saw him being dropped off in the car park across the road where I waited for you. Beside the library. Got out of a Jag. The whole thing didn't look right to me.'

Christine chuckled. 'What do you mean, exactly?'

'Cop in a uniform gets out of a flash car, across the road from where he needs to be, then walks the last part of the way in the rain? Seems dodgy. Not necessarily because I have a dislike of Jag drivers, but because that's just not normal. The driver could have pulled up a lot closer to the entrance than they did, like I did for you. So I believe Beattie didn't want to be seen, either at all, or at least not with that person.'

'It could have been his wife dropping him at work, and she doesn't like to do that right at the gate,' replied Christine. 'And? Did you follow the car?'

'Didn't need to. I got a photo of the driver, and the number plate, sent them both to Tom and Barry. They told me all we need to know at this stage.'

'So?'

'Your Inspector Beattie was late to an appointment with you because he was consorting with a man by the name of Liam MacNeath, the owner of a couple of golf courses not far away. MacNeath's on just about every committee in the area, and is also thought to have digits in multiple pies.'

'Do I take it from your tone these are questionable pies?' Christine thought it best to be clear.

'There's no other sort of pie worth knowing about.'

Christine sat silently, focusing on the way the rain washed down the side window. She'd done the right thing – she'd trusted a senior police officer – but the impression she'd got of him during their meeting was that he was being evasive. Slippery, even. And now this? A connection to a potentially criminal local entrepreneur wasn't good. She pulled out her phone.

'Can I do anything to help?' asked Alexander, his eyes on the rain-soaked road ahead.

'I'm going to give Carol the information you just gave me, so she can do a bit more digging.'

'The Case of the Golf-club-owning Gangster?'

'Ha, flamin' ha!'

TWENTY-SEVEN

Carol reckoned she was doing pretty well; she had her second load of laundry of the day in the machine, a line full of clothes drying in the summer sun and a good few hours' of research under her belt. Not that she was wearing a belt – indeed, she couldn't imagine herself being capable of wearing such an accessory for a considerable amount of time.

Albert was napping; he'd given her a poor night's sleep. While sitting up with him she hadn't been able to resist following lines of enquiry on her tablet. She'd wondered about the light bothering her son, but it hadn't seemed to make any difference to whether he slept or not, so she'd passed the time singing Welsh hymns, quietly enough so they counted as lullabies, and simultaneously screen-swiping.

Mavis had asked her to carry out some basic background digging into everyone on both of the croquet teams, including Henry; of course Althea knew nothing about Mavis's request and Carol planned on keeping the work she'd done on the duke private. But she'd done it, nonetheless. An early start had then allowed her to finish up what she'd been working on for Christine, and she'd been able to send an initial file of information to her colleague in Ireland in time for what she knew was an important meeting with the police there.

'Mam doesn't like to be smug, Albert, because there's a lot of truth in the saying that pride goes before a fall, but I have to admit, I'm having a good day,' she whispered as she lifted Bunty off her lap and moved toward her son's crib to make sure he was comfy.

She, Annie, and Mavis had a telephone conference scheduled in half an hour, so she set herself up at the dining-room table and was ready to go at the appointed time.

'Annie and I are in the office together, but we'll each use our own screen so you can see us both and we can access documents independently,' announced Mavis when the women connected.

'Have you both managed to read everything I sent?' asked Carol, hoping they had; she hadn't seen Annie since the previous day and wasn't sure what sort of mood she'd be in.

'I certainly have,' replied Annie, 'and we're just back from the hall where Althea, Mavis, and I managed to conduct interviews with all the main players too, so we'll be able to give you insights you haven't been able to get off the Internet, Car.'

Carol was pleased to hear Annie sounding so positive, and threw herself into her own line of questioning. 'Great stuff. So, what have you discovered, Annie?'

'Althea's a natural gossip, did you know that?' began her colleague. 'I mean, I know I'm good at it, even though I think I might have met my match in Mair Jones. But Althea? Great at it. She's so innocent-looking and can sound as thick as two short planks when she wants. It works. She talked to everyone, and we'd both also seen your notes so we were able to ask critical questions. It went well.'

'And?' asked Carol feeling a little impatient.

Annie sighed. 'Didn't get diddly.'

'What?' Carol was disappointed.

'Now hold your horses a moment, Annie,' intervened Mavis, 'that's no' exactly true, is it?'

Annie grinned. 'Nah, Mave's right, we did get hold of a few nuggets. I suppose I should be more formal about this and let us all get on the same page as each other. Mave and I have agreed we're *not* working on paid cases, but we are carrying out an investigation, off our own bats, that will run parallel to the police investigation – as far as possible. We're talking about the vandalism, the possible tainting of all the food at the tea hosted by Henry at Chellingworth and the death of Dr Priddle.'

Mavis waved her hand at the camera. 'I should say at this point that we're no' certain that Dr Priddle didnae die by his own hand. We're only aware of the preliminary toxicology report about the poor man, and that strychnine is indicated—'

'But isn't that a horrible way to die?' interrupted Carol, unable to contain herself. 'Wouldn't someone take an easier way out? Falling asleep with a bottle of something and a handful of pills, for example? In any case, how would he have got hold of strychnine?'

Mavis hooked her hair behind her ears. 'He might have been retired for some time, but he could still have had access to an old store of poisons. Maybe he inherited a poisons cabinet at his surgery, and took it all with him when he moved on. Many people, doctors especially I've found, hang onto some incredibly strange things as the years pass. But, even if we discount that, I will agree that imbibing a dose of strychnine is not what I would think of as a "normal" way to take one's life. Not that there's anything "normal" about such an act at all, of course. But I do believe we can discount suicide for our purposes of enquiring.'

Annie turned her face from her camera, and Carol realized she was giving Mavis a bit of a strange look. 'So, as I was saying,' said Annie forcefully, 'we're looking into the backgrounds of the people connected with the croquet teams, because we think one of them might have painted the "Vengeance is Mine" message at the vandalized pavilion, as a sort of announcement that they were going to kill Priddle. First off then, the Chellingworth Champs: let's discount Henry as being a prime suspect for murder to start with, and I'm saying that even though Althea's not here.'

'Agreed,' said Carol. Her research had confirmed what she'd believed, and hoped; Henry's life was blameless.

'Then we've got Edward the butler,' continued Annie, 'who I still reckon had the means and opportunity to poison all the food at the hall if he'd wanted to, and could have been the vandal, but there doesn't seem to be anything connecting him with Dr Priddle at all and I'll be honest, I know I don't know the bloke well – as a person – but he's such a calm, coping type, I can't imagine him rushing about the estate with a tin of paint and a vengeful soul. Also, he was definitely at the hall the entire time between the tea on Sunday and the discovery of Priddle's body on Tuesday morning, so couldn't have poisoned him. The same can be said of Ian Cottesloe, though he was at either the hall or the Dower House the entire time, taking him out of the frame for killing Priddle, and, again, we cannot find any real link between the two men – though Priddle was Ian's father's doctor. None of us can imagine why Ian would vandalize the pavilion, or want everyone to become ill either – and Ian did report a dicky tummy on Monday morning, it seems.'

'Reporting an upset stomach cannot exclude a person from our list of suspects,' observed Mavis.

'I agree,' said Annie, 'but if you recall, Althea already knew Ian had been poorly, and Ivor had kicked up quite a stink about it. I don't think Ian would have gone that far unless he was really sick. The same can be said of Bob Fernley; as estates manager we all agreed he would be unlikely to cause damage to the estate, and, although he wasn't known to have been taken ill, he was either working, or with his wife at all the pertinent times. He was also insistent that he's never been sick a day in his life and has never used a doctor.'

'True enough,' agreed Mavis, 'that's what he said, but I believe that latter point was pure hubris.'

'Finally,' said Annie with a sigh, 'and even though I don't like to admit it, young Aelwyn Thomas might be annoying, and might be one of the very few people who didn't suffer some sort of sickness after the tea, but there's nothing to suggest she wanted everyone to fall ill. Also, there's nothing to connect her to Priddle. At all. Nor her parents, or even her grandparents, according to your research, Carol; given that she's not originally from these parts, Priddle didn't tend to any of her family at all, and she claims not to know the man, never having met him other than during the tea on Sunday. As for the vandalism? Well, she'd be much more likely to Tweet a message like that than paint it.'

'Aelwyn's social circles and Priddle's – judging by her online presence – don't intersect at all,' agreed Carol. 'And you believed her when she said she didn't know him?' Annie and Mavis nodded their agreement. 'So what about Bronwen?'

'Now that's where it gets interesting,' said Annie. Carol thought she looked rather gleeful. 'She was one of Priddle's patients, back before he retired. She certainly had access to the food at the hall, and wasn't seen by anyone after the tea stuff was cleared away on Sunday. She said she was in her room, but there were no witnesses.'

'Hang on a sec', Annie, are you saying that just because the man was her doctor once upon a time, Bronwen Price might have wanted to kill Dr Priddle? That seems a bit of a stretch to me,' said Carol.

'I agree with Annie,' said Mavis sharply. 'At the moment we're looking for any connections between the vandalism at the pavilion, everyone becoming ill, the death of Dr Priddle and the people on the croquet teams. We've identified a connection. That's significant.'

Carol decided to not say anything and allowed Annie's original point to stand. 'What about the Anwen Allcomers team?' she asked.

'I'll speak to that subject,' replied Mavis. Carol wondered if that meant Mavis was keen to add her own subjective input about Huw, and thought this a good division of labor to allow that to happen.

Mavis referred to her notes. 'Althea's questioning – chatting as she called it – revealed to us that not only has she an aptitude for getting information out of people who owe her their living, but she's also no' bad at winkling secrets out of those who don't directly owe her anything at all. Tudor, for example, would make any pub a welcoming place, and I'm sure the Chellingworth Estate is pleased he leases the Lamb and Flag from them, but he'd no' go short of a place to run a business anywhere else, if he chose to. He knows that, so he didn't need to be as open with Althea as he was. That being said, the only real insight we gleaned from him was that he was pretty poorly himself after the tea, he was never a patient of Dr Priddle, though he accepts he knew the man somewhat. He did, indeed, carry about several plates of goodies on Sunday, allowing him – possibly – the chance to tamper with the food. However, when it comes to the vandalism, he was at pains to point out he'd have been either working, or else unable to enter the estate during the hours when the vandalism occurred. That's a point that could be claimed by many, though.'

'Come on, Mave,' interjected Annie, 'we agreed there was no reason for Tude to go painting all over the pavilion, or smashing it up, especially if he thought for one minute that would spoil the Anwen Allcomers' chances of winning the tournament. The same thing goes for him knocking off Dr Priddle – Tude says he was a useful player.'

'Aye, all true,' conceded Mavis.

'I agree,' said Carol. 'What about Aled? I sent you a lot of information about him, I know. It seems it's much easier to find out all about youngsters who use social media than those a bit longer in the tooth who keep themselves to themselves – as far as the Internet is concerned, in any case.'

'You did a great job on him, Car,' said Annie with a grin. 'I've got to be honest, the look on his face was a picture when Mavis asked him how his swimming lessons were going. He couldn't work out how she knew he'd signed up for a course at the public baths at the Builth Wells Sports Centre.'

'I don't think most people under the age of thirty have anything like the desire for privacy, or are aware of their lack of it, as those who grew up in the pre-Facebook, Instagram and Twitter age,' said Carol.

'When we explained how we knew – that the sign-up list is on the website – he didn't seem to mind the world knowing what he was doing,' added Mavis. 'Maybe that's a healthier approach to life – being prepared to have anyone know almost anything about you. I cannae say it appeals to me, however.'

'Don't worry, Mavis,' said Carol with a wink, 'your online footprint is tiny.'

'Aye, like my actual feet then,' said Mavis, looking gratified. 'So, back to the Anwen Allcomers,' she continued. 'Aled is, truly, an open book, and his sickness after the tea, his being in his bed all day and evening with his mother hovering over him, and the fact Dr Priddle didn't even attend to him when he was a bairn, all suggest he's not connected to anything we're looking into. Of course he knew Priddle as both a teammate and as a frequenter of the pub where he works, but Tudor suggested they had no more than a nodding acquaintance. Dr Priddle was more inclined to talk to Tudor – someone nearer his own age – rather than Aled, if he were inclined to talk to anyone at all.'

'And what about the vandalism?' asked Carol.

'Aled offered his mother as an alibi,' said Mavis with a tilt of the head, 'quite sweet, really. He was working at the pub the night that happened, then was in his bed. His mother was in the next room. We believed him.'

'And Althea managed to get out of him that he's got a poster of Gareth Bale on his bedroom wall,' added Annie. 'He made us all promise to not tell a soul. I'm going with the idea you don't count.'

'And then there are the others on the team,' said Carol. 'I have to say, I was surprised that Marjorie Pritchard is a participant in so many online forums,' she said, 'especially when you consider how involved she is in face-to-face village life. I don't know where she finds the time.'

'She suffers from insomnia,' said Annie quickly.

'Really? That explains a lot,' replied Carol.

'Aye, it does that, but that's something Althea managed to find out that I don't think should go further than we three here. Poor thing, it's a terrible affliction. So debilitating, and isolating. I've suffered from it for periods of time in my own life. In the forces, especially when you're part of an on-call medical unit, you find yourself doing a lot of traveling and working some strange hours. Once you compromise your sleep patterns, you can face all sorts of problems. I've never been one to use sleep aids, and I gather Marjorie shares my suspicion of them, which is a good thing. She spoke candidly about how isolating the experience can be.'

'That might explain why she's so "involved" with everyone else's life when she's out and about,' said Carol, feeling sympathy for the woman who usually managed to make her annoyed just by arriving in a room.

'Marjorie once had Dr Priddle as her GP, while she was a schoolgirl, but not since then, so there's at least a link there,' said Mavis, 'and she was his teammate. The good doctor has been involved in village life for decades, as has Marjorie, so their paths have crossed a great deal. She claimed they had a cordial relationship, but not close.'

'She also said she had no idea why anyone would want to kill him because he was, when all's said and done, a harmless type of person,' added Annie.

'Doctors often know a great deal more about a person than that person might wish the world to know,' said Mavis, sounding a note of caution.

Carol gave her words some thought. 'Might there be an incident from Dr Priddle's time as the Anwen doctor that's led to his death? Have you two moved away from thinking it might be connected with his late wife's suicide?'

'Althea asked Marjorie about that,' said Mavis.

'No, she didn't – and that was her skill at work,' interrupted Annie, 'she led Marjorie to the topic and Marjorie brought it up herself. That's the sign of an excellent interviewer – we covered that in my training, and I use that device when I'm engaging suspects myself.'

'As you should,' replied Mavis. Carol wondered if she was going to reach over and pat Annie on the head any minute; it appeared Mavis had decided to be extra-supportive of Annie since her mini-meltdown.

'So what did Marjorie have to say about Edna Priddle, as opposed to Clive Priddle?' asked Carol.

'Maybe Annie could respond to that one,' said Mavis.

'Having listened to what Mair Jones had to say about Edna, and what Marjorie thought of the woman, I'd say the two perceptions line up pretty well. Of course, when Edna killed herself, Marjorie was just a teenager, while Mair was a grown woman – so there'd be some difference in perspective. According to Marjorie, Edna Priddle was the perfect doctor's wife, and no one could believe she had the slightest reason to kill herself. When Althea mentioned the fact Huw Hughes was a regular visitor to the Priddle household, Marjorie agreed with Mair's impression that chess was likely to be all that was in play. She was a school friend of Huw's at the time – and we know Mair mentioned that she, Bronwen Price, and Huw Hughes were close friends. Marjorie confirmed that, and even talked about happy times the trio had enjoyed together.'

Carol took a deep breath and asked what she knew would be a significant question, 'Did you ask Marjorie if she thought either Bronwen or Huw could be connected with the vandalism, the tainting of food or Dr Priddle's death?'

Mavis took over. 'I did that, and she gave the matter some thought before she replied with a pretty convincing negative answer. She told us she couldn't imagine Bronwen doing anything remotely violent – her having always been as mild as milk, though she said she wouldn't put it past Huw to "do something stupid as a joke" as she put it – referring to making people ill – but she staunchly defended him when it came to vandalism and murder.'

'And did you think she was telling the truth?' asked Carol.

'Yes,' replied Annie and Mavis as one.

'Who was next?' asked Carol.

'Sharon. She's good at talking, but not about herself,' observed Annie. 'Of all the people Althea chatted with, she was the most cautious.'

'Too good at being on the other end of gossip,' noted Carol.

'Maybe,' said Annie, 'but she's a good person, you know. Yeah, yeah, I know I've got a lot of time for her, and I probably know her better than most people I've met in the village, so maybe I'm biased, but I don't see her in the frame for any of this. Dr Priddle was her parents' doctor, and hers when she was a small child. She also knew him as a customer and a team mate. However, she runs the post office so could get a message seen by any targeted group of people she wanted to by methods other than painting words on an obscure building on the Chellingworth Estate. As for tainting food up at the hall – yeah, I'll admit that she and I were a bit jealous at how much more grand everything was that was being served there than what we'd been giving our team, but, come on, why would she want to make everyone ill? Just so she'd have a run of sales on Milk of Magnesia or Imodium at the shop? I don't think so.'

'Might Dr Priddle have come into the post office to send something off to someone that maybe posed a risk to her in some way?' asked Carol.

'Ach, I chastise this one,' she nodded toward Annie, 'often enough about reading those American PI novels where everyone is on some sort of "shoot first, ask questions second" mission, so I suppose I'd better ask you the same thing – what have you been reading, Carol? Away off with Miss Marple in St Mary Mead again? This is Sharon Jones and Anwen-by-Wye we're talking about. It's a place where sheep farmers work themselves into a heap by the end of the day, then drink a gallon of beer to help them recover, not a place where genteel artists come to slather over the sight of the ankle of the vicar's daughter, or some such.'

'That's not what Miss Marple books are like at all,' said Carol, feeling hurt that Mavis was poking fun at at least three of the last books she'd read. 'Besides, when do you imagine I've got time to read novels at the moment? I'm a working mother, for goodness sake. Every waking minute of my time is filled with at least ten things to do.'

'Aye, I recall what it's like to be a young mother with bairns and career,' said Mavis quickly, 'but nonetheless, I would suggest you're being fanciful, Carol. Annie and I agree Sharon's not in the frame for these matters.'

Uncomfortable that it felt very much as though Annie and Mavis were ganging up against her Carol said, 'So we're left with Huw Hughes then.'

'Aye, that we are,' replied Mavis wearily. 'He's a complicated man, is that one. We witnessed a real charm offensive when he was with Althea, but she was immune.'

'She was,' agreed Annie.

'I know Annie and I have dug up quite a lot about Huw, but did anything new come to light?' asked Carol.

Mavis replied thoughtfully, 'He was extremely forthcoming about why he would have no earthly reason to destroy the pavilion, couldn't understand what all the fuss was about just because a few people had a touch of the runs after the tea at Chellingworth and categorically denied any part in Dr Priddle's death. He acknowledged he used to play chess with Edna Priddle, and was open about the tragic deaths of his three wives. He shared their places and causes of death with us, which confirmed what you'd both discovered. He was charming and affable.'

'And had the air of an innocent man throughout,' added Annie with what Carol deemed to be a worrying tone of finality.

Carol said, 'So when you said we "haven't got diddly," you meant we've gathered information, but none of it points to anyone as a suspect for anything.'

Mavis and Annie nodded.

Carol sat back in her chair and pondered all they'd done so far. 'So I ask again – do we really believe these events are linked? Could one person have vandalized the pavilion, another put something in the food at the hall and a third administered strychnine to Dr Priddle?'

'Come on, Car,' replied Annie, 'what you're talking about there is a crime spree of ridiculous proportions for a place this size. It would be extraordinary.'

All three women sat silently for a moment. Mavis spoke first, 'I'm inclined to think the vandalism was a victory cry about having made a good number of people sick at the tea; the vandalism and painting were at the croquet pavilion, the sickness occurred only in those attending the croquet tea. There's a clear, and I would say direct, link between them. It's Priddle's death that's the outlier.'

'I agree,' said Annie with a sigh. 'It makes most sense to see those two things as being connected with each other.'

'And neither is truly "serious," agreed?' said Carol.

'Well, I can tell you it was very unpleasant to feel the way I did,' replied Annie, 'and let's not forget that Marjorie ended up in hospital because of it, but I suppose you could say they were at the same sort of level as each other. Vindictive. Nasty. But not deadly.'

'So, let's focus there for a moment. Can we see anything that's come out of our research, or Althea's questioning, that suggests someone who had access to both the pavilion and the food at the tea, and had a bone to pick with someone – or even everyone – on those two teams?' pressed Carol.

More silence.

'Several members of the teams could have done both those things, but why would they?' asked Annie.

'What if it's someone on the Anwen team getting vengeance for never having won the tournament in many years, and maybe only the Chellingworth Champs were supposed to become ill?' offered Mavis. 'Annie, you were on the spot – was there any way in which some of the food was supposed to only be for some of the players?'

Annie pictured the set-up at the tea. 'I didn't see anything like plates of vegetarian food being kept away from non-vegetarian options, and, as far as I could tell, the platters of sandwiches and sweet treats were all arranged across a collection of tables in a well-presented, but nonetheless haphazard way. No, I don't think anyone could have been certain that particular items would have been eaten by just one team.'

'What about the make-up of the teams, Mavis?' asked Carol. 'From a medical point of view, are there distinguishing differences between them that could suggest that something introduced to the food might have affected the Chellingworth Champs to a greater extent than the Anwen Allcomers?'

Mavis was jotting down notes. Finally her head popped up and she announced, 'The Chellingworth team had more players who are older, but that's about it. Dr Priddle's age alone would skew the average age of the Anwen team, but if age were a factor, there were more older players on the Chellingworth team.' She looked thoughtful for a moment then added, 'If something was done to the food to induce the sort of symptoms we saw, it might be expected that it would more adversely affect older people, whose systems can be less able to deal well with that sort of attack. We know that Marjorie suffered from a sufficiently dangerous level of dehydration that she was taken to hospital; she's in her mid-fifties, is generally in good health, and I believe she's conscious about her weight, so she's not as portly as some others of her age on the teams. We now also know she suffers from insomnia, which in itself can compromise the immune system. But the police haven't told anyone, yet, what it was that made people ill at the tea. Indeed, they might never be able to, unless there's a significant residue of such material on the leftover food. Bear in mind, ladies, that the waste food had been put into bins and left out in what were, after all, warm conditions; the development of various bacteria could have happened after the food had been dumped so, if something were used that might have developed quite naturally in a rubbish bin, we'll never know.'

'We need more information,' said Annie.

'I agree,' added Carol.

'So which of us will go cap in hand to the police to try to winkle such information out of them?' asked Mavis.

More silence.

TWENTY-EIGHT

'Lady Clementine has arrived, Your Graces,' announced Edward. 'She's making her way to her rooms and will join everyone for dinner. I took the liberty of telling her Ladyship you were meeting for drinks at six fifteen.'

'Thank you, Edward, that might mean she'll join us at some point after six thirty when the rest of us will gather. Good idea,' replied Henry.

Edward left the dowager and her son alone in the library; Henry nursed a scotch and a book he had no intention of reading, while Althea drummed her fingers on the arms of her chair.

'It's all quite dreadful, Mother. First the moles, then the vandal, then everyone being sick. Now I discover you've been grilling half the staff as though they were common criminals. It's all left me quite unsettled.'

Althea guessed her son was hoping the scotch would put him back on an even keel.

'There you are, Henry, oh, and Althea too, how lovely,' said Stephanie as she entered the room. 'I've been looking for you.'

'Well, you've found me,' said the duke. 'How are you, dear?' The couple exchanged a kiss.

'I'll be glad to sit down,' said his pregnant wife, as she did just that.

As her son rose to refill his glass Althea internally applauded his wife as she said, 'Darling, if you keep on knocking back the booze this child of ours won't have a father for very long. Please try to moderate your intake.'

Henry retook his seat, looking guilty. 'Shall I ring for tea?'

Stephanie checked her watch. 'There isn't really time. I should think about going up to dress for dinner. I understand Clemmie has arrived, and the whole gang will be here too, so it should be a jolly evening. Not too long though, I hope.'

Can't be short enough for me, was what Althea thought, but she managed to say aloud, 'It'll be splendid. A good chance to spend time with both my children.'

Stephanie rose and threw her husband what Althea could only interpret as a warning glance. She walked across the room to take her leave. 'I'll be down in twenty minutes. I know you'll have another drink between now and then, but maybe you could make it a weak one and lengthen it with water?'

'Yes, dear,' replied Henry, eyeing up the decanter. 'I'll have my scotch over a good deal of ice,' he called, but Stephanie had gone.

'And I'll take a large sherry, thank you.'

'You're starting a bit early, aren't you, Mother?' Henry attended to her drink.

'It's not often I get to spend time with you and Clemmie together, but, if memory serves, things always seem to go more swimmingly if I have a glass in my hand.'

Lady Clementine Twyst was the last person to join the assembled group for drinks. Althea had expected no less, but was genuinely pleased to see her daughter. She greeted her warmly, complimenting her on how well she was now walking with no aid at all. Althea decided to go the whole hog and even commented that lime green hair was an excellent choice of color for the summer.

Althea hugged Clemmie much more tightly than she'd meant to, and was a little worried that her daughter seemed to have lost some weight.

'My dear child, you're skin and bones. Have you been eating properly now that you're back at the house in Belgravia?'

'Yes, Mother, I am. I put on so much weight while I was sitting about in that wheelchair for months after my leg was shattered, I thought I should do something about it; I have to attend physiotherapy in any case, so I've also started to attend classes at a gymnasium.'

Althea was agog. 'Really? Good heavens, I find it difficult to imagine you surrounded by sweaty beefcake and thumping great weights. Where is this gym?'

Clemmie laughed gently at her mother. 'It's not like that. It's all pastels and designed to appeal to women. It's a bit of a hike, being out in Fulham, but the people are delightful. A girl I know has shares in it. Abbie was at school with me. You never met her, but Daddy knew her father at the House of Lords, when Daddy still went there; he's Middleshire.'

Althea wracked her memory. 'Charles, isn't he?' Clemmie nodded. 'I recall I met him when I lunched at the House with your father once. Let me think . . . the Duke of Middleshire . . . short, round and completely bald. Terribly serious about politics. Always making sure Chelly turned up to vote, when he had to. The sort of chap who'd spin in his grave if he knew how little interest Henry has in politics. It's just as well they only nominate a few members to do the voting these days; Henry wouldn't have thrived in that world. Your poor, dear father found it exhausting and worrisome, but he did his duty up until 1999. Then, of course, they didn't want him any more. He was relieved. But I still say you're getting too thin, Clemmie.'

'It's all muscle, Mother. I also do hot yoga, and I'm now a vegetarian.'

'That's nice, dear. Did you think to relay that information to Cook at all?' Althea suspected her daughter hadn't, not being naturally predisposed to consider the needs of others.

'I telephoned a couple of days ago, so she'd have time to plan for my requirements,' replied Clemmie airily.

Althea was amazed. 'That's uncommonly thoughtful of you, Clemmie. Well done.'

'Peter's also a vegan, and he suggested I should do it. He says I should be more considerate of the staff. He's very wise, Mother.'

Althea almost choked on what was her second sherry. 'Peter? And who might that be? Are we scheduled to meet him at some point?'

'He's coming here on Saturday morning. Can't get away from work until then. Be nice to him, Mother?'

'Hello, Clemmie. Out of that old wheelchair good and proper, eh?' said Henry as he joined his mother and sister.

'Clemmie's a vegetarian now, and she's invited a young man for the weekend who has a job he cannot escape from until then,' announced Althea.

'He's not that young, Mother. He's almost sixty, so quite mature,' said Clementine.

'And he's got a job? An actual *job*?' Her son sounded as surprised as Althea felt. 'So he's not one of your usual coterie of disillusioned artist types who want nothing more than to swan about stressing over the concept of art rather than creating something that might actually sell, then?'

'Mock me if you must, brother dear,' retorted Clemmie, 'but I admit that having turned fifty, and also having stared death in the face quite recently, I now find I'm drawn to a different type. Peter has made a success of his life, and I'm proud of him for that.'

'What does he do *exactly*?' asked Henry more bluntly than Althea might have hoped.

'He's a professor of mathematics at the London School of Economics.'

'A what?' chorused Althea and Henry loudly, drawing the attention of Annie, Mavis, and Carol who were sitting with their heads together at the other end of the room.

'He's a mathematics professor who specializes in game theory and its application to financial markets. He's terribly well-respected in his field.' Althea thought Clemmie sounded as though she'd been coached.

'I look forward to meeting him,' said Althea, who wondered how on earth she'd be able to carry on a conversation with such a brilliant person. 'Does he enjoy croquet, or is that not the sort of "game" he's involved with?'

Clemmie smiled broadly. 'He loves croquet. He used to play it when he was a child, in Nigeria.'

'So he's from Nigeria?' asked Henry, sounding puzzled.

'Originally, yes. He's got two PhDs.'

'Eton?' asked Henry.

Clemmie shook her head. 'Harrow, Cambridge, Princeton in America, then teaching at the LSE.'

Althea's heart sank as her son replied, 'Oh dear.' He wandered off to join his wife.

'So, has there been much going on here while I've been away?' asked Clemmie.

'There's the gong,' replied Althea, 'let's walk through together and we can talk at the table.'

'I see that three of the four WISE women are here,' said Clemmie. 'Where's Christine?'

'Over at the family seat in Ireland, on holiday. The rest of us are working on some challenging cases.'

'Go on then – what? Something along the lines of The Case of the Lost Left Luggage?'

'I'll thank you to not use that disparaging tone, young lady. Old Dr Priddle was killed with strychnine earlier this week, and we've had a terrible time with sickness a-plenty both at the hall and in the village; someone possibly poisoned food here, at the hall. Though not with strychnine, I'm relieved to say. And we've had a vandal. And moles. *And* there's a man hereabouts who might have murdered three of his wives. So don't mock us until we've told you all about it.'

'Good heavens, Mother – it sounds like there's nothing but crime here these days. Am I the only person who has spotted that nothing like this happened in these parts until this detective agency opened its doors on our estate? There's a famous film all about the saying "if you build it, they will come" – is that what's happening at Chellingworth and in Anwen? We now have detectives in situ, so an infestation of criminals has engulfed the place.'

'Don't be facetious, dear, it's unbecoming in a young lady.'

'Come off it, Mother, I don't think you can call me "young" any longer, even if it makes you feel less old when you do so. Poor Dr Priddle. I remember him as smelling of linseed oil and having excellent sticky lollipops. Strychnine, you say?'

As Carol caught up with Althea and Clemmie she whispered, 'Stephanie just told me Chief Inspector James just phoned her and absolutely confirmed it was strychnine poisoning that killed Dr Priddle. And we now have two more critical pieces of information: the confirmed time of death was late Sunday evening. He would have died almost immediately after ingesting the poison; so the fact they found remnants of undigested lemon segments in his stomach contents is telling.'

'Lemons? Who on earth eats segments of lemons?' asked Clemmie as they proceeded toward the dining room.

Annie drew up alongside the three women. 'Dr Priddle liked lemons. He asked me to get him a few segments for his barley water at the tea. I saw him chomp right into one. I've never known anyone else to eat them like that, rind and all.'

'It sounds quite disgusting,' agreed Althea, 'but what a good way to disguise the taste of a poison. I expect it means his killer knew him very well. Knew his habits.'

Annie pounced. 'You're right,' she said, and stood stock still.

Althea felt it polite to ask, 'Are you quite well, Annie?'

Annie seemed to return to the present and said, 'Yeah. Fine, ta. But I just had a thought. Hang on a mo.' Althea watched as she darted to grab Mavis by the arm, and dragged her to join the group of what then became five women. 'Mave, is it possible to tell one type of lemon from another?'

Althea noticed that Mavis looked puzzled. 'Aye, I dare say. I'm no expert on lemons, but I'm aware there are different types.'

'No,' said Annie, 'I mean when they're in stomach contents, not on a tree.'

'Ach, I see. Again, I dare say you can. There must be tests which could ascertain the botanical variety of such items. Why, is it important?'

'It might be,' replied Annie. 'Althea, do you happen to know what type of lemons were served here on Sunday? They were small, sweeter than usual. I don't know the first thing about lemons – other than you need them for a G&T – but I know enough to be able to say the ones on the plates beside the drinks were fresh, small, and sweetish. For lemons.'

'Meyer lemons,' said Clemmie, to general amazement, 'they sound like Meyer lemons. Or possibly Eureka lemons.'

'Really?' said Althea. 'You know about such things, dear?'

'Oh Mother, you know very well I spent years in the south of France, painting and studying art. A place there called Menton holds an incredible festival of lemons every winter. We'd go along there for inspiration, and these lemon aficionados find it hard to shut up about their passion. I learned more about lemons than I thought I'd ever need to know.'

'You could ask Cook, Annie,' said Althea. 'Or maybe Bronwen. She might know more, because I dare say she'd use them more in her baking than Cook would in her dishes.'

'I'll do it in the morning,' said Annie, 'and I'll ask her what happened to all the leftover ones. There were bowls of them there, at the tea, untouched – they were cutting them as they were needed. Maybe it's a clue. After all, if that's what they found inside him, then that's likely where the poison was.'

'Wonderful source of vitamin C,' said Clemmie as the group began to move toward the dining table.

'My, my, you're full of surprises tonight, aren't you, dear,' said Althea, holding onto her daughter's arm. 'It's lovely to have you back at home for a few days. Have you by any chance given up alcohol as well as meat?'

'Don't be silly, Mother, I still enjoy wine – that's good for you.'

'I'm delighted to hear it,' replied Althea, 'I think I might need the odd glass or two of something as the weekend approaches.'

TWENTY-NINE

Thursday 25th August

Christine sat silently at the kitchen table with Alexander to her left, Tom and Barry opposite and Brid hovering with a teapot at her elbow. She wondered if she could be more miserable; even Brid's wonderful homemade bread seemed floury and bland, a far cry from its usual taste and texture.

'We've made it through another night with no incident,' said Alexander cheerfully.

'But there's still no news of my Callum,' said Brid, her voice cracking with emotion. 'My poor man could be in a ditch somewhere and we be none the wiser. Why hasn't anybody got in touch with us at all? What can have become of him?'

'There, there, Brid,' said Christine with as much compassion as she could muster after an almost totally sleepless night. 'I'm sure he's fine. We'd have heard if he wasn't.'

'They might be waiting until they can shift that potcheen,' suggested Tom. 'We'll hear about it if they try to sell it, you can be sure of that, so you can. Maybe Callum will be let go when they have a pocket full of cash.'

'But that could be ages,' wailed Brid. 'Do you think he'll be eating proper? Would they take good care of him, do you think?'

Christine could tell by the woman's expression she was pleading for some sort of comfort. 'I'm sure they will, Brid. They'd not want to deal with a sick man, would they?'

She felt utterly inadequate, and the reason she hadn't slept much was because of what she and Alexander had gone over and over again the day before; if Inspector Beattie was chummy with a shady character like Liam MacNeath, might he have been entirely the wrong person through whom Christine should have made enquiries about Gadfly?

'We'll see to the chickens for you, Brid,' offered Christine when the breakfast dishes were cleared away. 'Come on Alexander, let's do it together.' She found she couldn't force herself to sound enthusiastic any longer; she just had to get through the day until, maybe, Carol could come back to her with some helpful research insights.

The morning light filtered through clouds which promised rain. Again. Christine felt much older than her less-than-thirty-years, and she creaked louder than the gate of the coop as she bent to tend to a chicken.

'You can't dwell on it. It's done,' said Alexander as he awkwardly threw food for the birds. Christine felt a smile break out on her face as she watched his trepidation with the creatures. He wasn't terribly keen on country living, that much was clear.

'I feel I've taken a step which might lead to an unpleasant place,' she replied. 'I'm the sort who innately trusts the police, you're not. I think, on this occasion, you were right and I was wrong. I'm sorry.'

'Not all coppers are bent. Just some of them are,' replied Alexander, stepping over a bird that was sitting motionless, ignoring all the fuss and squawking surrounding it. 'We can't even be sure Beattie *is* bent, but we know he's consorting with a man who's decidedly dodgy. It might be nothing.'

'I don't even think Carol will be able to help,' said Christine, throwing the last of the food at the excited birds. 'After all, I know she won't break the law, and how on earth could there be anything she could possibly find out about a serving officer of the PSNI? It's not as though security isn't at the top of their list for people like that; they'd be easy targets if anything personal could be discovered online, even in these peaceful times.'

'Let's just see,' replied Alexander, showing her his empty bowl. 'Have we finished here now? I don't like the smell. I'll never look at an egg the same way, I promise.'

Making sure the gate was shut behind them, the couple strolled across the springy grass toward the rear of the manor.

'I thought I was doing the right thing, asking Beattie about Gadfly.

I didn't expect him to stonewall me like he did. Now I'm wondering if he did that because he's far from above-board, rather than just being a policeman who can't discuss certain topics. It's a worry.'

'I know it kept you awake,' said Alexander, gathering her into his arms. 'We're safe, Christine. We're here, at your home, with Tom and Barry to call upon if needs be. They could frighten off pretty much anyone. And I can be pretty forbidding too, if I have to be.'

Christine pulled away and walked ahead. 'I don't like violence, you know that. It never solves anything. But we just seem to be sitting about, being afraid. I want us to be able to do something – something positive – to get Callum back, safely. It's all about Callum. And Brid.'

'I know,' said Alexander. Christine could tell he was using his soothing voice, but it wasn't working on her.

'Maybe I should phone Daddy. He might be able to do . . . something.'

'Like what?' Alexander sounded cross. 'He's in London, not here. He doesn't know people in the underworld here. He doesn't even know people in the underworld there. I do. Sorry, but I do. And that's a good thing right now. Let's allow Tom and Barry to keep probing their contacts in the local area who might know something – that's our best bet. That and Carol. Tell you what, instead of waiting to hear from her, why not give her a call when we get inside?'

Christine nodded, knowing Alexander was right. 'I don't like to keep bothering her, but you're right. I'll check my phone for emails first, then phone her. But I'll go to our room to do it, I don't want all and sundry overhearing me.'

'Good idea,' replied Alexander as he gave her a hug.

THIRTY

Carol had been at her desk since four in the morning, with Albert in his car seat beside her. He'd refused to go back to sleep after a feeding, so she'd carried him about for an hour, then discovered he would only settle in that specific spot, so there he'd remained.

She'd used her time well, and was bubbling with excitement when her phone rang. It was Christine.

'Ha! I just sent you a link to a file I've put in the cloud for you,' she said before Christine had spoken, 'and here you are. Good.'

'Thanks, Carol. I saw it. You've done a lot of work, but it's difficult to read it all on my phone, so I'll need to have a look on it on my laptop, which is downstairs at the moment. Could you give me the highlights? What's the connection between Gadfly and that list of names of property-owning companies you put in the covering email? I'm sorry, I don't get it. What have I missed?'

'Don't worry, it took me a while too. But I did some background digging into the book you told me about, *The Gadfly*. When I was researching, I noticed a pattern that I thought odd, for your neck of the woods; there seemed to be a lot of companies with Russian or Russian-sounding names with property interests that appear to all be warehouses, or rundown parts of farms or industrial estates in Ulster. That didn't make sense to me, so I worked backwards, and, in several cases, the name of the company was – somehow – linked to a Russian artist who'd created something to do with the original Gadfly book. Ethel Voynich wrote it, Shostakovich wrote the score for a film made of it, Prokofiev wrote an opera based on it, and so on. It's been adapted and used as the basis for many artistic interpretations in Russia. I believe that making this connection is a valid interpretation of the facts.' Carol was feeling proud; she'd had a real breakthrough.

'You're so clever,' remarked Christine, making Carol glow. 'But what about the other companies? They don't sound Russian.'

'You're quite right; I did a bit more digging and discovered that Socrates and Plato used the term "social gadfly," and it's seen as a concept related to pragmatic ethics. The key names in that field include Dewey, Mill, and Nussbaum, three more names used for companies that also each hold a small portfolio of such properties. The clever thing is, not one of these companies is large – they'd not appear to be anything out of the ordinary, if you weren't looking for them. When you put them all together, there's a significant amount of land and property being held.'

'And you were able to get the names of the directors of some of the companies involved, I see,' observed Christine.

'Yes, but interestingly, only where I could find older records for companies that have been owning property the longest. It seems our Gadfly has become more careful of late, with holding companies being used to create a buffer. I sent the addresses of those properties owned by the companies I could find.'

'I see the three recurring names on those lists of directors are Colleen White, Moira Sheehan, and Bridget Moynihan; the ones you listed in your covering email, right?'

'Correct. Know any of them?' asked Carol. 'Any of the names mean anything to you at all?'

'I can get Tom and Barry to ask around.'

Carol thought Christine sounded quite unlike her usual, vibrant self. 'You OK?'

'Not really,' replied Christine, her voice was flat. 'I think I've put my foot in it with a dodgy copper, Beattie. Did you manage to find out anything about him? I didn't see anything in what you sent me.'

'Nothing. As you suspected, it's impossible to find out anything but the basics about serving officers over there. Name, rank, role, career notes, that's it, really. Once you're off the PSNI network, their senior officers "don't exist." I dug around as much as I could and discovered Beattie's from Belfast, served for a few years over on the mainland in Birmingham, went back to Ulster when he was promoted to inspector, and enjoys golf. That's about it. There's a link on a page at the end of what I sent you.'

'Birmingham and golf. That's useful, thanks.'

'Really?' asked Carol.

'It's more than I knew before; we can pursue the Birmingham angle from here, through Alexander maybe, and the golf thing might give Beattie a reason to be seen with Liam MacNeath. What did you find out about him?'

'All above board. He might have a locally questionable reputation, but as far as I can see at this stage, on paper he's squeaky clean.'

'You've done a grand job, Carol, thanks. We'll follow through at this end. How's everything else going with you over there?'

Carol gave her the highlights, but knew Christine had her plate full with her own troubles, so didn't burden her too much. The colleagues ended their call, and Carol was able to attend to Albert's needs.

THIRTY-ONE

Annie couldn't explain why she felt so excited when she woke. She knew she had slept well, and that helped, but there wasn't any suggestion this would be anything but an ordinary day, so she wondered what was going on; she felt different, but didn't know why.

Determined to not let herself get bogged down with useless self-analysis she noticed that, as it had done for weeks, the clear blue sky promised a sunny day; she wondered what on earth she could wear that would help her keep cool – and was clean and ironed.

As she and Gertie set out for the office she felt fresh and well-presented in a smart, dove-gray cotton two-piece her mother had found in a little shop on Putney Hill and had popped in the post for her; it perfectly matched a pair of ballet flats she already owned and, for once, she felt truly well put-together.

By the time she arrived at the office she had tripped off the kerb outside her cottage and had scuffed a shoe, Gertie had almost pulled her arm off when she'd tried to run underneath a bush and she was feeling decidedly sweaty.

'Mornin', Mave,' she called as she and her puppy lurched into the office. 'Sorry I'm a bit late, doll. Lovely day for it, innit?'

She looked up, having released Gertie from her lead, and was surprised to see Althea, Mavis, Stephanie, Carol, and Albert and Chief Inspector Carwen James all, basically, standing in an awkwardly-formed line in front of her. She felt for a moment as though she were facing a firing squad.

'Gordon Bennett – did I miss a memo?'

'I can only imagine you did,' replied Mavis tartly, 'the one telling you we had a meeting that was due to begin fifteen minutes ago. It's the only reason I can think of for you being late; it's so unlike you.'

Annie was thrown by Mavis's weird demeanor and bald-faced lie; she knew very well she was late often enough that it was almost expected of her.

'We've made small-talk and tea to fill the time until you arrived,' said Althea, 'but I'm glad you're here now because I've had quite enough of one and I'm dying for a cup of the other.'

Annie spotted the flaring of Mavis's nostrils in Althea's direction, and quickly deduced the team was expected to be on its best behavior in the company of the Very Important Policeman.

'Well, maybe someone could pour me a cuppa, 'cos I really have to, you know . . .' said Annie, and shot off to the loo.

By the time she returned, with a freshly-washed face and hands, and a quick squirt of Yardley's Lily of the Valley cologne to complete her revitalization, Annie could see everyone was settled; even McFli and Gertie were sitting nicely – both staring at the policeman as if he were about to perform a trick. Given the look on his face, Annie felt she wouldn't be surprised if he did; he looked decidedly smug. As the sun flooded the vast space of the barn, she noticed the dust glittering in the air – something she would always connect thereafter with Carwen James's announcement. 'We have arrested Huw Hughes on suspicion of murdering Dr Clive Priddle. You'll be delighted to hear we apprehended him without incident at his home this morning, and he is currently helping my officers with their enquiries at our headquarters. I expect him to confess within the day.'

'You're kidding,' said Annie, louder than she'd meant to. As everyone looked at her – including the dogs – she gathered herself and said, 'What evidence have you got?'

'We have enough to break him,' said the chief inspector with a Cheshire Cat grin.

'Where did Huw get the poison? How did he get the lemons to Priddle?' Annie allowed herself to sound as indignant as she felt. She ignored Mavis's rolling eyes and continued, 'Most importantly, *why* would Huw kill the doctor?'

'I'm afraid I'm not at liberty to say more,' said the policeman.

Annie felt herself getting hot, and looked to her female friends with eyes that were silently screaming, *'Help me out!'*

Annie could have hugged Stephanie when she said, 'Oh, Chief Inspector, you're among friends, and I happen to know the WISE women have done a little investigating of their own. How about you let them ask you a question, then you can ask them one? It would be a sort of detecting game – not an official release of facts, or anything like that. I'm sure they'd be happy to learn from a professional like yourself.'

Annie watched the man's face crease into an even more smug smile, and she couldn't help but notice that Mavis was almost twitching. She could imagine what was going through her colleague's mind at that moment. As Albert inserted a rather loud squeal into the proceedings, it seemed to Annie that Carwen James was giving serious consideration to the duchess' request.

'So long as it remains between us, Your Grace, I don't see how it can hurt.' He picked up his cup and beamed icily at the five women, two dogs, and one infant surrounding him, then took a sip of tea. 'Ask away,' he said. To Annie, it sounded like a challenge.

'Where did Huw get his hands on strychnine?' demanded Annie with as little aggression in her voice as she could manage; it was a question to which she couldn't even imagine the answer.

'Moles,' said the policeman calmly. 'I understand you've had something of a mole problem recently at Chellingworth Hall, Your Grace?'

Stephanie nodded. 'It's to be expected.'

'Indeed. And with such a venerable croquet lawn to maintain, and moles having always been the sneaky little creatures they are, fighting them will have been a constant battle at Chellingworth for many decades. I spoke with your current head gardener, Ivor, who admitted there might still be remnants of now-illegal strychnine-based mole poison lurking about in various sheds on the estate. Bronwen Price admitted, when pressed, that she saw Huw Hughes disappearing in the direction of a couple of the more ramshackle potting sheds on the day of the tea at the hall. We're pretty certain that's where he got hold of the poison he used to kill Dr Priddle. Of course we wouldn't expect to find the poison at his home, he would have discarded it. Now it's my turn. How did you know Priddle was poisoned with lemons? That's something our laboratories have only just ascertained.'

Annie half-heartedly waved her hand in the air. 'That was me; I saw Dr Priddle eat a segment of lemon at the tea as though it were a slice of apple. Turned my stomach, just the thought of it, but anyone who'd seen him do it, or who knew about his "little treats," could have used the flavor of the lemon to conceal the taste of the poison. All they'd have to do would be inject a lemon with strychnine, and, by the time he'd eaten one segment, he'd be dead. That was why he had undigested lemon in his stomach.'

'Ah yes,' said James with a wink toward the duchess, 'I granted you that small morsel of information when we spoke last evening. How clever of you to make the connection. You're right, it's a highly unusual habit for a person to have – eating a lemon that way. And I'm afraid you're quite correct that it proved fatal for the good doctor.'

Mavis jumped in. 'Now I'd like to ask you something.' Annie noticed her colleague's eyes were glittering, and not just because the barn was so sunny. 'You say Huw had access to the poison, and I dare say he could have made off with some of the spare lemons from the tea, plus the poison, added one to the other, and he could have given a lemon to Dr Priddle later that evening as a treat he delivered by hand—'

'That is exactly what we believe happened,' interrupted the policeman.

'Yes, I see,' continued Mavis, unfazed, 'but that's no' my question. My question is, *why* would he want to do that? What was his motive for killing Dr Priddle, Chief Inspector?'

Annie noticed a slight shift in the way the man held his body; the rigidity softened, and he didn't look at the women as boldly as he had done earlier. 'We have a couple of working theories, but we're hoping the man will tell us in his own words, when questioned.'

'So you don't know,' said Carol sounding as annoyed as Annie felt.

'I believe it's my turn to ask you a question now,' countered James, 'and I'd like to know what *you* think might be the reason. If, as Her Grace has indicated, you've been researching this case – in the background, so to speak – what have you uncovered by way of motives? Your discoveries might tally with our own.'

'We believe it was the result of a lovers' quarrel,' said Althea quickly.

'I beg your pardon?' Was all James could manage.

The other women managed to clamp their mouths shut. Mavis finally said, 'Yes, do please explain to the chief inspector what our thinking was, Althea.'

Althea looked around the room furtively, then leaned into the man. 'We believe that Dr Priddle and Huw Hughes were lovers when Huw was just a youngster here, and their affair – though not illegal – would certainly have been frowned upon. We also believe that, having put this youthful indiscretion behind him, Huw was keen it not be brought to public attention, so he killed Clive Priddle to keep his secret life just that – secret. Had your detectives worked that out?'

Annie silently applauded Althea's vivid imagination, as well as her utterly convincing delivery. She wondered how James would react. It was certainly interesting to watch the external evidence of the mental gymnastics he was performing.

'It's a line of enquiry some of my people have been following, but I can't say more than that.'

Annie didn't need to hear the man say another word to be certain the police had absolutely no idea why Huw might have committed murder.

'What about the vandalism?' asked Carol.

'A triumphant statement by Hughes for all to see about his killing of Priddle,' snapped the man, who seemed to have settled again, 'and we found a rag with remnants of the same paint that was used at the pavilion hidden in a shrub just inside the wall surrounding his property. Does that fit with any of the other theories you might have had about Hughes's motivation?'

Annie had to admire the way he was trying to winkle useful information out of them, but she reckoned none of them were about to play ball.

'I'm no' sure that's what a guilty man would do,' said Mavis sharply, then she added, 'though maybe you have a point.' Annie thought Mavis suddenly sounded as though she was stroking the man's ego, and suspected that to be a wise move. 'Do you believe Huw also tainted the food served at the tea in some way?'

Annie noticed James's demeanor shift, he finally looked as though he was enjoying himself. 'Our laboratories eventually found some traces of certain chemicals in a couple of the remaining bottles of lemon barley water concentrate. We believe that was the source of the illness experienced by many who attended the tea, and it also explains why not everyone had the same symptoms. Only those who drank lemon barley water were taken ill, and some drank a good deal more than others, it seems. I can tell you we found several empty plastic bottles of over-the-counter eye drops in a rubbish bin in one of Hughes's bathrooms; the stuff's not difficult to get hold of, and he could have introduced their contents to the bottles of concentrate at a convenient moment.'

'Don't you think someone would have noticed him doing that, in front of everyone, right there at the drinks tables in the middle of the croquet lawn?' Annie couldn't help herself.

The chief inspector flashed a toothy grin. 'It was busy, people were mingling and chatting, he could have done it in a surreptitious manner. Besides, we think he's developed an adeptness at hiding his actions and motives; what would you say if I told you we're also looking into the possibility he might have poisoned one of his late wives?'

Annie stared at her friends and colleagues. Mavis answered, 'So that wouldn't be the one who died while driving drunk in the south of France, nor the one who fell off a balcony in Amsterdam, but the one who died as the result of participating in a religious ceremony in Kenya?'

Annie's tummy flipped with joy as she saw the policeman visibly deflate. 'I see you have been doing your homework.' His tone was that of forced politeness. 'Would you care to share what you've discovered about those circumstances?'

Carol regaled him with a comprehensive overview of the research she and Annie had gathered about the circumstances surrounding the deaths of Huw's three wives. Annie had to give the man his due, he looked impressed. 'Would you be prepared to make your detailed findings available to our team?' he asked when she'd finished.

'So long as my colleagues and our client are happy for me to do so,' replied Carol. A nodding vote was taken and she added, 'If you give me an email address I can send a link to a cloud file I've created, if our client agrees.'

'Most kind,' replied James, sounding truly grateful. 'That might help us along on that front, where I'll admit our investigations are at an early stage. Thank you.'

'You see, Chief Inspector, working *with* the WISE women can sometimes be useful,' said Mavis quietly.

'I agree,' said Stephanie.

'I'm afraid time is pressing. I wanted to deliver this news myself, but I must get back. Is there anything else you feel you should tell me?' After everyone agreed there was nothing more, Chief Inspector

Carwen James took his leave of the gathering, and the women sat in silence for a few moments.

Annie wanted to shout aloud that she didn't believe for one minute that Huw had killed Priddle, or vandalized the pavilion, though she had to admit to herself she didn't like the sound of what James had told them about the eye drops. Instead of protesting his innocence, she tried to picture Huw's actions on the day of the tea – had she seen him doing anything that could have been a way of covering up tipping little bottles of eye drops into large bottles of squash?

She closed her eyes and imagined herself there again, the sun on her skin, Gertie pulling at her lead, chatting to Dr Priddle. She herself had gone to the drinks table, to get some barley water for herself and Dr Priddle, and some lemons – where had Huw been then? Across the lawn talking to Bronwen as Marjorie passed them, and Dr Priddle was talking about something to do with . . .

Annie leaped to her feet; Gertie rushed to her side. 'He's got it all wrong. The moles, the lemons, the vengeance thing, the eye drops, the wives, everything – all wrong.' She looked down at the upturned faces surrounding her. 'Look, I think I've cracked it. All of it. But I've got to talk to three women – my next-door neighbor, Mrs Iris Lewis who used to teach in the village school, Marjorie Pritchard and Bronwen Price. I've got to do it face to face. Will all of you just trust me on this? Just for a few hours.' Everyone nodded. 'Ta. I'll phone you when I know if I'm right. Come on, Gert, let's get your lead on – we're going for a bit of a walkabout.'

She gave no thought to how the conversation might go when she left the office, and focused on framing her questions for the women she needed to see. She knew she wanted to see Mrs Lewis first, then Marjorie. She'd save her face to face with Bronwen until last thing.

THIRTY-TWO

Christine knew she was being grumpy, but she couldn't help it. She and Alexander had just left the third ugly, crumbling, disused building on the list of places owned by Dewey Properties Ltd. and they had found nothing of interest, except the fact that – for disused properties – they seemed to be exceptionally well secured; tall fences, corrugated iron hoardings and padlocked gates had barred their entrance to each site.

'They must have something to hide because they are, literally, hiding the buildings so well,' she moaned. 'If only we could find one we can get into. This is hopeless.'

Alexander kept his eyes on the road ahead. 'You insisted we did this so we weren't just sitting about doing nothing to find Callum, and I've agreed with you because I think this, at least, is a start. But we can't expect to hit pay-dirt off the bat. We'll just have to try the next one, then the next, and so on. Come on, Christine, buck up. What's the exact address we're trying to find?'

Christine swiped her phone and said, 'You're right, I know. Just keep going straight ahead for now. We could stay on the A4 and bypass Maguiresbridge, or we could swing into town and try to find a pub or café; I could do with a loo, and my tummy's rumbling.'

'That'll happen if all you have for breakfast is half a piece of toast and three cups of tea. How do I get to Maguiresbridge?'

Ten minutes later the couple found themselves the only customers at The Coach Inn, with a half of Guinness and a slightly limp ham sandwich in front of each of them.

'It's a bit quiet,' noted Alexander.

'There's a beer garden out back,' said the young barman who seemed to have lost battles with both acne and bonhomie.

'That'll be grand,' said Christine, picking up her lunch and leading the way across the wide-planked floor, past the pool table and out into the rather underwhelming area where a collection of weather-beaten tables, concrete pavers underfoot and a huge number of wheelie-bins passed for a beer garden. 'At least it's a bit less oppressive out here,' said Christine, hoisting her feet, one at a time, into the bench-seat that was attached to the table.

'You've got to wonder how places like this keep going,' said Alexander, trying to stop the table from wobbling, but failing. 'Best you take a few sips of that or it'll end up all over you.'

They ate and drank in silence for a few moments, then Christine popped back inside the pub to use the facilities. She returned refreshed and, she hoped, with a better attitude. 'You were right, I needed something to eat. I'm feeling much more positive about the next three places on our list. While you finish that, I'm just going to check in with Brid to see if there's any news on the home front.' There wasn't, though there were tears a-plenty from Brid who, Christine suspected, had hardly slept since her husband had been spirited away.

'If nothing comes of today – and bearing in mind I'm usually the last person to suggest this – do you think we should tell the police about Callum's disappearance?' asked Alexander. He brushed crumbs from his snugly-fitting jeans onto the floor, where sparrows that seemed to have appeared out of thin air gobbled them up greedily.

'It might be a bit challenging to explain why we didn't tell them during one of my previous two interviews,' replied Christine. 'We've painted ourselves into a bit of a corner, in that respect, haven't we?'

Alexander nodded. 'Look, sitting here, not being able to make decisions about what to do next, is stopping us doing what we said we'd do next – which is to visit the place that's just out beyond here on the Belfast Road. Come on, we should get going again.'

Back in the car, they found it only took a few minutes to locate their next target, another fenced building. This one looked as though it had once fulfilled some sort of farming requirement, built entirely out of corrugated iron sheets, and a bit rusty around the edges. However, for the first time there was an open gate. They drove past slowly, and Christine spotted activity. 'There are a couple of transit vans in there, and I saw one chap standing up against the wall having a smoke. What do you think – should we come up with some ruse and waltz in there, maybe ask for directions? Or should we try to sneak in?'

'Let's drive past again, and take another look. Just give me a minute to turn around.' The road was narrow for an A road, but there wasn't any traffic. Finally heading back toward the building Alexander added, 'With all these sheep in the fields it looks a lot like Wales. Do sheep and crooks always hang out together?'

'Not necessarily, but Carol's always telling me sheep are stupid and untrustworthy – and she grew up on a Welsh sheep farm herself, so she should know. Maybe in that respect sheep and criminals do have something in common, but let's not mention that to any sheep farmers we know, OK?'

Alexander agreed, then slowed to a snail's pace as they passed the open gates in the fencing for a second time. Christine craned her neck. 'There's another bloke, and him and the first one seemed to be getting into one of the vans each. Someone was opening up one of the giant doors. Maybe they're going to drive off, or go inside. I say we pull over and do the sneaky thing. We can always pull the posh English "lost tourist" thing if we need to.'

There being no lay-bys or even real verges, Alexander pulled the car onto the slightly shorter grass at the edge of the road and switched on the hazard lights. 'Should be obvious enough for no one to hit it,' he said as they walked toward the gate.

'They've driven the vans into the building,' said Christine quietly as she peered around the corner. 'Come on, there's no one about, let's head for that old water butt over there,' and she was off, Alexander trailing behind her.

When they were tucked behind the ancient, rusty tank, Alexander pulled on her arm. 'Don't go off without me like that. We've no idea what we're getting ourselves into here. I will not have you running into danger.'

'Be quicker and keep up then,' replied Christine over her shoulder. 'Look, over there; there's an old set of iron steps leading to what looks like a door in the wall. I might be able to get a look inside from there.'

Alexander tightened his grip on her arm. 'Oh no you don't; you stay here, I'll go,' and with that, he darted away.

Christine's heart thumped as she watched him run across the open ground between the tank and the ramshackle building, then creep up the stairs. She hoped they'd hold. He bobbed up and down a few times, then she could tell he was using his phone to take photographs. He was back at her side in no more than five minutes, though it felt like a good deal longer.

'The door had a glass panel at the top, so I was able to see inside,' he announced.

'What's going on in there? Can I see the photos?' hissed Christine. She took Alexander's phone and stopped breathing; the entire hanger-like building was piled full of crates and plastic drums. It was clear there was an industrial-scale production of potcheen going on, and the men with the transit vans were loading crates into the rear doors of their vehicles. In one corner was a table with a few chairs surrounding it, and, on one of the chairs was Callum, a cigarette in one hand, a mug in the other. He was quite clearly smiling and chatting with the men doing the heavy lifting.

THIRTY-THREE

When she'd first moved into the tiny thatched cottage overlooking the green in Anwen-by-Wye, Annie had been ecstatic; she'd always liked the look of cottages on chocolate boxes, and was excited she'd get to live in one. Having spent the past eight months coming to terms with being a woman who was almost six feet tall living in a house designed for the short, sixteenth-century Welsh people who'd been its original inhabitants, she was now quite proud that she could use the tiny front door without hitting her head anymore.

Mrs Iris Lewis was the perfect next-door neighbor; she was well into her eighties, but not so infirm that Annie felt compelled to offer her help about the place. The only misgiving Annie had about the woman – who was always polite, and welcoming – was her penchant for budgerigars; her home was filled with cages of all styles and dimensions housing the birds. Knocking at the front door, Annie steeled herself for what she was about to face; birds in cages made her feel nervous – she had no idea why, they just did.

'Hello Annie, *cariad*,' said Iris. 'There's lovely to see you. To what do I owe the pleasure?'

Annie held out the packet of shortbread biscuits her mother had purchased at Marks and Spencer and had felt compelled to post to her daughter. 'I wanted to pick your brains for a few minutes. I brought biscuits. They're good ones.' Annie had decided it would be best to be open and honest with the retired school-teacher, still believing that particular breed could spot a lie even when it was being whispered, behind their back, a hundred feet away.

'Oh, shortbreads,' said Iris, taking the tartan-patterned box, 'my favorite. You shouldn't have, but thank you. Come on in and I'll put the kettle on. Make yourself comfy.'

The front door opened directly into the main sitting area of the tiny cottage, whereas Annie's at least had a little hallway. She immediately felt the space close in about her – the fluttering of wings against bars was a horrible sound, and the tweeting took some time to subside. Amazed and relieved that the entire place didn't smell like a zoo, Annie settled into a yielding rose-upholstered armchair, and tried to work out what to do with her long legs so they wouldn't get in the way of the elderly householder when she returned.

Finally settled, Annie put milk in her tea and accepted a biscuit which she placed in her saucer.

'Now, what was it you wanted to ask about? Am I about to help you with your detecting? You do realize how thrilling this is for me, don't you? To be quizzed by a private enquiry agent. Just like a book. Is this about poor Dr Priddle? The village has been a-buzz since he died. I'm afraid I haven't seen anybody acting suspiciously, not at all. More's the pity. I'd tell you if I had.'

Annie decided to be straight with the woman. 'It is to do with the doctor, and it isn't.'

'How intriguing, go on, eat that biscuit; if you don't help me out, I'll guzzle them all myself.'

Annie nibbled the biscuit then said, 'I know you taught in Anwen for decades, and that you eventually became the headmistress of the village school.'

'Indeed I did, a dream career.'

'Well, back in the 1970s, I understand Dr Priddle was the village doctor, and was married to Edna, who killed herself.'

'She did. It was a tragedy. Only suicide ever in the village, though one is one too many, of course.'

'Indeed,' continued Annie, determined to not be sidetracked. 'Now around that time Huw Hughes, Marjorie Lloyd – Pritchard as she now is – and Bronwen Price were all in school together. Not your school, because they were too old by then, but would I be correct in assuming you'd have known them when they were at your school, and that, as children of the village, you were still aware of them even throughout their teens?'

'I was. They were once my charges, you are correct in that, but, as you say, when you've overseen the care, education, and general wellbeing of children, you never lose interest in them completely.

Many of the people who live here were once my pupils; I enjoy being part of the continuity of the village, even though I am no longer an educator. It's wonderful to see what people make of themselves.'

Annie made sure she didn't sigh or sound impatient as she added, 'Of course it is. What I'm interested in is anything you can tell me about how exactly that particular threesome seemed to be connected when they were about seventeen, eighteen, and what their interactions with Dr Priddle and his wife might have been. Can you help?'

'It's all a very long time ago,' said Iris Lewis slowly, 'and, while I do recall pupils with clarity, I'm not so sure I can be certain of particular timeframes.' Annie watched as the woman narrowed her eyes and sipped her tea. 'So this would be the late 1970s?' Annie nodded. '1976 was that tremendously hot summer, I recall; the Queen visited Swansea as part of her Silver Jubilee in 1977 and I took all the children from the school, on a bus – that was great fun; Ken Follett wrote *Storm Island* in 1978. I love his books. Can't wait to read them. Good Welsh writer, he is. I think my favorite books by him are The Century Trilogy, though those Elizabethan ones he's writing now are . . . well, you know.'

Annie had to admit she didn't know, nor did she even know that Ken Follett was Welsh.

'Oh yes, born in Cardiff. Plymouth Brethren parents, so I suppose he had to exercise his imagination from an early age.'

'So you clearly recall the late 1970s,' said Annie, trying to get the woman back on track. 'What about Huw? Do you remember him? Was he a particular friend of Dr Priddle's back then?'

Iris Lewis put down her cup and saucer and leaned forward. 'You know something, don't you?' she said quietly.

'I'm not sure what I know,' replied Annie. 'As a professional investigator I try to have my information confirmed by several independent sources. Some people, Mair Jones included, have given me various insights into the way Huw interacted with Priddle and his wife, but I'll be honest and tell you I'd prefer to have yet another source to tell me about it.'

'I know what you mean, Annie. Mair's a woman given to hyperbole. Did she suggest to you that Huw and Edna might have been having an affair?' Annie shrugged. 'Well, they were, of course, but they managed to keep it quiet. She wouldn't have known about it, but gossips like to suggest things they don't know to be a fact just to see where it leads. I don't gossip, but, since you've asked me directly, I shall tell you what I know – what I saw with my own eyes. I saw Edna Priddle crying like a baby at the bus stop just after Huw Hughes had left the village. She didn't know I knew anything, of course, so maybe she thought she was being opaque when she told me she was upset because "a heart is a vulnerable thing." But I'd seen them, you see. Her and Huw. Together. If you were to look out of my front bedroom window you'd be looking across the green at what used to be the doctor's house and surgery. It's where your friend Carol lives now, though maybe she's not aware that the room she's using as a nursery is the one where poor Edna took her own life. The Priddle's curtains weren't as substantial as the ones hanging there now. One could see . . . shapes and shadows through them. When Dr Priddle was away from home, making house calls at night, you know. They still used to do that back then. Make house calls. Not any more, of course.'

Annie's heart fell. 'Did anyone else know about Huw and Edna?'

Picking up her cup, and another biscuit, Iris Lewis replied, 'Well, dear, I always imagined the doctor himself had found out, and that was why Huw left the village as abruptly as he did. And I can tell you he left more than one broken heart behind him. You mentioned Marjorie and Bronwen? They were both head over heels in love with him too; most girls were, I recall, but he showed some interest in those two. Saw themselves as The Three Musketeers, or some such, I suppose. Young people like labels. In any case, after Huw left, Marjorie rallied, and settled down with a new young man rather quickly. Bronwen Price, however, never seemed to recover. I recall she and the Priddles became closer after Huw left. Though it wasn't terribly long before Edna took her own life, of course.'

'Do you think Edna killed herself because she was broken-hearted? Over Huw?' said Annie, hardly believing she'd needed to speak the words aloud.

'Clear as the nose on my face, dear, but I would never say that to anyone. Nor will you, I trust.'

'Not unless I have to,' said Annie.

THIRTY-FOUR

'What do you make of it?' asked Christine nervously. 'Callum, in that photo, what's he up to?'

'He looks like he's having a brew with a bunch of his mates, which he was,' replied Alexander quietly. 'They were laughing, joking about how they'd manage to make such a lot of money because they'd diluted the potcheen. I don't think Callum's a hostage, or being held against his will at all – I think he's part of something Brid doesn't know anything about. And it's something that's not good.'

'Poor Brid.'

'Yeah, poor Brid. What's Callum mixed up in? That's a huge amount of potcheen. Look at all those crates. It must have taken them an age to make it all, if they did it the way you described to me.'

'Let me see those photos again,' said Christine, reaching for the phone. 'Oh no – look at this one. See there, at the back of the place? That looks like it might be a radiator in a giant container.'

Alexander squinted at the picture. 'That? Why would they do that?'

Christine stood and brushed down her leggings. 'It's a way to make more potcheen, faster. You use a radiator from a lorry as the condenser. It's really dangerous. The alcohol can dissolve all sorts of nasty things like lead from the engine parts, and then there's the possibility of anti-freeze getting into it too. It's a terrible way to make the stuff. My daddy would brain them, so he would. The stuff in those bottles could kill people.'

'So what are we going to do about it?' asked Alexander, also rising to his feet and grabbing Christine by the arm.

Looking into his wonderful eyes, she said, 'Don't panic, I'm not going to go running off and doing anything stupid. This is a big operation, and if these companies that Carol believes are connected with Gadfly own so much property – remote and rundown like this – we could be seeing just the tip of the iceberg. Could you phone

Tom and Barry, and ask them what the price of potcheen's been doing over, maybe, the past six months? If there's an industrial supply, the price might have gone down. It would be a good way to squeeze the small, local producers out of the market, meaning the person responsible for this would then have a much greater amount of business coming their way. If they're cutting costs by speeding up production, who knows, maybe they're even adding methanol – wood alcohol – which is cheap and easy to purchase in quantities that could mean you'd need to make less actual potcheen. That would be a deadly mix. Can you phone them now?'

'I'd rather do it when we're in the car,' replied Alexander. 'I know I was once renowned for my ability to disappear into the city-scape, but I have to admit I feel dangerously exposed out here, in the middle of nowhere, spying on an illicit distillation plant.'

'Come on then, let's go back to the car.'

Just as they had exited the gateway and were back on the road heading for the car, one of the white transit vans nosed its way out of the gate. Christine couldn't help herself; she turned and looked at the driver. It was Callum. She could see his fingers tighten on the steering wheel as he recognized her.

'Get in, quick,' shouted Alexander, unlocking the doors.

Christine moved as fast as she could, but she still wasn't fast enough; she hadn't managed to close her door by the time the van hit the back of the vehicle with a thump and a crunch.

'Shut it now, we're off,' shouted Alexander, grappling with the gear stick and revving the engine.

Christine dragged the door closed and pulled on her seatbelt as they shot along the still-empty road, heading back the way they'd originally come.

'We'll be faster than him on this road,' said Alexander, 'especially since he's got a full load in the back of his van, but he knows we've seen him and, of course, he knows where to find us. Let's see if he gives chase, or if he stops to get in touch with someone for instructions.'

'You don't think Callum is very high up in whatever criminal management system runs this enterprise, do you?'

'Come off it, Christine, he's not the brightest, is he? And it seems he's not the nicest, either. Imagine doing what he's done to his wife of – how long?' He crunched the gearbox and pressed the accelerator with his toe. 'I wish I had the Aston, not this knarly old thing.'

'This Land Rover will still be running long after the Aston's had its day. Besides, look at it now, we've hit eighty without a problem. Just keep going.' Christine stuck her head out of her window to try to see if Callum was behind them. He was, but the grubby white van was losing ground, which pleased her greatly.

'Home?' asked Alexander, using his side mirror to check behind them.

'Home. We need to talk to Brid, and that can only be done face to face.'

'Poor Brid.'

'Exactly,' said Christine sadly. 'Look, I don't think he's going to chase us all the way back to Ballinclare, so maybe you could slow down a bit – just so we don't get done for speeding – and I'll phone Tom about the potcheen side of things. I'll also tell Brid we'll stop on the way back and pick up some fish and chips, so she doesn't have to cook.'

'That won't tip her off that we've got a bombshell to drop on her?'

'I don't think so; there's a place in Belcoo she swears has the best fish and chips in the world, she won't turn her nose up at us bringing them home, though she might make us eat them in the kitchen, so's we don't "stink up the place," as she loves to say.'

'Didn't mind the potcheen-making stinking up the place, did she?' said Alexander without taking his eyes off the road.

'There's a romantic notion that making potcheen is something in the Irish DNA.'

'Not if it's lethal,' said Alexander quietly as he raised his foot a little off the accelerator.

Christine felt sick. 'You're right, and not if it's being turned out in such quantities that it's a massive business. Carol was right – all these premises owned by companies designed to be small enough, individually, to not raise any flags – it's clever. The Gadfly wouldn't need to use all the sites he owns all the time – he could move the production from one place to another. Maybe he can swap to a better center for distribution for a few months, or just keep the operation shifting around the area so as not to raise local suspicions. The Gadfly – biting, nipping away all the time. Turning out potcheen all over this county and, if Carol's research is anything to go by, in every other county in Northern Ireland too.'

'So, what shall we do? Phone Beattie? Should we trust him even though I saw him with that MacNeath?'

'What do you think?' asked Christine.

'You know what I think, or at least you can guess. I saw so many bent coppers in my time when I was an illicit courier, it wasn't funny. Truly, it wasn't funny. But that was Brixton and south London in the 1980s not rural County Fermanagh in the twenty-teens. It's a different time. I'm absolutely certain they've cleaned up their act back on my old patch, but here? I have no idea. This isn't what I'd imagined Ireland would be like at all. Well, your estate is, and the villages close by are – you know, green, pretty, lovely people all enjoying life. But that police station in Enniskillen. That was like a war zone.'

'It's not long since it was. When I was very little, we spent almost no time at all here at the manor; it wasn't safe, especially for a family with a title. Then there was the Good Friday Agreement in 1998, and we came here more often after that. I was still young enough to enjoy the freedoms I was given by Mammy here, though I'll admit I probably recall those days by looking in a rose-tinted rear-view mirror. When I was older, in school in England, I spent a fair amount of time studying what had gone on in this part of the world. Both sides did terrible things. That pub we were in today? It used to be called the Talk of the Town Bar. The IRA walked in and shot an off-duty RUC officer as he stood at the bar. Got the barman too. Both dead. That was in 1986, before I was born; about the time you were skulking your way around back streets and alleyways transporting all sorts of God-knows-what from one part of Brixton to another. Maybe drugs, maybe guns, maybe just dirty money, but definitely illegal things.'

'I've changed. Brixton has changed. Why not County Fermanagh too?'

'Oh Alexander, you're not Irish, you can't understand.'

'You're right, I'm not, and I never can be. But, look, let's tackle what we can, and not allow huge problems and challenges to overwhelm us? I'm still struggling with why Callum would be driving a van full of potcheen, having staged, presumably, the theft of his own potcheen *and* his own kidnapping. I mean, what would be the point of that? It was his stuff to sell in the first place. I'm beginning to think all the argy-bargy Brid overheard about borrowed money and an ever-increasing debt was all a load of tosh spouted for her sake and put about "on the street" for cover. But why would he want it to look like his potcheen had been stolen?'

Christine pulled out her phone. 'It might be that Callum was originally making the potcheen for someone else – with someone else's money and so forth, so, in order for it to end up where it has, it had to appear to be "stolen." Anyway, that aside, you're right, I must focus.'

Alexander slowed to what felt like a snail's pace as they entered a built-up area, 'Remind me to never get on your bad side. Your mind works in convoluted, evil ways. Does Mensa know that's what you use it for?'

Christine thumped him on his thigh and dialed the manor's landline.

THIRTY-FIVE

Annie had never visited Marjorie Pritchard's home before, and didn't really expect the woman to be there, but she couldn't think where else to begin. A severely-trimmed hedge surrounded neatly-planted borders; she rapped the brilliantly-polished brass door knocker. There was no response. A disembodied voice called, 'She's gone over to the shop, I think.' Annie looked around; there was no one to be seen.

Looking down, she spotted the top of a sun hat on the other side of the hedge between Marjorie's garden and that of her next-door neighbor. Annie peered over the angular boxwood divider and saw a tiny, elderly woman in a shapeless gardening apron.

'Hello Mrs Evans,' she said. 'Did Marjorie go out long ago?'

'Won't be back for some time, I shouldn't think. Going around telling everyone what a terrible time she had in hospital, and how honored she was to have tea at the hall yesterday. In her element she is.'

Annie thanked the woman and headed off across the green to

the shop, where she found Marjorie poking about on the shelf where Sharon displayed tinned soups and the like.

'Hiya, Marj, I wondered if I could have a word . . . in private,' she whispered.

'Don't mind me,' said Sharon from behind the post office counter. 'Coming to the end of the week, have to do my maths now.'

Annie knew she didn't want Sharon to be privy to her conversation with Marjorie, so wracked her brain to come up with something that would draw her target away from the danger zone.

'It was good of you to come to the hall and chat with us all about the things going on around here,' she opened, addressing the divorcee with a beaming smile. 'I was just about to wander over to Chellingworth Hall, for a sort of "Thank You" tea, and they asked me to track you down and invite you. Will you come?'

She knew her ruse had worked when Marjorie put down the tins of cream of mushroom and cream of tomato soup she'd been considering and replied, 'Now?'

'Well, in about an hour.'

Marjorie gave the idea no more than a second of thought. 'I wouldn't mind changing into something a bit more suitable for tea at the hall,' she said, looking down at her open-toed sandals. 'It's always such an honor.'

'How about I collect you from your house in half an hour? We'll walk over together,' offered Annie.

'Don't forget a newspaper for me in the morning,' called Marjorie to Sharon as she rushed out of the shop.

'And don't let the door smack you on the backside as you leave,' called Sharon, but Marjorie had already left. 'What are you up to, Annie?' she asked, circling the counter.

Annie decided it was best for her to attempt a quick escape. 'Nothing really. I just wanted to give Marjorie a treat, since she's been so poorly.'

Annie tried to maintain an air of innocence as Sharon replied, 'No you're not. You're investigating, and you don't want me to know what you two are going to talk about, that's what's going on here.'

Annie backed toward the door, feeling hot. 'Nothing of the sort.'

Sharon grinned. 'Never kid a kidder. Don't worry, I'll find out all about it, soon enough. Have a nice tea.' She paused and raised her eyebrows. 'They *have* really invited her, have they?'

'Of course they have. Anyway, I'd better run now,' Annie scuttled out. Striding across the green, she pulled out her mobile phone and called Stephanie, who agreed to fall in with her plans and invite everyone Annie listed to take tea at the hall at four thirty.

Cantering up to Marjorie's front door again at the appointed time, Annie saw that dressing more suitably for her appointment had required Marjorie Pritchard to don a summer-weight twinset in daffodil yellow and a box-pleated white skirt. 'I had to change my shoes,' said Marjorie as the women set off. 'Can't have my toes on show at the hall.'

Annie replied, 'You only have to wear close-toed shoes when you meet the Queen, not when you have tea with the Twysts,' then told herself off for sounding snarky.

As they walked to the hall along the lane which led from the church, Annie allowed some time for the exchange of general chit-chat before getting to the meat of her conversation, then she threw herself into her enquiries; she hoped she might be able to get something out of Marjorie that the woman wouldn't have been prepared to divulge in front of a dowager duchess.

'I've had a nice chat with Iris Lewis today,' she opened. 'She was telling me how close you were with Huw when you were at school. It must be nice for you to have an old friend return to the village.' She wondered if the news that her 'old friend' had been arrested on suspicion of murder had reached Marjorie yet. It had.

'I cannot believe they think Huw could have killed Dr Priddle,' said Marjorie huffily, 'but I trust the investigative process. There might be the odd one or two dim policemen, but innocence will prevail. He'll be out before supper time.'

'Maybe not,' said Annie ominously, 'the evidence against him looks pretty damning. We had a sit-down with Chief Inspector Carwen James earlier today, and he laid it all out for us.'

Annie had known such a statement would pique Marjorie's interest, so she freely exchanged all the highlights of the suspicions held by the police.

Marjorie fell quiet for a few moments – something Annie knew to be extremely unusual. Finally she said, 'He didn't say exactly how his wives died. But even so, why on earth would they think he would kill the doctor?'

'There's a theory that he and the doctor were lovers and he killed him because of that,' said Annie, throwing out Althea's concocted story to see what would happen.

Marjorie actually stopped in her tracks. 'Well, there you are then, that just goes to show.'

'What?'

'There's more than just a couple of stupid policemen. I've never heard anything so ridiculous in my life. Huw was always a ladies' man; anyone who knew him back then, or even today, would know that much. He's had three wives, for goodness sake, and – between you and me – I think he'd be happy to have a fourth. A man needs looking after, don't you think? We've been getting along ever so well since he came back. We've seen quite a bit of each other. He even took me to a lovely place down in the Gower for dinner, you know.' She sounded proud, triumphant, even.

Annie's innards plummeted. 'Do you mean Fairy Hill?'

Marjorie looked surprised and curious, as she replied. 'I do. But how do you know—'

'He took me there too. Monday night. The night you were in hospital. And we've also been out for a few lunches. Even a picnic.'

The two women continued walking side by side. The silence proved painful for Annie.

'I still don't know why he'd do it. It must have been someone else,' said Marjorie eventually. Annie believed Marjorie's tone suggested they were experiencing a similar range of emotions; they both felt hurt, but equally certain the man wasn't a killer.

Annie screwed up her professional courage, and ploughed on. 'Were you two ever an item back when you were in school?'

'Not really, though we were close. I suppose . . .' When Annie looked at Marjorie she saw a woman who was grappling with inner turmoil. 'I suppose I had a bit of a crush on him even back then. But I think a lot of us girls did. He was handsome, and worldly; seemed to know so much about places none of us had ever been. Still haven't. I don't know how he did it then, or even more recently, but he made me believe I was a very special person to him.'

Annie swallowed her pride. 'I understand Bronwen Price was a close friend too. That you were all at school together.'

Marjorie nodded. 'Yes, she was, but in a different way. She and I were close, so that's why we always went about as a threesome. She didn't seem to be interested in Huw at all.' She laughed. 'When you're young, things are so black and white, aren't they? Bronwen and I were best friends, and we truly believed we always would be. But, after school, we both changed so much. I took a secretarial course and went to work at a place in Builth Wells where I started going out with Owain, who worked there too. It wasn't too long before we were married. Bronwen went to the hall to work. She'd always been so vivacious, and fearless in many ways. I didn't understand why she took herself off there – and to do such menial jobs. It was almost as though she'd run off to a nunnery – you know, she cut herself off from everyone in the village. But I dare say we all grow up differently than we think we will, don't we?'

Not wanting to share just how true that statement was in her own case, Annie pressed on. 'When you and Althea were chatting yesterday, you said you knew that Edna Priddle and Huw used to play chess together.'

'Chess? Yes, I remember he was on the chess team at school, so I suspect he was very good. Edna Priddle was an odd woman, a bit stuck-up in a way. At least, that's how I always thought of her. Wore gloves to church. Mind you, a lot of the older ones did at that time.'

'But she wasn't old, was she? I mean, she was only in her thirties when she died.'

Marjorie gave the matter some thought. 'You're right. To me, a teenager, I suppose everyone over thirty was "old." Funny how the young think, isn't it?'

'So she really wasn't that much older than you. Or Huw. Less than twenty years. Women in their thirties – or even their fifties like us, eh? – are still vibrant. Have needs,' Annie added, daringly.

Marjorie waved off her suggestion. 'Edna and the doctor came over like a proper "old" married couple. No children ever, but set in their ways, you know? Are you suggesting there was something going on between Huw and Edna Priddle? That's just silly. He'd never have done that. Nor would she.'

Annie decided it was best to not share what Iris Lewis had told her. 'And you can't think of any other connections between Huw and the doctor?'

'I know Huw had tea with him a couple of weeks ago, but that's the other thing, see; if Huw had wanted to hurt the poor man, why wait until now? He's been back in the area for a couple of months; surely if there was any bad blood between them – from back when he was here growing up – he either wouldn't have come back at all, or maybe not until the doctor was dead. Clive Priddle was getting on; Huw wouldn't have had to wait very long until the coast was clear.'

'Has Huw told you why he *did* want to come back here to live?'

'*Hiraeth*, he said. I know, you're English, so you don't know about *Hiraeth*. It's a word we Welsh have for a desperate longing in your soul for Wales – something you can't shake off, no matter how you try. It gets to a lot of Welsh people, in the end. They might go away, but a lot of them come back. Some see it as a failure to come back to Wales after having roamed the world; I think it's because people come to their senses and finally work out what's important. Community. And there's nowhere like Wales for a sense of community. No one else in the world understands what it is to be Welsh. They think it's all sheep and beer and rugby and *Eisteddfods*. It *is* all that, I suppose, but it's a lot more too. Though maybe we Welsh aren't very good at having the words to explain it to others. We just know.'

Annie yearned to share how she longed for London, and her life there, but edited herself, to keep on track. 'So he came back because he missed the place?'

'The place, the people, the life. That's what he told me.'

'So he wasn't running away from anything, but toward something?'

'What would he have to run away from?'

'The specters of his three dead wives?' replied Annie tartly.

'Oh rubbish. He was devastated by their loss, he told me so. Even had a tear in his eye when he talked about how the same thing kept happening to him over and over again. It's really hurt him that he hasn't been able to keep a woman in his life that he truly loves.' Marjorie's voice was tender. 'Poor thing. Being victimized by the police, he is. Can't you lot do anything to convince them he didn't do it? Like find out who really did?'

'We're on the case,' replied Annie. 'Do *you* have any ideas?'

'Well, between you and me, I've never trusted Mrs Davies-Duster. I certainly wouldn't have her in my house. People have said things have gone missing after she's been around. The doctor might have found her trying to rob him, and *she* did him in. They say it's often the person who finds a body is the one who's done it, don't they?'

'They might do – on TV,' replied Annie. 'Anything else you can think of?' They'd almost arrived at the hall.

It seemed to Annie that Marjorie was acting very much like Gertie when she had a stuffed animal; she wouldn't let go. 'Mrs Davies-Duster was on the spot. She could have got the poison from her son-in-law; he works at a chemist's in Brecon, he does. There, see? She could have done it, easy.'

'Maybe,' replied Annie, as they walked along the drive toward the imposing façade of Chellingworth Hall.

'Tea here, again, but this time a few of us? I'm honored,' noted Marjorie. 'It'll be lovely.'

'Yes, I hope it will,' replied Annie.

THIRTY-SIX

With the difficult job of breaking the news about Callum to Brid behind her, Christine wandered to the stables in search of a moment or two of relative peace. She knew she had to be the one to make the decision about calling in the police, and, although she'd been happy to talk it over with Alexander, the knowledge that what she chose to do, or not do, would have significant consequences for her family, and her family name, weighed heavily upon her.

Ciara was happy to see her, something she demonstrated by stamping her hooves. 'No time for a ride-out right now, dear girl,' whispered Christine, 'maybe later, if the moon's out, or maybe tomorrow morning.' She stroked the muscular, warm neck that was within reach, then picked up a brush and went inside the stall to work on Ciara's coat. Her long, smooth strokes allowed time for Christine to think, the rhythm of her motions, and Ciara's reactions to her attentiveness, soothing her, and lulling her almost into a daze.

It was a warm afternoon, and Christine's forehead was soon filmed with moisture, but still she couldn't decide what to do; to trust Beattie, or not – that was the question. As her brushing became just a little too vigorous for her beloved horse, she dragged herself back to reality, and finished up. She realized there was a third option available to her, and decided to put it into action via a series of phone calls she made as she walked back to the manor.

Christine told herself she might end up looking like a terrible fool, but she felt she owed Brid, and her own family, a chance to sort the mess out once and for all, so – if she was wrong – she'd just have to stick out her chin and accept her fate.

An hour later, the crunching of pea-gravel announced the arrival of Inspector Beattie's car; Alexander, Tom, and Barry hid themselves in the scullery. Looking around the sitting room, Christine was pleased with what she saw; her paperwork and laptop were neatly stowed on top of the sideboard, all looking utterly professional. As she made her way to open the front door to the policeman, Christine wondered if he'd be accompanied by the same youthful minion as before; he was. The two men's shoes clattered across the entrance hall as they strode into the manor, and Christine led them to the sitting room, where they set their hats to one side, and took the seats they were offered by Brid as she set down the tea tray.

All finally settled, with cups and saucers, and Brid's homemade drop tea scones, Christine took a deep breath, and plunged into deep, murky waters.

She began by explaining the original story of Callum's disappearance; this drew the expected admonition from Beattie, and an immediate offer to 'get some men onto it.' Christine managed to prevent him from making any phone calls by explaining that her story wasn't over yet. Beattie showed he was ready to listen by taking a second drop scone, and complimented Brid on her baking skills. She nodded her red-eyed thanks, and sniffled into a hankie that had seen better days.

'As you know, I work as a part of the WISE Enquiries Agency, and I've been in touch with my colleagues back in Wales, who've been able to help out with this case,' said Christine.

'Hardly a case for private investigators,' replied Beattie. 'A kidnapping is something for the professionals.'

'Of course,' agreed Christine, putting on her 'sweetness and light' voice, 'and we'd be most grateful for your help. But, you see, there have been a number of lines of enquiry that have opened up as a result of Callum's disappearance, one being his possible connection with this Gadfly character.'

'I told you to not go poking your nose into that,' said Beattie sounding sternly patronizing. 'That's a local matter, which we're already looking into.'

'It's a terrible shame we never seem to find much,' said the young constable, drawing a steely-eyed glare from his superior. He retreated into his shell, and sulked his way through a scone.

'That's as may be,' Beattie's flat accent had already begun to grate on Christine, 'but sticking your nose in where it's neither wanted, nor where it can stand any chance of sniffing out anything of which we're not already aware, is counter-productive. In the extreme.'

Sensing his annoyance Christine decided it was time to push Beattie. 'So the following company names, associated with Gadfly, would already sound familiar to you, would they?' She stood, picked up a sheet of paper onto which she'd neatly written about half the list Carol had emailed to her, and read them aloud. She handed the sheet to the inspector, who all but snatched it from her hand.

As he peered over his teacup, the constable looked genuinely puzzled. 'That's a strange-sounding list of names, so it is. Exotic. Are they foreigners doing business with Gadfly over here?'

A curt: 'No need to wear out that brain of yours by thinking too much, constable,' from his superior silenced the young man. 'To be sure, it's an interesting-sounding list,' added Beattie, looking up at Christine. 'Where'd you get it?'

'A colleague at the agency. She's exceptionally good at online research.'

'And she's found all this in – what – a couple of days?' Beattie sounded amazed.

Christine could tell that the young constable wanted to say something, but was thinking better of it. Beattie spoke. 'And in what way do you believe these companies are connected with Gadfly? Indeed, what makes you think they are at all?'

Christine explained the route Carol had taken from the book, to its author and those who'd created works based upon the book.

Round-eyed, Beattie said, 'Clever. And what, exactly, do all these businesses do? I expect your colleague has ascertained that much?'

Christine talked through the properties held by the companies, and passed Beattie another handwritten list of some of the addresses Carol had sent her. 'As you can see, they range across every county in Northern Ireland.'

'If what your friend suggests is correct, that makes this Gadfly chappie a great deal more powerful than we'd previously thought,' mused the inspector.

'It would be a great feather in your cap to bring him to justice, don't you think?' said Christine, closely watching the man's facial expression. 'Your wife would be married to, perhaps, a chief inspector if you could do that, don't you think? Or maybe you'd get a commendation?'

'I've never been fortunate enough to find the right woman,' replied Beattie, deflecting.

'Mrs Sheehan could come to the medal ceremony, wearing one of her hats,' said the constable brightly. Beattie half-smiled, and nodded. 'That's Inspector Beattie's sister, Moira,' added the young man, looking more comfortable than he had since he'd arrived. 'Famous for her hats, she is. Got a lot of grand, big ones, so she has.'

Christine's mind was racing. She could feel her heart beating faster as she put two and two together. She glanced at her watch.

'Expecting someone?' asked Beattie.

She was cross he'd noticed her actions. 'Just a phone call from Daddy. He usually rings about this time each day.'

'Good to know,' said Beattie, with what Christine judged to be an insincere smile. 'So, maybe you'd prefer we took all this information away with us, so we can get on with hunting for this poor woman's kidnapped husband.'

'Oh, he hasn't been kidnapped, inspector,' said Christine, retaking her seat.

'But you said—'

Christine held up her hand. 'I know what I said. What I told you was what Brid was able to tell me the other morning. As I also mentioned, our enquiries have led to other discoveries, and one of those discoveries was Callum Ahearn.'

'So he's back? Safe and well?'

'No, he works for the Gadfly, and this afternoon he was hauling a van-full of potcheen along the Belfast Road from an old agricultural building out near Maguiresbridge, that housed a near-industrial sized distillery where a lorry's radiator has been used to intensify production levels.'

'You don't say,' said Beattie slowly.

'I do say,' replied Christine. 'I saw him with my own eyes. I have photographs of the operation, and of Callum and his accomplices stowing the potcheen into the van for hauling.'

'The little devil,' said Beattie. He turned to Brid. 'I'm sorry, Mrs Ahearn, it sounds as though your husband has got himself mixed up in something that might lead to his arrest.' Brid hid her face in her hankie

'And the arrest of Gadfly,' added Christine.

'If only,' said Beattie. 'How do you think Callum and Gadfly are connected, then?'

'The property where I saw the potcheen still is owned by one of the companies I told you about. One of the companies owned by Gadfly. A list of directors of several of the companies on that list makes for interesting reading.'

Beattie moved closer to the edge of his seat; his eyes steely. 'And would you have that list of directors?'

'His name might be on it, sir. We might finally get a break,' said the constable excitedly.

'Zip it,' barked his superior. 'The list, Miss Wilson-Smythe.'

'It's short. Just three people. All women. Colleen White, Bridget Moynihan, and Moira Sheehan.'

The constable's face was a picture of amazement. 'Is that not exactly the same name as your sister, sir?'

Beattie leaped to his feet and snarled. 'I've told you to shut it, sonny, so if you know what's good for you, you'll do just that.' He stood within inches of Christine's face. 'And what do you think that means?'

'I think it means that the reason the Police Service of Northern Ireland has faced such insurmountable challenges in discovering the real identity of the Gadfly, is that the Gadfly has always been one step ahead of them. His hundreds of property holdings, through dozens of small companies across every county, means he's been able to corner the potcheen market by moving his operations from site to site, never allowing the coppers to catch up with his production base. It's been a clever plan. But he's also used his unique opportunities to ensure that key pieces of information have never been seen by the police. He must have made a great deal of money over the years; the Irish do love their potcheen, so they do. And what a clever move to have the women as the company directors, because then he couldn't lose those properties if he were ever found out. Nice. So tell me, just how much money have you got hidden away, Inspector "Gadfly" Beattie? Hundreds of thousands? Millions?'

'Don't be ridiculous, woman,' snapped Beattie. 'You might be the daughter of a viscount, but you've no idea what you're talking about. Sheehan's a common enough name in these parts – not that you'd know that, because you're never here; your family just takes money from this estate and piles it into your fancy lives in England.'

'I live in Wales, and England. Sometimes I rent a cottage in Scotland, and, of course, my family home has always been here in Ireland. I don't think you're being fair in your characterization of me, Inspector Gadfly Beattie.' Christine was finding the confrontation oddly calming, and – even as she stared down the man in front of her – she wondered what that said about her. She noticed that the exchange was appealing less to the young constable, who was half out of his chair, with a look on his face that told her he wasn't sure what to do.

His boss's next move seemed to make his mind up for him; Beattie reached to his holstered service firearm and removed it, ready for action.

'Sir?' said the young constable nervously.

'What's your name?' asked Christine looking directly into the young man's terrified eyes.

'Say nothing,' snapped Beattie.

'Flynn. Constable Gerry Flynn, miss. Sir – what's going on, sir?'

Beattie smiled at Christine. 'Now listen to me, constable, I want you to go to the front door, walk outside, and prepare the car for us to take our leave of these two ladies. Mrs Ahearn, would you come and stand next to your employer over here, please.'

Christine's heart went out to Brid; the poor woman had been a tearful mess all day, and now she was a quivering wreck.

She sidled toward Christine who put her arm around the woman's shoulders. They huddled together, Christine not taking her eyes off Beattie's.

Christine felt Brid trembling as she whispered, 'So this is the Gadfly?' Christine nodded. 'And he's the one who my Callum's been working for? The one who forced Callum to make me believe he'd been kidnapped?' Christine squeezed her shoulders; she didn't think it was the right moment to remind Brid she thought Callum was a good deal more complicit than his wife was making out. 'And he owns lots of places where they make the potcheen, using engine radiators?'

'Not always, Mrs Ahearn,' replied Beattie airily, waggling his gun. 'We only resort to such methods when we have a large order to fill in double-quick time. That's why I needed Callum to make his "contribution" to my stocks on this occasion. It turned out he was very amenable to my offer. Seems you and he haven't been getting along too well for some time, and he saw an opportunity to make a fresh start. Without you.'

Christine's heart sank at the cruelty both in the man's tone and etched on his face. She felt deeply sorry for Brid, and hugged her closer.

'Jeysis, Mary and Joseph you're the Devil himself, sure you are,' spat Brid and, without hesitation or warning, she launched herself at Beattie with a wailing scream that almost deafened Christine.

As Brid leaped forward the gun made a cracking sound, then Alexander magically appeared in the doorway and threw himself at Beattie from behind. The gun went off again, then Tom and Barry joined the fray. Finally, Barry managed to grab Beattie's gun and handed it off to Tom, Beattie himself was on the floor with Christine sitting on top of him and Brid was in a heap on the floor beside the inspector, sobbing her heart out and still screaming. Christine nodded at Alexander so that he could melt away to the kitchen and remain unseen.

'And what do you propose now, young lady?' said Beattie from his prone position beneath Christine's rump. 'You've got nothing on me, yet I am bloodied and being held at gunpoint. My junior officer here will back me up when I give a statement saying you made an unprovoked attack on me – right, laddie?'

The constable looked panic-stricken. 'Sir? I don't know what's going on, sir. Are you the Gadfly like she said? It sounds to me like you are. You admitted as much yourself, so you did. And that's not good.'

'Shut your trap and I'll make sure you and your family are well taken care of. Got it?'

'I don't think so, sir. This isn't right. Look – you've shot her. She's bleeding.'

Christine looked at her upper arm. The constable was right, her blouse was ripped a little and there was blood. She hadn't felt a thing. Still didn't.

'What have you done, sir? I'll call for an ambulance. I'll tell it like it was, so I will.'

'Don't worry,' said Christine, 'your chief inspector will be here in—' she checked her watch – 'five minutes, and I have recorded our entire encounter on my handy-dandy laptop there. You've done yourself a heap of good by not agreeing to allow this man to bribe or bully you, Constable Flynn.'

'You've what?' screamed Beattie.

'I've recorded our entire meeting, since you arrived,' replied Christine. 'We private enquiry agents know how to use technology to our advantage, inspector. It's all been captured, and is sitting safely in the cloud. Now please stop wriggling, or I shall take the shotgun Tom is pointing at you, and get him to take my place sitting on top of you.'

Beattie sagged beneath her, and she saw Tom and Barry exchange a proud smile as Barry shoved the inspector's gun into his jeans' pocket, and wrapped his big arms around Brid – who was sobbing again.

'This'll be a tale they'll not believe at the pub,' said Tom.

'What, how it was us who caught the Gadfly? Sure they will, when they've bought us enough drinks for us to be able to tell them every detail,' said Barry.

'You'll get them to pick up that eejit Callum too, won't you?' asked Brid who was finally on her feet. 'I'm sure he's been taken terrible advantage of in all this,' her chin trembled, and she hid her face in Barry's comforting chest.

'I'm certain the police will have more people than just your Callum to nick, because I have a suspicion our Inspector Beattie here might find himself choosing to cooperate with his former colleagues, once they have him in custody,' said Christine, 'won't you, Gadfly?'

A gruff, muffled noise came from the man she was sitting on, and Christine felt absolutely marvelous.

THIRTY-SEVEN

The hastily arranged tea party at Chellingworth Hall was being held in the long portrait gallery on the second floor. Annie was delighted to discover that, by the time she, Gertie, and Marjorie arrived, Mavis, Althea, and McFli, Stephanie and Henry, Carol and Albert, Cook Davies, Bronwen Price, and Edward were all already either seated, or in attendance. In order to allow time for Marjorie to exchange pleasantries with the other attendees, and bring them all up to speed about her terrible time in hospital, Annie invited Bronwen to join her in a small anteroom at the top of the stairs.

'Thanks for all the lovely cakes and pastries, it'll mean a lot to Marj that you've made such a fuss,' began Annie.

Bronwen smiled and bobbed her head. 'No problem, Miss Parker, my pleasure.'

'You and Marj were good friends, she was telling me. In school together, Girl Guides, church choir and all that. And you both went about a lot with Huw Hughes, I understand. What do you think of them arresting him?'

Bronwen looked at her fingers, which Annie noticed were long, extremely clean and had nibbled nails. 'Oh, I don't know. I suppose they must know what they're doing, though I don't like to think of him killing anyone.'

'I expect he'll be having a terrible time, locked up in a tiny, dark cell, all alone.'

'I expect he will.'

'He's a man who likes his freedom. Likes to roam.'

'So I understand.'

'Marj was telling me she had a bit of a crush on him, when you were all in school together. I bet a lot of the girls did. He's very handsome even now, and I expect he was then, too.'

'Maybe, I don't really remember.'

'Did you ever have a crush on him, Bronwen?'

'Him? Me? No, never.'

Annie nibbled her lip. 'Did you know that Chief Inspector James is coming to join us here shortly?'

'No – no, I didn't.'

'Well, he is, and when he arrives I plan to tell him why I think Huw didn't kill Dr Priddle, and who really did. Would you like to stay while I explain everything, and get Huw released?'

'I should really be getting back to the kitchen. There's such a lot to be done.'

'I'm sure Cook Davies will be alright with you staying, if you'd like to.'

Bronwen continued to study her fingers. 'I'm sure it'll be very interesting.'

'Yes, I think it will. Come on, I can hear the chief inspector arriving now; Edward's bringing him up the main staircase. His voice carries. Shall we?'

They rejoined the group just as the chief inspector was being given a seat, a cup of tea, and a slice of cake. The entire gathering looked quite delightfully social, and polite. Not at all the sort of setting for the unmasking of a killer, thought Annie as she surveyed the room.

Annie motioned to Bronwen that she should sit, drawing a glare from Cook Davies, who seemed mollified when Henry suggested she should also take a seat. Edward remained at the door, which was what Henry had requested. Annie was delighted that the duke and duchess had agreed to set things up just the way she'd asked.

Annie faced the group, her back to the inner wall of the long gallery. Keenly aware that everyone was staring at her, she spoke with more confidence than she felt.

'Thanks to my colleagues, Mavis, Carol – and Althea – who are trusting me to do a good job with this one. I know it's all a bit odd, but, you see, this hasn't been like a normal case from the beginning. Indeed, it really hasn't been a case for us at all, because the police have handled it all so beautifully. So, chief inspector, please understand, this isn't usually how we do things. As a rule we enquire, find out something, then that leads to another line of enquiry and so on. We usually work through cases like you'd peel an onion, with one layer being revealed at a time, and us making discoveries and decisions as we go along. This time? Well, it's been different. But we're finally where we need to be now, I'm sure of that.'

'Thank you for your kind invitation, Your Graces,' said Carwen James nodding at Henry, Stephanie, and Althea – Annie noticed that he did it in the correct order to acknowledge their relative importance, 'but I am rather puzzled. We have the culprit for Dr Priddle's murder in custody, and it really *is* just a matter of time before he confesses.'

'So he hasnae coughed to it yet?' asked Mavis pointedly.

'Not quite yet.' Chief Inspector James's smile was politely cold.

'And he won't, because he didn't do it,' said Annie, bringing everyone's interest back to her.

'Oh, do tell,' said Althea, biting into a slice of coconut cake. 'Lovely,' she whispered to Bronwen, and gave the cook a wink.

'Never having done this before, I'll just tell it like it is,' said Annie. 'The person who killed Dr Priddle took some old mole poison from a shed on the estate and smeared it onto a lemon they gave him, knowing he'd ingest the strychnine when he used it as an accompaniment to the lemon barley water he was known to adore. Just like you said, Chief Inspector.' Carwen James nodded graciously. 'But it wasn't Huw who did it. I agree it looked as though he could have, but I reckon the main reason some people think Huw could have killed Dr Priddle is because they believe he's a killer with three deaths to his credit already – they think he killed his three wives and, once a killer, always a killer, right?' Annie bristled as the chief inspector nodded.

Annie straightened her back. 'Well, I don't believe he did that either. I've studied the facts and I've come to a different conclusion than you all did; Huw is a man who breaks women's hearts, and, when they are utterly bereft, they do stupid, foolhardy things that end up with them dead.'

Annie knew what the expression on Carwen James's face meant – he felt sorry for her, and not in a good way.

'You've all got me pegged as another woman in love with Hughes, haven't you?' Annie searched the faces of her friends and colleagues in the room, and knew she was right. 'Well, I'm not. But I have got close enough to him to be able to see him for what he truly is; he's a man who's in love with love, with romance. He cannot help but do whatever he can to make every woman he's with feel as special as he wants her to be. I've only felt that for a few short weeks; I cannot imagine how drunk on it a woman would become if she were with him for a good deal longer. It would be overwhelming. But then the question arises – what happens if he stops acting that way? Stops making a woman feel so special? I'll tell you what happens when it stops – their heart is broken in the worst possible way – because they haven't just lost *him*, they've also sort of lost themselves.'

Annie looked around the room. Carol was attending to a squirming Albert, but managed to make eye contact with her friend, and threw her a supportive look.

Annie took another deep breath, channeled every episode of *Perry Mason* and *Crown Court* she'd ever seen, and pushed on. 'I put it to you that's what happened with Edna Priddle. I have found an eye witness to the fact that Huw and Edna were enjoying a passionate relationship when Huw was about eighteen years old. Maybe Dr Priddle found out about the affair, or maybe it was just time for Huw to move on. Either way, not long after Huw left Anwen – and Edna – the woman killed herself, leaving a note that blamed her husband for making her life miserable. Some here might say hers was the first corpse on Huw's conscience, except I don't believe for one minute he was aware of what happened. I certainly don't think he believes his actions have led to the deaths of at least four women we know about, and maybe more we've never heard of. There was the wife who hopped off the wagon, then drove off a cliff; the one who chose to have some disgusting concoction put into her mouth as part of a "cleansing" ritual; the one who "fell" off a balcony and cracked her head open. Poor women.'

Annie allowed the pictures she'd painted to take hold in her audience's imagination. 'I know the general belief is that all these deaths could have been murders committed by Huw which he made look like accidents. But I would suggest that each death could also have been caused by each woman herself – not in the planned, traditionally suicidal way that Edna Priddle chose, taking her life by purposely overdosing on pills and leaving a note – but while they were in a generally depressed state, not feeling special, or loved, anymore. Look, I'm going to talk as though I'm among friends here – which I believe I am, in large part – so when I tell you that I know from personal experience how heartbreak can rob a person of the belief that their life is worth living, please don't let it leave this room. I know it's the truth, because I've felt it. I know how appealing it can be to act recklessly, truly not caring if you live or die. I was fortunate, because I had a good friend who helped me when I needed it most, helped me find the joy in life again, and I stopped taking stupid risks.' She winked at Carol, who smiled and wrinkled her nose affectionately.

Annie paused as Chief Inspector James cleared his throat, making it obvious that he intended to speak. 'You make some sober, interesting points, Annie but, all of that aside, I should remind you we haven't charged Hughes with anything other than Dr Priddle's death. Our investigations into the deaths of his wives are ongoing. If nothing comes of those enquiries then so be it. But we've got him for the murder of the doctor.'

'No, no he *didn't* kill Priddle,' replied Annie, working hard to control her emotions. She paused and silently counted to ten. 'I don't believe Huw did it. All you've done is suggest how he might have done it – you still have no idea of why he would. So, let me tell you a story. A long time ago, a handsome young man lived in a little Welsh village, and all the girls fell for him. He enjoyed the attention, and the girls enjoyed being with him because of how he made them feel – what he made them believe about themselves. Huw won over Edna Priddle, but he also had Marjorie and Bronwen hanging on his arms and his every word, and he led them a bit of a dance. Marjorie admitted to a crush – you don't mind me saying that, do you, Marjorie?'

Marjorie shook her head and spoke quietly, almost sadly Annie thought. 'No, Annie. Any attention Huw's ever paid to me is water under the bridge now.'

'Thanks, Marj. After Huw left the village in the late 1970s, you met and married your Owain; you "moved on," Marjorie. But you didn't, did you, Bronwen? You stayed in the area, yes, but you chose a new life-path for yourself that took you away from your friends, and even your family. You moved, here, to the hall, and you've never left. I asked myself why a girl might do that. Why a fun-loving, outgoing youngster would stop being what she always had been. So suddenly. A girl who'd also probably been in love with Huw, who'd certainly spent a good deal of time with him – enough to feel the effect of his charms, without doubt. I recalled a half-heard comment Dr Priddle made at the tea. He was looking over at you and Huw, your heads were close together and you both looked happy; I thought you were talking about the cakes you'd made for the tea, Bronwen. When he spotted you together, Dr Priddle wondered aloud if you were truly happy, then said something along the lines of, "she could have had it. No need for that, there wasn't." I thought nothing of it at the time, but, when I heard that Bronwen had told the police she'd seen Huw going off toward an old shed where he might have found some ancient mole poison, and I put that together with her hiding away at the hall all these years, I understood what Dr Priddle might have meant.'

Althea gasped. 'No!' she said, drawing puzzled looks.

Annie nodded, then took a deep breath and said, 'I believe you loved Huw very much when you were young, Bronwen. I further believe you had a relationship with him, and you fell pregnant. After he left the village – never knowing what had happened – you terminated your pregnancy. Priddle was your doctor, so he'd have known. It was clear to me at the tea that he felt sorry for you . . . *that's* what he recalled and commented upon when he saw you and Huw together again on Sunday. When I left him, you went over to sit beside him. Did he ask if you'd told Huw about your pregnancy? Were you frightened word would get out? And did that all get mixed up with the love and the hate you'd been feeling toward Huw since he'd returned to the village because he hadn't sought you out – hadn't remembered his "special girl"?'

As Annie had suspected, all eyes turned to look at Bronwen, who was pale. Annie was especially interested to note the chief inspector's expression.

She continued, 'I don't think you'd decided to poison Dr Priddle until after your chat with him at the tea, and I suppose it's to your credit that you were able to come up with a plan so quickly. Tell me, did you see Dr Priddle eating lemon segments that afternoon?'

'I never saw him do anything of the sort,' said Bronwen with passion. 'I . . . I wish I had.'

'I understand,' said Annie. 'I'm pretty sure someone like yourself – who's lived on the estate for almost forty years – would be well aware of all sorts of ancient stores of yukky stuff about the place. All you had to do was coat a lemon with old, illegal mole poison and deliver it to Dr Priddle. Was it a peace offering, when maybe you dropped in on him that Sunday evening? You said you were in your room, but no one could vouch for that. He wouldn't have been surprised if you'd turned up to beg him to not say anything until you were ready to speak for yourself. "Vengeance is mine" was what you painted at the croquet pavilion – you knew everyone connected with the tournament would be bound to hear about it, and possibly even see it, if it couldn't be cleaned up properly. But it wasn't a triumphant victory shout, was it? That's what everyone thought, but no.' Annie paused and looked around. 'Most of us connected the vandalism with the illness at the tea, but that was the wrong connection – the vandalism was connected to the poisoning of Dr Priddle. Indeed, the message you painted was a warning, to Dr Priddle himself, wasn't it? Both you and he are regular church-goers. You knew he'd be familiar with the rest of that text: "Dearly beloved, avenge not yourselves, but rather give place unto wrath: for it is written, Vengeance is mine; I will repay, saith the Lord." I looked it up and read around it, see, and it's not a threat of vengeance about to be wreaked by a person – it's the exact opposite. It's a plea for people to *not* take vengeance on each other, because vengeance is God's business. As I say, your painted message was a warning to Priddle telling him to not take vengeance upon you by telling your secret to Huw.'

The chief inspector harrumphed. 'Excuse me, but what you are saying is nonsense, Annie. As a professional, I feel forced to point this out to you, and this assembled group. You're saying this woman left a message – a plea as much as a warning – for a man she had killed. What on earth is the point of that? The message was painted on Sunday night. What would be the point of the message? The doctor was already dead by then.'

'Exactly. But Bronwen didn't know that,' said Annie.

'Explain,' snapped the policeman.

'Bronwen planned to make Priddle very ill, but didn't plan to kill him. She coated the lemon with the poison imagining that he would, at most, put a slice in his drink. She had no idea he would eat an entire lemon in one go – who would? It's such an extraordinary thing to do. She thought he'd get a little bit of poison, but he got a lot.' Annie looked across the room at Bronwen, and she wasn't alone – eyes bored into the woman, who didn't look up from her hands, folded in her lap.

'When you found out that Dr Priddle had died you were as shocked as everyone else, if not more so. But – and this is really telling, Bronwen – you came up with a wicked way to frame Huw for a murder he never committed. To allow the message to be connected with Huw, you dumped a paint-stained rag over the wall surrounding his house. And, when you had the opportunity, you mentioned to the police that you'd seen Huw moving toward a possible location of old mole poisons. Your contrived actions led to Huw becoming the prime suspect for the doctor's murder.'

Everyone stared at Bronwen – teacups in mid-air, mouths open.

'I just wanted Huw to notice me, like he used to,' she said quietly. 'If Dr Priddle had told him what had happened to me, he wouldn't have ever looked at me again. At all. Huw always hated the idea of a woman being pregnant. Talked about it a lot, he did. He said women's bodies were for pleasure, not procreation. Never showed the slightest interest in a woman who'd had a baby. Never wanted kids. And then Dr Priddle told me, that night at his house, that Huw was interested in you. Yes, you, Miss Annie Parker. That was it for me.'

Carwen James's cup rattled in its saucer.

'Couldn't you just have asked the doctor to keep your confidence, Bronwen? Why on earth did you do something as stupid as poisoning him?' Annie spoke softly.

'Dr Priddle said it was wrong at the time that I hadn't told Huw about the baby, but he helped me get an abortion anyway. But at first I was afraid to say anything, and then no one knew where Huw had gone to, see. But as soon as the doctor saw us together at the tea, he brought it up again. Said Huw deserved to know what had happened all those years ago. He was very insistent. Said I should pray about it at church, and search my conscience.'

Althea said, 'Maybe the man wasn't as sensitive as everyone thought, after all. But you should not have killed him, Bronwen. He didn't deserve that.'

'I didn't think he would die!' The distraught woman wrung her hands. 'He was only supposed to have a little bit of poison, see? I thought he'd be ill, but that he'd hear about what I'd painted at the pavilion. See it even. I just wanted him to be frightened. To not say anything to Huw. To know God would know.' Bronwen's voice cracked with emotion.

'Wait a minute, what about everyone being ill after the tea?' wailed Marjorie. 'Did you do that too, Bronwen? You did all the baking. Did you put something deadly in the cakes?'

Bronwen shook her head. 'I don't know nothing about that.'

'Any theories about that?' asked the chief inspector, staring pointedly at Annie.

'I think Huw will confess to having done that, if that's *all* he's being accused of,' replied Annie. 'You found the empty bottles of eye drops inside his home where Bronwen couldn't have planted them, and it's exactly the sort of thing his ego would make him do – try to knobble the opposing team to give the Anwen Allcomers a better chance of winning. For all that he says he's brilliant, he hadn't worked it out that members of both teams would become ill.'

The chief inspector rose and Bronwen burst into tears. 'I never meant to kill him, honest I didn't. Doesn't me painting the message for him to see prove that? Annie, you believe me, don't you?'

Annie nodded. 'I do, but I think it'll be for the courts to decide.'

'I say,' were the first words Henry uttered, followed by, 'that's awful.'

'Oh, Bronwen,' said Stephanie sadly.

Bronwen looked up. 'Should I go and get my handbag from the kitchen? Should I come with you now?' she was speaking to Carwen James.

'I'll come with you,' he said, and helped her from her seat. As the pair walked toward the door Annie overheard the chief inspector giving Bronwen a formal warning, and telling her that she was being arrested on suspicion of murder. It was only then that the importance of what she'd done hit her. She reached out for a chair and sat down with a thump. Gertie put her paws on her lap, and Mavis handed her a cup of tea.

'Congratulations on what you've just achieved,' said Mavis quietly. 'The Case of the Lethal Lemon?'

'Nah, you can't go giving away the solution in the title of the case, can you?' Annie shook her head sadly, but managed a wink.

THIRTY-EIGHT

Sunday 26th August

The rain everyone had been praying for finally arrived at the least convenient moment for the members of the Chellingworth Champs; a somber start to the croquet tournament had given way to a highly competitive situation, and the entire championship rested upon the final round. Henry was to play against his mother, and the crowd was rapt.

As the opponents took their opening positions the rain began to fall; plastic macs were pulled over heads and a few umbrellas opened. The atmosphere was tense, though it was clear to all that Henry was doing his best to make it appear he wanted nothing more than a fair game against an inferior opponent.

But the game didn't progress that way. As Althea's aggressive play put her farther ahead of her son with each shot, Annie leaned over to Mavis and whispered, 'How does she make the ball go that far? She's only little. I know she told us she used to play a long time ago back in London, but does what I'm seeing here mean she's really that good?'

Mavis didn't take her eyes off the field of play. 'Aye, she told everyone she used to play a bit in London. What I don't think most people know is *where* she played; it was the Hurlingham Club in Fulham. Do you know it?'

Annie nodded. 'I know where it is, but I've never been there. Posh. Private. Do they play croquet there?'

'I've been there once; when I was Matron at the Battersea Barracks I had occasion to take tea there, as the guest of the well-heeled offspring of one of my wards. Splendid place it is, but you're right, exceptionally private. A little jewel on the banks of the Thames, for those with the background and money to be able to afford to belong. Althea told me Henry's father joined up for her sake when they were first married; she said he wanted her to have somewhere in her beloved London to be able to meet her old chums. The Croquet

Association had their headquarters there right up until 2002. That's where she played, against some exceptionally good players, I understand.'

Annie stifled a giggle. 'Poor Henry.'

'Aye, poor Henry, right enough,' agreed Mavis. 'That wee woman's been hiding her light under a bushel for a long time. A bit like you, really. Now I think we're about to see her give her son a bit of a lesson on the lawn today.'

'Tude'll be in a good mood,' added Annie.

'Aye, but for more reasons than it looks like the Anwen Allcomers will take the trophy away with them today. He'll be looking forward to that dinner you've promised to cook for him at your cottage tomorrow night, won't he?'

Annie looked shocked. 'How d'you know about that?'

Mavis took Annie's hand in her own. 'He might have mentioned it a time or two about the village, and you know how Sharon likes to make sure everybody knows what's going on. Don't be surprised if the residents of Anwen-by-Wye have the two of you married off by the end of the week.' She winked at her friend, whose expression showed she was more than a little taken aback at the idea that, for once, she was the subject of village gossip.

'It's just dinner, Mave,' said Annie.

'You're already friends, so dinner is an excellent next step,' replied Mavis. 'Oh look, Althea's knocked Henry's ball right off to the far side of the lawn, and now he's got to come all the way back to get through that hoop.'

'That's bad for Henry, right?'

'Aye, I believe so, but it's good for your Tudor.'

'I keep telling you all, he's not "my" Tudor.'

Mavis patted Annie's hand. 'Aye, well, you keep telling yourself that, my dear, but allow us all the right to know different.'

Althea was having great fun, especially every time she looked at Henry's face. Clemmie's screams of support from the steps were a delight to hear, and, although she knew she shouldn't have enjoyed it so much, she did think her son could do with being taught that it's not polite to belittle one's elders, especially in company, nor to turn down an offer of help from one's own mother.

Using her tiny foot to secure her ball so she could smack it with her mallet and allow the force to transfer to her opponent's ball, she gave her shot all the strength she had. Henry's groan as he saw his ball go past the target hoop and off to the far side of the lawn told her he knew he'd all but lost the match. She then happily passed her own ball through the hoop and prepared for the final, triumphant thwack that would allow her to hit the stick at the center of the field of play, winning the tournament for the Anwen Allcomers. She could see Tudor was already on his feet, and caught an unmistakable glance pass between him and Annie. She believed they'd make a delightful couple, now that Annie had finally come to her senses and allowed herself to see what had been in front of everyone else's noses for some time.

Carol and David were sitting on the top step overlooking the croquet lawn, with Albert in his portable car seat beside them. As the rain began, they made sure their son would stay dry, then attended to themselves.

'There's no way we're leaving now,' said Carol, pulling a plastic poncho over her head. 'When Mam spotted this in Carmarthen market, she said I'd be glad of it one day and she was right. Mind you, I'm not sure the leopard-print pattern is what I'd have chosen.'

David laughed. 'Leopards are cats; I suppose she thought you'd like it for that reason.'

'Never thought of it that way,' replied his wife. 'Look at Althea, she's brilliant at this. Who knew?'

'Not me for one,' said David.

'Not me for two,' replied Carol. Albert gurgled his agreement. 'And not him for three,' she added. 'I like being three. Are you happy?'

David put his arm around his wife's shoulders. 'Are you?'

'Oh yes, I am.'

'There you are then. That saying "Happy wife, happy life?" You are one, so I have one. Tell you what, though, I'm glad you're here, safe at home or in the office, doing what you do with your research, rather than getting caught up in all sorts, like Christine. That could all have gone very badly, couldn't it?'

Carol nodded. 'Sometimes she just doesn't even seem to *see* danger, or, if she does, she should learn what that means, and walk away. She seems to have a pathological desire to get herself into circumstances where it's fifty-fifty how things might go. Even when it comes to men.'

'According to what she told you, and what you told me, she got off lightly this time,' pondered David, 'which means she might think she can get away with it again.'

Carol looked down at her son. 'Not here, she won't. I'm going to have a chat with her when she gets back about bringing danger to our doors. That's not the sort of thing I want happening anywhere near this one. Guns? Never.'

'If your chat with her works out as well as the one you had with Annie, that wouldn't be a bad thing. She seems happier now – more like her old self.'

'Working out who's a murderer and who isn't, when no one else can, must help a person's self-esteem, I'd have thought. I'm pleased she and Tudor are going to take a step forward together, even if it's only a dinner date to start with. She deserves to be happy.'

'As do we all,' said David. 'Best feeling in the world, this.'

'It is,' agreed Carol, then she stood to cheer as Althea's ball hit home, and the winners began to celebrate.

Tudor Evans did his best to not gloat during his speech after being handed the trophy by the vicar, and everyone agreed, when they congratulated him, that he'd been gracious in victory. As he and Annie walked to his car, the trophy was in one hand and he reached out for Annie with his other. He was delighted when she didn't pull away. He felt as though the weight of the world had been lifted from his shoulders, and was in no doubt which of his hands held the most valuable prize.

Christine looked up into Alexander's eyes from her hospital bed. The machine beeping beside her was annoying, and the drip in her arm made her feel inadequate. Mortal.

'I might never let you out of my sight again,' said the man she loved, and who had saved her from possible death. 'You're too headstrong by half. Mad, even. If you don't grow out of that wild streak soon you're going to end up in more trouble than this.'

'I don't usually mix in circles where guns are used,' said Christine quietly.

'Good.'

'But I do mix in circles where you're involved, and some might say that's wild enough in itself.'

'A day or so and we can get you out of here and back to the peace and quiet of rural Wales. It'll be safer there.'

'You're talking about a village where a poisoner was just apprehended, you realize that, don't you?' countered Christine.

Alexander shook his head slowly. 'Well, there's peace and quiet, and peace and quiet, and right now I think Chellingworth Hall is a lot safer than Ballinclare Manor. That said, I think the back streets of Brixton at three in the morning would be safer than Ballinclare Manor.'

'You'd know more about that than I would,' said Christine sleepily.

'Not as much as I used to,' acknowledged Alexander, 'and that's a good thing in itself.'

'Getting soft in your old age?' quipped Christine half-heartedly.

'Not on your Nellie,' replied Alexander, but Christine was already asleep.

He kissed her forehead.

It was past midnight when Stephanie finally sat up in bed. 'Henry, would you please stop fidgeting. It's difficult enough for me to get comfortable as it is, and you're making things ten times worse.'

Henry also sat up. 'Sorry my love. Is the baby making you sleepless?'

'No, you are. You haven't been still for more than twenty seconds at a time since we came to bed. What on earth is wrong with you?'

'I still cannot believe what Mother did to me today. I saw the look on her face as she took that last shot; she was thrilled. Mothers shouldn't undermine their sons like that. I'd never do that to my child.' He tenderly touched his wife's baby bump. 'No child deserves that.'

Swinging her legs out of bed, Stephanie held them out in front of her and twirled her ankles. 'Henry, dear, your mother's a much better croquet player than you, and she deserved to win. You'll have to admit that to yourself and accept it. She didn't beat you out of spitefulness, she beat you because she could. Why shouldn't she? It was a competitive situation, after all. It's not as though she was like that horrible Hughes person, who slithered through people's lives making them so miserable they couldn't take it anymore. Nor vindictive and unhinged, like poor Bronwen. You could have picked your mother to take Bronwen's place on the Chellingworth Champs team, but you declined her offer of help and decided to call upon her own ladies' aide, Lindsay, believing her to be the superior player. That must have hurt your mother terribly. Think on that. Tudor was being kind when he allowed her to take Huw Hughes' place; you were being mean when you turned down her offer to play with you. Let's be honest, dear, there's a lesson to be learned; people are not always what they seem to be on the surface – sometimes they have hidden talents, and other aspects to their personalities they've chosen to hide too, which is unfortunate and can be damaging.'

Henry snuggled back under the sheet, which was all he could cope with on such a humid night. 'I didn't mean to hurt Mother,' he said feebly.

'And I dare say Huw Hughes might say the same thing about Edna Priddle, his three late wives, and Bronwen Price. But actions have unintended, as well as intended, consequences. Just think about the way those moles have messed up the croquet lawn and take to heart what Ivor told you after the tournament; he's going to have to dig up a good portion of the lawn to repair those mole tunnels. They might not be visible, but they have seriously undermined the turf, and the lawn is hiding unseen dangers.'

'The Case of the Malevolent Mole,' said Henry.

'Don't start,' warned his wife.

'Yes dear,' replied Henry sleepily. 'No, I mean, no, dear. Are your ankles still swollen?'

'Less so than earlier this evening, I'll put a pillow under them. I'll be fine.'

'Our child already has a good mother,' he added.

Stephanie sighed. 'And a well-intentioned father, which is, I suppose, a promising start.'

'Yes, dear.'

ACKNOWLEDGEMENTS

Thanks to my family for their love and encouragement, which keep me going. Thanks to the entire Severn House publishing team for their professionalism and support, and to my agent, Priya Doraswamy, for hers. A host of reviewers, bloggers, librarians and booksellers have helped get this book on to bookshelves, and I thank them for noticing my work. Finally, my thanks to you for choosing to share time with the women of the WISE Enquiries Agency. Happy reading.

CPSIA information can be obtained
at www.ICGtesting.com
Printed in the USA
BVHW030852230519
549122BV00003B/4/P

BOOKS BY ANTHONY HECHT

POETRY

Flight Among the Tombs 1998

The Transparent Man 1990

Collected Earlier Poems 1990

The Venetian Vespers 1979

Millions of Strange Shadows 1977

The Hard Hours 1967

A Summoning of Stones 1954

TRANSLATION

Aeschylus's Seven Against Thebes 1973

(with Helen Bacon)

ESSAYS AND CRITICISM

On the Laws of the Poetic Art 1995

(Andrew W. Mellon Lectures in the Fine Arts)

The Hidden Law: The Poetry of W. H. Auden 1993

Obbligati 1986

EDITOR

The Essential George Herbert 1987

Jiggery-Pokery: A Compendium of Double Dactyls 1967

(with John Hollander)

The Darkness and the Light

The Darkness and the Light

poems

ANTHONY HECHT

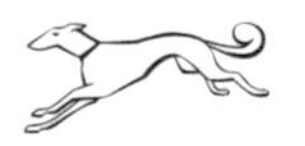

Alfred A. Knopf *New York* 2001

THIS IS A BORZOI BOOK
PUBLISHED BY ALFRED A. KNOPF

 Published in the United States by Alfred A. Knopf,
a division of Random House, Inc., New York, and simultaneously in Canada
by Random House of Canada Limited, Toronto.
Distributed by Random House, Inc., New York.

www.randomhouse.com/knopf/poetry

I am deeply grateful to Dorothea Tanning for her munificence, as well as her invincibly high spirits; to the Bogliasco Foundation and their Centro Studi Ligure, where a good number of these poems were written; to the Atlantic Center for the Arts, for their hospitality; to the Poetry Society of America, for the award of the Robert Frost Medal; and to the following journals in which recent poems have appeared: *The Forward, The Hudson Review, The New Republic, The New Yorker, The New York Review of Books, The Oxford Quarterly Review, The Paris Review, Pivot, Princeton University Library Chronicle, Rattapallax, The Sewanee Review, Sewanee Theological Review, The Southwest Review, Stand* (UK) and *The Yale Review.*

Grateful acknowledgment is made to Alfred A. Knopf and Faber and Faber Limited for permission to reprint an excerpt from "The Sun This March" from *Collected Poems* by Wallace Stevens, copyright © 1954 by Wallace Stevens. Rights in the United Kingdom administered by Faber and Faber Limited, London. Reprinted by permission of Alfred A. Knopf, a division of Random House, Inc., and Faber and Faber Limited.

Library of Congress Cataloging-in-Publication Data
Hecht, Anthony, [date]
The darkness and the light : poems / by Anthony Hecht.
p. cm.
ISBN 0-375-41194-1 (hc) — ISBN 0-375-70946-0 (tpb)
I. Title.
PS3558.E28 D37 2001
811'.54—dc21 00-062007

Manufactured in the United States of America
First Edition

For Helen

and

In Memory of Harry and Kathleen Ford

and of William and Emily Maxwell

Aye, on the shores of darkness there is light.

—John Keats

The exceeding brightness of this early sun
Makes me conceive how dark I have become,

. . . .

Oh! Rabbi, rabbi, fend my soul for me
And a true savant of this dark nature be.

—Wallace Stevens

Contents

The Darkness and the Light

Late Afternoon: The Onslaught of Love

At this time of day
One could hear the caulking irons sound
Against the hulls in the dockyard.
Tar smoke rose between trees
And large oily patches floated on the water,
Undulating unevenly
In the purple sunlight
Like the surfaces of Florentine bronze.

At this time of day
Sounds carried clearly
Through hot silences of fading daylight.
The weedy fields lay drowned
In odors of creosote and salt.
Richer than double-colored taffeta,
Oil floated in the harbor,
Amoeboid, iridescent, limp.
It called to mind the slender limbs
Of Donatello's *David.*

It was lovely and she was in love.
They had taken a covered boat to one of the islands.
The city sounds were faint in the distance:
Rattling of carriages, tumult of voices,
Yelping of dogs on the decks of barges.

At this time of day
Sunlight empurpled the world.
The poplars darkened in ranks
Like imperial servants.
Water lapped and lisped
In its native and quiet tongue.
Oakum was in the air and the scent of grasses.
There would be fried smelts and cherries and cream.
Nothing designed by Italian artisans
Would match this evening's perfection.
The puddled oil was a miracle of colors.

Circles

Long inventories of miseries unspoken,
Appointment books of pain,
Attars of love gone rancid, the pitcher broken
At the fountain, rooted unkindnesses:
All were implied by her, by me suspected,
At her saying, "I could not bear
Ever returning to that village in Maine.
For me the very air,
The harbor smells, the hills, all are infected."

I gave my sympathy, filled in the blanks
With lazy, bitter fictions,
And, feeling nothing, won her grateful thanks.

Many long years and some attachments later
I was to be instructed by the courts
Upon the nicest points of such afflictions,
Having become a weakened, weekend father.
All of us, in our own circle of hell
(Not that of forger, simonist or pander),
Patrolled the Olmsted bosks of Central Park,
Its children-thronged resorts,
Pain-tainted ground,
Where the innocent and the fallen join to play
In the fields, if not of the Lord, then of the Law;
Which decreed that love be hobbled and confined
To Saturday,
Trailing off into Sunday-before-dark;

And certain sandpits, slides, swings, monkey bars
Became the old thumbscrews of spoiled affection
And agonized aversion.
Of these, the most tormenting
In its single-songed, maddening monotony,
Its glaring-eyed and nostril-flaring steeds
With perfect teeth, but destined never to win
Their countless and interminable races,
Was the merry, garish, mirthless carousel.

Memory

Sepia oval portraits of the family,
Black-framed, adorned the small brown-papered hall,
But the parlor was kept unused, never disturbed.
Under a glass bell, the dried hydrangeas
Had bleached to the hue of ancient newspaper,
Though once, someone affirmed, they had been pink.
Pink still were the shiny curling orifices
Of matching seashells stationed on the mantel
With mated, spiked, wrought-iron candlesticks.
The room contained a tufted ottoman,
A large elephant-foot umbrella stand
With two malacca canes, and two peacock
Tail-feathers sprouting from a small-necked vase.
On a teak side table lay, side by side,
A Bible and a magnifying glass.
Green velvet drapes kept the room dark and airless
Until on sunny days toward midsummer
The brass andirons caught a shaft of light
For twenty minutes in late afternoon
In a radiance dimly akin to happiness—
The dusty gleam of temporary wealth.

Mirror

for J. D. McClatchy

Always halfway between you and your double,
Like Washington, I cannot tell a lie.
When the dark queen demands in her querulous treble,
"Who is the fairest?," inaudibly I reply,

"Beauty, your highness, dwells in the clouded cornea
Of the self-deceived beholder, whereas Truth,
According to film moguls of California,
Lies in makeup, smoke and mirrors, gin and vermouth,

Or the vinous second-pressings of *Veritas*,
Much swilled at Harvard. The astronomer's speculum
Reveals it, and to the politician's cheval glass
It's that part of a horse he cannot distinguish from

His elbow; but it's also the upside-down
Melodies of Bach fugues, the right-to-left
Writing of Leonardo, a long-term loan
From Hebrew, retrograde fluencies in deft,

Articulate penmanship. An occasional Louis
Might encounter it in the corridors of Versailles;
It evades the geometrician's confident QE
D, but the constant motion from ground to sky

And back again of the terrible Ferris wheel
Sackville describes in *A Mirror for Magistrates*
Conveys some semblance of the frightening feel
Of the mechanical heartlessness of Fate,

The ring-a-ding-*Ding-an-Sich.* Yet think how gaily
In the warped fun-house glass our flesh dissolves
In shape and helpless laughter, unlike the Daily
Mirror in which New Yorkers saw themselves.

It's when no one's around that I'm most truthful,
In a world as timeless as before The Fall.
No one to reassure that she's still youthful,
I gaze untroubled at the opposite wall.

Light fades, of course, with the oncoming of dusk;
I faithfully note the rheostat dial of day
That will rise to brilliance, weaken as it must
Through each uncalibrated shade of gray,

One of them that of winter afternoons,
Desolate, leaden, and in its burden far
Deeper than darkness, engrossing in its tones
Those shrouded regions where the meanings are."

Samson

There came to the nameless wife of Manoah
In annunciation an angel who declared:
"Like Sarah who was barren, even so shall you
Conceive a child; you also shall bear a son."

Almost every day at the Boston Lying-In
There are births defying expectation, all
Medical wisdom; almost daily a mother thinks
Her child God-given, a miracle and a wonder.

And the angel said: "You must both abstain from wine,
You and the child; from all contact with the dead;
Nor let your hair be shorn, for he is God's,
And he shall be a Nazarite from the womb."

In the Hebrew shul at Lodz the little boys
Studied the Torah, and let their sidelocks curl
And sway to the rhythm of reading. They too have
been
Sacrificed, like Nazarites before them.

An Orphic Calling

for Mihaly Csikszentmihalyi

The stream's *courante* runs on, a *force majeure,*
A Major rippling of the pure mind of Bach,
Tumult of muscled currents, formed in far
Reaches of edelweiss, cloud and alpenstock,

Now folding into each other, flexing, swirled
In cables of perdurable muscle-tones,
Hurrying through this densely noted world,
Small chambers, studio mikes, Concorde headphones,

And from deep turbulent rapids, roiled and spun,
They rise in watery cycles to those proud
And purifying heights where they'd begun
On Jungfrau cliffs of edelweiss and cloud,

Piled cumuli, that *fons et origo*
("Too lofty and original to rage")
Of the mind's limpid unimpeded flow
Where freedom and necessity converge

And meet in a fresh curriculum of love
(Minor in grief, major in happiness)
As interlocking melodies contrive
Small trysts and liaisons, briefly digress

But only to return to Interlaken
Altitudes of clear trebles, crystal basses,
Fine reconciliations and unbroken
Threadings of fern-edged flutes down tumbling races.

An Orphic calling it is, one that invites
Responsories, a summons to lute-led
Nature, as morning's cinnabar east ignites
And the instinctive sunflower turns its head.

Rara Avis in Terris

for Helen

Hawks are in the ascendant. Just look about.
Cormorants, ravens, jailbirds of ominous wing
Befoul the peace, their caws
raised in some summoning
To an eviscerating cause,
Some jihad, some rash all-get-out
Crusade, leaving the field all gore and guano
Justified in hysterical soprano

By balding buzzards who brandish the smart bomb,
The fractured atom in their unclipped talons.
Ruffling with all the pride
of testosteronic felons,
They storm the airwaves with implied
Threats and theatrical aplomb
Or cruise the sky with delta stealth and gelid
Chestsful of combat-decorative fruit salad.

It's the same in the shady groves of academe:
Cold eye and primitive beak and callused foot
Conjunctive to destroy
all things of high repute,
Whole epics, Campion's songs, Tolstoy,
Euclid and logic's enthymeme,
As each man bares his scalpel, whets his saber,
As though enjoined to deconstruct his neighbor.

And that's not the worst of it; there are the Bacchae,
The ladies' auxiliary of the raptor clan
With their bright cutlery,
sororal to a man.
And feeling peckish, they foresee
An avian banquet in the sky,
Feasting off dead white European males,
Or local living ones, if all else fails.

But where are the mild monogamous lovebirds,
Parakeets, homing pigeons, sundry doves,
Beringed, bewitching signs
of the first, greatest loves
Eros or Agape gently defines?
God's for the ark's small flocks and herds,
Or Venus incarnate as that quasi-queen
Of France known as Diane de la Poitrine.

They are here, my dear, they are here in the marble air,
According to the micro-Mosaic law,
Miraculously aloft
above that flood and flaw
Where Noah darkly plies his craft.
Lightly an olive branch they bear,
Its deathless leafage emblematic of
A quarter-century of faultless love.

A Fall

Those desolate, brute, chilling sublimities,
Unchanging but as the light may chance to fall,
Deserts of snow, forlorn barrens of rock,
What could be more indifferent to man's life
Than your average Alp, stripped to the blackened bone
Above the tree line, except where the ice rags,
Patches, and sheets of winter cling yearlong?
The cowbell's ludicrous music, the austere
Sobrieties of Calvin, precision watches,
A cheese or two, and that is all the Swiss
Have given the world, unless we were to cite
The questionable morals of their banks.
But how are people to live in dignity
When at two p.m. the first shadows of night,
Formed by the massive shoulder of some slope,
Cast, for the rest of the day, entire valleys—
Their window boxes of geraniums,
Their cobbles, pinecones, banners and coffee cups—
Into increasing sinks and pools of dark?
And that is but half the story. The opposing slope
Keeps morning from its flaxen charities
Until, on midsummer days, eleven-thirty,
When fresh birdsong and cow dung rinse the air
And all outdoors still glistens with night-dew.
All this serves to promote a state of mind
Cheerless and without prospects. But yesterday
I let myself, in spite of dark misgivings,

Be talked into a strenuous excursion
Along one high ridge promising a view.
And suddenly, at a narrowing of the path,
The whole earth fell away, and dizzily
I beheld the most majestic torrent in Europe,
A pure cascade, over six hundred feet,
Falling straight down—it was like Rapunzel's hair,
But white, as if old age and disappointment
Had left her bereft of suitors. Down it plunged,
Its great, continuous, unending weight
Toppling from above in a long shaft
Or carven stem that broke up at its base
Into enormous rhododendron blooms
Of spray, a dense array of shaken blossoms.
I teetered perilously, scared and dazed,
And slowly, careful of both hand and foot,
Made my painstaking way back down the trail.
That evening in my bedroom I recalled
The scene's terror and grandeur, my vertigo
Mixed with a feeling little short of awe.
And I retraced my steps in the secure
Comfort of lamplight on a Baedeker.
That towering waterfall I just had viewed
At what had seemed the peril of my life
Was regarded locally with humorous
Contempt, and designated the *Pisse-Vache*.

Haman

I am Haman the Hangman, the engineer
And chief designer of that noble structure,
The Gallows. Let the Jews tremble and beware:
I have made preparations for their capture
And extirpation in a holy war
Against their foolish faith, their hateful culture,
An ethnic cleansing that will leave us pure,
Ridding the world of this revolting creature.
I shall have camps, *Arbeit Macht Frei*, the lure
Of hope, the chastening penalty of torture,
And other entertainments of despair,
The which I hanker after like a lecher.
And best of all the gibbet, my friend, my poor
One-armed assistant, in stiff, obedient posture,
Like a young officer's salute, but more
Rigid, and more instructive than a lecture,
Saying, "I can teach you to tread on air,
And add another cubit to your stature."

A Certain Slant

Etched on the window were barbarous thistles of frost,
Edged everywhere in that tame winter sunlight
With pavé diamonds and fine prickles of ice
Through which a shaft of the late afternoon
Entered our room to entertain the sway
And float of motes, like tiny aqueous lives,
Then glanced off the silver teapot, raising stains
Of snailing gold upcast across the ceiling,
And bathed itself at last in the slop bucket
Where other aqueous lives, equally slow,
Turned in their sad, involuntary courses,
Swiveled in eel-green broth. Who could have known
Of any elsewhere? Even of out-of-doors,
Where the stacked firewood gleamed in drapes of glaze
And blinded the sun itself with jubilant theft,
The smooth cool plunder of celestial fire?

A Brief Account of Our City

for Dorothea Tanning

If you approach our city from the south,
The first thing that you'll see is the Old Fort,
High on its rock. Its crenellated walls,
Dungeons and barbicans and towers date back
To the eighth century. The local barons
Of hereditary title moved their courts
Inside whenever they were under siege
With all their retinues, taxing the poor,
Feuding with neighboring baronies, masterful
Only in greed and management of arms.
Great murderous vulgar men, they must have been.
The fort, history records, was never taken.
It might be worth a visit when you come.
For a mere thirty kroner you can ascend
The turrets for a quite incomparable view.
From there our forests look a lot like parsley
And cress; there the wind enters your throat
Like an iced mountain stream. Piled here and there
You will find pyramids of cannonballs
In the great courtyard, stacked like croquembouches,
Warm to the touch where the sun glances off them
And chilly in the shade. The arsenal,
Containing arquebuses, fruitwood bows,
As well as heavy mortars and great cannons,

Is open to the public. The furniture
Is solid, thick and serviceable stuff,
No nonsense. But what may strike you most of all
Is the plain, barren spareness of the rooms.
No art here. Nothing to appease the eye.
And not because such things have been removed
To our museums. This was the way they lived:
In self-denying, plain austerity.
As you draw nearer to the city itself
You will make out, beyond the citadel,
The shapely belfry of Our Lady of Sorrows.
Then you will see, in the midst of a great field,
Surrounded on all sides by acres of wheat,
A large, well-cared-for, isolated house—
No others neighboring, or even within view—
Which is given free of charge by the city board
To the Public Executioner. His children
Are allowed a special tutor, but not admitted
To any of our schools. The family
Can raise all that's required for their meals
Right on the grounds, and, if need be, a doctor
Will call on them, given half a day's notice.
The children are forbidden to leave the place,
As is, indeed, the entire family,
Except when the father alone is called upon
To perform official duties. And by this means
Everyone is kept happy; our citizens
Need have no fear of encountering any of them,

While they live comfortably at our expense.
Whenever you visit, be certain that you dine
At one of our fine restaurants; don't miss
The Goldene Nockerl, which for potato dumplings
Cannot be matched, and our rich amber beer
Is widely known as the finest in this region.

Saul and David

It was a villainous spirit, snub-nosed, foul
Of breath, thick-taloned and malevolent,
That squatted within him wheresoever he went
And possessed the soul of Saul.

There was no peace on pillow or on throne.
In dreams the toothless, dwarfed, and squinny-eyed
Started a joyful rumor that he had died
Unfriended and alone.

The doctors were confounded. In his distress, he
Put aside arrogant ways and condescended
To seek among the flocks where they were tended
By the youngest son of Jesse,

A shepherd boy, but goodly to look upon,
Unnoticed but God-favored, sturdy of limb
As Michelangelo later imagined him,
Comely even in his frown.

Shall a mere shepherd provide the cure of kings?
Heaven itself delights in ironies such
As this, in which a boy's fingers would touch
Pythagorean strings

And by a modal artistry assemble
The very Sons of Morning, the ranked and choired
Heavens in sweet laudation of the Lord,
          And make Saul cease to tremble.

Despair

Sadness. The moist gray shawls of drifting sea-fog,
Salting scrub pine, drenching the cranberry bogs,
Erasing all but foreground, making a ghost
Of anyone who walks softly away;
And the faint, penitent psalmody of the ocean.

Gloom. It appears among the winter mountains
On rainy days. Or the tiled walls of the subway
In caged and aging light, in the steel scream
And echoing vault of the departing train,
The vacant platform, the yellow destitute silence.

But despair is another matter. Midafternoon
Washes the worn bank of a dry arroyo,
Its ocher crevices, unrelieved rusts,
Where a startled lizard pauses, nervous, exposed
To the full glare of relentless marigold sunshine.

The Hanging Gardens of Tyburn

Mysteriously fed by the dying breath
Of felons, by the foul odor that melts
Down from their bodies hanging on the gallows,
The rank, limp flesh, the soft pendulous guilts,

This solitary plant takes root at night,
Its tiny charnel blossoms the pale blue
Of Pluto's ice pavilions; being dried,
Powdered and mixed with the cold morning dew

From the left hand of an executed man,
It confers untroubled sleep, and can prevent
Prenatal malformations if applied
To a woman's swelling body, except in Lent.

Take care to clip only the little blossoms,
For the plant, uprooted, utters a cry of pain
So highly pitched as both to break the eardrum
And render the would-be harvester insane.

Judith

It took less valor than I'm reputed for.
Since I was a small child I have hated men.
Even the feeblest, in their fantasies,
Triumph as sexual athletes, putting the shot
Squarely between the thighs of some meek woman,
While others strut like decathlon champions,
Like royal David hankering after his neighbor's
Dutiful wife. For myself, I found a husband
Not very prepossessing, but very rich.
Neither of us was interested in children.
In my case, the roving hands, the hot tumescence of an uncle,
Weakened my taste for close intimacies.
Ironically, heaven had granted me
What others took to be attractive features
And an alluring body, and which for years
Instinctively I looked upon with shame.
All men seemed stupid in their lecherous,
Self-flattering appetites, which I found repugnant.
But at last, as fate would have it, I found a chance
To put my curse to practical advantage.
It was easy. Holofernes was pretty tight;
I had only to show some cleavage and he was done for.

Illumination

Ground lapis for the sky, and scrolls of gold,
Before which shepherds kneel, gazing aloft
At visiting angels clothed in egg-yolk gowns,
Celestial tinctures smuggled from the East,
From sunlit Eden, the palmed and plotted banks
Of sun-tanned Aden. Brought home in fragile grails,
Planted in England, rising at Eastertide,
Their petals cup stamens of topaz dust,
The powdery stuff of cooks and cosmeticians.
But to the camel's-hair tip of the finest brush
Of Brother Anselm, it is the light of dawn,
Gilding the hems, the sleeves, the fluted pleats
Of the antiphonal archangelic choirs
Singing their melismatic *pax in terram.*
The child lies cribbed below, in bestial dark,
Pale as the tiny tips of crocuses
That will find their way to the light through drifts of snow.

Look Deep

Look deep into my eyes. Think to yourself,
"There is 'the fringèd curtain' where a play
Will shortly be enacted." Look deep down
Into the pupil. Think, "I am going to sleep."

The pupil has its many-tinctured curtain
Of moiré silks, parted to let you in,
And the play will present a goddess you used to know
From the glint of sunlit fountain, from beveled mirror,

A goddess, yes, but only a messenger
Whose message is the armorial fleur-de-lys
She carries in her right hand, signifying
The majesty of France, as handed down

From the royal house of Solomon and David:
Wisdom, music and valor gracefully joined
In trefoil heraldry. Nearly asleep,
You settle down for a full-scale production

Of *The Rainstorm* in its grand entirety,
Which, greater than *The Ring,* lasts forty nights;
Everything huddled in one rocking stateroom,
A saving remnant, a life-raft-world in little.

Dream at your ease of the dark forests of spruce
Swaying in currents of green, gelatinous winds

Above which the classless zoo and zookeepers
Weather the testing and baptismal waters;

Dream of the long, undeviating gloom,
The unrelenting skies, the pounding wet
Through which a peak will thrust, a light, and over
The covenanted ark, an *arc-en-ciel.*

Nocturne: A Recurring Dream

The moon is a pearl in mist and sets the scene.
Comfort seems within reach, just over there,
But rocks, water, and darkness intervene.

Incalculable dangers lie between
Us and the warmth of bedding, the fire's flare.
The moon is a pearl in mist and sets the scene;

She's not, as claimed Ben Jonson, heaven's queen.
More ghostly, an omen of death hung in the air.
Rocks, water, and darkness intervene

Between that shadowy dwelling, barely seen,
And something not at all unlike despair.
The moon is a pearl in mist and sets the scene

For—secret rites? Ensorcellment? Marine
Catastrophe? Before we can declare,
Rocks, water, and darkness intervene.

Oystery pale, anything but serene,
Our goal seems cloaked in the forbidding glare
Of moonlight as a pearl that sets the scene
Where rocks, water, and darkness intervene.

Lot's Wife

How simple the pleasures of those childhood days,
Simple but filled with exquisite satisfactions.
The iridescent labyrinth of the spider,
Its tethered tensor nest of polygons
Puffed by the breeze to a little bellying sail—
Merely observing this gave infinite pleasure.
The sound of rain. The gentle graphite veil
Of rain that makes of the world a steel engraving,
Full of soft fadings and faint distances.
The self-congratulations of a fly,
Rubbing its hands. The brown bicameral brain
Of a walnut. The smell of wax. The feel
Of sugar to the tongue: a delicious sand.
One understands immediately how Proust
Might cherish all such postage-stamp details.
Who can resist the charms of retrospection?

Public Gardens

"Flow'rs of all hue," a sightless Milton wrote
Of Paradise, which doesn't mean "all flowers."
An impoverished exile in his loneliest hours
Knows that not everybody makes the boat.

He has not mastered the language, he still retains
A craving for some remembered native dishes;
These sorrowful foreign skies, all smoke and ashes,
Remain uncleansed by the pummeling winter rains.

Jobless, he mopes in the shabby public gardens
Where importunate pigeons harry him for food.
Back in the dark unwelcome solitude
Of his attic room, he can view through the daisied curtains

The pantile roofs of this dirty little port.
But without passport or valid papers his fate
Lies with officials. Immense reasons of state
Conjoin to deny him permission to depart.

His is a sad but not uncommon lot,
Familiar to border guards, to police and such.
Even plantain, spleenwort, lichen, tuber and vetch
May be found in Paradise; the teasel not.

Sacrifice

I
ABRAHAM

Long years, and I found favor
In the sight of the Lord, who brought me out of Ur
To where his promise lay,
There with him to confer
On Justice and Mercy and the appointed day
Of Sodom's ashen fate;
For me he closeted sweetness in the date,
And gave to salt its savor.

Three promises he gave,
Came like three kings or angels to my door:
His purposes concealed
In coiled and kerneled store
He planted as a seedling that would yield
In my enfeebled years
A miracle that would command my tears
With piercings of the grave.

"Old man, behold Creation,"
Said the Lord, "the leaping hills, the thousand-starred
Heavens and watery floor.
Is anything too hard
For the Lord, who shut all seas within their doors?"
And then, for his name's sake
He led me, knowing where my heart would break,
Into temptation.

The whole of my long life
Pivoted on one terrible day at dawn.
Isaac, my son, and I
Were to Moriah gone.
There followed an hour in which I wished to die,
Being visited by these things:
My name called out, the beat of gigantic wings,
Faggots, and flame, and knife.

II
ISAAC

Youthful I was and trusting and strong of limb,
The fresh-split firewood roped tight to my back,
And I bore unknowing that morning my funeral pyre.
My father, face averted, carried the flame,
And, in its scabbard, the ritual blade he bore.
It seemed to me at the time a wearisome trek.

I thought of my mother, how, in her age, the Lord
Had blessed her among women, giving her me
As joke and token both, unlikelihood
Being his way. But where, where from our herd
Was the sacrifice, I asked my father. He,
In a spasm of agony, bound me hand and foot.

I thought, *I am poured out like water, like wax*
My heart is melted in the midst of my bowels.
Both were tear-blinded. Hate and love and fear
Wrestled to ruin us, savage us beyond cure.
And the fine blade gleamed with the fury of live coals
Where we had reared an altar among the rocks.

Peace be to us both, to father Abraham,
To me, elected the shorn stunned lamb of God—
We were sentenced and reprieved by the same Voice—
And to all our seed, by this terror sanctified,
To be numbered even as the stars at the small price
Of an old scapegoated and thicket-baffled ram.

III
1945

It was widely known that the army of occupation
Was in full retreat. The small provincial roads
Rumbled now every night with tanks and trucks,
Echoed with cries in German, much *mach schnell,*
Zurück, ganz richtig, augenblicklich, jawohl,
Audible in the Normandy countryside.
So it had been for days, or, rather, nights,
The troops at first making their moves in darkness,
But pressures of haste toward the end of March
Left stragglers to make their single ways alone,
At their own risk, and even in daylight hours.

Since the soldiers were commandeering anything
They needed—food, drink, vehicles of all sorts—
One rural family dismantled their bicycle,
Daubed the chrome parts—rims, sprocket, spokes—with
  mud,
And wired them carefully to the upper boughs
Of the orchard. And the inevitable came
In the shape of a young soldier, weighted down
With pack and bedroll, rifle, entrenching tools,
Steel helmet and heavy boots just after dawn.
The family was at breakfast. He ordered them out
In front of the house with abusive German words
They couldn't understand, but gesture and rifle

Made his imperious wishes perfectly clear.
They stood in a huddled group, all nine of them.
And then he barked his furious command:
Fahrrad! They all looked blank. He shouted again:
FAHRRAD! FAHRRAD! FAHRRAD!, as though sheer
    volume
Joined with his anger would make his meaning plain.
The father of the family experimentally
Inquired, *Manger?* The soldier, furious,
At last dredged up an explosive *Bicyclette*,
Proud of himself, contemptuous of them.
To this the father in a small pantomime—
Shrugged shoulders, palms turned out, a helpless, long,
Slow shaking of the head, then the wide gesture
Of an arm, taking in all his property—
Conveyed *Nous n'avons pas de bicyclettes*
More clearly than his words. To the young soldier
This seemed unlikely. No one could live this far
From neighbors, on a poor untraveled road
That lacked phone lines, without the usual means
Of transport. There was no time to search
The house, the barn, cowsheds, coops, pens and grounds.
He looked at the frightened family huddled together,
And with the blunt nose of his rifle barrel
Judiciously singled out the eldest son,
A boy perhaps fourteen, but big for his years,
Obliging him to place himself alone
Against the whitewashed front wall of the house.
Then, at the infallible distance of ten feet,

With rifle pointed right at the boy's chest,
The soldier shouted what was certainly meant
To be his terminal order: *BICYCLETTE!*

It was still early on a chilly morning.
The water in the tire-treads of the road
Lay clouded, polished pale and chalked with frost,
Like the paraffin-sealed coverings of preserves.
The very grass was a stiff lead-crystal gray,
Though splendidly prismatic where the sun
Made its slow way between the lingering shadows
Of nearby fence posts and more distant trees.
There was leisure enough to take full note of this
In the most minute detail as the soldier held
Steady his index finger on the trigger.

It wasn't charity. Perhaps mere prudence,
Saving a valuable round of ammunition
For some more urgent crisis. Whatever it was,
The soldier reslung his rifle on his shoulder,
Turned wordlessly and walked on down the road
The departed German vehicles had taken.

There followed a long silence, a long silence.
For years they lived together in that house,
Through daily tasks, through all the family meals,
In agonized, unviolated silence.

The Witch of Endor

I had the gift, and arrived at the technique
That called up spirits from the vasty deep
To traffic with our tumid flesh, to speak
Of the unknown regions where the buried keep
Their counsel, but for such talents I was banned
By Saul himself from sortilege and spell
Who banished thaumaturges from the land
Where in their ignorance the living dwell.

But then he needed me; he was sore afraid,
And begged for forbidden commerce with the dead.
Samuel he sought, and I raised up that shade,
Laggard, resentful, with shawl-enfolded head,
Who spoke a terrible otherworldly curse
In a hollow, deep, engastrimythic voice.

Indolence

Beyond the corruption both of rust and moth,
I loaf and invite my soul, calmly I slump
On the crowded sidewalk, blissed to the gills on hemp;
Mine is a sanctified and holy sloth.

The guilty and polluted come to view
My meek tranquility, the small tin cup
That sometimes runneth over. They fill it up
To assuage the torments they are subject to,

And hasten to the restoratives of sin,
While I, a flower-child, beautiful and good,
Remain inert, as St. Matthew said I should:
I rest, I toil not, neither do I spin.

Think how this sound economy of right
And wrong wisely allows me to confer
On all the bustling who in their bustling err
Consciences of a pure and niveous white.

The Ashen Light of Dawn

Reveille was bugled through army camps
As a soft dawn wind was fluttering streetlamps.

It was that hour when smooth sun-tanned limbs
Of adolescents twitched with unlawful dreams,
When, like a bloodshot eye beside the bed,
A nightlamp soaked oncoming day in red,
When, weighted beneath a humid body's brawn,
The soul mimicked that duel of lamp and dawn.
Like a face dried by the wind of recent tears,
The air is rife with whatever disappears,
And woman wearies of love, man of his chores.

Here and there chimneys smoked. The local whores,
Mascara'ed, overpainted, slept a stone
And stupid sleep, while the impoverished crone,
Breasts limp and frigid, alternately blew
On embers and on fingers, both going blue.
It was the hour of grief, of chill, of want;
Women in childbirth felt their seizures mount;
Like a thick, blood-choked scream, a rooster crowed
Distantly from some dim, befogged abode
As a sea of fog englutted the city blocks,
And in some seedy hospice, human wrecks
Breathed their death-rattling last, while debauchees
Tottered toward home, drained of their powers to please.

All pink and green in flounces, Aurora strolled
The vacant Seine embankments as the old,
Stupefied, blear-eyed Paris, glum and resigned,
Laid out his tools to begin the daily grind.

BAUDELAIRE

The Plastic and the Poetic Form

Let that Greek youth out of clay
   Mold an urn to fashion
Beauty, gladdening the eye
   With deft-handed vision.

But the poet's sterner test
   Urges him to seize on
A Euphrates of unrest,
   Fluid in evasion.

Duly bathed and cooled, his mind,
   Ardorless, will utter
Liquid song, his forming hand
   Lend a shape to water.

GOETHE

The Bequest

Good folk, my love's abandoned me.
Whoever gets her, willingly
(Although she's kind as well as fair)
I give her to him as my heir,
Blithe, easy, unencumbered, free.

She wields her graces cunningly,
And God knows her fidelity.
Let him who wins her next take care.
Good folk, my love's abandoned me.

Let him look after her and see
She's kept from smirch and calumny
Because the darling thing might snare
Any man's heart who's unaware.
Forlorn I make my threnody:
Good folk, my love's abandoned me.

VAILLANT

Once More, with Feeling

The world has doffed her outerwear
Of chilling wind and teeming rain,
And donned embroidery again,
Tailored with sunlight's gilded flair.

No beast of field nor bird of air
But sings or bellows this refrain:
"The world has doffed her outerwear
Of chilling wind and teeming rain."

Fountain, millrace and river spare
No costly beading nor abstain
From silvered liveries of grosgrain.
All is new-clad and debonair.
The world has doffed her outerwear.

CHARLES D'ORLÉANS

Le Jet d'Eau

My dear, your lids are weary;
Lower them, rest your eyes—
As though some languid pleasure
Wrought on you by surprise.
The tattling courtyard fountain
Repeats this night's excess
In fervent, ceaseless tremors
Of murmur and caress.

    A spray of petaled brilliance
        That uprears
    In gladness as the Moon-
        Goddess appears
    Falls like an opulent glistening
        Of tears.

Even thus, your soul, exalted,
Primed by the body's joys,
Ascends in quenchless cravings
To vast, enchanted skies,
And then brims over, dying
In swoons, faint and inert,
And drains to the silent, waiting,
Dark basin of my heart.

A spray of petaled brilliance
That uprears
In gladness as the Moon-
Goddess appears
Falls like an opulent glistening
Of tears.

You, whom the night makes radiant,
How amorous to lie, spent,
Against your breasts and listen
To the fountain's soft lament.
O Moon, melodious waters,
Wind-haunted trees in leaf,
Your melancholy mirrors
My ardors and their grief.

A spray of petaled brilliance
That uprears
In gladness as the Moon-
Goddess appears
Falls like an opulent glistening
Of tears.

BAUDELAIRE

Taking Charge

Back off, clear out, the lot of you,
Vile Melancholy, Spleen, and Woe;
Think you to dog me to and fro
As in the past you used to do?

Not anymore. "Begone. You're through,"
Says Reason, your determined foe.
Back off, clear out, the lot of you,
Vile Melancholy, Spleen, and Woe.

If you resurface, may God throw
You and your whole damnable crew
Back where you came from down below,
And thereby give the fiend his due.
Back off, clear out, the lot of you.

CHARLES D'ORLÉANS

A Symposium

Only a Thracian goon would lurch from tippling
To brawling. Barbarians one and all. For our part
Let's preserve the rites of Bacchus, our seemly and civil
Devotions in the calm service of pleasure.
Good wine imbibed by lamplight has nothing to do
With bashed-in cups or swordplay. Subdue your clamor,
My friends, and use your well-connected elbows
For hoisting moderate drinks. You ask that I
Knock back my own full share of Falernian must.
Then let's hear Megylla's brother tell us who knocked him
All of a heap with the heavy weapons of bliss.
Suddenly tongue-tied? Well then, I'm swearing off,
Not a drop more. Those are my fixed conditions.
Whichever beauty it was that sent you reeling,
There's nothing to blush about, since you only go
For the classy and high-toned. Come on, just whisper
Her name in my ear.
O you poor silly kid,
You've bought yourself a regular Charybdis;
You deserve better. What can Thessalian spells,
Wizards or magic ointments do for you now?
Snagged by the tripartite, hybrid beast, Chimera,
Not even Bellerophon, mounted on Pegasus, could save you.

HORACE I.xxvii

A Special Occasion

O *mise-en-bouteille* in the very year of my birth
And Manlius' consulship, celestial spirits,
Instinct with ardors, slugfests, the sighs of lovers,
Hilarity and effortless sleep, whatever,
Campanian harvest, well-sealed special reserve
For some fine and festive holiday, descend
From your high cellarage, since my friend Corvinus,
A connoisseur, has called for a more mature wine.
Soaked though he be in vintage Socratic wisdom,
He's not going to snub you. For even Cato the Elder,
All Roman rectitude, would warm to a drink.

You limber the dullard's faculties with your proddings;
With Bacchus the Trickster you break through careful
 discretion,
Making even the politic say what they mean.
You resurrect hope in the most dejected of minds;
To the poor and weak you lend such measure of courage
As after a single gulp allays their palsy
When faced with the wrath of monarchs, or unsheathed
 weapons.
Bacchus and Venus (if she will condescend),
The arm-linked Graces in unclad sorority,
And vigil lamps will honor you all night long
Till Phoebus, with punctual bustle, banishes starlight.

HORACE III.xxi

A Prayer to Twin Divinities

Let the girls sing of Diana in joyful praise
And the boys of her twin, Apollo unshorn, shall sing
And honor their sacred mother, whom Jupiter, king
Of gods, so favored, honor with song and the bays.

Of Diana let the girls sing, goddess of streams
Who loves the icy mountain, the darkened leafage
Of the Erymanthian woods, the brighter boscage
Of Lycian heights, young girls, give her your hymns.

To Tempe, to Phoebus Apollo's native isle
Give praise, you boys, and praise many times over
His godly shoulder slung with both lyre and quiver,
His brother's instrument, his festive, sacred soil.

Hearing your prayers, Apollo, god-begotten,
Will fend off war and plague and all ill omen
From Caesar and his people, and banish famine
To the lands of the barbarous Parthian and Briton.

HORACE I.xxi

Miriam

I had a nice voice once, and a large following.
I was, you might say, a star.
Of course, today, no one would ever know it.
My brothers have managed to corner all the attention
In spite of some rather dubious behavior.
O I could sing and dance with the best of them,
Pattern my feet to the jubilant hosannas.
But now I am always silent, always veiled,
Not only in public but in my private chambers
Where there are no mirrors or polished surfaces
In which my white affliction could be reflected.
I've even given up going through my scrapbooks;
The past is past; it's no good to anyone.
Many were lovely once, at least as children.

Witness

Against the enormous rocks of a rough coast
The ocean rams itself in pitched assault
And spastic rage to which there is no halt;
Foam-white brigades collapse; but the huge host

Has infinite reserves; at each attack
The impassive cliffs look down in gray disdain
At scenes of sacrifice, unrelieved pain,
Figured in froth, aquamarine and black.

Something in the blood-chemistry of life,
Unspeakable, impressive, undeterred,
Expresses itself without needing a word
In this sea-crazed Empedoclean Strife.

It is a scene of unmatched melancholy,
Weather of misery, cloud cover of distress,
To which there are no witnesses, unless
One counts the briny, tough and thorned sea holly.

Lapidary Inscription with Explanatory Note

There was for him no more perfect epitaph
Than this from Shakespeare: "Nothing in his life
Became him like the leaving it." All those
Who knew him wished the son of a bitch in hell,
Despised his fawning sycophancy, smug
Self-satisfaction, posturing ways and pig-
Faced beady little eyes, his trite
Mind, and attested qualities of a shit,
And felt the world immeasurably improved
Right from the very moment that he left it.

—

Quintus, as what is called a man of the world,
You know how we keep the wheels of progress oiled
By what we call *prospicientia*,
Vorsichtichkeit, the prudent Boy Scout way
Of being prepared. For the obituary notice
When you shall slip behind the Great Portcullis,
I have prepared the modest sketch above
Conscientiously while you are still alive,
Omitting your worst features, as it behooves,
Not out of some *de mortuis* piety
But simply because they wouldn't be believed.

Long-Distance Vision

How small they seem, those men way in the distance.
Somehow they seem scarcely to move at all,
And when they do, it is slowly,
Almost unwillingly. I bend my head
To my writing, look up half an hour later,
And there they are, as if

Engaged in boring discussion, fixed in a world
Almost eventless, where it is somehow always
Three in the afternoon,
The best part of the day already wasted,
And nothing to do till it's time for the first drink
Of the uneventful evening.

I know, of course, binoculars would reveal
They are actually doing something—one doubles over
(Is it with pain or laughter?),
Another hangs his jacket on the handle
Of his bicycle, tucks in his Versace sport-shirt
And furtively checks his fly.

But the naked eyesight smooths and simplifies,
And they stand as if awaiting the command
Of a photographer
Who, having lined them up in a formal group,
Will tell them to hold even stiller than they seem
Till he's ready to dismiss them.

In much the same way, from a palace window,
The king might have viewed a tiny, soundless crowd
            On a far hill assembled,
Failing to see what a painter would have recorded:
The little domes, immaculate in their whiteness,
            At the foot of the cross.

Secrets

The number of witches and sorceresses [has] everywhere become enormous. —JOHN JEWEL, BISHOP OF SALISBURY, 1559

When they fly through the air they turn invisible
But may sometimes be spotted by patient birding questers
At the witching hour in woods on the darkest possible
Moonless nights at the regular secret musters
Of their kindred spirits, these horrible Weird Sisters.

It is widely believed that lust is their ruling passion,
A legacy maybe of Puritan tradition,
Or because they are ugly, for they use some glutinous potion
To lure young farmhands into abject submission
Or orgies of loose sabbatical possession.

For their foul rites they render the fat of babies;
Spider and warted toad mix in their simples;
Heartless they are, and death is among their hobbies;
Nothing on earth is vile as their mildest foibles,
Cold as their tits, delicate as their thimbles.

Poppy

It builds like unseen fire deep in a mine,
        This igneous, molten wrath,
This smelting torture that rises with the decline
        Of reason, signifying death.

As when, fueled with suspicion, the coal-black
        Othello is wrought forge-hot,
Or when pouting Achilles lashes back
        At the whole Trojan lot

For the death of Patroclus: the one prepared to die
        In fury, to pit his life
Against a well-armed equal, the other to slay
        An innocent young wife;

Both, curiously, heroes. It is like that seething
        Pit, pitch-black, at whose lip
A petaled flame spreads crimsonly, bequeathing
        One or another sleep.

The Ceremony of Innocence

He was taken from his cell, stripped, blindfolded,
And marched to a noisy room that smelled of sweat.
Someone stamped on his toes; his scream was stopped
By a lemon violently pushed between his teeth
And sealed with friction tape behind his head.
His arms were tied, the blindfold was removed
So he could see his tormentors, and they could see
The so-much-longed-for terror in his eyes.
And one of them said, "The best part of it all
Is that you won't even be able to pray."
When they were done with him, two hours later,
They learned that they had murdered the wrong man.
And this made one of them thoughtful. Some years after,
He quietly severed connections with the others,
Moved to a different city, took holy orders,
And devoted himself to serving God and the poor,
While the intended victim continued to live
On a walled estate, sentried around the clock
By a youthful, cell phone–linked praetorian guard.

The Road to Damascus

What happened? At first there were strange, confused
accounts.
This man, said one, who had long for righteousness' sake
Delivered unto the death both men and women
In his zeal for the Lord, had tumbled from his mount,
Felled by an unheard Word and worded omen.
Another claimed his horse shied at a snake.

Yet a third, that he was convulsed by the onslaught
Of the falling sickness, whose victims we were urged
To spit upon as protection and in disgust.
Rigid in body now as in doctrine, caught
In a seizure known but to few, he lay in the dust,
Of all his fiercest resolves stunningly purged.

We are told by certain learned doctors that those
Thus stricken are granted an inkling of that state
Where *There Shall Be No More Time,* as it is said;
As though from a pail, spilled water were to repose
Midair in pebbles of clarity, all its weight
Turned light, in a glittering, loose, but stopped cascade.

The Damascene culprits now could rest untroubled,
Their delinquencies no longer the concern
Of this fallen, converted Pharisee. He rather
From sighted blindness to blind sight went hobbled
And was led forth to a house where he would turn
His wrath from one recusancy to another.

Elders

Ein dunkeler Schacht ist Liebe

As a boy he was awkward, pimpled, unpopular,
Disdained by girls, avoided by other boys,
An acned solitary. But bold and spectacular
The lubricious dreams that such a one enjoys.

He wandered apart, picked at his scabs, pinned down,
In the plush, delirious Minsky's of his mind,
High-breasted, long-thighed sirens who served his own
Terrible lusts, to which they became resigned,

And he thought himself masterful and accursed
As he pumped his flesh to climax, picturing wild
Virgins imploring him to do his worst,
And every morning he left his bedding soiled.

And so it went year by tormented year,
His yearnings snarled in some tight, muddled sensation
Of violence, a gout of imperiousness, fear
And resentment yeasting in ulcered incubation.

When he was old he encountered someone else
Enslaved by similar dreams and forbidden seethings,
Another dissatisfied, thrummed by the same pulse,
Who brought him where they both could observe bathing

In innocent calm voluptuous Susanna,
Delicate, and a quarter of his age,
Her flesh as white and wonderful as manna,
Exciting them both to desires engorged with rage.

Sarabande on Attaining the Age of Seventy-seven

The harbingers are come. See, see their mark;
White is their colour, and behold my head.

Long gone the smoke-and-pepper childhood smell
Of the smoldering immolation of the year,
Leaf-strewn in scattered grandeur where it fell,
Golden and poxed with frost, tarnished and sere.

And I myself have whitened in the weathers
Of heaped-up Januarys as they bequeath
The annual rings and wrongs that wring my withers,
Sober my thoughts and undermine my teeth.

The dramatis personae of our lives
Dwindle and wizen; familiar boyhood shames,
The tribulations one somehow survives,
Rise smokily from propitiatory flames

Of our forgetfulness until we find
It becomes strangely easy to forgive
Even ourselves with his clouding of the mind,
This cinerous blur and smudge in which we live.

A turn, a glide, a quarter-turn and bow,
The stately dance advances; these are airs
Bone-deep and numbing as I should know by now,
Diminishing the cast, like musical chairs.

I.M.E.M.

To spare his brother from having to endure
Another agonizing bedside vigil
With sterile pads, syringes but no hope,
He settled all his accounts, distributed
Among a few friends his most valued books,
Weighed all in mind and heart and then performed
The final, generous, extraordinary act
Available to a solitary man,
Abandoning his translation of Boileau,
Dressing himself in a dark well-pressed suit,
Turning the lights out, lying on his bed,
Having requested neighbors to wake him early
When, as intended, they would find him dead.

“The Darkness and the Light Are Both Alike to Thee”

Psalms 139:12

Like trailing silks, the light
Hangs in the olive trees
As the pale wine of day
Drains to its very lees:
Huge presences of gray
Rise up, and then it’s night.

Distantly lights go on.
Scattered like fallen sparks
Bedded in peat, they seem
Set in the plushest darks
Until a timid gleam
Of matins turns them wan,

Like the elderly and frail
Who’ve lasted through the night,
Cold brows and silent lips,
For whom the rising light
Entails their own eclipse,
Brightening as they fail.

Notes

"Mirror": *A Mirror for Magistrates,* a sequence of poems by many hands concerning the theme of the Fall of Princes, of men of great authority and power, containing an *Induction,* and an account of the downfall of Henry, Duke of Buckingham, both by Thomas Sackville, Earl of Dorset.

"Samson": Judges 13:1–5

"Rara Avis in Terris": The poem was composed to accompany the anniversary gift of a brooch described in the final stanza.

"A Fall": *Pisse-Vache,* mentioned by Byron in an October 9, 1816, letter to John Murray as "one of the finest torrents in Switzerland."

"Haman": Esther 3:5–11

"A Certain Slant": The poem had its origin in a sentence in a story called "The Boys," by Anton Chekhov.

"Saul and David": I Samuel 16:14–23

"The Hanging Gardens of Tyburn": The poem is based on folklore concerning the mandrake plant, which was long believed to have magic properties. According to one botanical handbook, "its roots were an integral part of every witch's cauldron, its berries . . . used as an opiate and love potion. It was common knowledge in medieval times that the mandrake grew under the gallows from the dripping semen of hanged men. Pulled from the ground the root emitted wild shrieks and those who heard them were driven mad" (*Folklore and Symbolism of Flowers, Plants and Trees,* by Ernst and Johanna Lehner, p. 91).

"Judith": Judith 10:1–23

"Lot's Wife": Genesis 19:15–28

"Sacrifice": Genesis 22:1–19

"The Witch of Endor": I Samuel 28:3–25

"The Bequest": Vaillant, a.k.a. Pierre Chastellain (though by some these are held to be two entirely different persons) was a member of the circle of Charles d'Orléans.

"Miriam": Exodus 15:20f; Numbers 12:1–15; Deuteronomy 24:9

"Secrets": One of the folk names for the foxglove is "witch's thimbles."

"The Road to Damascus": Acts 9. See also *From Jesus to Paul,* by Joseph Klausner, pp. 325–30.

"Elders": Daniel 13; Minsky's was a striptease/burlesque theater in the Times Square area of Broadway in the late 1930s.

A Note About the Author

Anthony Hecht is the author of seven books of poetry, among them *The Hard Hours,* which received the Pulitzer Prize for poetry in 1968, and, more recently, *Flight Among the Tombs.* In 1984 he received the Eugenio Montale Award for a lifetime achievement in poetry, and in 2000 the Robert Frost Medal from the Poetry Society of America. He has written a critical study of the poetry of W. H. Auden, and *On the Laws of the Poetic Art* (Andrew W. Mellon Lectures in the Fine Arts). He taught for some years at Bard College, the University of Rochester and Georgetown University, and now lives in Washington, D.C.

A Note on the Type

This book was set in a typeface called Walbaum. The original cutting of the face was made by Justus Erich Walbaum (1768–1839) in Weimar in 1810. The type was revived by the Monotype Corporation in 1934. Young Walbaum began his artistic career as an apprentice to a maker of cookie molds. How he managed to leave this field and become a successful punch cutter remains a mystery. Although the type that bears his name may be classified as modern, numerous slight irregularities in its cut give this face its humane manner.

Composed by NK Graphics, Keene, New Hampshire

Printed and bound by Edwards Brothers, Ann Arbor, Michigan

Designed by Soonyoung Kwon